Symphony of Power

Lyndie Swedersky

W & B Publishers
USA

W & B Publishers
For information:
W & B Publishers
Post Office Box 193
Colfax, NC 27235
www.a-argusbooks.com

ISBN: 978-0-6923184-4-7
ISBN: 0-6923184-4-5

Book Cover designed by *Samantha Tarkington,*
and Kate Rhodes,

Printed in the United States of America

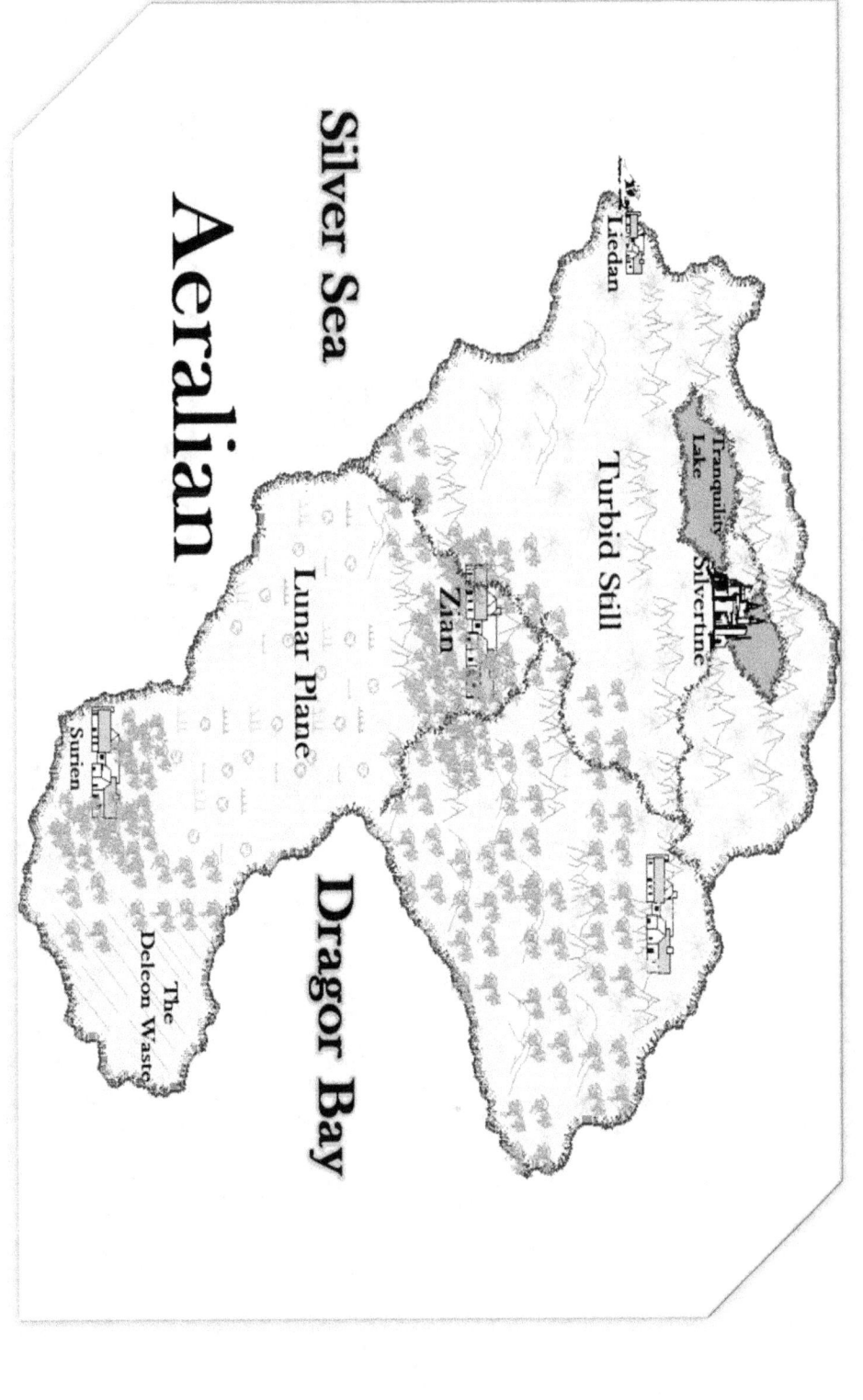

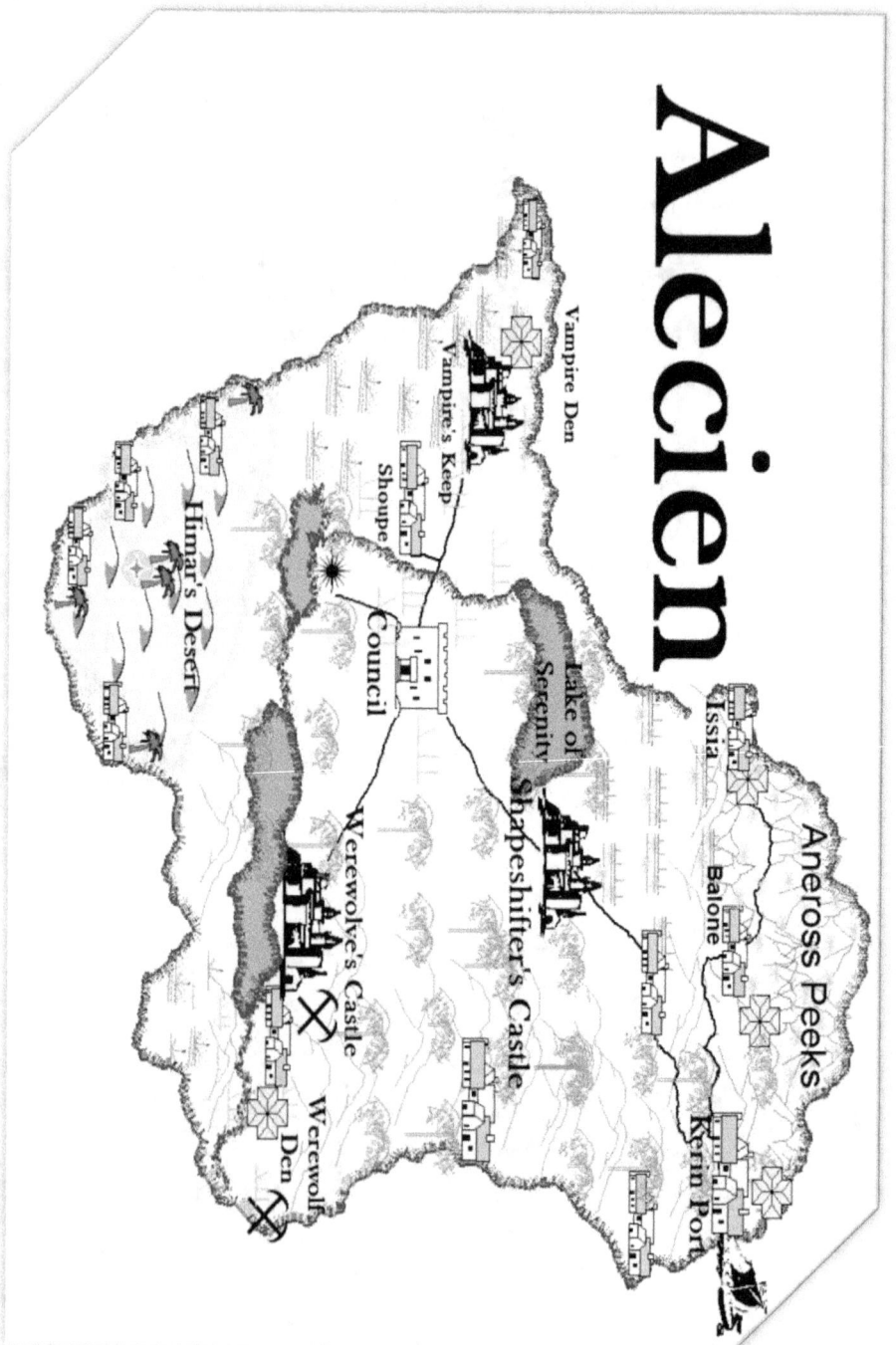

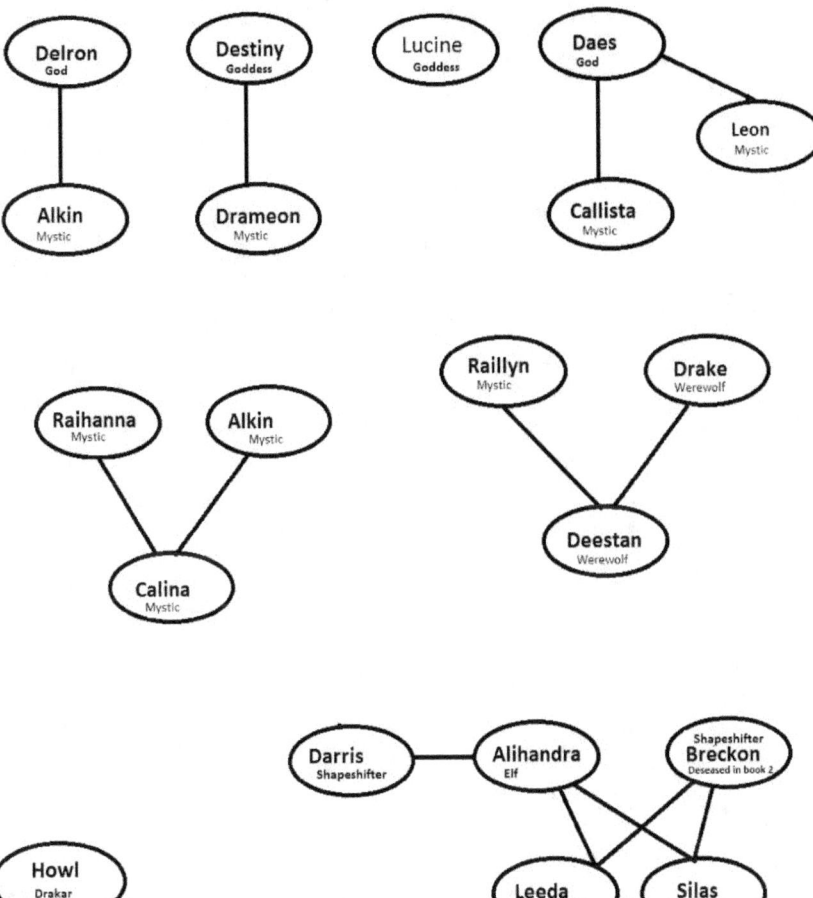

~Dedication & From the Author ~

Over the past years I have written down the story of Raillyn & Alkin, along with their many friends. It is not only a story of their life but a reflection of, the dedication of friends and family. Always sticking together through thick and thin. Thank you for sticking with me for all these years, and thank you for giving life to these wonderful characters.

Thank you Samantha Tarkington, and Kate Rhodes, my wonderful Artist and Illustrator! Dieter Steffman, thank you for uploading and sharing amazing fonts that help authors like me! And lastly thank you Nahdia, my wonderful niece who shared her quote and helped wrap things up!

Even now, after the war has ended, there are those who die because of the hatred that it sparked. The few mystics who remain fight for the Gods and hope to restore peace. Any race across the Silver Sea would tell you the meaning of a Mystic means one who is of many blood. In actuality the word Mystic is referred to "one who is born with the blood of the Gods," also known as a Demigod. This Ancient guardian race born of mixed blood, either from a God and a lesser race or between two Mystics, protect the land.

Sealed by a brand, infused with magic and blood, these mixed-blooded brood are bonded to their God. At times, they are nothing more than pawns used to govern the rules held true by the heaves; never able to intervene with anything other than a light hand. If caught interfering or playing a larger role in the natural events of the world, their appointed God would punish them.

Along with the Dragons, the God's first creation, they maintain a magical harmony in the land and all things created. As the laws of the Gods held true to the mystics, the Dragon race was not bound by any rules and often became the Mystics assistants. Through this bonded attachment, purposes that were implausible to fulfill by one of God blood was able to be fulfilled by their Dragon companion while in human form. This loophole was one of many that Gods and Mystics alike used to play their ultimate game of life. Even now the game is played, less so with their Dragon companions and more so with the mortal races.

Mystics allow the natural flow of their God-kin's magic to flow freely in the world and realm while the Dragons and their half-blood kin helped control the natural flow of this magic. Together these two races served the Gods, as carefully balanced ropes hold up a basket, keeping balance and order to their accustomed god or goddess. The war however disrupted this flow of magic and ripped the bond between the land and the Gods themselves, banning Daes from the land asunder. A single rope was cut and, chaos erupted in Alecien and Aeralain, the world began its descent into darkness. Balance was dismantled. I had tried desperately to stop Daes' power from leaving the world. I had tried to save Leon before his death but was not successful, and when Daes teleported me out of The Keep and into his realm, I witnessed the struggle the world now would face.

The child who remained with Daes' power was in ruins, her tiny body lashed out and tried to destroy those around her. Her emotions and power no longer in balance, she now reigned in chaos. Daes himself tried to desperately control his last lineage child, but was not successful. Eventually, the decision was made to place her into a deep sleep. This sleep would allow her to hopefully heal and restore her magic and mind to its normal balanced state. This was the hope, if it worked would be another story.

~Howl~

Reunion ~ Raillyn

Thinking back so much had changed... In a way it felt like saying goodbye to a part of myself. Knowing there was no going back. Alkin and I had left The Keep together, to meet the Wolves. It had been six years since I had last stood as an ally in their halls. And now it felt foreign. Like I was an outsider.

I finally remembered my father was Drameon, and he had watched me grow up under Chaimh and Liliana's care. He protected me and advised me, and helped kidnap me... After the portal fell Alkin and him had been the ones who devised the plan to take me from Death's Realm, and place me into The Keep. There I spent six years of my life. Raised my Wolven daughter and entwined myself with my captor inevitably by having another child, with him.

However he wasn't my captor, he was my friend and I felt confused and saddened by our now strained friendship. I felt rejected, by him.... Why....

Standing in my father's arms a rush of emotions hit me. Something was changing inside. It made me antsy and put me on edge. The way my magic seemed to flow around my emotions, like two different temperatures colliding together, was unsettling.

I felt off kilter, in a way, at rock bottom. Except, I was expected to pick myself up and move on like nothing happened. But, how could I? So much had happened and I was sure so much still would occur. My mind stuttered briefly, everything went hazy almost staticky, even my hearing faltered momentarily. Taking a deep breath, I tried to steady myself.

Mentally, I had made up my mind on what was going to happen. Part of me was determined to return to my prior life and speak with Drake. I was happy to be alive, eager to talk to him with full knowledge of who I was, yet something deep inside ached. It hurt so bad I wanted to fall to my knees and cry. It was as if a piece of myself, was ripped out and nothingness replaced it. Looking around the room, my gaze fell on Alkin, who now stood back out of the way as if he was unsure what to do now. For a moment the smell of pine filled my nose while flashes of a lush, dense forest filled my mind.

Again something stuttered inside me, this time more violently. The intense green canopy high above and the dampness of its cool embrace forced itself on me. Making another memory cross my mind, of a time when I was young.

My parents were away and I was left in Alkin's care. When my parents weren't there, he was responsible for me. I loved him, even then, and I felt the love he had for me.

One day when my parents were out we took a walk in the woods. Being a mischievous three-year-old, I ran on ahead laughing as I padded my bare feet across the soft forest floor. Alkin told me to be careful and not get too far ahead.

Turning to listen I ran on, not watching where I was going I slipped down an embankment, towards a cliff. In an instant, Alkin was there, holding me close as we somersaulted towards the edge. Thorns, branches, sticks, and brush tore at our skin as we tumbled head over heels. Alkin held me tight as he tried to take the brunt of the fall. I cried out as I held onto him for dear life. Finally, we stopped, looking at Alkin's dirty scratched face I saw his other hand gripping a tree.

Looking behind me, I saw how carelessly close we had gotten to the edge. Tears welled up in my eyes as I shied away from the open sky of the sudden drop and clung desperately to his chest. Thankfully he took the easy way out and he summoned a portal that we rolled through to home.

We landed gently onto the floors hard oak surface. Sluggishly he got up and set me down. My eyes stung with the burn of tears and as I wiped them away smudges of dirt marked the back of my hand. That only made me cry more, fearing he was going to punish me. I felt the brief touch of his fingers brushing my hair aside, and gazing up at him he briefly met my eyes, relief in them.

Watching, his feet shuffled across the floor and as he sat in the nearby chair he let out a groan of pain. He slouched back so far his head was nearly staring at the ceiling. He looked tired, and I could tell he didn't have the heart to punish me. Instantly my tears stopped as I looked at him closer.

He was dirty from head to toe, and glancing down so was I. While I only had small scratches, he had tears. He had protected me from the more hurtful damage. Blood ran down his leg from a gash on his knee, the material was ripped off and missing, leaving the skin bare and torn flesh visible.

Standing, I didn't say a word but instead I went and got a bowl of cold water and a few rags. Going to Alkin, I saw him watch me curiously. I was a Mystic, and even though I appeared young I had the mentality of a six-year-old, non-ancient. I had seen my parents care for each other and knew it was only right to do the same for people I loved.

Carefully I carried the bowl of water to him. Walking slow, it slopped over the edge and splattered my hand with tiny droplets. Slowly I set it on the floor and gathered the rag, gently placing it under the water. As soon as it was submerged and had soaked up enough, I gently wrung it out and reach out to touch Alkin's leg. His muscles rippled and tensed briefly under my touch, as if I surprised him. Carefully I wiped the dirt away from his wound. He didn't complain, but I felt him stiffen as if in pain.

Re-soaking the rag, I wiped his wound again until it was clean. When I was satisfied, I did something my mother often did, and others of my kind. Something I had seen done many times between family. Barely bleeding anymore, I carefully leaned forward and kissed his wound. His skin was warm and soft. Almost instinctively I felt myself lick my lips, tasting his blood. It was sweet, almost like honey, and powerful. I felt my eyes change color and reflect my magic, blue in color. Looking up at Alkin his face looked shocked and he pulled me onto his lap.

"I will heal, child, don't worry about me. Let's get you in the bath and clean, then I will finish attending my wounds." He said as he picked me up and carried me down the hall. "Also you shouldn't kiss wounds unless they are your family's." He said trying to hint that what I did was almost wrong.

"But you are family." I retorted back seriously, the memory faded.

Suddenly his eyes met mine, almost like he had seen what I had. He laughed at something Briar said, then looked away. The stuttering started again, my soul felt a need to go to him, and it frightened me. He had been the reason I was removed from Drake and my old life. Yes, it was for a justified cause, Daes and the Gods demanded it, but still. He had manipulated me, kidnapped me, laid powerful spells upon me that I still didn't understand, and in turn killed me, and not just once but twice!

My heart skipped a beat at the thought of the dagger plunged deep inside Raihanna's construct body. It sent shivers up my spine. Yet, it also sent waves of sadness through me. *Why?* My emotions tipped from one extreme to another, like a pendulum swinging back and forth.

Was it because Alkin and I had spent over six years together? That as Raihanna I was familiar with him, and loved him? Or was it because the mental connection we shared through our Mystic bond, was now gone.

I felt a tear escape my eye as I realized I was still looking at him. For a moment, a shaky sensation began to creep through me. My stomach ached and my throat burned. Bile rose in my throat, I wanted to scream, kick, fight, or just run and hide. I didn't know, I was so confused and the unrest in my soul was so uneasy. It made the world around me spin, making me dizzy, and wanting to shed more tears. My father noticed my response and leaned down to whisper in my ear.

"Relax dear, it's normal to feel that way after such a traumatic event." He said lovingly.

Looking my father in the eyes calmed me. His mimicking ever-changing eyes reflected my own and brought a semi-calm to my mind. Taking a deep steadying breath I pulled back from his grasp and looked to see where Drake was.

He had come up behind me. His sturdy yet gentle face, with familiar green eyes that our daughter shared with him, looked at me. However, he seemed upset, not happy about the situation and why should he be? The people I had called into our lives had manipulated him also, yet I felt the compassion of why. I lived through it.

Having my mother killed so violently and brutally was not what I expected when I was three. Grieved, my father went against everything Mystics were taught and sought revenge, killing those who committed such a ghastly act against his mate. I never wanted to be taken away from my parents or have them completely removed from my life, along with the friends I was used to having around me.

"You're her father?!" Drake's voice shouted breaking my inner thoughts. "Why didn't you say anything? We have been working for over six years together and not once did you feel the need to let anyone know Raillyn was your daughter! There better be a reasonable explanation for all this!" He yelled as he crossed his arms in front of him. Near black hair fell around his face, framing it.

His face tightened, his chin seemed set, and his lips were hard pressed. For a moment, I felt I wanted to go comfort him, but I feared being rejected. I had been in The Keep for six years, with another man. He had probably been fighting to get me back. But being Raihanna then, and myself now, I wasn't sure how to react to all of it yet.

As Raihanna I loved Alkin, the man who placed me in a construct body, and killed me not just once but twice. I lived in the Vampire's Keep, hunted and killed people with no remorse. Till my normal personality started breaking through... However I don't feel whole, and not my prior self. It feels like something changed, or is missing and needs to be found. It scared me, and clutching my father's arm tighter, I almost felt like my world was spinning.

"You already know the reason, Drake." I heard Howl's smooth whimsical voice say. Almost like notes on a breeze his tone always got my attention.

Yet, it was so different now, our link was broken and it seemed odd to not feel the emotions behind his words. Even though I could clearly see them on his face, it displaced me. My head spun as I felt my magic reach for the link that was no longer there. My father's hand on my shoulder kept me physically in the world, even when my mind was on the verge of blacking out.

"Raillyn was Daes' last Mystic. She was the one who was taken from this world to be kept alive. You and I have already had this conversation. As I said we have to let the Mystics do what they do best, and in my case help them in any way I can." Howl said before turning towards me and meeting my gaze. "That being said, Raillyn, since we had a bond while you resided in Raihanna's body, it's now broken. I am more than happy to reinstate it, and do a blood exchange with you; in turn, helping you and Daes." Howl said smirking mischievously.

Looking at Drake, who sounded like he gasped out loud, he appeared appalled. Either from the fact that Howl was so blunt or the fact that he wanted to do a blood exchange with me. Remembering Howl's blood flowing down my throat as I resided in Raihanna's body caused my mind to shudder again.

I originally thought I was drowning. Instead, I was panicking and Howl had saved me. Securing me to the living world when all my spirit wanted was to escape from the immense magic I had cast.

Nodding my head sharply, I knew he would know what I meant and would want to reestablish the blood bond. At that thought a sensation crept through me, almost like a tickle, like something nagging at my brain. Biting my lip a little, I realized it was in the air.

Something I smelled was causing the unnerving nagging. The smell of an open pine forest on a warm spring day fluttered into my nose. It smelled like morning rain. It made my stomach tighten and quiver. The familiarity of it caused my mind to feel like it was jolted from drinking too much Dragon Fruit. An energy infused creamy drink.

My nostrils flared as I sniffed the scent, it was Alkin's. Taking a deep breath, I realized it drowned out the scent of everyone else around me. No longer could I smell Wolf, Drakar, or even the flowery purple lilacs beyond the walls. Pressure built up. I felt a shift in my eyes, something changed even though I couldn't put my finger on it. My mind blanked and everything became hazy. Stepping away from my father a primal feeling encompassed me.

Out of my peripheral vision I saw Drake tip his head curiously, Howl stood smirking. His bright blue eyes looked at me mischievously. Vaguely I heard Drake question something. *Was it "what's wrong with her? Or "what's she doing?"* I wasn't sure my mind was so focused on the smell. It drove me forward.

Alkin stood speaking to Briar, he leaned against a column with his arms crossed, unaware of my pursuit. His chestnut hair hung perfectly over his Elvin-like face. I felt the need to reach out and touch it, run my fingers through it. Memories of my time in The Keep, as Raihanna, flooded my mind.

My breathing picked up as I approached and he suddenly became aware of my ever closer presence. Briar met my gaze as I felt myself smile almost wildly. Static filled my ears, all sound was lost, and all focus was set on the need to just touch Alkin.

I saw his nose flare and his eyebrows flinch as if he recognized something in the air. Meeting my eyes, he tipped his head and took a step back. I felt my body tense as if I wanted to jump forward, like a cat stalking its prey.

Then memories of my so-called dream came flooding back to me and Alkin standing in Death's Realm saying that it wasn't just a dream. My heart stuttered as I felt nervousness buildup inside.

Like a snapping twig, I felt it. My eyes shifted again, I was unsure how but I just knew they did. My hearing returned and the static left replaced by an awkward silence. Meeting Alkin's eyes I noticed they were dilated and he was fully focused on me.

My predacious nature changed at that moment, and all of a sudden I was unsure of myself. Swallowing hard, I felt myself take a step back, too uneasy to turn away.

Alkin had started out on the Vampires' side, or so I had thought. In reality, he was preparing The Keep and Hunter for my arrival. Why? I still didn't know, but it had to do with me being Daes' last Mystic. Until I found out more information, I wasn't sure what to think about Alkin.

Yes, we had a child together, but that was when I was in the construct body. A body he created and in turn one that had memories and emotions, again from him. Yet there was something else, the nagging sensation. It wasn't part of either my mind nor body, it resonated from my soul. Feeling my eyes begin their strange shift and my hearing begin to static. I shook my head and stepped back further. *I can't touch him.* If I did, I feared what might happen.

"Raillyn?" Drake said while placing his hand on my shoulder, breaking me from the strange trance. Almost shaking I let him pull me into his embrace. "Are you ok?" he asked while lovingly brushing my hair.

Again something shifted inside, some inner fight vs. flight response resonated into my body, I wanted to leave. My body shuddered, as I felt like a bird trapped in a cage. My mind slipped from me as it seemed to stutter. I felt myself briefly lash out, pushing myself away from Drake as if he burned me. Darkness foreshadowed me as instinct took over.

Next thing I knew I was on the floor, panting heavily, my father was beside me, arm on my shoulder. A deep blue haze emanated from me nearly concealing me in its grasp. *My magic.* I thought to myself.

Taking a deep breath I noticed even the air coming out was a deep blue color. Raising my hand to my face, I trembled and my mind changed once more. I felt like I was being swung, back and forth, up and down, from one emotional high to another. My body began shaking uncontrollably as I felt it shift again and tears began to pour down my face. It felt like being ripped in two.

My mind reached for a connection that was no longer there, only causing me more grief. The now blue air around me felt heavy, making me feel claustrophobic. *Why!* I cried out loud mentally knowing no one was connected to me to hear. *Why was I feeling this way?* Again a shift occurred in my body, causing more tremors to envelop me. Heart nearly pounding out of my chest, I swayed as I noticed my hearing was already gone. *Now that I think of it... I don't remember ever hearing anything after Drake's voice.*

My skin crawled like a thousand tiny fire ants trying to burrow into me. My nerves felt like they were charged with such electricity they might burn up. Everything hurt, mind, body, and soul. Then I felt something snap inside me, like a tree falling in the forest, I stood swiftly terrified and fell into darkness.

Tension ~ Alkin

Seeing Raillyn's eyes, I knew what it meant. Even though mentally she didn't understand the bond between us, her body did. It wanted desperately to reconnect with me and my body felt the same way.

Her eyes dilated, as large as saucers, I knew she smelled my scent in the air. Her scent hung heavily around her, and as she approached me, my body stiffened, recognizing her.

Never had our kind experienced an issue such as this one, our bodies and soul recognized the need for each other yet her mind wasn't able to understand why. She never grew up Mystic, this more primal side of our race was foreign to her.

The overdriving need to just touch her and begin re-establishing our bond was nearly too much to handle. I began feeling myself move forward unintentionally, driven to just grab her hand and whisk her away. However, the Wolf stopped her and got in the way.

My primal mind growled at his closeness towards my mate. Briar flinching near me said I had done it out loud as well. Taking a step forward Drake met my eyes with hatred in them. We were getting along, in a sense while I worked in The Keep. Now however with Raillyn being in the same room as us, that was changing. Both of us wanted to prove our dominance over the other, to prove who she belonged to.

Raillyn too felt it. The way she jumped backwards as if Drake was on fire was in a way funny. I felt myself smirk as she began to panic from his touch, her mind said he was fine, but her body couldn't stand his touch anymore. I knew it was the opposite for me, her body craved mine but her mind was still frightened, unsure.

As her magic harmlessly whipped out around her, it sent a warning. I could feel a shift in the air. Her magic was telling everyone she didn't want to be touched, to leave her alone. It was sinking into the minds of those around her, changing their actions and dampening their need to assist her. Only the Ancients were immune to its altering effects.

Exhausted, she went to her knees. I felt myself move forward, wanting to go to her. However, I stopped myself. If I touched her, it would set aflame our bond, meaning it would drive me to mark her and bind her as mine. A problem for the current situation we faced. She had to get to Daes, and soon, so she could finish the task she was placed on long ago.

Taking a deep breath. Drameon tried to calm her, but to no avail. Finally, her body and mind gave up, succumbing to unconsciousness. A tingling sensation filled me with dread, I hated not being able to help her. Meeting Howl's gaze, however, we both knew it was for the best. Lips thinly pressed, Howl wandered over to me. As he walked he pulled a sky blue rag from his belt.

"You need this." He said while tipping his head towards mine, brow raised.

Running the cloth across my forehead I realized how sweaty I was and not just my head, but my neck and chest also. I felt hot and uncomfortable, the need to go and take Raillyn away with me was powerful and it took a lot of self-control not to give into those needs.

A bead of sweat danced its way down my chest and caught on my pants line. I would have to bathe after this. My body was excreting too much pheromone to be around Raillyn safety. Taking a deep breath, I looked at Drameon wondering what he was planning on doing. Before I got a chance to ask anything Drake swept down to take Raillyn away from her father.

Unintentionally a challenging growl emanated from my throat. I was still worked up over the situation. Raillyn was mine and I wasn't going to let some halfwit Wolf have her regardless of what happened in the past. *She has been mine for over six years,* and I was not in a sharing mood.

"Stop." Drameon said recognizing what was going on. "Howl, take her to the small den, please." He spoke while standing, and cradling his daughter to him, before passing her to Howl. A wild smirk crossed his face briefly, almost too fast for anyone to see. *What was he up to?* I wondered as he quickly left the room. His piercing blue eyes seemed to dance mischievously.

I met Drameon's eyes for a moment and wondered if he knew what the Drakar planned. His face softened as if stress crept from his body. Meeting my gaze he frowned, but seemed understanding. We had our moments, of understanding and regret, and this was one of them. He was still uneasy about his daughter being my mate and that I understood her better.

Clenching my fists so tightly I almost drew blood, I looked towards the door where Howl had taken Raillyn. Part of me was half-tempted to go after her. However, I knew I had to stay and address the situation that was caused after returning her to what I had believed at the time was her rightful place. How wrong my mind had been though.

"What in Death's Realm was that all about?!" Drake cursed, almost shouting and slightly shaking.

"That my friend was something anticipated, but not entirely expected." Drameon began carefully before looking towards me. "While I cannot say everything I can say the path she is walking is very narrow and demanding. Her magic lashing out and her mind shifting the way it was proved that."

Drake seemed confused, as if someone tried to push him over and failed. I stood still knowing if I said anything it would start a fight. Instead, I seethed in my own anger.

"I have never seen Raillyn act in such a way. That was animalistic, like my people on a full moon. Your race doesn't shift so why was she acting like that?" He questioned as everyone stood tense and quiet around him.

I fidgeted uncomfortably, shifting from one foot to another. Internally my mind wanted to leave still, and make sure Raillyn was ok, but physically I knew I couldn't. It just pissed me off further.

In that instant Howl strolled back into the room. Smiling cockily, he walked past me, patting me on the shoulder before stopping in front of Drameon, who scowled at him. Whatever was going on he knew and wasn't happy.

"I took the liberty of swinging by my room before the den and asked if Lyth and Celeste could take Raillyn. As you know, they have been visiting my place in case we needed them on short notice. After explaining a quick version of the unsettling events they happily agreed, and took her to the small den." Howl said to Drameon before turning to face me. "And you my friend, they want to see right away." My eyes narrowed at that request.

"Perhaps we can all go meet them, and when we get there someone can tell me what's going on." Drake said unnervingly.

Before waiting to hear more I turned and walked out the door. I knew if I stayed I'd cause a scene and that wasn't possible. Already too many buttons were being pushed about this situation, causing more grief than anticipated.

I had hoped I could bring Raillyn here, leave her with the Wolves and let her catch up a little. Later when Daes called her she would go and do her duty, completing the task he had laid out for her and learning what it entailed. Even though it wasn't ideal for me, it was what I wanted. To see her happy, I could put my own selfish feelings aside if she could smile for a while. However, that didn't happen and the protective male inside me was not going to let my mate be handed over to another man.

Entering the red-carpeted halls I almost blindly made my way to the den. I didn't care if the others followed or not and as I entered, Celeste caught on right away that I was in a dark mood.

The small-framed, strawberry-blonde lady was kneeling near Raillyn as I came into the door. Her fire-like evergreen eyes met mine momentarily. "Calm down, she's fine." She said gently brushing a strand of Raillyn's hair out of her face. "However this is only going to get worse, and you know it. You cannot fight what is, Alkin. No matter how hard you try, you just can't do it and neither can she." Celeste said, while standing and reprimanding me.

I was already backpedaling from my original idea of letting Raillyn stay in the Wolves castle, it was beginning to look like a horrible plan. Her badgering me wasn't helping matters it only caused more anger to spread throughout my body. I couldn't take

Raillyn away, even though she didn't hate me outright I knew, mind wise she was highly upset for everything I had done to her.

Why shouldn't she be? I thought to myself. I would be pissed too if I found out my actions were manipulated and then the life I had taken from me. I would be beyond pissed at the person who had a hand in it. To make matters worse we had spent over six years together in The Keep, she was slowly starting to come out of her shell and put her full trust in me. That however shattered as she discovered the truth and with our bonds broke, that only made the situation worse. She couldn't tell what I was thinking or if I was telling the truth anymore. Instantly I hated myself for landing in this situation. If I had only controlled my anger in the first place and not tried to kill Lord Drake, none of this would have happened. Or at least not in the fashion it had.

The door closing behind me made me realize I was pacing the floor and inching closer and closer towards Raillyn. Now within arm's reach, my body stilled as I smelled her overpowering scent. *This is going to be a problem...* I thought as I tried to calm myself and reconnect with the real world and not my natural instincts.

"Is she ok?" I heard Drake ask genuinely concerned for her. Part of me seemed relieved he cared, the logical part. However, the more primitive part wanted to rip his heart out and shove it down his throat.

How was it I had kept such control of my anger till now? I thought to myself before I knew the truth. It was because Rai was mine in The Keep and I never had a rival vying for her attention. Now it was different.

Drake rushed by me, shouldering me out of the way. However, before he reached her I grabbed his arm. Slamming him into a nearby wall, unconsciously I drew my dagger and pressed it against his neck. *Isn't this behavior what caused this terrible situation in the first place?* My logical side asked.

No, this was different. Drake was the leader of the Werewolves, and human-like or not they still were primitive and possessive when it came to females in their care. He blatantly shoved me away from her, challenging me.

"Challenge me again Wolf and I will make you regret it. While I cannot kill you, I can sure make you think twice about what you are doing." I said threateningly before releasing him, tossing him away from my mate.

Standing between Raillyn and Drake, the Ancients in the room tensed. They had seen situations such as these before. An unbound pair often caused such problems, especially when the female was around males, not of her kind, who didn't understand the underlying situation.

The fact was that Raillyn was my everything, that without her I didn't feel whole or like myself, and her the same with me. Regardless of her not growing up Mystic instinctively she knew. Making Drake understand that sooner would be better, however how do you get a protective Wolf to listen to reason, when I myself was even unreasonable. At the moment Raillyn had to remain safe, and she had to get to her grandfather, Daes as soon as possible.

"Alkin! Isn't this what started this whole mess? You two don't need to fight." Drameon said, trying to calm my inner demons. However, I ignored him, my eyes were on Drake. We circled the room, before he sprang into action.

Drawing his sword I saw it a split second before he brought it down on my head. Calling my shadowed blade, I parried his attack. Pushing him back away from Raillyn, the sound of wood knocking against stone floors resonated in the room.

Out of the corner of my eye, Lyth grabbed a few toppled chairs and moved them aside. Everyone seemed to jump back, unsure what to do; everyone but one. Howl stood directly behind Drake and seemed to stay there. Casually he crept around the room eyes aglow and grinning. I couldn't see the others maybe that was because only Lyth and Howl were Raillyn's primary Drakar guards.

Celeste's voice broke my thoughts. "Boys! My Goddess, stop this right now before I whip magic at both of you!" She yelled, clapping her hands together loudly. With that echoing single clap, magic boomed with power and resonated like thunder in a dense forest.

Glancing at her to see how serious she was, she looked mad. Her usually calm face was set seriously against the pale of her hair. In her hands sat two menacing deep green near black orbs of cracklings magic. Like lightening dancing in a jar, she held them ready to toss as us. Yes, she was a healer, but this was not meant to heal, this was meant to cause us to go unconscious. On another occasion I had been subject to such magic before and was not about to let it happen again. Shoving Drake away, I jumped back and dissipated my blade. Howl and Lyth were there to grab me and hold me back, should I decide to attack again. Clenching my fists in anger, my temper felt volatile.

"I can tell you that everything I did, even the stuff you hate me for, I did for her!" I shouted, shaking with anger, and pointing towards Raillyn. "With that being said I'm not sorry for the events that lead to Callina." I said in a calmer tone shoving Howl, and Lyth off me.

Turning I glared at them, I knew my eyes were blazing red, and looking towards Rai I had a moment of weakness. My pupils dilated and the overpowering need to take her away from this madness encompassed me. Ultimately she was my responsibility until she went to Daes, regardless of her father being there. Or the guards she had with her. She was well over the age and he knew what it meant under our laws. The sound of a snap and Howl's hand in front of my face broke my trance.

"Go jump in Tranquility Lake for a while, we will watch Raillyn." Howl said as I caught the meaning of his words. *Go cool off someplace else.*

If it were anyone else it would have angered me more; however, I knew Howl meant well. Still the primal side wanted to be sure they knew I meant business. Leaning towards Howl, I emanated a low growl.

"You better or you will have more to worry about." I said before stepping back through a portal to leave.

Unsettling Information ~ Drake

As Alkin disappeared through the portal, I allowed myself to sigh with relief. However it is short-lived as Raillyn begins to stir. Shakily her hand goes to her forehead, covering her eyes. Taking a step forward, I found myself wanting to go to her, to comfort her. Taking a quick glance around the room made me stop. I was unsure what the Ancients in the room would do. Watching instead the golden-haired woman named Celeste, who must have been the Den Healer, rushed to Raillyn's side. Her azure blue pants pillowed around her legs as she walked.

"How are you? Do you feel OK?" She asked helping Raillyn sit upright. Her fiery green eyes seemed to glow.

Raillyn nodded, but rubbed her head as if she was nursing a dull throbbing ache at her temple. For a moment her nose twitched, almost like our women's when they pick up a familiar scent. Removing her hand she stood swiftly, her eyes glowed a deep magenta color before fading and resuming their ever-changing hue. Celeste flinched momentarily before standing and backing up cautiously, allowing Raillyn room to walk.

Uncharacteristically she smelled at the air. Again it reminded me of my people, who often took in the scents of those around them. She was acting as if she was one of my Wolves, more animalistic than her usual nature. *Why was she acting like this?*

Looking around the room no one met my gaze. All eyes were on Raillyn. Drameon had a look of unease on his face, his silver hair fell across his creased lined furrowed face. Pain almost reflected his eyes. Lyth seemed worried as well and stood ready to move into motion. Only Howl appeared relaxed, but even his stance seemed ready. Like a snake waiting to spring into action, Howl seemed curled up in the corner. One leg bent, foot on wall, and arms folded. He looked at me and smiled almost sarcastically, before his attention turned back to Raillyn and her unsettling behavior. She stood unmoving almost as if she was taking every-thing in.

She never acted this way until she was in The Keep. As I've heard it was a place that was accustomed to living off the scent of others, just like Wolves and Shifters. Chaimh had once stated that it was vital to survival, to know the scent of those you trusted aside from those you didn't there. *Maybe there was more to her behavior than what I was seeing...I couldn't think straight on it though there were more important things than worrying about her behavior.*

This must have been what Howl meant when he said she would change. Her eyes grew wide for a moment almost fearful, flashing purple. Shaking her head, I saw her tense.

"Where are the girls?" Asking no one in particular.

Drameon seemed to shy away from the question I knew where Deestan was, she was here in the castle. However, I didn't know where the younger one was. Alkin took her the instant he came to tell us Raillyn was alive and healing after the ordeal in The Keep.

"Deestan is here, she's probably studying in the library as we speak. Callina is with her father in Silvertine." Drameon said calmly. Raillyn tensed as his words hit her.

"Why? Who said he could take her? I left her in the care of the Den for a reason. Not for him to get his hands on her." She said distraughtly. Everyone looked towards me. It was my fault he took her.

"Alkin and I got into an argument and he left with her, say-ing if he was such an inconvenience that he would remove his presence from my castle." I said summing up the situation. Alkin and I often argued, since he was the one who kidnapped Raillyn and my daughter over six years ago. Regardless of him assisting us, we didn't get along very well. Yes, I understood it was an or-der from Daes, Howl told me that much. Still, it bothered me how close he had become with her, and that they had a child together.

For a moment, Raillyn twitched her head, as if something was wrong. Slowly she walked towards me with a jerk in her step, like a marionette tethered to string. She was closer to me now, our body inches from each other. Standing on her tiptoes, she leaned in to whisper softly but audibly, in my ear.

"Alkin drew blood didn't he? I can smell his scent on you." She said before withdrawing, and smiling menacingly, leaving me confused.

"What is wrong with you?" I asked. This wasn't the sweet Raillyn I remembered, nor was it Raihanna, or at least the Raihanna I had seen.

Shooting a questioning glance at Celeste who appeared expressionless, I saw her arms were crossed in front of her as if she was waiting for me to make the first move. Drameon appeared expressionless. Lyth smirked slightly, but it faded quickly when Celeste shot him a glance. Raillyn made a frustrated almost whine which brought my attention back to her.

Glancing back down at her, I saw her fists balled up tightly. Her chin was tilted upward defiantly. Her eyes looked hard, glassy, almost watery, as if battling some inner demons. Shaking, a blue haze began to radiate from her body. Meeting my gaze, her eyes now a stunning shade of blue, swam with confusion and newly found emotions.

She let out a long drawn-out breath through her nostrils. Raillyn's eyes, still blue, softened a bit, seeming less glassy, and her face relaxed. Unclenching her fists the tension in her body evaporated.

"Something inside is…" She paused grasping for words and tilting her head to the side. "I feel like I'm being pulled and pushed in too many different directions at once. I feel so lost… I feel… " She trailed off, placing her head in her hands. For a moment, she appeared as if she might cry. Strangely enough, at that moment I could feel Raillyn. The Raillyn as she had been years ago. I wanted to comfort her, tentatively reaching out my hand, the burn of energy made me pause.

Like a whip snapping a horse in motion, some unseen force lashed out. A maniacal grin spread across her face that turned to an angered sneer. Startled, I flinched, withdrawing my hand. The Raillyn I knew was gone.

"I can't believe you just let him walk out and take her like that!" She yelled as she lunged towards me, a blue haze seemed to engulf her hands.

Startled, I backed away as Howl and Lyth both sprang forward. Grabbing her by the arms and waist, they pulled her back with them. Both men gripped her arms tightly as she kicked out her legs angrily, her chest heaving as she struggled. In the time it takes a lit room to go from light to dark, Raillyn's demeanor changed again. Just like before she went still.

Howl and Lyth gave each other a questioning look. Glancing around I saw Celeste with a purple bottle in hand standing back against the wall. Drameon had made his way to her during the commotion and they whispered to one another.

Raillyn's body relaxed and a watery confusion settled back into her eyes; she seemed to not stare at anything in particular. Cautiously Lyth released one of her arms, Howl did the same, but neither stepped away from her. Again her gaze became unsettling as it darted upward. Raillyn's blue eyes shined malevolently with a distinct reddish undertone. The haze of blue seemed to spread from her hands across her body like an eerie reddish blue fog. Strangely enough the colors didn't blend. Stepping back, I had seen the look before, it was the look Raihanna gave before she did something devious.

Her eyes began searching, and meeting mine once more, I had a pretty good suspicion of what was going to happen next. The air around me tingled with power just as Raillyn lunged for me again. Howl was prepared this time. Grabbing her around the waist, he pulled her back. Both fell onto a pillowed bench. Raillyn kicked her feet wildly trying to break free. Lyth grabbed her arms and tried to restrain them, however it didn't help. Her elbow connects sharply with Lyth's face, smashing him in his cheek, just missing his eye. Howl shifted to get a better grip. Howl managed to pin her hands under his muscular arms. The air around them crackled and steamed, both men appeared red faced and sweaty, but appeared unaffected by her behavior. Drawing a dagger Howl handed it to Lyth who was rubbing his face. Taking it he nodded in understanding. All I could do was watch helplessly.

"Good! I was going to say if you weren't going to form a bond with her I would, because this is ridiculous." Lyth snarls while holding the knife and running it across Howl's free hand. His blood beaded at the wound and began to seep out.

Bringing it near Raillyn's face, she paused. Another change was occurring inside and this time I saw it in her behavior; she relaxed. The swirling red-blue haze faded as Lyth slowly let go and looked towards me.

"Trust us, she will be way better off if she has a Mystic binding with one of us. She's overloaded and running on instincts due to it. To make matters worse she isn't bound to Alkin anymore and he was the only one keeping her sane." He said carefully.

Not really understanding what he meant, I just nodded. I heard his words, but my eyes were on Raillyn. She took Howl's wrist in her hands and brought it to her lips. Instantly she took a deep breath before closing her eyes and sucking at the wound feverishly. She began making noise, she was enjoying it. She was acting like the Vampires in The Keep. Complete disgust must of shown on my face because Howl explained.

"Think of it as a blood lust, while she's not driven for the blood in my veins she craves the power. Her power hasn't been complete in so long she doesn't know how to deal with it or how to replenish it. As I've said, Ancients cook with blood, it helps keep us sane and our energy levels steady. However, Raillyn wasn't raised Mystic and since leaving The Keep, she hasn't replenished any power since before Raihanna's death. This is what happens if we don't." Howl said.

He had mentioned this in his story of how he was tied up with the Mystics. That often they cooked this way, because blood was power and power was magic. It made sense, even my race knew it resided in everything living, even the land itself was em-powered.

Finally, Raillyn began to take blood slower, and reached behind her back, where her dagger lay. Pulling it from its sheath, she ran it across her own wrist, before turning slightly to place it in Howl's mouth. Now both drew each other's blood.

Another change occurred; this time I felt it in the air. It seemed to stir with electricity. My skin tingled and my heart picked up pace. It was almost invigorating. Drameon met my gaze as I smiled. Walking towards me, he patted my shoulder.

"It's their magic, its resonating in unison, in harmony. Howl is trying to steady her emotions and bring her back in check. This is only a temporary fix though. There are a few other things that need to occur before it becomes permanent."

Looking him in the eyes I wondered what he meant. "What other things?" I questioned.

"Things I will not say in full right now. She has to find her balance and she can't do that if she refuses to acknowledge certain situations that are natural to our kind." He said, as I saw Howl slip his hand down the collar of her shirt.

Slowly he moved it towards her left shoulder. Raillyn in turn did the same. Slipping her hand under Howl's low collared shirt she quickly found his shoulder.

A blue light began to permeate from their resting place, almost simultaneously. Bright blue lines, traced in an ancient pattern that held no language or meaning to me. Leaves, vines, and swirls drew in cerulean across the exposed skin. As the glow faded they opened their eyes and released each other's wrists. Raillyn licked her lips, wiping her mouth clean, removing any trace of blood left behind.

"Thank you." She said to Howl before hugging him and standing. Smiling, he stood as well.

"It's only a temporary fix, you will still feel the shift of your emotions, but not as dramatically. Hopefully, for the time being, it will keep your magic from lashing out. It won't be permanent though, not until Daes' power is flowing back in this world and in order to do that you need to find your new balance." He said as he flicked her nose.

"What do you mean by finding my new balance? How can I find my new balance if I need Daes' magic in the world to keep from feeling crazy?" She said.

"For that, you have to speak to Daes." Drameon said as she looked unsurely around. Spotting me, she looked towards the ground.

"I'm sorry. I was mad that you let Alkin take Callina. However, He's never hurt me or the girls. However, there is something unnerving about him. That causes my core to tremble." She said as she came to give me a hug. For a moment, she pulled back before hugging me again.

"What was that for?" I asked. I still felt a bit wary of her new "normal" behavior. She shook her head against my chest.

"I don't know. You smell different." She said as she inhaled my scent deeply.

Leaning down I did the same. For a moment, we both stood taking in the scent of one another. Something had changed on her also. No longer did she smell like sweet honey and vanilla. It smelled almost like lemons with a hint of pine. This subtle change irritated me.

Was it the time she spent in The Keep? The change in her magic? Or even that she had been Alkin's lover for over six years. At that thought, I felt myself possessively hold her tighter. She stilled in my arms.

"I'm sorry for what happened." She said breaking my train of thought. "I never knew I was going to have to live in The Keep. I didn't know any of it. I know you're mad about what happened there and I don't blame you." She said almost guessing why I was upset. Leaning down I kissed her head.

"I'm not mad at you, I'm mad at that Demon." I said.

She giggled at my response. "He's not a Demon. He's a Mystic, like me, and my father. We live very hard lives and I'm only just now seeing that. I don't know what to expect or what will happen. Only that I need to speak to Daes and do what he asks me to do. Even if it's not what I want, he knows what's best for the world as a whole." She said while looking me in the eyes seriously.

Putting my hand on her cheek, she looked up at me almost frightened. Leaning down I stole a kiss and pulling back she seemed almost surprised. "Whatever happens we will get through it. Together this time." She nodded her head, almost apprehensively.

"Raillyn, if you want to learn more then I think you should come with me. My mother just sent me a call asking to speak with me, and if you come along I am sure you will get answers." Drameon spoke as Raillyn looked towards him hopeful.

"Go." I said. "I'll be here when you comeback."

Smiling she went to her father and left through a shadowy grey portal.

"I think we will also go." Celeste said to Lyth, who pulled at his arm.

I gave a nod. Assuming they probably wanted to go check on Alkin, or they had business elsewhere. Closing the door behind them, I found myself alone with Howl. Sighing I went to sit on the bench, shrugging his shoulders Howl came to join me.

"Can you tell me more about the old ways? How do Mystics live? Other than what I know, what else does it entitle?"

Taking a deep breath, and leaning back in the chair, he seemed tense. "That I really shouldn't impart to you, but I can tell you Mystics and Drakar live very much alike. All the Ancient races live very similarly." He said. Closing his eyes and rubbing the bridge of his nose momentarily, I listened.

"We are tied to the Gods, like Mystics who naturally let events occur, and only play a subtle hand in getting them to shift accordingly. We listen and obey the Gods and their plans. We pray daily to them for the balance we need to get through the day, to do what is right, and to have them lead us along the correct path. At the end of the day, we thank them for the life they gave us, the friends and family we have and for all the fortunes they bestow upon us. Raillyn is learning this. But that is only part of it."

Looking at him, our eyes met. I could tell he was choosing his words carefully, considering this was perhaps turning into a sensitive topic.

"Well, what else? I can see that you are similar to us, praying, listening, and following the gods. Even though, it's on a deeper level than us, it still is the same. Right?"

"Yes, as you know Mystics carry out the Gods plan and Drakar assist them. We have a saying, the Ancient's. **Blood is power, blood is everything...** Literally blood and power is everything to us. It's in the air we breathe, the food we eat, in our drink, in the earth. It's used in healing, when bringing a new life into the world, and in death when delivering a soul to Delron. Festivals, sowing crops, cooking, imbuing gems and other items, nearly everything we do involves blood, involves power. Nothing is simple, nothing is like how you do things. I believe the only blood spell we share is how you speak to the Goddess." He said eyeing me carefully.

Nodding my head, I knew he was right. I saw that much when he was able to bring Raillyn under control through the Mystic bond they created. "Yes, we use blood to summon the Moon Goddess. There are a few spells that require blood, but not many. When Raillyn carried Deestan, Luca used a blood spell to identify that the child was mine. Other than that our race isn't centered on it."

Howl diverted his gaze at the mention of Deestan. Something was not being said that he kept from me. It's what Alkin hinted at as well, and Drameon.

"What? You, Alkin, and Drameon have been bothered every time I mention Raillyn and her tie to my kingdom. I know she's Mystic, she is bound to no throne, but that doesn't mean she can't love who she chooses." I was getting angry again. Speaking about Raillyn had become a delicate subject that angered me and brought fear to my mind.

Howl stood and paced the room before taking a seat again. I followed his every move and quietly watched. "I guess you will learn sooner or later anyway. Especially if the talk around Silvertine is serious…"

Sighing he continued. "Ancients typically do not get a choice in who they love. It's a reason for the betrothal. We are bound to one person, one mate, who we are drawn to, who we crave, and our body, magic, and mind live for. We are told this from a young age, we grow up with the knowledge that we are meant for only one person. Meeting them for the first time is said to trigger unimaginable feelings, emotions, and energy. It literally is love at first sight, it's inescapable, and encompassing, everything changes. Like two halves becoming whole, light meeting dark, good creating peace with evil, we are one. Neither can escape its force and if they try, well their magic forces them into situations to be together." He paused unsure either what else to say or waiting for me to respond.

Shock must have crossed my face, I had never heard of this, our race was different. We always had a choice for everything. I was beginning to see how limited the Ancients lived, they required blood, power and had limited choices in everything they did.

"All Ancients have this? Even Mystics? Do you have a mate?" I asked suddenly curious to know more about what I was dealing with, what Raillyn was dealing with.

He paused and his eyes softened slightly before he shook his head no, and hardening his face. "No, not yet, I still have the luxury of not being tied down." He said wantonly smirking, but his tone spoke otherwise.

Looking at him skeptically, he seemed to be deep in thought, brow raised he met my eyes. "You're lying." I said knowingly, his behavior told me he was hiding something.

His typically mellow demeanor took on a different appearance. Eyes open wide, his breathing picked up pace as he seemed shocked, almost frightened. "Stop looking at me like that, Wolf." He said before running his fingers through his hair. "At this time

I don't have a mate I'm tied down to. However, that doesn't mean I don't know who my mate is." He said calmer.

Frowning I apologized, I didn't mean to unnerve Howl in such a way. "Sorry, it's just how you said it made me realize you were lying."

"Keh." He said casually, before going on. "Her name's Ayanna, she's living with the Shifters in the north, actually. I placed a friend of mine in her village to retrieve her. She was too close to Zion for my comfort, and there are less Vampires in the north so it's safer there."

Furrowing my brows I was confused why the Shadow Walker would care about a Drakar woman. That's when it dawned on me, *she must be a half-breed...* Like Howl originally was, she must of been the result of two different races.

Glancing at Howl he saw me staring at the fire deep in thought.

"Yes you're right, she's a half-breed, just like me. The details are unknown, and this is only speculation but from what I know her mother is a blue Drakar, and a rogue Shadow Walker male took her mother. During the time, everywhere was in an uproar, because of the war in Alecien. The war threw the world and it's energy into chaos. During this time she must have met her mate, but was taken away. Ayanna was the last Drakar of Daes' line born into this world after the war broke out." He trailed off.

"So why are you not with her? If you know who she is I mean?" I asked curiously.

Howl slightly laughed. "Because she's like Raillyn, she didn't grow up knowing the ways of the Ancients. And seeing how Raillyn acts makes me want to wait a little longer, slowly have her learn Drakar ways instead of pushing them on her." He paused before going on. "I'm giving her time," He said halfhazardly. "And I sympathize with Alkin in a way because I know how it feels. Thankfully for me I haven't had actual contact with her." He finished while twisting at his blue teardrop amulet around his neck.

Before I had a chance to ask what he meant about Alkin, he continued. "And yes all Ancients, including Mystics have this. It's one reason why we follow no throne, only follow the Gods and their ways. We have no desire to do otherwise, no one's ever complained about our ways, even if they are a bit hampering to those who do not understand it. We enjoy how we live, the Gods created us this way and we live to serve them. That being said, I know it is foreign to you, but as I said we live very differently."

"Living differently and living how you live is not the same. You are so limited to what you can and cannot do. Why?"

Raising his eyebrow he seemed surprised. "Why, you ask? Because, you see it as limited but we see it as endless. The magic and bond between mates is a rush of energy that heightens every sense of your body and mind. You do not want to live any other way. Mates come to depend, wholeheartedly on each other. They are so tied together that their very lives depend on each other. The power and emotions in everything we do bring us closer. Our lives are not easy, by no means are they like yours. As you know when our females become with child, they lose their magic. This is not only unsettling, it's dangerous, and only brings more dangers as it goes on." He said with his old bravado.

What he said was true, Raillyn had lost her power when she was pregnant with Deestan but I didn't think that was dangerous. She was fine and nothing bad had happened. "What do you mean it's dangerous? Raillyn was fine the whole time and her magic returned with no issues after Deestan was born."

Howl slightly laughed and shook his head at my words. I looked at him upset by his reaction. "Oh, you don't understand, do you? First off, females are not able to have a child until they find their mate. Second, it's their mate who ensures their safety, during this time. It's their blood that keeps them strong. If they didn't, things would end badly, and lastly, their magic just doesn't comeback. It's their mate who helps in that as well. Females are most vulnerable after the birth of a child, not only do they lack their magic, but they are not able to focus, their mind is hazy, and their spirit borders between the barriers of life and

death. Often it can cause irrational behavior. You saw similar behavior earlier with Raillyn. It's due to the trauma of their magic
being absent for so long and shock. To be brought back, they
need blood, and power from their mate. Only they have the force
needed to hold them in the living. He was there when Deestan
was born, and I'm sure he was following Rai around to make sure
she was safe. Or he had someone helping him."

Shock must have crossed my face again. *Her mate was
there when our daughter was born? Raillyn was not able to have
a child until she met her mate?* Guilt gripped my mind at the
thought of this, and Howl saw it. I loved Raillyn but if what
Howl said was true… and she belonged to another…

"That means, Raillyn's mate has been around us this whole
time, even before Deestan was born. Does Raillyn know? Why
didn't she tell me? And who?" I asked curious to know what I
already suspected, and being reminded of Howl's comment. *That
he understood how Alkin felt…*

"She didn't know. Remember Raillyn wasn't raised to
know the old ways. Chaimh and Lillian raised her but left out
certain details about her life. Alkin was supposed to remove her
from Alecien, and take her to Aeralain, or even the God's plane
of existence. There she would learn about who she was and the
Ancients' way of life. However, that didn't happen." He said before going on smirking. "You know who her mate is, you two
disagree so much and now you know why."

It was all making sense. He was mad at me, and it was
worse when we argued over Raillyn. "So Alkin's known this
whole time and never said anything to anyone?"

Looking me in the eyes, he shook his head. "Alkin didn't
say much. However, after speaking to several people in
Silvertine, the ones who just left in fact, I realized he had his
friends assisting him. You and Briar intervened and took Raillyn
away before Alkin could. It left her in a confused state. Feelings,
emotions, and magic danced across her. Emotions she didn't
know how to control, and the one person who could control them
wasn't able to get to her. However, I did find out that on the night

of the full moon, Raillyn sought Alkin out. She opened a portal to his home in Silvertine. From what I know it didn't go well, since Raillyn was never raised as an Ancient, the situation of them exchanging blood, marking each other and Alkin claiming her created anxiety. She panicked in what she thought was a dream and left, going to you instead. Deestan was proof of that. If she knew who her mate was and knew what she was, she would have never carried another man's child."

Placing my head in my hands, my thoughts swirled. "If she sought him out why did he let her leave?" I asked trying to understand why this had all occurred in the first place.

"Because he panicked, and when she left he couldn't go after her. Your world was blocked to outsiders at the time, unless they were invited." Howl said, almost desperately.

That made me pause, he was right. As I remembered back to that time, I did remember smelling blood, and the scent of pine. In my more feral state I didn't care and wanted to eradicate that scent. Alkin's scent. I made a terrible mistake, and I knew it. *Even rulers are not exempt from moments of stupidity...*

Howl patted my shoulder before going on. "Yes, I know." He said understandingly. "However, Alkin placed many people in Raillyn's life, Celeste and Lyth were here in the Wolves' Den when Deestan was born. Nora was in The Keep caring for the girls and even Alkin and Drameon were around, unseen to everyone. What all they did I am not sure of, but I can guess how far they had to go to keep Raillyn safe. I think if you want the truth you need to ask them, maybe with Celeste and Lyth."

"Ok?" I was unsure of what to do with the information I had received and still curious to know the rest.

"Just wait, I am sure you will get answers when Raillyn returns. Until then just relax, remain calm, and don't let it get to you. I have seen into Raillyn's mind. She loves you, she really does, and even though she doesn't understand the situation yet, when she does she will be hurt. She will be torn between what her mind wants. Yet, her soul, magic and body desire something different. I think for now you decide if you can live with the idea of Alkin being Raillyn's mate. He has sacrificed so much because of her love for you. I would ask Alkin what he plans on doing, if he is going to bind her to him or not. Meaning Raillyn would only respond to him. It's a precarious path they walk and one that will need to be worked out together. You need to talk to him, maybe you two can begin seeing eye to eye." Howl said as he got up and walked towards the door.

I got up and followed him out into the hall, frowning. Whether I liked it or not, I would have to come to terms with all this information.

Lessons of Their Own ~ Raillyn

As I left the portal, I walked into what appeared to be a familiar room. I had been here before. We had visited, when my mother – my real mother – was still alive, long ago.

A fireplace lay to my right. A tall staff similar to Delron's stood nearby, leaning against the wall. Its phoenix and dragon carvings spiraled upwards in the same manner, but instead of holding a large red stone as Delron's did, it held a huge forest green emerald. Chairs dotted the room, and various bookshelves filled with ancient tomes lined the walls. Old paintings, artwork, and tapestries hung where no shelves were while beautifully crafted rugs lined the floors. Destiny and Chaimh stood as soon as the portal closed, both a portrait of worry.

Destiny stood immediately, her braided, long silver hair, hung loosely down her back. Bright green eyes, high-cheekbones, pointed ears and Elf like features met my ever-changing eyes. Chaimh stood beside her, his familiar brown hair, pale Elvish features and brown eyes met mine as he smiled. Full heartedly I returned his smile. It felt good to see him again after so long and everything that had happened.

Drameon beamed genuinely as he went to his mother and embraced her gently in his arms. "Hello, mother, all is well." He said stepping back and placing a hand on my shoulder. Looking at him, we smiled at each other.

I couldn't help but feel happy, more like myself. For once I was not fearful of what I should or shouldn't say, and felt I could speak freely here. Yet, I still worried about my unsettling behavior from earlier.

"Hello, grandmother." I said bowing slightly. "Hello, Chaimh." I said as he took me into a tight embrace.

"How I have worried about you, my child." He said into my hair as he kissed the top of my head.

When Chaimh released me Destiny quickly pulled me into a tight hug. "I wasn't sure if you would even survive The Keep, I was so fearful the Vampires would kill you." She said as she released me and motioned for us to sit.

"Please come and sit, join us. Is there anything I can get you?" My grandmother asked very host-like, eager to please.

Smiling I shook my head and took a seat. "I am just happy to be here in one piece." I replied while laughing slightly. "When I lay outside your house as Raihanna I really didn't know if I would make it this far." I said remembering back to my teleporting travels, now able to place my location.

Remembering the realization that struck me, and knowing I had to die in order to stop the pain. Even then I was still unaware that Alkin would be able to reverse the spell, but he was my only choice. He had created the construct body which I was residing in at the time, and from what Howl said only the creator could deconstruct the spell.

Taking a seat, my grandmother went on. "Yes, I was unaware at the time what the outcome would be. I still am, in a way. You are at a turning point, child. There is still much work that needs to be done. So much you must learn." She said while looking at my father and Chaimh.

Nodding my head, I agreed, Hunter still wanted to use the portal to summon evil beings. Shadows and dead creatures that would destroy Alecien and eventually the world, it was a frightening feeling, knowing my hands played a role in helping this.

"Other than that, how do you feel?" Chaimh asked breaking my train of thought.

Looking at him and meeting his eyes, my mind went blank. The last time I had spoken to him was just before Alkin took me from Death's Realm and the last time I had seen him was as Raihanna. When I poisoned him with my darkened blade.

"I'm so sorry. When I was Raihanna, I poisoned you." I said regretfully.

"Don't fret about it, it was all part of the plan. I'm more concerned of your feelings and how you are handling all of this." Chaimh asked again more seriously.

For a moment I pondered how to answer, my emotions tipped from regret to sadness, as I felt myself reach for the mental link between Alkin and I. Shaking my head they tipped again, to anger.

"In a way I'm furious, and confused. You knew, didn't you? When I came to first visit, when Deestan was little, you were so quiet about Alkin and said nothing. I should've known you knew him. Especially after Delron said he was his son, you two work so close together. But I still don't know what draws me to him. Is it magic? A spell? Either way it nags at my mind, and I don't like it nor understand it."

Chaimh looked at Drameon, who avoided his gaze. Even Destiny stared at him expecting an answer. My father's eyes flashed silver, matching his hair. The air around him changed and became thick, something was up. Something unsaid.

"None of us can, nor will we say anything about the matter. Daes has the answers you seek and he's the one who wishes to speak to you about them. Just know everything was done for a reason. Alkin taking you away, and your time in The Keep was valuable. Even the things that bother you, the bad things you've done." My father said while pacing the floor.

"Yeah, I know, and Hunter still has that staff, which bothers me. I bet he's ready to open the portal at any time and if that happens, terror will be unleashed on the world. Auran cannot handle an army of undead shadow beings. If they get out they will destroy everything." I said while standing and pacing. I shook my head before going on, a dizzying feeling lightly brushed my mind. "I can't believe that I had a hand in the events creating those items. Both of them are nothing but trouble." My power rose in a new more powerful, frightening way. The room spun slightly. The uneasy feeling was returning as I felt my emotions begin to sway back and forth again.

My magic felt so different, I could feel it penetrate so deep it pierced my very core. Emotions controlled it now. I felt it tipping my magic in favor of chaos or harmony, depending on my mood, making it feel like a constant tug of war. Balance was a struggle.

It angered me, I was on the verge of shaking, and I knew my eyes flashed red. My vision hazed as I paced and thought about the events that lead to this moment. That Hunter had knowingly ordered the portal to be erected, and planned to unleash an army of undead on the world. Subtly I felt a shift in the air around me but disregarded it.

Rage boiled inside me. "I hate him, hate him to the core. Hunter is evil and his intentions are madness."

Another shift occurred, this time inside, around me my family sat quiet and listened to my rambling. I felt something amiss, but my rage stopped me from putting my finger on it.

"You're right, grandmother, much work is still left to be done. It infuriates me. The portal needs to be dismantled, the staff needs to be destroyed and Hunter must die! I will not stand by while he destroys lives and kills more people." Something cracked deep within, my anger spiked furiously and with it so did my temper. Like a volatile substance catching fire, my anger peaked. "If need be I will be the one to kill him! I will personally drag him into the cellar of The Keep and torture him to death!" I yelled before realizing my mistake. It struck me as if I was punched in the stomach, the very air left my lungs, and a chill crept across my burning hot skin. Something changed in me, I was so angry I was blind in my fury, essentially acting like Raihanna. Now my mind was blank, as I realized a new presence had entered the room. One that I instinctively knew had listened to my rampage of anger.

Suddenly I was slammed against the wall, strong rough hands held my neck pinning me in place inches off the floor. Vibrant blue eyes glowing red with anger filled my vision, and long black hair fell into my face. *Daes.*

His magic was encompassing and overwhelming. It pierced my core, penetrating my soul. Everything stopped, my magic immediately leveled out and my mind blanked in horror.

"You will not kill Hunter nor have a hand in any of the events that you speak of! Control the anger to stop your madness, and cease acting in chaos." He said, releasing me from his grip.

As my feet touched the floor, I collapsed. My body shook, either from the overload of my magic combining with my anger or out of fear. Closing my eyes I tried to desperately gain some control over the rage. My body burned and pain echoed in every fiber. I gripped my head trying to stop the horrors it wrought.

Then like butterfly wings I felt fingers lightly dance upon my cheek. Gently they brushed my hair behind my ear, and rested on the nape of my neck. Pure magic seeped into me and spread down my body. My breathing seemed haggard and rough.

A calming peace took over, rage was no longer felt. My body calmed and stopped its shaking. The burning and pain subsided. Relief... Taking a calming breath I finally felt able to open my eyes.

Daes sat with me on the floor, his dark hair fell over his subtle Elf-like feature while his hand rested on the nape of my neck. The very air seemed to crackle and spark around us, holding a blue hue. The foggy like substance felt charged with enormous power. With every breath I took, the energy flowed into me, encompassing my mind. Like a cold winter's day, my breath hung in the hair, in a darker shade of blue. Frightened, I scrambled to my feet, pushing myself away from Daes.

Touching his shoulder and shoving myself backwards triggered a reaction. Forcefully, another vision took hold of my mind. My mother and I had spent much time with Daes while my father was away. We studied, trained or just talked in his home. When I opened my eyes, I found myself on the floor. Daes once again knelt, in all black beside me. My mind felt hazy and I blanked out for a moment. When I came too, his hand rested on my shoulder and I felt the steady beat of his magic running through my body once more.

My thoughts and emotions calmed, bringing my magic in control. Deep down I felt a part of me understand, however consciously fear began to boil up inside, winning. My heartbeat picked up pace, as I felt my body begin to shake violently. Panicked I jumped back out of his reach.

Like a dagger piercing my head, a burning sensation took over and pain exploded throughout me. I felt my magic violently lash out in a whip-like action. Glass shattered and the dull thud of objects hitting the floor echoed in the silence of the room. Eyes closed from the pain, I felt myself hit the floor hard. As darkness began to encompass me, I heard my grandmother cry out. Physically my body felt scalding hot, as if I was on fire.

It was just like before. My body felt unstable and volatile. Exhausted I allowed my mind to slip into the unconsciousness of an ancient spell, still residing deep within.

~~*~*~*~*Drameon*~*~*~*~*~*

Even now I feared for my daughter, and as I watched her fall to the ground and the Gods' spell grasp her once more forcing her into the sleeping trance of her toddlerhood. I knew I couldn't do anything to save her. She had become Daes' most carefully guarded lineage heir, and no other power could rival him or his care for her.

Just as in the Wolves castle I could only do so much, she was not of my lineage. I was powerless in controlling her seesawing emotions and magic. If her mother were still alive, she would easily be able to realign her but I had to rely on others.

Regretfully I had missed much in Raillyn's life, I had known the Gods had taken her but where I had no knowledge. She was whisked away from everyone who had a hand in the start of the war and kept away from them. I still was learning the extent to which they went to keep her sane and alive. The Gods spoke little of that time, and my mother, Destiny, only said that they had done what was needed to be done.

During that time, Raillyn's magic threatened to strike out and kill everyone and everything around her. Thankfully the Gods were immune to such magic, but still she lashed out at them. Her mind was in shambles from the death of her mother and my rampage of slaughter.

Still even to this day I felt ashamed for what I had done. If only I had kept a clear head Raillyn might have been able to stay with me. Sadly during that time, Daes held little control over her tiny immature mind that tried desperately to understand and grasp the uncontrollable magic which pulsed through her.

Destiny said the decision was made to place her in a sleeplike state, a magical coma. Halting her age, thoughts and magic until a later time, but I know this was not all that was done. They locked most of her magic away, making it inaccessible to her.

The spell Alkin and I were told to place upon her while in The Keep would only fracture the spells grasp on her. It would be left up to Raillyn to finish the process and continue on the path to become her real self. The Raillyn she should have been before the war and the hatred had spread so violently across the land.

Only the Gods themselves knew the reversal spell and what it entitled. It made me fearful for what she would be put through, after already being put through so much. So much still had to be explained. Much work had been done to right the wrong, but there was still so much left unfinished. Power had to be restored and there were not many ways to replace its loss.

Without saying a word, Daes scooped Raillyn up. My mother and he both looked at me as if I would try and stop him. I knew what had to be done, and I knew my place in the matter.

"I know." I said calmly. Daes nodded his head in under-standing, created a portal, and went through with Raillyn.

~*~*~*~*~*~*Raillyn*~*~*~*~*~*~*~

The steady vibration and crackle of magic woke me from my sleep. Opening my eyes, I gazed up at a vast, deep dark blue orb, which made up a skylight dome high above the bed I laid in. Looking around the room felt strange, its dim features didn't really reveal its natural beauty but in its own way revealed a twilight world. Bookshelves, filled with various objects and bottles lined the room, while a large blue crystal sat on a nearby table, pulsing with magic. Each flare of power, the crystal, gave would cause it to glow slightly before dying back to its dull features. *I've been here before*, I thought.

As I sat up in an equally deep-blue bed with its intricate elven patterns and leaf-like features, the crystal seemed to pick up pace and beat faster. Equally my heart began to take up with and match the rhythm of the crystals beat. I felt my eyes change color, and could only assume the glow matched the crystals.

The pain was gone and so was the burning sensation. Finally, I was beginning to feel normal again. Taking a deep breath, I smiled momentarily amazed, before gazing around the room further. This place was comforting.

On a nearby chair I spotted a large bag. Pulling it onto the bed, it felt as if it was full of clothes. Opening it revealed what contents it held. My Elite gear from The Keep, the Mythril black chestplate, blackened leather armor and long black leather cloak. Their familiar thick but soft texture made me frown. Like touching a rabid mink, I flinched and shoved the items back into the bag. I didn't want to see them or be reminded of the time I had spent there. Lifting the bag over my head I threw it onto the floor before laying back and closing my eyes trying to rest a little more. Not ready to confront those demons, I tried to block it out. But it didn't work.

Alkin had lied to me, stolen me away from everything I knew, and not once told me why. It was unnerving, even though I understood it was because of who I was, it didn't matter. I wasn't prepared to deal with what was to come on those terms, not yet anyway. Suddenly the door opening broke my thoughts. Blinking my eyes to clear my head, I looked to see who was entering.

Daes slowly walked into the room, the hall outside was dim and seemed to glow in a blue haze. Seeing him come into the room frightened me. His immense power radiated from every pore in his body. It was shaky, unstable, and yet balanced. It caused my own emotions to react wildly. Quickly I jumped from the bed and stood across from him. He smiled and carefully bent down to pick up the pack. I watched his every move, his black clothes moved with him fluidly. Powerful muscles rippled, hidden below the surface. Instinctively I knew that even though he appeared normal, he had emanated strength and power. It was frightening. Carefully he took the pack, placing it atop of the tussled blue elfin blanket, before turning towards me.

"Where am I?" I asked trying to sense where my father was with my magic, getting nothing in return.

Daes frightened me to the core, the magic pouring from him was intense and chaotic, but at the same time so pure and harmonized. It made me confused yet calm at the same time, and while my magic seemed to be controlled. My mind was racing while I was around him. It was exactly how I felt when I was at the Wolves' castle. Calm yet frantic, like a small bird trapped in a cat's cage.

Slowly and fluidly Daes brushed his long black hair behind his ear, I noticed it was slightly pointed much like the Elven race and Deestan's.

"You're in my home," He said in a smooth voice. "I need you to understand something." He began saying almost restlessly. "You will do as I say child; too much has been put into this for you to mess it up now. You are a Mystic and you will obey. With that being said, I do not want you having contact with the Wolves at this time. You walk a precarious line due to the situation you caused. Know this: you **cannot** take the Wolves throne. Opening that portal is the most important thing you can currently do." He said in a calmer demeanor. "And this," He said while holding up the pack. "Is imperative to you at the moment." He said while tossing the pack to me gently.

Automatically I caught it and looked at him, upset. I had enough of The Keep, and the Vampires. Throwing the pack back at him, I felt my anger rise, and my power.

"I don't want that stuff, I never want to see it again! And what do you mean the situation I caused?!" I yelled as I saw his cool blue eyes take on a red appearance. "I hate The Keep, I hate Hunter and I especially hate what is going on right now!" I carried on, unaware that the crystal in the room glowed fiercely with my rising anger.

My emotions were tipping again, I felt it deep within. The unsteady sway was building up and this time my mind was becoming staticky. My body began shaking once more as anger encompassed me.

The once blue color of the crystal began radiating an iridescent rusty red hue. Daes turned, noticing the stone. before I saw him grab the pack off the floor. Strongly he tossed it back across the bed and into my arms, knocking me back a step or two. Before meeting his gaze I felt his anger, it beat at me as sea waves beat at a rocky cliff. Suddenly I knew things were not going to go well. Like two powerful lightning storms his anger trumpeted mine with its sheer power.

"You will listen to me and listen well. I will not have you going and killing anyone, let alone Hunter or the Elite. No one will die at your hand, do you understand me? You will not torture or maim anyone either." He shouted angered by my outburst. "Aside from that, you are to return to The Keep and continue working for Hunter and finish the portal that Alkin and you began your work on."

Shock crossed my face and mind. Not only did Daes want me to return to The Keep, he wanted me to continue working with them and open the portal. Again I felt my anger rise, I didn't want to listen. My mind couldn't comprehend why this was important. Instead I felt myself reaching for my magic. Determined to leave I called a portal and went through not wanting to hear any more from him.

~~*~*~*Drameon*~*~*~*~*~*

Daes opened a portal and entered the room. Looking at me with hurt and anger in his eyes he spoke.

"You will go after her, Drameon, and this time you will not mess things up. It's too important to have things go amiss now. She must return to The Keep and finish the portal spell with Alkin. My magic must be free to roam in the world once more and that portal is the only way to do it. I can never return without it nor can my power enter the land." Daes said as he spoke, I felt his anger rise and could only assume Raillyn had left before he was able to explain the situation further.

Inwardly I had to chuckle. Obviously the time away from his kin resulted in him forgetting how two similar personalities often clashed. Calista and him were the same way, they got along great until something angered the other, then they would clash for a time, before going back to normal.

Standing, I nodded my head in agreement. This was the whole purpose for placing Raillyn in The Keep, they had the means in order to erect a portal and summon beings from another realm. Even if the means they used were unsettling. Raillyn was the only one able to create the portal that would begin to bring her grandfather's power back into the realm. "What did you tell her if I may ask?" I said calmly.

He seemed to be contemplating the situation at hand. "Raillyn's magic is controlling her, it appears when she is enraged. It was my fault in this case. I told her to return to The Keep and to open the portal, leaving the Wolves alone for now. I should have explained more, but she left before I could do so. I tried to remove some of the overwhelming power she was encompassed with, but it still wasn't enough. Her magic has a strong influence over her and can overwhelm her mind. If that's the case, she will sleep it off and awaken normal once more." He said regretfully as he came to stand in front of me.

Bowing, I understood and would have to ask Alkin if he would track her for me. "I will ensure she does as she's told." I said creating a portal and going through it to the Wolves' castle, unsure what to expect.

Confrontation ~ Alkin

When I received Drameon's mental call, I was still furious. I had escaped the Wolves' castle and entered the large den inside Drameon's house. Bookshelves stood everywhere as deep red chairs were spaced perfectly between them. Beautiful artwork dotted the walls and the ceiling was lined with low-hanging rafters. Walking around the large mahogany table, I left the room. My anger was getting the best of me and I would not allow it to lash out here.

Too much was happening already and situations were beginning to happen that I had no control over. It was infuriating, and annoying. Raillyn was mine, we had a deep history together. Like in The Keep she was not only my student when she was young, she was my mate. There was no way I would allow another to think he could have his way with her. Walking into the hall, I followed the blue carpet dotted with stars to the last door on the left.

Various tapestries hung from the walls, a large four-poster bed sat in the middle, a chest at the foot, while a dresser lined the wall. A small table and two chairs sat near a large paned window on the opposite side of the room. Looking at the green satin blanket with the symbol of a sapling decorated the surface made me think of Raillyn. This was her room.

The scent of vanilla, honeysuckle, and thyme still lingered here. I needed this little reprieve, and allowed myself to sit on her bed, taking in her scent I hoped it would calm me. *How was I going to make Drake understand?* Remembering back to our argument caused my anger to rise again.

Standing swiftly, I walked around the bed, clenching my fists I knew I was becoming furious. Her smell lingering in the room didn't help matters, she was mine and I was not going to let anyone else touch her ever again. I flung one of the chairs to the floor, it crashed to the floor in a crack. *No!* I would not destroy her room.

Calling my magic, I left to the one place that I didn't care for, knowing if I destroyed it, I wouldn't have any regrets. I went to my chambers in The Keep. The deep blue colors of its darkened furniture and tapestries remained dim. I despised Lord Drake.

Even now the bond between Raillyn and I seemed to grow stronger. It would only be a matter of time before it boiled over and we would have a problem on our hands. Already I had dealt with that issue once and given her what she desired, I feared the next time, with us so close to the end. If a complication arose now, the portal might not be opened. We were fighting with time itself.

Out of sheer anger I flipped the small table that once sat in the middle of the room over. Its wood surface splintered against the nearby wall. Reaching out I slammed the nearby bookshelf down on top of its shattered remains.

Taking a deep breath I tried to still my thoughts, Raillyn had no idea of anything. No idea how dangerous the path she lived and walked was, how dangerous the path would become now that she returned to normal. Not only was I a danger to her but so many things she once took for granted. So many things, as she lived her life prior to The Keep, I had kept her safe from.

My mind went into another whirlwind of emotional uproar as I felt myself not only hate the world, but hate being the reason she was in this position. If only I had taken her away when I had the chance, before she got so tied up in the affairs of the Wolves.

Gathering my magic into a red ball of energy I sent it careening towards the fireplace, where it erupted, sending the logs inside aflame. Small pieces of charred wood burst from the fire as it roared into life, singeing the nearby rugs. I didn't care. Instead, I ripped at the other bookshelf. Toppling it over into a shattered mess upon the floor, books scattered. Grabbing one I tossed it into the fireplace as well, before I felt my magic begin to control my anger.

Swaying momentarily from the exerted force of my emotions, I sat in a nearby chair. *Gods, I loved her, and I couldn't lose her to the Mystic life. A life she had to live but a dangerous one for females. I would walk beside her to the depths of Death's Gate and back if it meant keeping her safe.* Nothing would keep me from that, *ensuring her safety.*

I didn't know what to do, I wanted to mark her, and bind her to me. Forcing her to only respond to me, and in turn leaving our minds fully open to one another, something we still hadn't done. Then maybe she would see the truth, but I didn't know. I knew what my instincts told me.

That primitive side of our lives stemmed from our mixed blood and magic, from the God's themselves. It made me want to go feral when I saw another man handling my mate, when I still hadn't marked her. To make it worse, our scents called to one another, demanding us to complete our bond. It was easier when she was mine in The Keep and I didn't have another male after her. Now, however, since I had fought these urges and instincts for years, I was falling apart, I couldn't do it much longer. Something was going to give.

Running my fingers through my hair, I felt the subtle call from Drameon asking to speak to me. Taking a deep breath, and closing my eyes, I called a portal and went through.

***

I had entered the Wolves' castle and stood in the small den where Drameon indicated to meet him. I wasn't happy about being back here but knew he had his reasons. Drameon sat in a nearby chair, next to the fireplace. He stood as the portal closed and dissipated behind me.

"I am glad to see you my friend." I said reaching out and clasping his hand.

"I hope all is well? And apologize for calling you here." He said nothing to my earlier behavior. Taking a seat and indicating for me to sit as well, I waited for him to finish. "There was a slight problem, Raillyn ran from Daes and disappeared. Even I can't track her. She doesn't want to be found." He said carefully.

Rubbing my hand across my face, I took a deep sigh. If she ran I doubted I could even track her since I never had a chance to bind her soul to me properly. Nervous and angered I thought of the places she would have gone. None of them seemed likely. The door opening broke my thoughts. Drake, Howl, and Saibal entered the room. Howl smirked slightly while Drake eyed me warily, only adding more stress to the situation.

"Are we to expect you around the castle more often?" Saibal asked curiously. Drake eyed him with authoritative eyes.

Howl still smirked before talking. "Alkin, don't leave. I'll be back, I think this situation is going to require another hand." He said disappearing out the door before anyone could ask what he meant.

The four of us stood in silence for a moment. "Should I stay or is everything going to be all right? I have a friend waiting on me elsewhere." Drameon said nervously while eyeing me and Drake.

"No, we'll be fine," Drake said. "Go meet your friend."

Nodding his head Drameon summoned a portal and walked through its smoky embrace. As it dissipated the door opened. Howl and Lyth walked into the room. Long crimson red hair hung in a loose braid around Lyth's elven face and watery blue eyes. He was dressed in simple blue billowy dancer pants, and a simple black shirt. A deep green sash hung around his hips, adorned with the Dancer charm, indicating he was from the Den. Saibal seemed tense and on alert.

Howl however held out his hand casually. "This is Lyth, Celeste's mate." He said matter of fact like towards Saibal.

"It's all right, Saibal; it's fine that he's here. His mate is a healer in the Den and helped Raillyn when Deestan was born." Drake said, surprising me.

What has Howl told him? I eyed Lyth and Howl knowing the two of them were more than likely conversing mentally to one another. *Damn Drakar, and their scheming ways.*

"I figured you two needed to talk and having him in the room might be beneficial." Howl said while taking a seat.

Lyth casually leaned against the wall near the fireplace. "Where is Celeste?" I asked Lyth knowing his mate couldn't be too far away.

Lyth seemed to grin mischievously. "At Howl's house, in case something goes wrong."

Daes' Drakar were annoying at times, they enjoyed causing chaos they could control. This situation needed to be handled and they seemed to lavish in the excitement that it brought into the room. Their magic would assist in keeping the peace. Still it put me on edge, knowing Drake knew who Lyth was and the fact that Celeste had a hand in Deestan's birth. He had no prior knowledge to this until now, and I had a feeling Howl or Lyth told him.

"So I can only assume, Howl told you about Celeste being in the local Den when Deestan was born. I don't see how else you would know she was a Den healer, unless he said something." I said cautiously, not knowing what was said and not wanting to say more than needed.

This game Drameon and I were playing, where we danced around the truth, seemed to turn. This time, however, I was caught in the middle. Words were being used against me, trapping me in their web. The Wolf Lord and the Drakar were scheming together this time and I was left in the middle.

Drake sighed as he paced the room. "Saibal, why don't you stand guard outside, I don't want anyone coming in or bothering us."

Saibal bowed slightly to Drake before leaving the room and gently closing the door behind him. For a moment, my heart picked up pace. I felt trapped, I wanted to escape but I knew this conversation would happen sooner or later anyway. Drake paced the room, I was sure to give him a wide berth. Crossing my arms, I waited.

"Yes, Howl told me that Celeste was there when Deestan was born. He also told me that **blood is power, that blood is everything.** About how important it is in life and everything you do. What I want to know is why? Why didn't you say anything about Raillyn sooner? Why did you let things get so out of hand?" Drake was angered but tried to hold his temper within.

"I told you, I went to great lengths to keep Raillyn alive and well. Everything was under control." I said choosing my words carefully, not wanting to reveal too much until I was sure of just how much Drake knew.

Drake began pacing even faster, I was upsetting him. Rubbing his hand across his face, he appeared agitated. *Good!* I knew manipulating him this way would upset him more. Howl and Lyth seemed to stay back, but I felt the subtle hum of their magic already trying to control his anger. Seeing their behavior, I knew they would only interfere if things became distraught. Maybe through Drake's agitation, I'd get him to tell me what else he knew. However with the Drakar's magic I would have to work around this and pick at him carefully.

"Not once did you tell anyone that Raillyn was your mate, and because of it you **had** to go to great lengths to keep her safe! I don't understand the full situation, but I know that much!" He yelled at me.

In an instant, my temper built up inside me and my eyes took on a red appearance. *OK, forget being subtle...* He angered me and pissed me off. I would keep to the facts, but I really wanted to vent some of my anger at him.

Tipping my head sideways, my nostrils flared and a low growl emanated from my throat. Sweat began to bead on my forehead and run down my cheek, onto my chest. The Drakar's spell had little effect on me at this time, and any grasp it had I shrugged off.

"Did Howl tell you how dangerous the situation was for Raillyn? That when she was pregnant, she was most vulnerable? Or about the fact that nearly forty percent die during their first pregnancy? It's a way our species weeds out the weak. Equally alarming about thirty percent of those who are strong enough to survive lose their first child. Did he tell you any of that?" I yelled equally angered. "Did he tell you that my blood and power was the only thing that would heal her and keep her from dying? That Drameon and I had orchestrated the timing when Deestan would be born to ensure Raillyn and the child's safety? Because we knew if any Wolves were there, we would be denied access to her and you would have neither of them? Or that Stasha assisted us in the whole thing?"

I saw it on his face. No, Howl had not said that. My blood began to boil with anger and my head felt like it would explode. I hated getting into dark moods, it was alarming. My father was the same way, it was our dark magic. Drake was equally angered I could feel it pouring off him in waves as he struggled to control himself. I could tell that Lyth and Howl had backed off and let us get it all out now.

"You orchestrated when Deestan was born? And Stasha's known the whole time about you two?" he asked, shocked.

For a moment, my anger calmed as well. "Yes, it was the only thing we could do. Raillyn never told you, did she? About everything that happened that night?"

Drake was recalling that night and what he was told, I could see it in his eyes. "I was told that Raillyn had wandered into the lower levels and was given a ring from a gemcrafter of the Den. When she was returning to the upper levels, she began having issues. Afterwards, she said a Denmate named Celeste and Hanna attended her."

So he knew part of it. It had been years since I was called a gemcrafter. "You're right, she was antsy, she went down to the lower levels because I was there. I gave her the ring, it was her mother's. After I had left, Drameon escorted her upstairs, and him being a healer, all it took was one touch. As he laid his hand on her back, he pulsed a magical spark into her. It sent her into labor and I bet Raillyn didn't mention that I was there in the room helping when Deestan was born or how after she became foggy. That all she wanted to do was sleep."

Drake was unsettled by this information. I didn't blame him it was nerve wracking. Howl sat quiet and listened, but Lyth spoke up.

"It's true. Drameon and I were in the room next door to ensure everything went smooth. What else wasn't said was that Raillyn told Leece to leave, leaving only the Drakar and Alkin in the room to attend her. That instinctively she knew who she needed around her."

Drake looked at him curious. Raillyn didn't tell him that either. "Leece never said anything about that." He stated trying to piece everything together. He was right, Raillyn had instinctively wanted only those who could assist her there, and no one else.

"She probably didn't say anything because she feared getting into trouble from you." I said sarcastically.

Lyth and Howl both seemed to agree with me. My anger began to calm once more as I leaned against the wall to further calm myself and appear less threatening.

Drake eyed me angrily as Lyth went on. "It's true, though Celeste and Alkin delivered Deestan, not Leece. Afterwards, Raillyn became foggy, slipping in and out of lucidness. However, after Celeste gave Raillyn a mix of Alkin's blood and healing herbs her moments of being aware became more often. Instinctively Raillyn reached for Alkin, and I'm sure he can agree. It was startling seeing how she remained in a haze and consciously unaware, but her subconscious was fully aware of what was going on."

Lyth was going to tell him, I knew he was. Raillyn was healing. After Deestan had been fed and cared for, Drameon took her, leaving us in the room alone. I had given her my blood cutting a small gap on my chest so it would bleed for her.

"You don't seem to understand the bond that is shared between mates. What Alkin did was not easy on his part. Yes, it involved blood but it also involved power, and love. He gave himself up for Raillyn's wellbeing. Allowing her to do and take what she pleased from him to heal." Lyth said as I saw Drake reading between the lines. He struggled with understanding our way of life.

I felt his anger rise, a split second before he drew his blade. Charging me, Howl swiftly stood from his seat, as Lyth prepared himself as well. I drew my crimson dagger from my belt, ready to deflect his blow. As our blades met, Howl grabbed Drake while Lyth pulled me back.

"You laid your hands on my mate?" he asked angered.

I was tired of this game. My anger had peeked into a fiery inferno, rage had built up. "Need I remind you she is not your mate! I had laid claim to her even before you touched her. You can even ask her, she knows I took her innocence. You are infuriating and arrogant! So, yes, I put my hands on her!" I yelled outraged.

To think he would suspect otherwise. Raillyn however was a different story. She naturally craved the touch of my skin under her hands, it was euphoric. Even though, she thought it was a dream it was the first time we kissed.

The surge of power from that single touch was enough to merely send anyone over the edge. She loved the tingle of power dancing over that single touch, it was what she needed, what she craved. As Drake struggled to break free from Howl, I felt the immense protectiveness I had for her envelop my mind. I had tried to contain it, but this man brought out the worst in me.

"So what do you plan on doing with her? She has a daughter here; you can't expect to take her away and have her not angry." Drake questioned as Howl let him go but stayed near him.

"If I was smart I would find where she is and bind her to me now. However, that is not an option. She has a task that needs to be completed and before that is done there can be no issues." I said once more allowing my silver tongue to slip into place, and do its trick. "Already she's becoming harder for me to handle. In The Keep, she was always around me and I didn't have the worry of another man trying to take her. Now that's different. Because my instincts see you as a threat everything is excelling. Meaning the likelihood of me binding her is greater. Already you saw a little display of what happens when mates resist the bond."

"Is that what was happening when you and Raillyn were acting strangely?" Drake questioned as he began visibly relaxing. Sighing I knew he had to know the truth, there was no way around it.

"Yes, we are made for each other and the more we resist this bond, the more it will drive us towards one another. Both of us remember the time we spent in The Keep, and when she died the mystic marks died with her. Now she's craving for them to be put back to feel that rush of closeness from those bonds." I paused a moment and looked towards Howl, I knew why he choose to handle Drake instead of me.

My pupils dilated slightly as I caught the scent coming from him, he had exchanged blood with Raillyn and she placed her Mystic mark on him, permanently marking him as her personal guard. Yet, there was something else. Focusing directly on Howl, he released Drake and walked towards me. Meeting me face to face, he knew what I was doing.

Leaning forward carefully, I sniffed where I smelled her scent the strongest. I knew her mark lay on his left shoulder, I could smell her touch strongest there. However, that wasn't what bothered me. What bothered me was that Howl had placed her in his lap as he exchanged blood with her. I could smell it on him.

A distinct scent I hadn't smelled since The Keep. It set all my nerves aflame and caused my pupils to dilate even further. Static began to fill my ears as I felt myself reaching towards our bond, a bond that was no longer there. Getting nothing, I turned away and tried to calm myself running my fingers roughly through my hair I hoped the pain would draw me out of this state of mind. This was bad, I thought as I felt my breathing pickup pace.

"Alkin?" Lyth said, but it was barely audible.

"What's wrong with him?" Drake questioned as he backed up.

I heard Lyth sigh, "Just that I wish we had a necromancer here to throw him into Death's River. Celeste and I suspected this was the reason for all their issues." He said as he walked towards me.

My vision was hazy; nothing mattered to me other than leaving and finding Raillyn. Every fiber in my body was aflame, it literally felt like I was thrown into a volcano and I couldn't die in its fiery lava. My body and mind were becoming overloaded. If this kept up I would either unconsciously do what it was commanding me to or fall victim to unconsciousness. Neither was an option at this time.

Briefly I saw Lyth in front of me. Sweat ran down my face and I knew I looked like a madman, for a moment I felt ashamed that others, non-ancients, had seen me behave so irrationally, but this was what happened between unbound mates when nearing that time. Usually it was short lived. However us fighting the bond was only drawing it out.

The sharp pain of an electrified slap lit up my right cheek sending the sparks of Lyth's magic throughout my body. It brought me out of my mind and instincts and back to the room.

For a moment the room spun and blurred around me. Leaning back, I steadied myself on the wall. "Thank you." I croaked as I felt myself regain control over my primitive behavior.

"How long has it been since Raillyn cycled?" Lyth asked as he crossed his arms. This was not something I wanted to talk about, let alone in front of Drake. However the look on his face told me he would not back off.

"A little over three years, almost four, giving the time Raillyn carried Callina." I said knowing what he was about to remind me of.

"What do you mean?" Drake questioned Lyth as Howl looked at me knowingly. Lyth sighed.

"I think that's the problem. The bond between you two is broken. Yet her body and mind remember what's supposed to happen. Her body's ready to cycle even though her mind's not, I doubt she remains unbound longer than a week." Lyth said before turning to address Drake's question.

"What that means is this. We all know females have cycles. Wolf females are attuned to the moon. They bleed monthly, giving you a chance each month for a child. Ancients are different it's every three to five years. Raillyn's body knows that time is close and it puts her on edge. To make it worse, since her mental link to Alkin is broken and so is his claim, her body refuses to cycle. So in a sense she's teetering on the edge of a rocky cliff ready to jump, but can't." Lyth said as Drake began to understand.

"So what's going to happen? Are you going to bind her?" he asked looking at me.

"No." I replied sternly. Both Howl and Lyth looked at me doubtfully.

"Yes." They both replied sarcastically in unison.

"You know what that means don't you?" Lyth stated as if I was stupid.

Of course, I did, but what choice did I have. There was no resisting the bond, every Ancient, who had a mate knew, even myself. It was too intense, too emotional and often when resisting it lead to inescapable issues which mates were forced to work together over.

"What do you think she will do?" Drake asked Lyth.

Sighing I saw Lyth weigh his words. "From seeing Howl's thoughts from Raillyn and hearing about her from others, she loves you. Do not think otherwise. She loves you as husbands and wives love one another. But, Alkin and Raillyn can't escape the inescapable. Ancients love differently; it's deeper, more emotional. With Celeste, I know her every thought, every need, want and desire. Her dreams and fears, I know everything, nothing is hidden between us. The mental and physical link we share is that strong, it entwines every fiber in our body and soul into one. It's so hard to explain..." Lyth said as Howl seemed deep in thought.

"Then let's not tell him." Howl began as we looked at him curiously. "Lyth, how long has it been since a Wolf Lord has visited Silvertine?"

My eyes grew wide at the thought. I had grown up there, was raised there with Opal and Solomn, my adopted mother and father. They kept order in the city and I had known it was well over a couple hundred years since the last Wolf Lord walked its walls. Drake seemed confused by the comment, and looked towards me. I held my tongue, I would not interfere and influence this decision.

"Come, let's go to my place." Howl said as he slowly lead Drake towards the door and into the hall.

Saibal still stood guard and looked at Drake questioningly as we entered the hall. I don't know what was going on in Drake's mind, but he remained calm and let Howl pull him along. Lyth and I followed quietly behind him as we left Saibal behind.

***

Upon entering Howl's home, I heard Celeste. "Lyth, what in Death's Realm are you two thinking? Alkin?" She shouted at us.

My eyes blazed purple, and I shook my head silently, she knew me well enough to know that it meant I would not discuss it. I was trying to think of any repercussions to this little endeavor. Lyth and Howl seemed to think of this as a game and enjoyed the conflict it brought. Drake still seemed unsure what to expect and instead stood quietly as Howl released his arm.

Going to his mate, Lyth pulled Celeste into his arms, kissing her lightly on the forehead. "Everything is all right. Howl just thinks Drake needs to visit Silvertine. If Drake is OK with that?" He said while looking towards Drake.

Thinking briefly, he replied. "If I will get answers and understand this situation better. why not." I heard the sarcasm in his voice and couldn't help but smirk.

Celeste whispered to Lyth, "Opal and Solomn will not be too happy about this. Winter Solstice is coming in a few weeks and they have been busy preparing for the festival. They will not enjoy an outsider such as this in their midst at this time…" Celeste began as Lyth kissed her gently on the lips stopping her from going on. Lovingly she looked into his eyes. "Lyth." She said quietly. I knew though that they probably were speaking mentally, trying to work the situation out.

"It's fine, if Opal and Solomn say they don't want him there we will bring him home. Please do this for me, love. Think of how much fun it will be, we'll just stick to the Den and central section." Lyth said, almost begging as he kissed her again.

Smiling, I couldn't help but shake my head knowingly. While the males of our race were used to being in charge, it was a different case between mates. Often whatever the female said went, because a happy home was an agreeable home and it was much easier to give in and compromise than to argue.

"I'll do whatever you want this evening if you let Howl and I have our fun this afternoon." Lyth whispered into her ear quietly.

Celeste smirked mischievously as she looked lovingly into Lyth's eyes. Drake gave Howl a questioning look and I couldn't help but smile myself. Already Drake was seeing how outwardly we were with our mates, unlike the Wolves who were more careful and kept things behind closed doors.

Celeste sighed indicating Lyth had won. "All right." She said giving in.

Howl smiled elated and attuned the door to Silvertine. Momentarily the room glowed bright blue. Drake looked cautiously around unsure what to do or what was happening. This would be a trip for him. While the Wolves shared similarities they were also very different from the Ancients, and going to Silvertine would show how different it was.

***

After the glow faded, Howl lead the way out the door and into the lush green forest surrounding Silvertine in the Turbid Still. The snow hadn't come to this region yet, but soon would.

The Winter Solstice marked the time when snow would arrive and with it the darkest days of the year.

Entering the forest was a sigh of relief in and of itself. I was happy to be home, though I had hoped it would be under different circumstances, and with Raillyn.

The walk was short to the tall palace door, Howl's house lay a mere thirty feet from the nearest door into Solomn and Opals giant house. However as we neared it a mental message entered my mind, it was Drameon.

"I will return later." I said, quietly excusing myself. Not stating the reason why I had to leave, I opened a portal and disappeared into its foggy embrace.

Revelation ~ Raillyn

My head hurt as I opened my eyes and blinked a few times. After I had left my grandfather, I went to the only neutral place I could think of, the Den and Stasha. Before losing consciousness I begged her not to tell Drake I was there, I was sure Daes would already be upset with me for this little endeavor but I didn't want to make it worse. Daes frightened me, and even though I should be listening to him, I really didn't want to at this time. Too many unanswered questions.

As I looked around the room, I was in the same small den, deep below, that I was in when having Deestan. The small table lay near the door, a cabinet, and few chairs along the wall. Memories of that day flashed through my mind, for a moment I smirked, and my stomach fluttered.

The door leading to the smaller room opened and Stasha entered quietly. Her long dark hair hung bound loosely around her. Feathers, beads, coins, and bells were worked interactively into its length. Amber eyes met mine, as she smiled, she didn't appear to have aged that much since I had seen her last.

"How do you feel? And just so you know I didn't tell anyone you were here. I'm sure I will hear about it later but at this moment that doesn't matter. What are you doing here? Last I heard you were healing after Alkin dispelled the construct spell." Stasha said causing me to look at her curiously.

How did she know about the construct spell...? Unless it was mentioned after Raihanna was destroyed. That probably was it.

"This was the only neutral place I could think of, I'm sorry. I needed a moment to myself, away from the hassle of prying eyes. I haven't had time to think alone, nor am I getting the answers I feel I need. I hope you don't mind." Tears threatened my eyes while my emotions tipped.

Stasha sat down beside me on the edge of the pillowed bed and patted my leg. "Of course you can come here to escape a little bit. The Den is always open to its dancers."

As she sat with me, I debated my choices. Who could I call that would not rat me out to my father? Then it struck me. *Howl.* Even in The Keep he had seemed neutral about the situation, and even gave me information that I didn't think Alkin wanted me to have. He was the one who told me about the war, my mother, my father and their roles in this whole mess. Even my role in it. If anyone could tell me more, it would have to be him.

"I'm going to call a friend here; I need his help figuring out this whole mess." I said standing before she could say anything. "He's a Drakar and I don't know if he's a Denmate. Is that all right?" I questioned trying to remember my manners. My mind went from wanting to take control and just do what I wanted. Primarily acting like Raihanna, while in The Keep. Barking out orders, doing as I wanted with no care and being ruthlessly detached. To trying be like I was prior to The Keep. Calm, caring, remorseful and understanding. But still taking my normal mercenary demeanor of being authoritative in certain matters. It felt painful.

Stasha looked at me almost blindsided, her mouth open and her eyes darting around as she searched for words. "Umm, that would be fine. Most Drakar are Denmates anyway. Also, no one will bother us, so there is no fear for intrusions." She said meekly while looking down at the floor.

Stasha was acting strange, and I couldn't place my finger on it. Her demeanor felt different around me, almost as if she knew more than what she was saying. For a moment, I disregarded it and began calling Howl.

Placing my left hand over the Mystic mark I tried to calm my swaying mind. It felt like an endless tug of war, between my emotions and magic. Taking a few deep steadying breaths, I was able to clear my mind. Then I thought of Howl, his deep blue piercing eyes, his Elf-like face, and his cedar wood, cherry blossoms, orchid, and sandalwood scent. All of it came rushing into my mind in a stream of memories. Reaching for our personal link, I sent a magical call out to him, just as the memories overcame me.

He had been my mother's personal guard, that much I remembered from my childhood. He followed her around everywhere, and helped her assist my grandfather in tasks. For a moment my mind panicked, I didn't want to think of Daes or any of that. As I felt myself pull away from the memories, my magic threatened to lash out around me.

Closing my eyes and imagining a bubble, I tried to encase the energy in a small radius around me, so not to harm Stasha. Instead, darkness tried to consume me. My heart picked up pace, and my breathing became haggard. Then I felt a portal open and someone enter the room. Their magic was relaxing, calming, and reached out towards me encasing my magic, safely within.

A hand fluttered across my cheek, causing me to smile, my magic and emotions aligned perfectly. Taking a deep sigh of relief I slowly opened my eyes. Howl stood in front of me, his hand rested on my cheek, smiling cockily. His piercing blue eyes seemed to glow with power, and twinkle with mischief.

"Hello, sweet cheeks, I can't be gone too long or trouble will ensue, but what can I help you with?" He asked showing me in his mind what he meant. Lyth and Howl had brought Drake to Silvertine and were escorting him around the Drakar city. My mouth hung open and my eyes grew wide in shock.

"What in the world were you two thinking?" I asked outraged, taking a step away from Howl and his outreached hand. A tingle of magic seemed to echo in the room, keeping my anger in check. "Why?" I asked him mentally.

Howl shrugged his shoulders and flattened his lips. "Why not? He's tied into this whole mess might as well educate him the best we can so he's better prepared." Howl said matter of fact like, before turning to Stasha, who sat quietly out of the way.

"Hello, Stasha, I owe you thanks for not telling Celeste and Lyth that Raillyn came here." He said while bowing.

Tipping my head sideways, I looked at him curiously. "What do you mean? Stasha knows Celeste and Lyth?" I asked suddenly feeling lost in conversation. *What's going on here? How is it that everyone around me knows more about what's going on than I do?*

Howl smirked wickedly at me; his eyes flashed a deep shade of blue as he grinned. "That's right, Alkin and Drameon never said anything did they?" He paused as he looked back at Stasha, who looked like she was trying to keep a hard to keep secret. She sat half-biting her lip nervously. "Stasha here has been working with Alkin and your father for almost seven years now. In fact, they enlisted her help around the time you became pregnant with Deestan."

My mouth fell open, and my magic retaliated against Howl's. I felt on the edge of a dark void of darkness, mind blank. Looking at Stasha, she seemed hurt. "I wanted to tell you but Alkin had me bound by ancient magic. I couldn't talk about it or say anything unless you knew. It was for your own good, I swear." She almost cried out, hurt.

"Why?" Was the only thing I managed to say.

Howl spoke up on that question. "Because I'm sure you remember by now, how dangerous things are with female ancients when they are carrying a child."

Sure I remembered a little, what I was told as a child, and what I remember seeing around Silvertine. Many women died during pregnancy due to complications, with magic, body, and overall health. My mother had said it was normal, a way of weeding out the weak. It was sad, but a necessary evil, to keep the balance of our people. Ancients couldn't overpopulate and this was a way to ensure we didn't.

My mind panicked as I remembered more. Even though, I was young when I was taken, my parents were teaching me the Ancients' way of life. Why it was essential and what it entitled. I was only just beginning to see and understand it all. I saw chil-

dren as young as three years of age, or fledglings acting differently around certain people.

Females were always guarded and protected in the Ancient
races. They were safeguarded and cherished, because they were
the ones who brought life into the world, at times at the expense
of their own. But there was more, something I didn't quite grasp
when I was little. It was nagging at me and pushed memories upon me.

Memories of me meeting Alkin. How he knocked me out of
the tree and how he looked at me with that sideways smirk. My
heart fluttered as the images of what I was seeing began to crack
like shattered ice. My mind couldn't handle the overwhelming
feeling and intense magic of the memories, and my teetering
emotions. The room spun around me as if caught up in a massive
wind. I swayed on my feet just as darkness consumed me. The
floor suddenly disappeared and I felt myself falling. Whisper like
I heard Howl curse just as his arms grabbed my upper body, halting my downwards spiral.

History ~ Drameon

Howl teleported into the den just before I left to search for Raillyn again. As the blackened portal ebbed away, I saw he carried Raillyn in his arms. A look of regret was on his face.

"I didn't mean to overload her with everything. Have you two told her anything about what's going on? She was shocked that Stasha had helped us, and from what I saw in her mind she's confused about everything." Howl said in a reprimanding tone.

"No, not much has been said. Daes told us it wasn't our place anymore. That she needed to be molded and shaped carefully so she can bring his magic back into the world." I stated regretfully. There was so much I wanted to tell her but was only given permission to let her know certain things. "I'm sure Daes has a reason behind it all."

Howl sighed as he made his way towards the hall and Raillyn's room. "I'm sure there is and I plan on finding out. Now that Raillyn has had contact with Daes, I should be able to use our link and speak to him." If anyone was going to figure out Daes' plan, it would be one of his Drakar. I nodded my head in approval, as we entered Raillyn's room.

Slipping around Howl, I pulled the blankets back so he could place her in bed. Gently tossing the green comforter over her brought me a sigh of relief. After everything that happened it made me worry *what else she was going to be put through*, but for now she was home.

"I think if anyone can learn what Daes has planned for her it's you, and I would greatly appreciate it if you found out. Maybe you can help speed this along. If you need Alkin's help he's in the Lunar Plane, speaking to an interesting consort. Recently Geirolf Koray, leader of the Lunar Planes Wolves, contacted Nora."

"Why did he want to speak to her?" Howl questioned as he placed his finger to his lip in thought.

"I don't know how he heard, but he knew she was in The Keep and in Alecien. So Geirolf went to Silvertine and asked Opal if he could speak to her. He had an interesting case to present with documentation to back it up. Apparently Lord Cyrin, Drake's father, was speaking to Geirolf about an alliance with the Lunar Plane Wolves. It even progressed to the signing of a betrothal between Geirolf's daughter Raven and Lord Drake, but never amounted to anything." I said trying to remember the details Opal and Solomn had passed onto me.

"Wait! What? A betrothal between Drake and Raven? But that means this would have been before Raillyn had contact with the Wolves, well over seven years ago." Howl almost shouted.

Smiling I nodded. "Yes you're right, but as I said nothing happened. Lord Cyrin was supposed to tell Drake about the betrothal, he promised Lord Geirolf, but died before he was able to. Drake's father was keeping this hushed, so he told no one, and I understand why. If word had reached the Vampires that the Werewolves in Alecien were working with the Aeralain Werewolves, another war would break out. It was supposed to be a surprise, tipping the tables for the Wolves to win and drive out the Vampires."

That's what Geirolf wanted. He said he had spent years trying to find a safe and easy way to speak to Lord Drake, and now that Silvertine was getting involved with Alecien, it allowed the Lunar Wolves to do the same. I bet he was fearful of what happened and was weary to send any aid after he heard no response from Cyrin. It only made sense, and made things easier for us. Lord Drake was promised to another, and so was Raillyn.

"That means, they're going to be speaking to Lord Drake while he's there, isn't it? That was why Opal was so willing to allow him into Silvertine. She's going to be the mediator between the alliance of the Lunar Wolves and the Alecien ones?" Howl asked, figuring it all out. He smiled from ear to ear. "Oh my, and that means, Drake actually has to take up his position as a leader and take a queen. I have heard of Raven, she's feisty and a head-strong leader, Geirolf already allows her to lead her own troops. What's Raillyn going to think about all this? Does Daes know?" Howl asked, going from a happy mood to a concerned one.

I nodded my head. "Yes, Daes knows; in fact he was thrilled to find out. I believe whatever his ultimate goal with Raillyn is, is tied to this alliance in some way. Why don't you go ask him and find out?" I mentioned hoping something would be said. I was already given the OK to show my daughter certain memories, but that was all I knew at this time concerning her.

Howl nodded his head and smirked as he called a portal. The smoky black mist swirled outward until it was large enough for him to pass through. Waving his hand once he passed into the portal and disappeared. Closing my eyes and shaking my head, I sat next to Raillyn. Howl was a good man, I was sure he would discover something to aid my daughter. Which brought me to another thing, Daes had given me permission to allow her to know a little of what was going on. Not everything, but bits and pieces. He also said I could place my Mystic mark back on her.

Invoking my magic, I would impart that to her, allowing her to dream about the events that led up to this moment. Just as she had seen previously, a ball of warm green energy gathered in my hand. I recalled all the knowledge and information that was vital to the current situation, into the ball. When I was sure it was all there, I released it into her mind. Slowly the green orb sunk in, absorbed by her skin. Lastly, I took her hand, once more summoning my magic, I pulsed it through her.

Raillyn was my daughter and it was in my right to place my Mystic mark back upon her wrist. A right every parent had with their child. Even though, that right was temporarily taken from me, I was thankful Daes was being lenient after everything that happened.

Faint green lines began to trace her skin in an ancient pattern. It was the oldest language, a sigil that marked family units. As leaves and vines spiraled about her right wrist, they drew across mine as well, it glowed bright green before fading leaving a pale almost white, green Mystic mark. When it was finished, I Brushed her hair out of her face, kissed her forehead before sitting back and watching her dream.

~~*~*~*~*Raillyn ~ past information*~*~*`*~*~*

Words and pictures entered my mind. Like water running between my fingers, I controlled none of it. It was as if someone was sharing memories with me, or telling me a story.

My mother had been Daes' last mystic born, at the time of her death she was already over a thousand years old. Daes often favored her over the other five children he had, allowing her to craft God blades and use spell components inaccessible to Auran dwellers.

After I was born, Daes was thrilled to learn I possessed his blood and became his youngest lineage heir. Due to the fact that my magic demanded balance and craved both harmony and chaos, my mother was granted a reprieve. Daes wanted her to spend her time raising me until I was old enough to begin training and controlling my magic, which began to prove true just before my second birthday.

During this time my mother constantly tried to keep me in balance, often shooing my father and her friends away. Teething, temper tantrums and learning the basic stages of controlling my magic proved to be testing for her. Often needing a reprieve herself she sought out her father for help.

"Teething is already hard for babies, why does it have to be harder for Mystics?" My mother asked as she paced the room. Her blackened hair fell into the golden haired child's on her hip.

"It's because it upset the natural balance of their bodies and therefore upsets the balance of their magic...." He began before he was interrupted.

"Blah...blah...blah... I know. I was being sarcastic. You have to forgive me but I haven't had much sleep. My little heathen has been keeping me up all hours of the night." She said exhausted while the child screamed in her arms.

Like a ghost I watched the scene unfold. My mother loving-ly brushed my hair out of my face. Leaning down she kissed the extract center of a ring of baby curls wisping around the top. Daes walked over to a shelf that seemed to take shape out of dark shadows and come to life before my eyes. Reaching out he re-moved what appeared to be a bracelet, and tossed it at my moth-er. Almost instinctively she grabbed it with barely a glance.

"Try that." He said casually as he sat in a nearby chair.

My mother turned the object over in her hands. It seemed to pulse with power. Water like blue gems, some tiny and others Okra sized, formed a circle bracelet. "What do I do with it?" She almost snapped at him. "It's too large for her to wear."

Sighing Daes stood and walked over to Calista. Gently he reached out and removed the still fussing baby from her grasp. Placing a hand to her head Calista seemed tired, and swayed briefly on her feet.

"This." Daes said as he slipped the bracelet over the tiny hand. Like rocks sliding over rocks the soft sound of grating sand echoed in the now still room. Everything was quiet, as the brace-let twisted and reformed, becoming smaller and fitting just right. The tiny hand holding it immediately brought it into her mouth and happily chewed on its smooth multi-shaped surface.

"That doesn't count, she's normally happy when you hold her anyway. You cheat, you calm her with your magic." Calista said swaying more.

Reaching out Daes put a hand on her arm, steadying her. "Go sleep, child, you've exhausted your power. I will take care of Raillyn, and when you awaken there will be a hearty meal await-ing you." He said gently pulling my mother into a loving hug be-fore kissing the top if her head and letting go.

Nodding her head she sighed. "Ok, father." She said in de-feat. "Wake me if you need anything."

Daes chuckled a little as my mother walked towards a twi-light blue lighted hallway. "I have cared for many babes, my dear, I think we will be alright." He said rocking the now drowsy baby in his arms. Calista smiled as she disappeared from view.

Darkness seemed to cloud everything from view and encompass me.

Daes was the best at controlling this fractured power of both chaotic and harmonious magic. My mother and I would spend days, and weeks with him, teaching me many of the same tasks and chores she had performed as a child herself. There I learned the basics for not only my magic, and how to control the forever teetering seesaw of power it brought, but also the beginning responsibilities that came with it.

"Concentrate, focus on the crystal and it's steady beat, push your magic into the hard surface. Visualize it entering it, like sunlight enters glass. Then you can control it, increase the pulse or steady it." Daes' cool voice said to a small child who sat criss-crossed on the floor, a large blue crystal beating like a heart in front of her.

Sweat beaded along the edge of her golden hair as she concentrated harder. Daes paced the floor around her, he moved like fog, stirring up nothing and making no noise. He was soundless and calm, the pinnacle of balance.

I remembered this, I was striving to be like my mother, and grandfather. Just like Howl and Leon, balanced and in control. An act that was only achievable by growing up and practicing. My aim though was to stop letting the outside chaos into my soul, to keep it at bay.

Meditation helped immensely. After I began to gain a small amount of control and I was able to stop the sway between the balance from being so erratic. My memories blurred and stuttered, rocking like an earthquake near a lake. Everything became uncontrolled but controlled at the same time, soon images began to appear. My mother speaking to Daes alone, my mother's tear-streaked face as she left home on her first task since my birth. These memories were not mine, but they were being shown to me.

My mother returned to work, and often left me with my father, Alkin, or Daes. As she always took Howl with her as her personal guard. This was when things went wrong.

The Vampires had learned that they could use Ancient blood to strengthen their deadly blood magic. Before too long they decided regular Ancients were never strong enough and Mystic blood would aid them in ways they could only imagine. So while my mother visited The Keep, she was drugged and placed in the cellar, the very place of nightmares.

In turn, Howl was immobilized by Drakar poison. The runed walls and floor of the area, omitted all sources of magic. Howl sat dying from the poison coursing through his veins as my mother was drained of blood. They had meant to keep her alive, but her mortal wound and the spelled room prevented any healing to be done and in turn sealed her fate. As soon as my mother had died, Howl felt the effects of her death. It pierced his body and wracked him with immense pain as he felt the Mystic mark she had placed upon him so many years ago fade. In turn, Howl knew Drameon and Alkin would know of her death. My mind stuttered as it seemed to take over its own memories of what happened. I remembered, what happened... the image cleared once more as my memories took hold again.

Howl was right, my mother's death hit not only Drameon and Alkin but myself as well. I was home with them and another mystic, Leon. His yellow hair always shone brightly in the sunlight, almost like golden wheat. He paced the floor with my father, both in what appeared to be sweat-covered stress.

Tremors took over my body, when the effects of my mother's death took over. The pain and emptiness flooded my body, my heart fluttered, and brought me to my knees. Tears flooded down my face and before I knew what was happening, my father left through a portal. His anger poured over me seconds before as realization sunk in. Alkin couldn't let him go alone, my father had gone to The Keep and already I felt him begin a mass slaughter. He didn't shelter his mind from me as he made his way to the cellar and the location her magic was last. Ruthlessly he sliced at the Vampires, cutting some in half. Their withered remains spilling like red and black ooze onto the floor. Alkin glanced at me and for a split second our eyes met, mine wide in horror at what I witnessed through my father's mental link. Sighing he followed my father through a portal of his own, leaving me home with Leon, another mystic of Daes' lineage. My mind blanked, as a staticky feeling took over, hazing and causing a ringing noise in my ears.

I cried, for how long I didn't know, everything hurt, every fiber in my body was on fire as frigid lightning shot through me at the same time. Leon, tried to calm me, but had no mental link other than the lineage we shared, so his words only went so far.

Eventually, Alkin returned to the house, I was still in the haze of pain, but he took me in his arms. Cradling me close, my mind slowly stilled, dismissing the static. I felt Alkin reaching out with his magic, soothing me. However he smelled wrong, instead of a calming forest he smelled like Death's River. Putting my head on his shoulder, I felt Leon leave through a portal, probably after my father and mother.

Alkin was hurt and covered in blood. I smelled it strongly, covering him. His neck was gashed open as if a Vampire intended to rip out his throat. I felt myself staring at it, trying to concentrate on anything but the anger and fear I felt inside me. Focusing on the wound, I felt myself needing to comfort him. My three-year-old mind only knew one way. How I was comforted.

Leaning forward, I closed my eyes and kissed his wound. Hoping it would heal like my father's kisses healed mine. Opening my eyes, I watched but knew deep down that I didn't have the magic to heal like my father. It disappointed me, I licked my lips in thought.

A feeling I didn't understand but one that stood out made me focus on the wound with more intensely. It needed to be healed, yet I knew I didn't have herbs or know how to mix them properly. The thought crossed my mind, I remember watching the healers in the Den mix their saliva and blood with herbs to heal, or watched as a mated pair would lick the wounds of their loved one, exchanging blood in the process; promoting them to heal with magic. My mother and father had even healed me in this *fashion so it wasn't foreign to me. Bonds and magic ties allowed the healing to be effective.*

Alkin rubbed my back as he held me close, not knowing my thoughts. "I am sorry child for this entire situation, but you are safe, do not fear. We will get through this." His voice quivered and I felt wetness run onto my shoulder. He was crying.

My heart lurched for a moment, Alkin was like family to me and I didn't like seeing family hurt. He needed help and I was the only one there to help him. I felt determined for a moment as I leaned towards his wound once more. Carefully I ran my tongue across it.

On contact I felt a change, my saliva increased as if my body knew what my mind wanted. His blood tasted sweet and I felt him tense as I lapped at it. For a moment, I thought he would remove me and reprimand me, but he didn't. I hoped he knew I just wanted to help.

After a few minutes, I felt him take a deep steadying breath as I noticed the bleeding stop. His skin was no longer torn, and instead just angry and red. Smiling I licked away the last remnants of his blood before pushing off his shoulder so I could look him in the eyes. He smiled back reassuringly as he brushed my hair away from my face. Knowing what else needed to be done, I was frightened for a moment but knew it would help him feel better.

Wanting to complete the healing ritual I had started, I felt myself reach for my little dagger on my waist. Alkin seemed worried and distant. Before he could do anything or stop me, I ran the blade over my wrist. Quickly he tried to grab my hand and knock the dagger away but it only applied more pressure, cutting my skin deeper.

His eyes flew open wide with fear as he sat with me in a nearby chair. For a moment I wanted to cry, my wrist hurt and blood poured from its wound, the blood vessel was cut beyond my body's natural ability to repair. If I sat here without being healed, I would die. Alkin shook as he inspected the wound.

"Faen!" I heard him curse loudly. My mouth fell open never hearing him curse in such a matter before. He was beyond pissed. "Your father's going to kill me for this but if I let it bleed you will die." He said as he brought my wrist to his mouth and tried to control the bleeding.

While my hand was in his mouth, he pulled his own dagger out and ran it across his hand, placing it to my mouth. Eyes wide open, I knew he had reversed the healing ritual and was now performing it on me. I felt his magic flow into me just as his blood filled my mouth. It was calming and refreshing, like a cool rain after a hot day.

A tingling sensation was felt in my mind, mentally I found myself curiously reaching towards it. As if imagining you are touching another individual the feeling exploded. I felt Alkin's concern towards me, his overwhelming need to help heal me and stop me from helping him. He needed to go to my father; he desired to help bring him home.

While it wasn't wrong, my father didn't want me connected to him so soon. He wanted me to be free and not uncontrollably tied to another "guardian." Alkin wasn't a guardian, Alkin was different. I felt it, something about him called to me and this bond only made me happy and thankful he was my friend.

My wrist ached but slowly that began to die away. I caught Alkin's thoughts. It was healing and soon would be gone. Interested I continued to watch him. Finally the pain vanished and he released my hand. He kept his hand firmly pressed to my lips as he checked my wound. After he was content, it was healed he pulled his hand free.

"You can let go now." He said as I was more concerned with his wounds than my own.

I felt myself looking at his neck. "See you're all better." I said smiling that I had healed Alkin.

Mentally he laughed while physically he had a stern look on his face. I couldn't help but smile knowing he wasn't outraged at me. Pulling me into his arms, he hugged me tightly.

"Never do anything so stupid again. OK? You really had me worried sick." He said kissing my hair.

"I know but you were hurt and needed to be better, you need to go find my daddy, and you couldn't do that with your neck like that." I said proving I felt his thoughts.

Shock crossed Alkin's face and mind, his body stiffened, as a knock echoed on the door. Marla my nanny walked in and bowed her head. She was a Drakar from Silvertine often called to watch me when no one else could. Standing Alkin closed his mind to me and handed me to her. Instantly I fought and screamed. I wanted Alkin. I needed his comforting touch even at this age. My tiny hands reached towards him as I cried out. Something about him drew me to him. A love I didn't understand yet. However he stood stiffly and left, saying he was going after my father. His mind felt wracked with grief as he did so, which only added to my own sorrow.

My power began to rage and grow intense from the unease of the world and the chaotic disruption its magic had fallen in. My magic began to lash out and attack anyone around me. It burned, my head was pounding, heart racing and sweat pouring out of me. With each beat my magic lashed out like a whip, slicing anything in its path.

The Drakar, who cared for me tried to desperately help calm me, but failed and lost her life to my power. How long I screamed and boiled in turmoil I couldn't recall... Eventually, my father returned. I was so distraught. Even though he was still angered over my mother's death, he gathered me into his arms and tried to comfort me. His grief and hatred for the events unfolding because of his actions were overwhelming and only caused me to fall further into chaos.

My body felt like I was being skinned alive, my mind felt like boiling lava was being poured into my skull. Shaking from the immense, overwhelming emotions that I was feeling I felt like I was going to die. That my tiny body wasn't going to be able to handle this. Instinctively I felt myself reach for Death's River, only to be ricocheted off an invisible wall.

My father was furious, and in that instance, a great sadness overcame me. Placing me on a large pillow my father's anger took him over once more and he threw objects, toppled furniture and tossed various vials about as if they were nothing. The one place I knew I could feel calm was unreachable. I continued to cry and my magic became more erratic, I felt it twist round me like a whirlwind. Becoming more violent as I became inconsolable. At one point a spray of blood splattered my face, as my father once more tried to comfort me. But it hurt. Everything hurt. Alkin was gone and my mind couldn't find him. My magic was beyond my bodies limit, and I knew it. Then someone came.

Like a dream my grandmother Destiny appeared. My mind refused to still but I saw her power lash out in invisible threads and suddenly my father became a statue. Powerless, as her silent spell took over. She removed me from his grasp. I screamed louder; her hands felt like knives digging into my skin. Thrashing in her grasp she took me outside into the bright moonlight.

Walking fast she made her way towards a massive portal which lay in front of her. Her voice was like a haunting melody on the wind. However I couldn't be calmed by it, everything I knew was falling apart. My whole world was becoming different. Glancing towards the moon, my breathing picked up, in that instant I wanted to die. I felt broken, hurt, and unable to move on.

Before we entered the portal, I saw my father step out of the house. He looked angry his jaw was set stiffly against his normally soft features. Violently he sent a deadly wave of mystic magic across the field. It toppled the purple lotus flowers I loved so much, killing them instantly. For a split second my eyes flashed open in horror, and my mind went still. Before spiraling once more into the chaos it had become. Out of overwhelming anger and grief I sent out my own wave of magic. Again warm blood splatters my face. For a moment I felt her pause, then Delron was there. My mind was fragmenting, and static driven. Only allowing me to catch half of what was happening.

Delron handled my father, as Destiny took me away and tried desperately to help ease the pain. Gently she caressed my head and sung lightly to me. I was in such an uncontrollable anarchy my power ravaged my tiny body. Making it feel like thousands of tiny glass shards. A red and black void filled my waken thoughts. Destiny was there, my grandfather wasn't.

She had rocked me for hours while Daes was away handling another situation. That much I caught as I screamed and thrashed in pain and turmoil. Finally, he returned and Howl was with him. He rushed towards Destiny and took me into his arms, just as I sent a wave of chaotic magic from my body.

"I can't control her." Destiny said between sobs.

Frowning, Daes laid his hand upon my head, Howl stood quiet and watched the events unfold. I hurt, the pain inside was intense. Yet Daes tried to use his magic to push harmony on me, a semi balance to what I was feeling. But the balance which this man tried to bestow upon me caused the pain to be worse. I felt like I was being ripped apart, my little mind would break before too long under this stress. Already I felt my body wanting to shut down, to drown out this pain in an ultimate end or in a fractured chaos.

"Hush my child, all is well you are safe. You are loved and everything will be fixed, you have to trust me on this." He said in a loving voice as he continued to try and use his magic to calm my raging mind.

Regardless I continued my onslaught, everything hurt, pain echoed through me like a raging ice storm and nothing would stop it from ripping me apart. The carefully created atmosphere which I had been raised in and had been learning to control my magic in had been ripped to shreds, leaving nothing. Chaos now reigned in my mind and body and the ability to control the balance was well beyond my power. I needed to heal from the death of my mother, the unimaginable fear of the war. The instability of magic Auran was left in only added fuel to the burning inferno in my soul. My father hadn't made things any better as he raged on and was now banned from the God's realm and my touch. And Alkin... Where was he? I needed him, even though my mind was probably beyond his reach I wanted him there.

My grandmother continued to cry, as Daes handed me to her once more. "What about Alkin?" She asked between sobs.

My grandfather shook his head. "If I can't get through to her he won't be able to either. He may be able to calm her, but her mind will still be fractured and we've seen the results of leaving that unattended." He said in sorrow and regret.

Something flashed through my mind, an image of a golden-haired boy no older than me. He raged and screamed in pain and chaos as well. In an instant it was gone, in a blood splattered memory of a time long ago.

"We have to do it." Daes said as I heard him speak in the ancient tongue and draw upon a deep dark magic. It bubbled around him making the air thick and sticky. "We will fix things after she is safe." He said as I was held close. Destiny nodded and seemed to glow with power. Tears ran down her face as she apologized, saying they would make it better. Then sleep overcame me. It consumed me in a matter I could not escape. Like an arrow piercing my soul, the darkness to embraced my chaotic filled mind.

Sitting up my eyes flew open, all the emotions of that day poured through me. I was in tears. Instantly my father's reassuring touch encompassed me in a deep hug. Silently we sat for a few moments in tears, before another memory gripped my mind.

A fireplace, the scent of lilacs. The image became more clear, my mother and I sat in the main den of the house. I must have been close to three, just before the unsettling events. My mother brushed out my tangled long coppery hair. She talked as mothers often did.

"I'm sorry honey, but Alkin had to attend other things," she began as I sat quietly and allowed tears to run down my face. "I know you like him, baby, but you will come to learn that being a Mystic is very demanding and that sometimes we have to do things we do not like. That means letting our friends and loved ones go and do their job." Calista said as she stopped brushing and picked me up. Taking me into her arms, her dark hair fell into my golden hair.

Gently she wiped away the tears. "Don't cry, child, he'll be back soon." My mother said as my father entered the room curious to know what was going on. Coming over he leaned down and gently kissed the top of our heads. Catching his gaze his eyes mirrored mine and my mother's ever-changing ones.

"Your mother is right. Alkin will be back so don't worry." He said before turning to speak with mother. "I never thought she would become so attached to another Mystic so early." He began as he went to toss another log on the fire. "I have a feeling if this keeps up we will never get rid of him." Father said in a joking tone while mother gave him a sarcastic look.

I, on the other hand, looked at my parents curiously and somewhat alarmed. Mother couldn't help but laugh slightly at my response. "When you get older if you want to keep Alkin around that is fine with us. All I want for you is happiness."

***

The memory faded as quickly as it began. I wanted to fight to run or scream, her words echoed through my mind as everything cleared to real-time.

"I'll never be able to fully get rid of him, will I? What does it all mean? Is this normal?" I asked as more tears fell from my face.

My father laughed slightly, just as a portal began to open up into the room. "Truthfully I don't think any of us will be rid of him."

My eyes focused on the blackened portal, tears still streaming down my face, and heart feeling heavy. Howl walked out of the shimmering black mass, and smiled as it faded. His face appeared etched in stone, and somber, as if someone had died. Even his mind was blocked from me, it was frightening and only added to the sadness.

"Who won't we be rid of?" He questioned while looking at my father and casually crossing his arms.

He sighed, "Alkin. She remembers more. Hopefully, soon she will know everything."

My father was right, I was remembering everything and I was hopeful that this teetering period would pass. I saw how co-ordinated my mother was with Daes, and I knew she would want me to be the same. I wasn't frightened of him as much anymore. Yet I was still so confused about Alkin.

"Is it normal?" I heard myself ask again with Howl here. For a brief moment, I felt Howl brush my mind. My body began to shake as I felt on the verge of tears. "Why do I feel like my whole worlds been ripped apart, and shattered to pieces?" I cried into my hands. "I feel like my hearts been ripped out of my chest and stepped on. I hate feeling so vulnerable!" I cried out as I felt Howl's reassuring embrace.

His strong arms circled me, as his magic encompassed me. The smell of cherry blossoms, and sandalwood filled my nose. I felt the bed shift momentarily.

"I will be right back, I think it would be best if you drank something." My father said as he left the room quietly.

"I'm so sorry, I wish there were an easier way..." Howl began as he watched my father go. "And is what normal? If I went through what you have I'd feel like my world was also shattered ." He said half smiling, and turning to look directly at me.

Shaking my head, "That's not what I mean." I cried into his chest. The subtle smell of cherry blossoms was calming but just reminded me of spring, and Alkin. Lightly pushing away from him, I glanced down at the green sapling embroidered comforter. I twisted it in my grasp, like a nervous school girl.

"Can I show you?" I asked frightened to relive and remember those memories of meeting Alkin.

Howl's eyebrows furrowed with concern. Glancing at him, he chewed at his lip for a moment, before taking a big sigh and answering me. "Yeah, show me, I will help if I can." He said while pressing his forehead against mine, and smiling mischievously.

Playfully I pushed him away, he raised his eyebrow and his eyes gleamed. Howl was like a brother to me, for some reason I felt I could share things with him I was too embarrassed to share with my father. Things such as this...

Carefully I reached my hand out and placed it on his cheek. Then I closed my eyes and concentrated on the memory that most confused me, and was bugging me for some time. The over-whelming feeling of not being able to breathe, of my heart stut-tering and the world falling away from my feet, engulfed my mind. The memory of the first time I touched Alkin came flowing back into me. My heart twanged and ached, as an overwhelming sense of grief beat at my mind.

Tears fell from my eyes, as I heard myself begin to cry. Not able to handle the feeling any longer I broke our connection and bawled into Howl's chest. Taking deep and what sounded like painful breaths, he reached out to comfort me. His mind poured his magic into me as he embraced me in a gentle hug.

For a moment, his mind seemed in turmoil. A girl with fiery red hair flashed across Howl's memories, she laughed and danced through a field of white flowers. Howl's mind then shift-ed to sheer grief, and the need to drown himself in Darah wine.

For a moment my tears stopped as I realized he had similar feelings for that girl. She was younger though, but he felt drawn to her. This, how I felt, was something normal, but what did it mean?

"That's why you were in Balone, wasn't it? That's why you said you needed to escape. What is that feeling?" I asked him meeting his eyes.

Sorrow filled them and hurt. His strong composure broke momentarily at the question and me pushing the mental image of the girl, smiling with a wreath of the white flowers in her fiery hair, on his mind. Tears swam in his eyes briefly, before he hard-ened his face and blocked me. Like a stone wall being thrown up everything, went mentally silent.

"That's something I will not talk about here. If you want answers perhaps you would like to go and speak to your grandmother in Silvertine. But we will have to be quick; she has other affairs to attend to soon." He said while turning towards the door that my father just entered. Smiling weakly, and seeming to know defeat, he nodded in agreement.

"Yes! Yes! I want answers, I want to know what that is and why it causes me to feel so uneasy. Knowing you have had a similar experience with someone younger than me makes me feel better. That means it wasn't any dark spell then was it?" I questioned as he pulled me out of bed and to my feet.

Pressing his lips together, he sighed. "No, it's not dark magic but I doubt you are going to like the truth. Come on, let's go." He said while pulling me into a portal.

Exploration & Understanding ~ Drake

A man crushes a variety of herbs in a pestle and mortar. Then the powder goes into a bowl, opening a nearby bottle and pouring its contents onto the herbs. Its blood-red liquid is thick like maple syrup, yet smelled like blood. Grabbing a nearby spoon he mixes them together murmuring a spell I cannot understand. Lastly water is added before it is put over the fire to simmer. *It's an amazing process.*

"Why are there four different bottles filled with blood?" I ask Lyth as I count the bottles that looked like the one the man had opened.

"There are four different mixtures of blood because we have four different Gods and equally four different attuned magic's to those Gods. Those of Daes' magic heal best with blood similar to their own, same goes with Destiny, Delron, and Lucine. Lucine being the Lunar Goddess. While we are not incompatible to heal with blood from another lineage, it's not as quick of an outcome."

Turning my head I looked at Lyth curiously, I had never heard the Lunar Goddess' name before. Not once did it cross my mind to ask her real name. None of our texts or history told us her name was Lucine. It made sense, Lucine meant moon's life in the Wolves language.

Smiling, I followed Lyth along the red, blue, silver, and green bricked streets. A couple walked by, the female relaxed in the male's arms. Watching them, they paused now and again looking at the different vendors. At times he whispered something to her, she would grab his hand or kiss him gently. His hands were constantly on her, holding her hand, waist or back, smiling and keeping her close. I could feel the love they shared for one another.

Silvertine was an amazing city, full of rich history and religion. It was much more focused on the Gods than my people were, everything revolved around the Gods. Lyth said that the Drakar never deny a request from the Gods, that they full-heartedly tried their best in fulfilling it when asked, often acquiring help from a Mystic of their lineage.

As we walked Howl caught up, he had excused himself shortly before arriving. His bright blue eyes met mine as he smiled wildly at us. "Sorry, for that little mishap, I cannot stay too long, there is a lot going on at the moment."

Lyth gave him a curious look but didn't question.

We walked quietly as we left the textile area and entered the heart of the city. A large dragon fountain stood in the center. Shimmering iridescent scales seemed to dance with magic in the sunlight. From different angles they seemed to change color, red, blue, green, and silver.

A young girl about nine or so sat on the fountain's edge while other children ran around or played in the water. She innocently splashed at them as they splashed back. A young man approached her and smiled happily before sitting and joining in the fun.

During the splashing, the girl lost her balance and precariously fell into the fountain. Almost instinctively she reached for the young man as he in turn reached for her. Carefully and lovingly he pulled her out, she was in tears and buried her face into his chest. He stroked her wet hair affectionately and rubbed his face across her head protectively.

Something stirred inside, as I saw him act this way. So similar to the Wolves, yet she was so young, a child. Shock must have crossed my face. *Surely they didn't claim ones so young?*

"She's ten, and still has a few years before her parents will let him court her. Yet, already she knows who her mate is. They allow him to help raise her, he becomes her protector, and mentor when they are not around. At times, mates meet when they are young and have the advantage to be raised together. They learn to depend on each other. In addition, they learn from each other, they learn magic, love, affection, respect and so much more. While she still lives with her parents, it is not unheard of for her mate to spend time there with her. However, he will not lay claim on her till she is much older. Nonetheless, she does know her fate." Howl said, clearing up my confusion.

"So their parents don't mind the closeness? What about abuse? Would he ever do something to her?" I was trying to understand everything, I wanted to know what Raillyn had missed growing up.

Lyth shook his head. "Celeste and I grew up together, I'm only four years older, so you can only imagine," he said with a smirk. "There is never a fear for abuse, because we feel what our mate feels. Even at such a young age I am sure those two have a blood bond between each other. Celeste and I had one when she turned four. It means mates share thoughts and emotions mentally between each other. It also means that once a blood bond is formed the pair begins to grow closer. Fledgling years are the worst for parents whose child grows up around their mate, they have to learn to start letting go sooner than those who aren't raised around their mates. However even so, Parents actually encourage this pre-mate behavior. That girl's life is in her mate's hands and his in hers and they know it. Their bond runs so deep even at a young age they will do anything for one another. She will grow up only knowing his touch, his love and affection. Plus there is no chance for an unexpected pregnancy, as with your fledglings. She will not have a cycle until she becomes of age to be marked rightfully as his mate."

"Then what about Raillyn? I know Ancients are similar to our women but it's years instead of a month between each cycle. What changed though?" I asked needing more information.

The man had his young mate in his lap and she clung to him as if the world was ending. He smiled down at her understandingly and lovingly before whispering into her ear. Almost immediately her face lit up as she jumped out of his lap and onto the dirt ground.

She began pulling his hands and willing him to stand quicker. Smiling he stood and patted her head, she grasped his hand, as any child would an adult. Then they disappeared into the city. That man loved her. I saw it in his eyes. They were soft and warm towards her. But I bet they would be different towards other people.

"Raillyn was taken away from her parents at a young age, or she would have had a life like that girl. However, since she was taken the bond between Alkin and her was severed. She grew up without her mate around. That being, as you could say, is the other side of the coin. Sometimes mates don't grow up together, Howl's a good example of that. They live their normal life, sometimes taking lovers that never amount to anything. Other times they search and try and find their mate. Or wait to be found. Females will have a cycle every three to five years, a low-key one that only makes their stomach flutter. Yet, even if they took a lover, they cannot become pregnant. I'm sure that was how Raillyn was until she met Alkin." Lyth said before pausing and pointing out a group of fledglings.

Five males and two females laughed and danced together, but there was no spark between any of them. None of them were mates. Yet they still treated the girls with respect and were careful with them. The boys you could tell were rough housing, they punched and pushed at each other.

One of the bigger boys, shoved a smaller boy hard into a petite curly blond girl. She fell backwards and scuffed her knee on the bricks. Her mouth hung open, shocked from the fall. The biggest boy next to her glanced at the other boy leaning against the wall and pushed himself up.

He went over and attended the girl while the biggest boy went over to the two boys who were on the ground rolling around in a small brawl. The last boy, helped and pulled at the smaller boy, who both flung around wildly as the one he fought was contained. The tall girl screamed briefly as the boys almost hit her. That's when two adults, males, came and intervened. They grabbed the two boys who were brawling, and escorted them into the crowd. The remaining fledglings settled down, and the boys checked on the girls before they went back to talking, and hovering around them. It was strange yet familiar, our males, even at a young age tended to be gentle and caring towards females.

"Did Alkin and Raillyn have a blood bond when she was young?" I asked not even realizing I had asked it. Howl and Lyth looked at each other curiously.

"I don't know if they had a blood bond at the time, but if they did, it would make sense why she never feared him. If she had a physical link to him through blood it wouldn't have been erased or hampered when her memories were. However, I don't know, you would have to ask him or Drameon. If Drameon even knew, that is. I will say this. Alkin was constantly hanging around with Drameon and Calista. Even then they allowed him to help care for Raillyn. I don't know how many times I visited and found him asleep with her in a chair or playing dolls with her quietly in her room. Even then he loved her and protected her. He would do anything for her and when she was taken it was devastating to him." Lyth said as if recalling the events mentally.

"Tell me about it? What happened?" I asked hoping to understand his actions more. Already I was seeing what should have been and what was.

"I don't know all of the details but I know he went to speak to his father, Delron. However, no one told him where she was. He felt her in the God's realm but could never find her. In his anger, he tore apart his house here in the city and left for a good hundred years or so. Where he went I have no idea, but he and Drameon didn't talk to one another again until after the end of the war. Then they both seemed to start working together again, like nothing had happened. I can only assume that was when the Gods told them their plan and gave them tasks to accomplish and make things possible." He said as we walked on. "Come on, it's getting late and Opal will expect you back before nightfall."

As we walked the main road back to Opal and Solomn's, I couldn't help but feel remorseful towards Alkin and Raillyn. Not only had her world been ripped out from under her at a young age, but the one person she trusted was banned from seeing her. Her parents were lost to her as the Gods took her into their care. Then, after all that, they placed her in a foreign land, with no memory of her prior life.

I was sure she felt the grief still over her loss of time and what should have been. After seeing Silvertine and its people, I felt I owed it to her to help her reclaim what she lost. It saddened me, but it's what she should have had in the first place.

***

As we walked I paid little attention to where we were until entering the palace, where Solomn and Opal lived. The building was the largest in the city, its white towering walls topped with the large golden dome atop the planetarium was amazing. It caught the sun's rays and shimmered, a dazzling luminescent hue. I followed Howl and Lyth through the large red arched doors and through the main halls and onto the ornate plush rugs.

The silver walls glowed subtle as orange magic lights hung from the ceiling. Tapestries of saplings, dragons, or ancient patterns lined the walls in various colors. Howl turned and smirked at me as we neared the four-dragon door.

A red, blue, silver, and green dragon each spiraled up its golden length. This door opened up into the main den where I had met Opal and Solomn. Pillows lined furniture and the floor while a large fireplace stood along the northern wall, making it cozy. Glancing at Lyth, he seemed nervous but smiled at me. Howl opened the door and walked into the room. Solomn's fiery red eyes met mine before anything else. His broad chin, yet elf-like appearance, made him standout. Opal, his mate, stood next to him her long brown wavy hair, bright blue eyes, and Elvin facial features smiled warmly at me. Three other figures stood in the room, I caught their scent immediately, and even before looking at them I knew they were Wolves.

Two tall masculine males stood around a petite female, with bright hazel eyes and blackish blue hair. The same features I had seen before over and over again. It was the girl from my dreams, however this time her hair was not tousled around her head. My eyes met hers and her lips seemed hard pressed. She wore the same light brown leather armor as before.

"You?" I said almost in shock. "You're the girl I saw along the shores near the plains."

My mind seemed to draw back to the time I first met this lady. It was along the shores of a large lake with shimmering blue water. An open plain lay beside it, tall grasses and brush grew as far as the eye could see. This girl stood along the shore, tears running down her pixie-like face. *This was the girl who had haunted my dreams for over twenty years.* When I saw her prior I wasn't sure if it real or a dream. It wasn't until I noticed I physically held her wrist that I realized it wasn't a dream at all. That she was real...

Even now I felt the connection from her lingering in my dreams and our first actual encounter, before she pushed me back home, shocking me back into my room at the castle. *She was no Alecien Wolf... Which meant only one thing, she probably lived here in Aeralain...*

Looking at her more closely – she closed her greenish-blue eyes and bit at her lip. Awkwardly she turned her pixie-like face towards the ground.

"Raven, what is he talking about? Have you two met before?" The sandy-haired gentleman, with a burly face and rugged trimmed beard, asked while crossing his arms.

Opal and Solomn seemed confused and glanced towards each other before looking at Howl and Lyth, who stood smirking. "Father, I didn't mean to. I was casting a scrying spell and I don't really know what happened." She said whimsically. "From what I can tell he was able to manipulate the magic I was casting and it pulled him to me. After I realized what happened I immediately sent him back. I didn't mean for things to get out of hand and apologize for using magic I wasn't familiar with."

"Raven Koray, you know we are forbidden to use dark magic spells, they are dangerous to those who are untrained. You could have gotten yourself killed by using such a spell!" The older man said authoritatively. The younger man, with blonde hair and deep violet eyes, glanced at him and nodded his head agreeing.

"Father, I know summoning spells are forbidden to our kind, but if you let me explain… I was trying to help! We needed to reach Chancellor Droggen after Lord Cyrin was killed and we lost all contact with Alecien. I studied the scrying spell for months before I even tried it. At first it was slow and I couldn't do much of anything, but over the years I learned all the information I was able to pass onto you…" She started defending herself.

"Which you lied about. You said you had an inside source working for you in Alecien, I believed it was one of the Drakar, and not this. You and I will have a very serious talk when we return to the Lunar Plane tonight."

Raven closed her eyes and stood submissively beside the older man.

"For now, Lord Drake, we are here to speak to you about a situation concerning your father and me. My name's Geirolf, and I am the leader of the Lunar Planes Werewolves. Before your father was killed, we were speaking about an alliance between our people. I have brought all the documents, here to Silvertine and will let you look them over as well, to ensure we are truthful." Geirolf said pulling out papers from a satchel he had swung over his shoulder.

For a moment I just stared at him, his deep brown leather armor seemed almost black, and his shoulder-length peppered hair reminded me of my own fathers. *How was he contacting him? From across the Silver Sea?* I stood shocked, unsure what to do, and feeling in a haze.

"Drake?" Howl said as he pushed me lightly on the shoulder. "Why don't you have a seat and look over the documents?"

Quietly I took the papers and sat down in the nearest chair, bewildered. "How were you and my father speaking to one another, if I might ask?" Turning them over, it was indeed my father's handwriting.

Geirolf sat beside me and leaned back in the chair. "We enlisted the aid of a Drakar to go between here and Alecien. He took our letters back and forth for us, using his home. As you already know from speaking to Howl, they can tie their houses to different locations for easy travel."

"Yes, Howl has his home tied to my castle at this time."

Geirolf smiled and went on. "This Drakar did that for us. However, things went wrong. Just after your father was killed, we sent him across the Silver Sea with a cryptic note stating to meet in Kerin Port on a certain day and time. It was stated on the note to send a reply. We hoped you or your Chancellor would respond, but nothing came, and the Drakar never returned. We believe the Vampires found him and killed him. After that we didn't dare try and contact anyone in Alecien. So we waited. Now however I see that my daughter became impatient."

As I skimmed the notes, I briefly saw the word betrothal, and peace. Pausing, I read a letter my father wrote to Geirolf. The letters were faded with time, however I would recognize his writing anywhere.

Geirolf,

Things have not been going well; I fear the Vampires plan to attack my people. Already I have lost too much to them, I refuse to lose more.

I will speak to my son about his betrothal to Raven, I believe it is long past time he settles down, even if it's for a peace arrangement. It will strengthen both our people and the ties for us will be beneficial to all. I am sorry this letter is short, but I wanted to let you know I am taking a small group of troops north to survey farmlands that have been ransacked by Renegades. If you do not hear from me within the month, try and get word to Chancellor Droggen or my son. I think showing him these letters would be proof enough of my intentions, should I fall in battle.

Lord Cyrin

My father must have sent this message just before his death. I was never aware of my father working with an Ancient.

"Can I ask who the Drakar was? I never knew my father was working with someone on this side of the Silver Sea. My father mentioned briefly before he left that it was time I settled down, but I never thought he setup an arranged marriage for me…" I said a little shocked, and confused.

Raven leaned down and met my eyes, distracting me for a moment with her smile. *This had been the girl who scryed for me even before my father died, yet she hid that from her own father. Why? I wish I could speak to her alone…*

"His name was Terrene; he was one of Lucine's Drakar. His house fell apart and crumbled not long after he disappeared. That's why we thought he was killed, his magic died with him and so did his spells." Raven said solemnly.

Her scent seemed to hang in the air, it was sweet vanilla, laced with cinnamon, honey, and an alluring flower I couldn't place. For a brief moment, I wanted to reach out to her and comfort her. However part of me felt ashamed.

Was I really going to toss Raillyn aside so haphazardly for this woman? Then the twang of guilt hit me, *she was promised to Alkin as I was promised to Raven. Raven had even gone as far as helping me stay alive when my mother died.* It drove me onward, that secret hidden connection we shared since we were young. It made me wonder. *Was this how the Ancients felt when they found their mate?*

"I'm sorry but can I speak to Raven alone for a moment?" I asked, shocking everyone in the room.

Her father looked at me, a subtle rumble emanated from his throat.

"Father I will be fine, you are the one who arranged marriage between us and insisted it stay in place if we were to ever make peace. We are making peace and I find that it is within my right to speak to my future mate alone. Opal, Solomn, do you object to this?" She said firmly focused on the two Drakar leaders.

Opal smiled and took Solomn's arm. "Of course not, dear, in fact, I think it's only natural that you two would need a moment to speak about such startling matters. Please let us give these two a moment of peace." She said as Solomn and her began leading everyone into the main hall. "We will be right next door, please come join us when you are done."

"Of course, my lady." Raven said, bowing respectfully. She stood silent until the door was closed.

"How…" I began before she shushed me, placing a finger to my lips. Even this close her scent was driving me crazy, it was exotic and seemed almost magnetic. Before saying a word, she went to the door and opened it just barely. She sniffed the air as it moved around the door, before closing it and coming to sit next to me.

"Sorry, I wanted to make sure, Eli wasn't outside guarding the room. He would tell my father everything if he knew what I hid from him." She said while folding her hands in her lap and looking at them.

Taking a breath, I couldn't help but ask. "You didn't tell your father you were dabbling in the dark magic even before my father's death. Why? You helped save me when my mother died, and even before that you haunted my dreams. He doesn't know, does he?"

She met my gaze, a look of shame in her eyes. For a moment I thought she would cry, tears seemed to pool in the corners of her eyes as she looked frightened. "No, my father doesn't know. I've been dabbling in the dark arts since I was eight after I met a red Dragon near the Deleon Waste. My father would kill me if he knew I was venturing there. But after I found him I couldn't resist the drive to learn about my necromancy. As you can tell I have necromantic blood, my skin gives it away." She said looking away from me.

For a moment, I didn't know what to say. Yes, her skin was leucistic, but I never attributed it to necromancy. "How do you have necromantic blood?" I heard myself ask before I could stop myself. I didn't mean for it to come out rude, but I was curious.

Raven silently nodded. "It's ok. I got it from my mother. She was a necromancer and a Mystic of Delron. She was born and raised in this city, she knew its laws, and traditions. However, she never grew up around her mate. When she was twenty-six that changed, they bumped into each other unexpectedly, and it triggered her cycle. She was scared and frightened by the sheer power of the bond that she left. She disappeared to the Lunar Plane and ran into my father. It was only for one night but it's how I came around." Her eyes met mine determined and truthful.

"Your mother was Mystic?" I questioned to be sure.

"Yes. After she had me she was forced by tradition to return me to my father's people. But she stayed in the village until I was fifteen, with her own mate. My father married and had a son when I was three, but he still considered me to be his heir. It is a great honor to be a child of a Mystic, even if we don't carry their mixed magic in our blood." She said smiling.

I was nervous of what to ask next, but it had to get out in the open. "Do you know about Raillyn and Deestan?" I questioned wondering how much she knew.

Reaching out she placed her hand on my cheek. "Of course, it's a very understanding issue outside the Ancients' law, on our part at least. On the other side, they try and keep issues such as me from happening, but we believe the Gods have a purpose for it. They would never kill one of their own—that's not how Mystics are—but they tend to be very busy for children not of their blood."

I nodded my head in agreement, Deestan had mentioned how Raihanna worked in The Keep and it sounded similar.

"It's sad, while you're growing up and trying to understand the difference, but I learned my mother always found time to be with me. My mother and her mate also have a son, of Delron's lineage. I often found myself jealous of him while I was growing up. She always seemed to take him everywhere, while I had to stay in the village. Like I said, when I grew up a little and became educated in my magic and culture, it made sense. Mystics don't get the luxury of raising a child not of their blood. They are forced to hand the child over and allow other parents to raise them. In a way, I think distancing herself from me made it easier on her. My relationship with my mother is better now that I'm not a kid, she's more like a friend than a mother though." Raven said meeting my eyes. Her soft features smiled lightly. I could tell she was truthful and thankful for what she had.

"Deestan is like that in a way; she's been educating herself in anything she can. Even in The Keep she began reading when she was four. In a way, I feel it was the only way she felt she could keep up. She seems similar to you and your situation. So why would your father not want you to embrace that magic?" I asked a little confused still on the necromancy part.

"Because it's dark magic, death magic. He thinks I'm going to get myself killed. What he doesn't know is that I've walked in Death's Realm since I was five and am not afraid of the magic or beings that dwell there. Delron accepts me as a disciplined user and allows me entry. So what do you think about our arranged marriage? Truthfully I knew since I first saw you something drew me to you. I know our race doesn't have the mate bond that the Ancients do, but I always believed that something brought two people together, even if it wasn't magic." She said, blushing and getting straight to the point.

I ran my fingers through my hair debating my words. Yes, I agreed, there was definitely something about her that kept my attention, but at this time I didn't need that. What I needed was to help Raillyn get what she needed to be done. And hope it was the right thing to do.

"So what can this marriage offer my people and yours for that matter? Right now is just a crazy time for all this. Raillyn and the other Ancients need help with stabilizing Daes' magic." I said hoping she understood.

Smiling she leaned forward. "That's the thing – this is the perfect time for this. My people can bring the old ways of life back to yours. I have my own troops in the Lunar Plane, my father would let me run more but I would need my own tribe to do so, and we are not separating our people meaninglessly. This alliance will allow my people to separate and come with me to Alecien, in turn strengthening your own troops. Believe it or not, I don't just sit at home doing housework. I'm a fighter and I'm not afraid to stand up for what I believe in. I heard stories and seen the aftermath in the elders' eyes of the war here. Many of them escaped the horrors, being wrought in your land. Some left with missing limbs or barely breathing but still they went, in hope that one day they could return." Raven stood and began pacing as she went on.

"I will not tolerate a race that is so stuck on terror and destruction that they disregard life so wantonly. They cannot be allowed to do what they want in that matter. They are nothing but a menace an ill-created race born from the destruction of themselves. Yes, I'm sure their creation had a purpose but they are running wild in Alecien and not caring what they do. It's time to put a stop to all this, and I hope to do just that with this alliance. Balance must be restored, it has been way too long since the blue dragons have awakened from the land and I fear if it goes on our world will die. I will do whatever it takes to keep those around me safe and to follow the Gods the best I can!" Raven stated while she stopped in front of me. "So will you allow my troops and me to reside in the castle and we can devise a plan to put an end to all this?" She asked while holding out her hand.

Smirking, I couldn't help but agree with everything she said. She was right, balance had to be restored. The Vampires were the main reason it was so unbalanced and the land was in ruin. Taking her hand, I agreed to her terms. She and the troops she commanded would accompany us to my castle, where they would meet and train with Saibal and my men. From there, we would work out the details.

Heartache ~ Raillyn

As Howl and I walked the silvery halls towards the main den, I failed to pay attention and nearly ran into a newly opened door. Seeing it approach my face suddenly made me jump backwards. When the door closed it revealed a woman, short, white-blond hair, ocean blue eyes and almost elf-like features that appeared to be more Fae like, met my ever-changing eyes. It was the lady from when I was dying as Raihanna.

Realization struck me as I made the connection, I must have teleported, on my own, to Silvertine. I knew now that the other lady had been Opal. She seemed surprised to see me as I was her, and nearly dropped the books she held in her hand.

"What are you two doing here?" She asked nervously. "I mean, does Opal and Solomn know you're here?" Correcting her tone.

"What do you think, Darcia? Would we be sneaking around the darkened halls of the palace alone if we were expected? There are not many people who know about Raillyn and I'm trying to keep it that way for the time being." Howl said while poking her forehead.

She swatted him away. "Oh, Howl, you are such a terror. Don't touch me I don't know where that hand has been!" She almost shouted. Howl smirked and leaned closer as if to annoy her more.

I couldn't help but giggle, the two of them fought like they were on two different sides of the spectrum. In a way, it was hilarious. "No, they don't know I'm here. We've just arrived. Perhaps you can take me to them?"

Composing herself, she bowed her head at me as she held onto her books tightly. "My names Darcia Gley and I would be happy to escort you to them." She said before leading the way down the hall, opening a door and waiting.

Smiling I walked through, into another copy of the hall we just left.

"So whose idea was it to come here, if I might ask? If you are trying to keep Daes' last Mystic a secret, Silvertine was a terrible choice to visit. Once word reaches the streets, everyone in Aeralain will know in a few days' time." She said as we passed a woman dressed in grey clothes; she bowed slightly as we walked by and avoided eye contact. Thinking she was a servant I kept my attention on Darcia, the lady seemed confused for a moment before turning away. Rounding another corner we stopped outside a remarkably crafted door. Howl followed silently behind us.

"It was his idea, I asked him something. Well, rather showed him something and he told me it was best if I asked my grandmother."

Darcia looked at Howl questioningly. "I could only imagine what kind of answer a barbarian like him would give you." She said tartly.

Howl looked at her as if he was about to say something rude.

"Stop don't even make her mad, she's being nice and taking us to my grandmother. So behave." I told him sternly along our mental link.

Sighing he quietly followed behind. Turning a corner, I saw a large red door with four Dragons spiraling up its length. They twined around one another, and each had a different color. *The color of the Gods,* I thought, as a slight memory of my mother talking about the different colored Dragons being in coalition to the Gods' eyes and magic color. White, Green, Blue, and Red dragons appeared to be dancing in a stormy sky. It was amazing.

Darcia opened the door and stood as I finished marveling at the work. Smiling at her, I followed her into the room. Two people sat near a large dragon-sculpted fireplace. The room was dotted with various pillowed chairs, benches and seats, all decorated in the four different magic colors. The two people seemed surprised by my appearance. They rose to meet me immediately.

Opal and Solomn stood before me. Opal stood with her long brown wavy hair, bright blue eyes, human-like ears but very Elvin facial features, and Solomn with his broad chin, fiery red eyes and ruff but handsome face. I felt frozen in place, unsure what to do or say. I had teleported here when I was Raihanna when the construct body which I had resided in was failing me. Here was my grandmother and the very people who raised my mother.

It was Opal who broke the silence, tears in her eyes she came to me and pulled me into a tight embrace. "Raillyn." She said as tears fell from her blue eyes. "I never thought I would see you alive." She said between light sobs. I found tears running down my face as well. "I don't even know where to begin. I haven't seen you since the Gods took you from your father." She said as she led me towards the pillowed bench where they sat prior.

Darcia and her mate Solomn talked quietly amongst themselves. Howl stood off to the side leaning against the nearby wall.

"I tried desperately to have Daes release you to me when your mother passed but he said no, he forbid it. I was devastated, but knew I would see you again.... And here you are." She said smiling, the tears vanishing as if they never existed.

My face matched her smile, as I finally found my words. "I don't remember much, it all happened so long ago, and I'm still bound by the spell..." I said trailing off as Solomn turned at those words.

Opal met her mate's eyes and then looked back at me. For a moment, my grandmother's eyes glowed vibrantly, an equally bright blue haze began to wisp off her in small tendrils. Slowly they reached for me and I felt her magic brush mine. Like lightning I felt my magic react and push hers away, my body shook and the air in my lungs took on a blue appearance before fading away and dying down.

"I knew the Gods had lain magic upon you but I didn't realize it was so strong. You're right, it seems as if Daes' spell still controls your magic." She said while brushing my hair back. "As far as the past, your father kept us up to date on the events happening across the Silver Sea with you. In addition, Howl brought us a child you released into the Vampire's Den. Callina, she's such a dear." She began to say as I met her eyes and glanced at Howl. A look of shock crossed my face.

Noticing, she met my eyes and stopped for a moment, unsure if what she said was wrong to say or not. "Alkin's daughter Callina, I was told you released her to the Vampire's Den, yes? I begged Alkin to allow her to stay here, but he insisted her mother wanted her in the local Den. I'm thankful I get to visit my granddaughter still…" She began as I interrupted her.

"Wait – what?" I asked confused as I looked at Howl for answers. Reaching out towards him, I grabbed him by the front of his shirt. *"You said I would get answers on what in the world that magic was."* I said mentally to him.

"And you will." He said gruffly and ill-tempered before he stormed off. "I need a moment's reprieve, to compose myself." Throwing his hands into the air, he exited through another door.

Suddenly confused, Opal and Solomn met me with worry in their eyes. "Is he ok?" They asked me.

My grandmother had a worried look to her face as she went to sit down. "I have never seen Howl so distraught. Whatever is going on must not be good." She said while patting her mate's lap as he sat.

Fuming briefly mentally, I took a seat near them,

Darcia was already in a chair reading near the fireplace. "Howl and his drama… That's all I have to say on that." She said pausing for a moment while I looked at her curiously.

Solomn seemed to laugh slightly at this remark. "Howl does have quite a personality but I am sure it's nothing." Opal seemed to agree, snuggling her mate before sitting back upright.

"What do you mean about that?" I asked Darcia.

Sitting upright she slightly closed the book before meeting my eyes. "He's a bit of a drama boy, always chasing the girls around till they want to actually stay around. Then he moves onto the next. God, when he was a fledgling he was a nightmare…"

She said as I looked at her confused. "He was big into throwing snogging parties in the local Den." Darcia said quieter.

"Darcia! Howl is a lot better now, it's not polite to speak of his ill-fledgling behavior like that." Opal said sternly.

She sighed, "She should know the truth is all. I bet he hides that side of his personality." She said as she lay back down and began reading.

Thinking back, no he didn't hide that personality, he seemed like a big horn dog at times. Always flirting and grabbing people. A smile crossed my face as I laughed slightly, remembering when we first met.

It was in the little northern town, I ran too fast across the icy road and slipped. He had grabbed my arm, stopping me from face planting the ground. Howl flirted with me then, and got me drunk. Nothing happened but it still made me laugh. *Typical Howl...*

"And I thought she'd be different." I heard Darcia say as Opal looked at Solomn lovingly.

For a moment, I was taken aback. It reminded me of my time in The Keep, of my time with Alkin. My chest ached for a moment at the thought. *Was I missing him?* I thought for a moment. I hadn't really thought about him, instead avoiding those feelings. Again I felt myself avoid them, pulling back almost shutting a door to them.

"So, tell me, how did you and Solomn meet? Was it a sudden thing or did you two take your time? Was it after you had my mother? And how is Callina?" I asked unsure if I should mention Howl's emotional turmoil that I felt before he closed his mind to me.

Solomn and Opal seemed to be eager to tell their story. They looked at each other with an intense love and passion. I was feeling at ease and calm here.

"It was before I had your mother. In fact, it was the issue of meeting Solomn that lead me to agreeing to give Daes a child." She began.

I looked at her curiously to hear such a thing. *If she was Solomn's mate how did it come down to her giving Daes, a child?*

"During my studies, I had trained in the art of a Matriarch, it is similar to what you would know as priestess except we are allowed to take mates and not remain celibate. I had taken my vows and began my apprenticeship. Over this time I met Solomn, it was a simple moment that I will never forget, a split second decision made me go to the High Patrons. I had discovered an item that belonged to Lord Ralos, immediately I brought it to him, and while I was there, I noticed his son, Solomn. Now Ralos was ancient, and had decided to pass the title of City Protector onto his son, who was over a couple hundred years old already. I was in awe of Solomn, to know he was taking on such a role at his age was amazing. Not only does city protector manage the guard they also govern the city. He essentially was becoming King. Failing to pay attention to my surroundings I stumbled. He quickly reached out and grabbed me, and in that instant I knew. The overwhelming sensation of not being able to breathe, where your own heart threatens to stop and where a single moment of time seems to last a century. That one single powerful event sealed our fate, neither of us spoke about it at first." Her words echoed in my mind, that was it.

She went on. "Instead we stood quietly looking at each other, unsure what to do. He was going to become ruler of the city in just a few days' time and I had just become an apprentice for the local magic school. There was no way I thought we could be mates."

As Opal spoke about how she felt when she met Solomn, she described the same feeling Howl felt. The same feeling I had long ago. I felt a shift in my mind and for a brief second I panicked. Standing shakily, Opal noticed my distress.

"What is it?" She asked stopping her story, suddenly fearful for me.

Feeling tense, I paced the room for a moment, Darcia sat up and seemed to take notice also. My emotions reigned from subtle calmness to chaotic distress. My breathing picked up pace and I felt myself begin to sweat. I knew Opal and Darcia felt it since they were both Daes' Drakar, my magic fluctuated within the room in waves of unease.

"What is that feeling? Who gets those sensations?" I asked tentatively.

Opal stood and walked towards the fire, grabbing my elbow to stop my pacing she met my eyes. "You don't know?" She questioned, worriedly. I shook my head and looked towards her for answers.

"It's the inescapable bond between one's mate. Think of it like a blood bond or when placing a Mystic mark on friends. It's that magnified and blood isn't the trigger in this case, your magic is. Forming a blood bond with your mate can intensify your feelings but at the same time it soothes the overall primal effects of your body. When you are bound to your mate, those feelings, and conditions are controlled even more. All Ancient races have the mate bond integrated into their being. People have fought it, but it only makes the bond fight back. Often putting mates in situations where the more primitive instincts takeover, forcing them together." Opal said matter of fact like.

Unsure what to do or how to proceed I looked at Darcia. "Mystics have this?" I asked hopeful for an answer. I felt I was approaching some new revelation.

Darcia stood and sighed. "It's the whole reason the Gods refuse to breed with Ancients. Why has something like this happened to you?" She asked suddenly making the gears in my head turn.

Something did happen to me. Was it the same? I had met Alkin, been saved by Drake and Briar all at the same moment. It was confusing, it all happened so fast. Then the dreams came, but they weren't really dreams. My body tingled as I remembered Alkin running his hands down my thighs. Shutting those thoughts out, I needed more answers, not comfortable with talking to my grandmother about this subject. Destiny, Chaimh and Daes came to mind. I quivered as the strange sensation picked up the scent of pine. *Had Alkin been here?* My insides began to quiver and my mind began going blank, I needed to leave before I did something I would regret.

"I think I need to excuse myself for a moment. Would it be all right if I returned here once I'm done to finish getting answers I need?" I asked knowing deep in my soul I had to visit my grandfather. Opal nodded her head understandingly.

Without another word, I turned and summoned a portal and went through. As I exited it my other grandmother, Chaimh, and Daes sat around a large fireplace sipping drinks talking amongst themselves. My appearance didn't seem to startle any of them.

"To what do we owe this visit?" Daes asked as I stood before them hands on my hips.

Meeting Daes' eyes he sensed the unrest deep in my soul, the anxiousness it brought. Those unsteady, unrelenting effects it wrought on my body. It was pure stress. I was confused I wanted answers and the truth.

"Do Mystics have a bonded mate?" I asked out loud, not caring what I said or did anymore. "Opal told me that all the Ancients had this inescapable mate bond that was so forceful and powerful it took your breath away and was unrelenting once put in motion. Do Mystics have this?" I asked again, Destiny seemed startled and Daes was unyielding.

Chaimh was the one who stood and spoke. "Calm down, child, is that why you have been so worked up lately?" He asked trying to sooth me.

He stood and brushed the hair from my face as I looked at him uneasily. "I showed Howl a memory of my past and something happened. His emotions ran so deep, deeper than anything else... and I remember feeling that myself, years ago." I said while Destiny and Daes kept quiet and listened.

Again I felt tremors shake my body as I remembered Alkin grabbing my hand in the forest so long ago. I tried to associate that feeling to whatever it was intended to be associated with. Then more memories flooded my mind, but they weren't mine. *My mother's thoughts, her memories, but how?*

Daes' words and Chaimh's were lost in the static of her memory. She had met my father when she was young. Drameon was almost three hundred years older than her, and she was a mere child. But she was drawn to him.

He had visited Silvertine on business for Destiny and Lucine. An image of a familiar person entered my mind, Nora, the maid from my days in The Keep. When Drameon went and spoke with Nora, Opal and Solomn. Calista came into the room, running from Leon, who she was playing with. She accidently ran right into Drameon and even then something was sparked. Even though, she was too young for the deeper connection, she felt herself drawn to him. She simply just stood staring at him. Like he was familiar to her.

The memory shifted, Drameon had spent several years in Silvertine and my mother would silently follow him around the city, spying on him. Her emotions were confused, she felt something for my father but was in denial and instead tried to divert the feelings. She tried to make him out to be a bad guy, someone who was disrupting the natural flow of her magic and mind. So she played tricks on him. Misplacing items he left in a room at her parents' house, tracking mud into his room, and putting too much pepper on his food. Anything to cause a controlled chaos, she did regardless of the punishment. She was driven to poke and prod him. Anything to be near him, or get a peek at him.

Eventually, Drameon left and wasn't seen in Silvertine for years. My mother was distraught, but as time went on she began to work for Daes. On one outing, she went to the Northern Plains the coldest continent Auran had. There while speaking to the giants she saw him again.

While exploring the town he turned a corner and ran right into her. She was no longer a child. Instead a young adult, and that deep soul wrenching feeling was felt. The air around them stilled, and so did time. My mother knew what this was, she had been raised to know this feeling and she felt Drameon did too.

Leaning down he gently kissed her lips, but in that instant my mother's wild magic lashed out for the first time in years. She moved away from him and fell onto the snowy ground. She struggled to breath, struggled to contain the uncontrolled chaos that echoed in her mind. She never planned this, never expected it. Drameon leaned down and gently pulled her up off the ground and into a light embrace. She shook with fear and shock, slowly she felt herself relax with him, as a mental connection was made through their magic. It steadied her, she found her center, and found herself wanting more. Already she knew she could never escape.

"You felt that before?" Chaimh asked quietly, looking towards Daes, bringing me out of her memory. "When? With who?"

Looking at the ceiling, I felt like I wanted to cry. A strong emotional force brought tears to my very eyes and slowly they ran down my cheeks uncharted. I was just like my mother.

"How is this possible?" I asked no one in particular, but I knew Daes would respond.

He witnessed everything that went on in my mind as I experienced it, like a watchful shadow. Chaimh and Destiny seemed lost, unsure what was going on. Daes, on the other hand, knew, I felt it in my soul and suddenly my eyes began glowing bright blue to match his own.

Another memory shattered my mind, another one of hers. My mother and father struggled for centuries for a child, and every time the child would not survive. My mother blamed the blood in her veins, Daes however blamed it on her magic. She was one of his few children, who because of the delicate situation of her creation, possessed necromancy. Such a combination resulted in her magic harming the child. Unless the child was lucky to possess necromancy, it often ended badly.

A time came when my parents stopped trying, and avoided their bond. Every three to five years they avoided her cycle, and instead of being together they stayed away from one another. For fifty years they did this and with each cycle the growing need to be together would only get worse. Something was going to break, was going to give, and that's what happened.

The burning need during a cycle was hard to forget and impossible to avoid. It went so deep that unless blood was exchanged in vast quantities and their magic branded one another with the magic brands, similar to Mystic marks, but strictly between mates. It marked them as a mated pair and tied them to one another inescapably bonding them together. So much that females would only respond to their mate. Only able to have a child with them and them alone.

Even then complications arose. Herbs were often used to prevent any unwanted children. A safeguard for many who didn't want to chance fate. But for my parents they had fought her cycle for so long, and things tipped to fast.

The information continued to pour into me, as if my mother was telling me, or I was watching the memories of when she learned it. Forty percent of all females died during their first pregnancy, it was a way to weed out the weak. In addition fifty percent of those who were strong enough to live, would lose the child. This made for hampering numbers in the Ancients' world.

If the child lived, the mother was at risk after its birth. Her magic gone, her body in shock, she needed the assistance of her mate to bring it back. Large quantities of blood and the touch of his magic was what she needed.

When I was born, it was in Daes' home, it was because my mother had so many complicated pregnancies no chances were being taken. Leon, Celeste, Lyth, Howl, Alkin, Daes and my father were all there. It was a typical birth, one that I had with both my girls. My mother kept me with her for over an hour before she began to grow tired and need blood.

So I was passed to Daes and we left my parents alone, so my father could heal my mother properly. It was coming back to me, I remember how I acted in The Keep after Callina was born. I was not Raihanna, not the uncaring, heartless bitch she was. For a few days, I lived as Raillyn, even though I lacked the memories I was myself. Even after I had Deestan I still reached for Alkin and needed his touch.

My breathing picked up pace, I felt like I couldn't catch my breath no matter how hard I tried. Sweat poured from every inch of my body, as my vision hazed and cleared like a swift moving fog. A crack wrenched through my soul as if pieces fell away from a large stone. It was the bonds around my magic, they were breaking.

"It's possible because I made it possible." Daes said cunningly, drawing attention to himself. "Your mother begged me to take her memories into a soul orb so one day you would see what you should have known all along."

Another memory ripped through my mind. Alkin had often been there when I was young. During one such occasion, I was left in his care for over a week. As night fell a storm began to brew. We were in his home, the rounded hive house, with the fireplace, chairs, the tree like staircase leading up to the second-floor balcony.

I was asleep in one of the rooms there, until lightning cracked in the sky and thunder echoed through the walls. Scared, I jumped out of bed and ran to find Alkin. He was reading a book near the fireplace and dozing.

Frightened I jumped into his lap, causing him to drop the book. "Raillyn, what's the matter?" He asked as I grabbed onto him for dear life. I buried my face into his warm chest, and tried to drown out the sounds with his heartbeat. Just as I began to calm down another bolt of lightning tore through the sky and thunder crashed above.

Shrieking in fear as he put his arms around me and held me close. I squeezed my eyes together as tight as I could, trying to concentrate on anything else. "Don't like the storm, huh?" He asked gently, before kissing my hair. Shaking my head, I knew he felt it. "Not going to go back to your room tonight, are you?" I shook my head no again, as another bolt lit up the room.

I pressed my tiny body against his till it hurt. I was so frightened and I didn't want him to let me go. Sighing he shifted his weight and picked me up. Holding me close, he began to walk towards the stairs. For a moment, I thought he was going to place me back into bed, but we passed the room. Continuing onwards towards the third floor enclosed stairs. Pulling back, I looked him in the eyes, as another bolt lit the room up. His room was normally off limits. My parents yelled at me anytime I would explore or venture there. Jumping at the crack of thunder, he smiled at me and kissed my hand lovingly.

"Regardless of what your parents say or think, I'm not going to let you sleep alone tonight. That would just be cruel. So for tonight, and tonight only you can come up to my room and sleep with me." He said as he carried me up the stairs and into the darkened room.

His room, I knew by heart, it was filled with deep blue linen and red tapestries. The canopy above the bed was satin silk, and white like clouds.

Gently Alkin lay down in bed, holding me against him. With his free hand he pulled the blankets over us, I remembered snuggling closer towards him and taking in his calming scent before falling asleep there.

He was my savior in so many situations, and he was my secret keeper. I knew he would never judge me wrongly for anything I did. Things were easier around him...

Daes broke my memory as he carried on where he left off. Time seemed to mean nothing as the memories came and went.

"Your mother knew you would not be raised with Ancients and she wanted you to have the knowledge when the time came. So what happened?" He asked cryptically to anyone but me.

Shaking violently, I felt his mind, felt what he mentally and physically asked. My mind was racing, chaos was breaking out, uncontrolled chaos on my part.

Daes however had complete control, I felt it in my very being. My grandmother and Chaimh sat quietly watching everything unfold. He must have told them not to intervene.

My body burned as I recalled the time he spoke of as if it was yesterday. It was when Drake and Briar "saved me" from Alkin. When I first met him and he threatened to take me beyond the gate with his magic. I had felt Alkin's thoughts and intentions even then, through our old blood bond.

How my dreams were not dreams and that Alkin had marked me before I marked him and how we exchanged blood. How I had been claimed by him taking my innocence even before Drake touched me. The realization struck me in that instant, as I whispered his name "Drake."

Daes rose in one swift motion.

"But we know what happened with Drake." Chaimh said trying to pull me back to the present.

Tossing a few more logs onto the fire, I heard Daes' smooth voice. "Chaimh, you are right. Lord Drake was there, but she is realizing something deeper than that. Mystics do have mates that they share an inescapable bond with, it's preset into their very existence. Call it a safeguard if you must, but it ensures the Ancient races live on. Meaning only Ancients have this bond." He said matter of fact like while coming to stand near me. "What Raillyn fails to tell you is that she knows a much deeper secret that only she can tie to its origin." Pacing in front, he looked at me. "I know you feel it in your soul, say it."

Internally I felt a struggle, I had known the whole time that my dream was real. Yet I chose to ignore it and pretend that Alkin hadn't laid claim to me, sealing my fate to him. The brief memory of Luca telling me that the child wasn't a wolf crossed my mind. The terrible feeling peaked. My mind was thrown further into chaos, causing my body to shake uncontrollably as my mother's did in her memory of finding my father.

"Did Opal tell you that it was because she tried to hide from her mate's bond she sought out a child? That she felt he would reject her and since she met him her first cycle started and she began to brood and desire only one thing, an infant? Those feelings she associated with Solomn she wouldn't bring out and instead she kept inside. She even tried to dilute them with herbs and alcohol, but that didn't work. In the end, she prayed for relief at the temple. Prayed that I would come take her pain away. This resulted in our fancy. All because she was in tears over the situation and her body burned for her mate. I felt bad and gave her the one thing she asked for. All because she refused to go to her own mate and told herself those feelings were fake." He said while meeting my eyes.

Then another thought occurred. Deestan! Luca's wolf magic had been wrong, she was a wolf. Even then I didn't hate Alkin. Instead we argued a little then I sought him out hours before her birth. I was driven by some unknown force to find him in the lower levels of the Wolves' Den. That was when he gave me my mother's ring, before Drameon escorted me upstairs and moments before the first waves of pain hit.

Realization was sinking in, I remembered Celeste, who had delivered the girls and how Alkin had been there for both their births, regardless. I was so oblivious to it at first and didn't think twice. In addition, the room reeked of Alkin's scent, all because Celeste brewed herbs together masking him from me.

After Deestan was born, I remember Alkin lying next to me, channeling his magic into me. Vulnerable, I had reached out towards him, wanting, needing, and getting anything I asked for. There was a moment where I was half awake. Celeste insisted he bind me to him, branding me so I would heal faster, and he said no. Instead, he gave me blood and stayed by my side. Even then I could sense his unease and love for me.

My anxiety rose for a moment, I had known what I did as Raihanna and I knew as Raillyn I did the same. Even before actually knowing Alkin I reached out for him, I needed him like needing air to breath. He was my rock, my savior in this world of chaos. He was my mate.

It was in that instant I knew, deep in my soul I had known all along, but I refused to acknowledge it. Still I refused to say it out loud and turned to walk away from Daes and the words he was speaking. The tremor picked up, as my body shook with such force as to topple houses, I felt on the edge of an emotional breakdown. My head pounded and my nerves felt charred. Chaos reigned inside me, and it knew no limits. For a moment, my power lashed out in waves. Placing my hands over my ears and going to my knees dulled out the sound of shattering glass.

"Control the chaos you have brought upon yourself." Daes said while Destiny and Chaimh watched on.

"I don't seem to understand." Chaimh said while looking towards me. Taking a deep breath, I stood just as the subtle magic from a portal opening was felt. However I barely noticed it, my mind and magic raged on.

"Say it out loud." Daes continued on.

Tears streamed down my face and the burning tremor rattled my very being, collapsing me to my knees I felt I had to admit the truth. Alkin had always been interesting to me, not once was I fearful of him, but instead I viewed him as an equal. Even early on he seemed different, not like he was really going to hurt me, and never had he. Even the first time I met him after being replaced in Alecien he intrigued me. In The Keep I found myself gravitate towards him and was not shocked when he agreed to my asinine plan. Instead I felt relief. I could never rid myself of him, and truthfully I didn't want to.

Seeing Alkin the first time as an adult sent the wild wave of uncontrollable magic through my very being, and I could only guess his as well. Sealing our fate, but not locking it in place, Drake and Briar had stepped in just as I was making a mental link to Alkin. They severed the bond that was being formed, and all the feelings and wild emotions were loose and free.

Tears streaked my face, and my soul cried out in pain. The barrier on my magic waned like a metal sword threatening to break. I was struggling with the emotional turmoil that raged in my soul. It hurt—more than anything else in the world, more than the pain of bringing a child into the world. It echoed through my very being and burned like a fiery ice storm.

It set everything in motion, my love for Drake, Deestan and later the inescapable feeling of not wanting Alkin to leave me alone in The Keep. It led to me housing him and going to him when I cycled there. I should have known then. He was the only one I could stand to think of touching me in such a manner.

While all the others brought whoever they felt into their chambers, I could only stand Alkin.

I knew I could never escape him even then, I never had a chance to resist. Even after everything we had been through, after he killed me, not only once but twice I knew I couldn't escape. And truthfully I didn't want too... *How can you walk away from your angel, even when he acts like a devil... You don't, you can't. No matter how much you fight it, you can't escape the inescapable.*

Head in my hands I let the tears run. A reverberating snap resonated deep within. I loved them both, I truly did, my soul cried out for Alkin while my heart cried out for Drake. Yet it wasn't the same, I loved Alkin on a much deeper level than Drake. I hadn't known Drake long enough to actually love him, not how I loved Alkin. Finally, I allowed myself to admit the truth.

"Alkin," I whispered almost unrecognizably. "Alkin's my mate." Looking at Daes and Chaimh told me what I already knew and confirmed. A feeling of calm suddenly seeped into my soul, icy, cold, and subtle. No longer was my mind in chaos, something changed deep within. Like dust in the wind, my mind and magic felt a releasing current that echoed deep in my soul. The last piece of the barrier surrounding my magic disappeared.

Glancing up, I saw my father near Chaimh, watching and waiting. It was all because of that one moment in time, and he knew it, I saw it on his face. Lips pressed thin he struggled for words.

"I told him not to tell you." My father said. "Alkin came storming in after they took you and said what I had suspected all along. It was the reason as to why your mother and I were so careful about your relationship with him. We weren't sure at the time, but we did suspect it was because you two shared an inseparable bond. Even Alkin suspected it when you were young." My father said while brushing his silver hair away from his face.

Standing I faced my father, unsure what to even say. "If you want more information about how he handled it I believe you need to go speak to him." My father said as I turned away slightly upset at the situation.

The feeling of calm was overpowering I felt something click inside my soul, no longer was I struggling to keep balance in sway, I automatically kept a tight grasp on the chaos and harmony in my mind. Like a heavy weight being lifted off my chest I felt like, I was able to breathe easier.

Daes felt the shift as well. Meeting his eyes I saw him smile. "Perfect," He said bringing attention away from me for a split second. "You broke the bonds that restricted your magic." Daes said proudly.

That was the sensation, it was real balance, true control, but still anxiousness. Like something was missing, thinking about Alkin I knew what that something was. Alkin never bound me to him, he marked me and claimed me but only as Raihanna had he branded me with his magic. It was what my soul was lacking and wanting. For a moment I felt broken, and off key. My emotions were neither chaotic nor harmonized, they were simply just blank. Then I felt them sway, snapping into anger.

"So all of you knew all along and no one felt the need to tell me?" Turning towards Chaimh I went on. "You knew I was Drameon's daughter and that Mystics were the same thing as Demigods? You knew about this mate bond and not once did you mention it to me?" I asked, heartbroken that in a sense things had been kept hidden from me since my childhood.

Chaimh paused for a moment, I could see it in his eyes, he was hurt by my words, and I regretted saying them out of anger. "Yes I knew, the moment you first saw Drameon in the library as a child, I knew you belonged to him. As far as not telling you the relationship between Mystics and Demigods, I felt we would tell you when you got older. Same goes for the mate bond. I didn't want you to feel different with your sisters, and I didn't want them to view you as different, I wanted you three to get along and not have to worry about such things. Even then I knew he watched you, Alkin that is. I felt his presence in our house after night fell. The evening you first met him was when you were five, do you remember?" Chaimh asked as I recalled the time I chased fireflies around the yard, and when Alkin came to visit my father. At first I was frightened but that quickly turned to something else. What I didn't know then, but I saw it now. It was because of our bond because as a child we had shared blood. I was never scared of him...

"I can see now that was a mistake, I knew the moment you summoned me to Lord Drake's castle that things had gone amiss. Drameon had kept tabs on you after Delron summoned me away. He told me you and Alkin had a run in and it sparked feelings you didn't understand. No one was able to intervene though because you chose to go with the Werewolves and their land was blocked off from the mortal realm. Lucine, the Lunar Goddess, even denied any Mystic access there, unless they were invited. Because things moved so fast. By the time you summoned your father there it was too late. No one felt it was right to tear you away from that life. So we let it be, knowing soon you would be removed and placed into The Keep and set on the path to unlocking the bonds that held your power and Daes.'" Chaimh admitted solemnly

The now gentle sway of emotions fluctuated again, tears ran down my face.

"I'm sorry." Chaimh said quietly. "I only wanted to see you happy, Drameon and I had tried effortlessly to deter you away from Drake when you were younger, in fact, it was half the reason it was decided children should not attend council meetings. Later I didn't find out until it was too late and you already carried Deestan. Nothing could be done."

As he spoke, I remembered back to the incidents. Drameon and Chaimh had, in fact, both tried to deter me away from the fleeting fancies of my youth and the emotions that accompanied fledgling's. Drameon even went as far as to state he would borrow me if I did anything stupid. Later after I was with child he even was the one to point out I was in a predicament that would cause issues. Only now did it all make sense.

"Then why the wild, irrational behavior?" I asked "Why is it when Alkin's in the room my mind sort of goes feral? Why didn't I have this issue before when I first met him?"

Daes smiled. Reaching for his mind I knew what his answer was before he spoke. "That's because the body you reside in died. The claims, marks, and blood ties you had to Alkin died with it. The reason you didn't go, how you put it, feral in the beginning was because you already had a blood tie to him." Daes said, reminding me of how I healed Alkin and slit my wrist causing him to heal me.

Looking at my father, I chewed at my lower lip.

"You had a blood bond with Alkin previously? When?" He asked looking at me shocked.

Sighing. I knew a look of nervousness crossed my face. *How was I going to explain this one?* "It was my fault. When you were rampaging through The Keep, Alkin came to check on me. Letting Leon leave, he tried to calm me. He was wounded and I felt the urge to help him. After seeing the healers in the Den and you and mother heal each other. I healed his wound with my saliva and took his blood. After that I slit my wrist, he tried to stop me but the knife dug in too deep. Alkin had no choice." I felt myself smiling as I remembered the bond the exchange created. My body and mind wanted that, I felt my very soul shutter with adrenaline. "After realizing I could touch his mind and feel his thoughts he closed me out. He called my nursemaid and left. It's what started my raging. I wanted to stay around Alkin, his mind and touch was comforting."

My father sighed yet seemed understanding.

"If you're going to open the portal you need complete balance. You have been able to restore your magic and mind, but your soul is still in turmoil. You know what needs to be done, and I'm sure you will be short on time afterwards." Daes said drawing my attention to him.

I knew what he meant; I needed Alkin – his touch, his blood, his magic and the constant presence of his mind. Reaching inside I searched my feeling, those bonds were broken again and my body was recognizing the need to be bound to him. I felt confused on what to do next. My grandfather's rough but gentle hands on my arms, drew me out of my inner thoughts.

"Let's try this. For now don't worry about the bond. Instead I want you to do something for me, child. Call it my first task to you. I need you to return to The Keep, listen to Hunter and don't kill anyone. I will speak more in depth with you later about the situation. But for now, just return to The Keep and show Hunter you are alive, that Raihanna is alive. Try and stay concealed. Unless the need is dire, don't let him know you're Raillyn again. That is the most pressing matter at the moment. Try and avoid contact with Alkin and don't let him know you broke your bonds or that you remember. Not yet anyway." My grandfather said while pulling me into a deep embrace.

His magic ran over me in waves, it was calming and I found myself smiling and wanting to obey. "Ok, I can do that." I said, wishing Daes and I could talk more about my mother and Ancients. Yet, I was thankful I didn't have to face those feelings or behavior at this time. I loved Alkin, I really did but I knew what my grandfather meant. If I touched him it would reinstate the bond we shared, and while I was in The Keep I was already close to brooding. Our bond would bring about that issue again, and I was sure Daes was right, we would be racing against the clock. We were biding as much extra time as we could by doing this.

Releasing me from his arms, he let me go to my feet. Calling a portal, I left to The Keep to follow his orders and do what Mystics were supposed to do. As I went I thought how much he loved me. He had given me my mother's memories, he nourished my mind and healed it when it was in turmoil. The least I could do was listen and do as he said.

The Lunar Wolves ~ Drake

Raven and her troops had gathered in Silvertine with the intention of using Howl's house to move to my castle. For me, each day was harder and the more time I spent here with Raven the more I found myself acting similar to the Drakar and their mates. Even now as we walked into the main den she snuggled into the crook of my arm, smiling up at me. Avice, Raven's guard captain, was hard at work in the council room preparing the troops for the move. It gave us a few short moments to ourselves before we left to my people and prying eyes.

"So you sure your people will believe you if you tell them, you felt the need to move on for their own good? I know it's logical, but I worry. And what about your daughter..." Raven said as we sat on the pillowed bench near the fireplace.

"I know. I worry also. Since she returned to us we haven't had much time together, and now this. She will be upset, I'm sure, but if we make it clear she will still see her mother and spend time with her, I'm sure it will be OK. Plus you can share your own stories with her, and bond a little." I said, smiling into her silky hair.

Spending time with Raven brought out feelings I had stomped out years ago, and almost given up on. Since we had been in Silvertine while we waited, I enjoyed being able to walk the streets openly with her. I could only hope Raillyn would be OK with it all, and would be able to come to terms with Alkin.

A twang of pain echoed in my heart. Raven and I had talked about Raillyn in great detail, and I have been able to see and know I was never fully in love with her. That it was more of a semi-love, we never seemed to have this deeper level of understanding between us that Raven and I did. She would always be important in my life, she was the mother of my oldest and my heir. However, deep down I knew she could never take the throne, nor be my true mate. I just needed to come to terms with my fears, and understand the truth. Regardless of how upsetting it might be. With Raven's help I was able to do so, or at least begin.

"Like you said, we need to take one step at a time. I don't regret my choice. However, I do feel sad that it has to be made without letting Raillyn know. We haven't even had a chance to talk alone since Alkin brought her out of The Keep. On that note, I should have known. I think Alkin and I need to sit down and talk as well. She belongs to him."

Raven looked up at me lovingly – we had a long history, even if it wasn't physically. She had haunted my mind and dreams while I grew up, she had saved my life and lead me to my mother as a fledgling. From those brief moments a connection began growing, and only continued to grow. Already I found my-self loving her.

"I'm sure she feels the same about you. Don't worry, we will all have to sit down and talk this out sometime. However, we cannot at this time. We're already going to have to explain a lot to your Chancellor about us and perform the marriage ceremony as soon as possible." Raven said nervously.

We had been careful, only daring to touch each other light-ly. However, I was beginning to feel the need to kiss her and make things move faster. So much depended on our union, we both felt pressured in a way. Bringing her feet up and under her, she snuggled into me further, and took a deep breath.

The door opened behind us, and we figured our time was up and Avice or Opal was coming to update us. Quietly it closed and nothing was said, the scent of pine entered the room, causing me to turn around, startled.

Alkin stood eyebrow raised at Raven and I.

Raven herself leaned up, sensing my unease. This was not how I wanted Alkin to find us, I only hoped he would understand and not judge too fast.

"Well, what is this?" He asked with a curious look on his face. "And you criticized…"

"Alkin, let me explain, this isn't what you think…" I began to say.

The air in the room seemed to become heavy, and thick, almost sticky. "Isn't what I think? I seriously don't care what you do, but if you plan on taking a Wolf mate the least you could do is let Raillyn know your plans. It isn't fair to her, and need I remind you about Deestan. If she seems to be a problem, I will take her." He stated, eyes flickering red. I could tell he was careful to stay in control. That this bothered him.

"No!" Raven shouted beside me. "What are you doing here, Mystic? Why are you butting your nose into places it shouldn't be?" She questioned boldly.

Alkin seemed to be taken back for a moment. Closing his eyes, he seemed to debate his words. "You're right. I shouldn't be nosing around in others affairs, but neither should he." Alkin said sarcastically while pointing towards me. "Plus, this is my parents' home, I have every right to be here! I'd like to know who you are and what you're doing here!"

Raven pushed off me and stood, she bit at her lower lip as she thought. "My father Geirolf is leader of the Lunar Plane Wolves. For over fifty years he and Lord Cyrin have been planning on an alliance between our people—going as far as arranging marriage for us. However, since Lord Cyrin died before those arrangements could be made things were delayed. I am here to follow through with the plan and help Lord Drake and our people bring peace back into the land of Alecien. In turn chasing out or destroying those damned Vampires." She stated, not hiding anything and being truthful about our intentions.

Alkin raised his eyebrows seemingly impressed. "If that's the case, then you two will be following through with these intentions, and soon I expect. The Vampires already plan on using their power for evil and to summon creatures of pure darkness. I'm sure Drake has told you that, however."

Raven looked at me, knowing the situation. "You're right, things will have to go a little faster. And I have already been speaking to Drake about the situation with the Vampires. We're going to join our troops and attack them before they have a chance to bring their undead army into Alecien. Speaking of which, I'm going to talk to Avice and make sure everything is in place. We need to leave to your castle as soon as possible to begin putting things into motion." Raven said, before bowing slightly and leaving the room.

Alkin and I stood for a moment just looking at each other. "So does this mean you are giving up on Raillyn?" He questioned while leaning against the wall.

For a moment I was surprised by his words, he was right. After six years of searching, it seemed surprising that I would give up so easily. But there were reasons for it. "I think so. After seeing Silvertine, and its people and hearing about Raillyn's childhood, I'm losing faith in her coming back to me. In addition, after I met Raven, and discovered she had used magic to speak to me and contact me for years from the Lunar Plane, it changed something inside me. I don't know what happened, but it made me realize Raillyn was never truly mine, and never would be. She's Mystic, she can take no throne, nor would she of ever been able to be my true mate. Don't get me wrong, I did love her, I do love her, I always will. It's nothing compared to what you two have, I'm sorry, I really am. I just want her happy, and from what I saw while she was in The Keep, she was." I said admitting the truth to him.

"Heh..." Alkin laughed briefly. "That's all I want, as well, to see her happy. I can only hope she forgives me after every-thing I've had to do. I feel so bad for everything she has had to go through. Sadly it was the only way, and I hope everything works out, for both of us." He said solemnly before turning to leave out the door.

Sighing, I hoped he was right, and in a sense I was thankful our confrontation went so well. For the time being I would con-tinue on with our plan and take Raven and her people to my home. Leaving the room, I went in search of Raven.

I found her near the entrance leading into the city. Avice, the tall, full-built auburn-haired woman who was Raven's captain, stood with her.

"Everything is in motion, my lady and we await your lead and command to travel to Alecien." Avice said happily.

Raven's face lit up. "Good I'm so happy to see everything in place." Pausing she turned, nose twitching, she recognized my scent. "Are you ready? We can wait a few more days if you think we need more time." She asked as she slipped into the crook of my arm.

Avice glanced at us, surprised. Raven was the type of woman to do her own thing, however when it came down to me she wanted everything perfect and often relied on me more than she realized. However, I was the same way, relying on her, it wasn't like me yet it felt so natural.

"No, I think it's time I head home. If I don't people will start to wonder what happened to me. Already Briar bought me an extra day. Plus he gets so bored running things alone." I said jokingly.

Raven smiled up at me warmly, as she nodded her head towards Avice. "Gather our troops in the courtyard. I want us ready to leave in a few minutes." She said as we slipped away back into the halls, and towards the courtyard.

Silently we walked the grey halls, across the ornate rugs and down darker hallways. The large opaque doors that lead into the forest yard beyond were paces away. However before proceeding I pulled Raven back, I wanted to ask her something before things began getting crazy again.

"Wait a moment." I said pulling her into the shadows. "Before we leave, can I kiss you?"

For a moment I heard Raven take a sharp startled breath, even her body tensed for a moment. "I'm not sure, I don't think we should, not yet anyway." She seemed uneasy. "You know how addicting our race can be between couples. I don't want to kiss you and find I don't want to stop..." She said meekly turning her head down.

Placing my finger to her chin, I brought her eyes to mine. "We won't have to worry about that soon if all goes well. It's just that you have been in my mind and dreams for so long, I have to know what it feels like. Placing her hands behind my head she pulled my lips to hers. They were warm and welcoming, momentarily she licked at my lips, as if memorizing my taste and scent. I felt myself doing the same, tasting her lips, her skin and sweat. It was like honey and hot herbal tea with vanilla and milk. I felt myself smile as she kissed me more feverishly. I matched her speed and found myself running my hands up the back of her shirt, under the leather armor.

Her skin was hot, and sweaty, my hands pulled the material up as she pulled at my shirt collar. Suddenly her mouth was on my chest in a euphoric feeling of bliss. Thoughts of marking her with tooth and claw came flowing into my mind. Never had I bonded with another Wolf, not on this level, and this was only the beginning. Wanting more, I felt my own body react, my lips traced her neck and shoulder, down her chest.

For a moment I paused, and felt my incisors enlarge. I wanted her, wanted to mark her and speed this up. She paused as if she caught my thoughts, and nuzzled her nose against my head. Before licking my lip I felt her own teeth were enlarged, playfully she scrapped them against my skin. A pleasurable grumble escaped my throat, as I continued my way across her chest. Her tender skin was hot, as my hands traveled across lower regions. An aching cry echoed from her throat as she pulled at my clothes.

"Raven?" Avice called out from somewhere down the hall.

Immediately Raven pushed me away cursing. "Shit!" She said as she tried to fix her clothes and hair. Cursing myself, I re-arranged myself and turned to await our company. Raven eyed me warily, her breathing was still quicker than normal, and she was taking in my scent more than before. Even I found myself more drawn to her scent.

"My lady, are you all right?" Avice asked, her amber eyes meeting my own and Raven's curiously and worried. The troops who were accompanying us followed closely behind.

"Everything's fine Avice, I just stumbled and Drake caught me." She said before turning and walking out the door and into the courtyard.

The vast green forest smelled like a welcome relief to the stressful situation. Heavy moss hung from trees and lined the forest floor. Birds chirped and rustling leaves echoed around us. Nothing would harm us here; most of the animals in this small area where deer, elk, and a few wild fowl. Going to Raven, I found myself pull her towards me as we walked towards Howl's house.

The small two-story house was not far from the exit and was easily found. Upon entering Howl stood smirking at me as the small brigade of troops and myself, Avice and Raven squeezed into his tiny den.

"Is everything ready? Because I am not going to be a personal chauffeur all the time." He questioned as he closed the door.

"Everything is all set, please align the door to my home." I stated as Howl smiled as he drew his dagger, and ran it over his hand.

Blood pooled out of the wound, beading in red droplets. Quickly he placed it over the large blue stone, atop a staff like structure near the door. It reminded me of the summoning spell when Briar and I would go and speak to the Lunar Goddess. In a resonating blue hue, the stone glowed briefly before dying down, and the blood on Howl's hand seemed to disappear along with the wound.

Smiling he opened the door, and the red-carpeted halls of the castle met my eyes.

Looking at Raven, she smiled at me. "Ready for this to begin?" I whispered into her ear.

Her smiled beamed from ear to ear as she leaned close to whisper something to me. "As long as you're ready for a long day, and an equally long night?" She questioned mischievously.

I looked at her questioningly before she continued. "We have a long day ahead of us and you made me can't wait for it to be done." She said hushed but determined

Smiling down at her, I lead the way and walked into the halls. Raven stayed at my side, but walked head high as my equal, Avice and Howl were just paces behind us. The footsteps of the troops were muffled by the ornate rugs, but their purpose echoed down the empty halls, that a fight was coming. When? No one could tell, but the gathering of troops was never a good sign.

Rounding the corner and approaching the main hall, a few servants stepped aside, wide-eyed and unsure. Word would spread quickly that strange new Wolves were within our walls and that I walked beside them. I was thankful when turning the last corner that the throne room doors were wide open. Beyond them, I saw Droggen and Briar sitting around the table with Saibal. Several maps were laid out on its surface, even before entering the room Briar looked up at me and smiled.

"Finally." He said standing and coming to greet us as we walked in. He eyed me curiously, smirking at the site of Raven.

She smiled up at me, her eyes glowed a feisty green and sparkled in the light. "This is Raven Koray, her father is leader of the Lunar Plane Wolves in Aeralain. Apparently father was negotiating a peace treaty with them." I said handing the documents to Droggen for his own verification.

As Droggen looked over the paperwork, I pulled a chair out for Raven to sit in. Smiling she took her seat and waited. "Saibal, this is Avice, Raven's captain of the guard. I want you to take her and the troops, and show them the training grounds. Get them accustomed to where things are, and I want you two to start working together on some strategic maneuvers." Raven nodded at Avice, I knew she had a similar talk with her captain before leaving.

Bowing, Saibal left accompanying the troops and their captain out. "Follow me, please." He said as they left the room.

Papers ruffled as Droggen continued to flip through the documents. "These are indeed your father's letters. Raven, if you don't mind me asking, how did Lord Cyrin and your father get these letters across the Silver Sea?" Droggen asked pausing to read the final letter from my father.

Raven shifted in the chair and crossed her legs. "We had a Drakar helping us, he used his house, much like Howl does here, to take the letters back and forth."

Droggen eyed me curiously at the mention of the house. I had touched briefly on the subject weeks prior but never went into great detail. Raising my eyebrows, he turned and finished reading the documents.

"I remember your father mentioning that if you refused to find a mate he would find one for you. However, I never knew he actually was being so meticulous about it. He was planning everything perfectly. I bet when he was surveying the land he was preparing to join forces and move forward." Droggen said placing the papers in his lap. "I should have seen this coming. I knew your father was speaking to allies for help, I just never thought those allies were in Aeralain…"

Raven smiled at Droggen and leaned forward. "I knew very little of what my father and he spoke about until I was older. But from what I was told this was a project that was in development since I was nine. Even after it failed, my father refused to let me take a mate, and I was told to keep pure. It was all because we knew that Daes' last Mystic would return to the world and that the balance that was lost so long ago would be restored." She said before a look of sadness crossed her face. "Or that is what we hope anyway. That's what the stories say…" She trailed off.

"Daes' last Mystic?" Droggen questioned a little confused.

"Yes, Daes' last Mystic. When the war broke out the Ancients were murdered, they were blamed for the start of the war by the Vampires, when in turn they actually started it. They stole away a Mystic of Daes' lineage and killed her so they could use her blood for a dark ritual. They planned to bring darkness and creatures of pure hate into the world and use her blood to do so. They took so much, she died. Her mate was furious and stormed The Keep. Because of that the Ancients were blamed and attacked. They fled to Aeralain, but in doing so Daes' Mystic line was slaughtered, they stayed around trying to control the outbreaking chaos." Raven started retelling the story Howl told me about Raillyn and her parents.

"But you said they were all killed. I don't seem to understand." Droggen stated.

"What she means is that all the adult Mystics of Daes' line were killed. Ancients don't have children often, and there was only one child of Daes' lineage at the time of the war..." I began.

"Raillyn..." Raven and I said together. I looked at her questioningly. "Howl told me, when he first came to the Lunar Plane to suggest we use Silvertine as a mediator for our alliance, and that she was placed back into the world to realign the peace. All I can say is that from what you've said the Vampires are trying to do the same thing as before. Bring darkness and death to the world through this portal. I don't see what else it could be used for and it has to be stopped before it gets out of control this time." Raven said while crossing her arms and pacing. I couldn't help but smile, she was right both of us shared this information with each other and we saw no other use for the portal.

"This alliance has to happen, we need to strengthen our forces and attack while we can, before another war breaks out or worse those creatures are summoned. Raven, did Howl say anything to you pertaining to what those creatures could be?" I asked hopeful.

She shook her head. "Just what we already know that they are dark death beings and monsters that spread evil and hate. He didn't even mention if they are bound here or in the Gods' realm."

That made me pause. "If they were in the Gods' realm wouldn't the Gods keep them secure there? They have to be somewhere else. I think we only have half the story on these things, I wish we could find out more. Maybe Howl can find out for us." I said deep in thought.

Raven nodded as Droggen sighed. "If it will stop another war then I see no choice. I will prepare for you two to be wed and mated tonight then." He said placing the papers on the table and standing to go. "But hear me out." He began and pointed at me sternly. "Once this happens you will not be able to go back. She's not Raillyn, she's a wolf and wolves mate for life. Make sure you are ready for that." Droggen stressed before turning to leave.

For a moment, I paused in thought, knowing I was sealing my life to Raven's. Even though, I had a connection to her it was still in a sense frightening. She was still so new to me, practically a stranger, but so familiar.

No, I can't think that way, this is how it was supposed to be... My father wanted this, and if it's been in the works since Raven was nine, then my mother probably knew too. This is right. I thought as I took Raven's hand and brought it to my lips.

Her scent lingered briefly and drove my mind wild, I was excited. "It's a risk I'm willing to take." I said as she snuggled into the crook of my arm.

Return to The Keep ~ Raillyn

Walking the darkened halls of The Keep I remembered what Daes had told me. *Wear your Elite armor as much as you can, and conceal your face to keep them from knowing Raihanna is dead.* So my gear was on and my hood enveloped my face in magical darkness.

Already I could hear whispers echoing down the hall from the servants. It had been weeks since Raihanna had last been seen at The Keep and Hunter would want a full report. Entering my chambers I realized not much had changed, and I recalled the last time I had been here. It was when my state of mind was on a suicide mission.

Even though at the time I was unaware of the task I had performed to break the spell, it still ate away at me. Guessing lead me to consider the task was to break the spell the Gods had placed on me as a child and to begin the process of returning to the balanced nature which I was destined to live. A knock at my main door interrupted my thoughts. Ash stood as I opened the door, Hunter must have sent him to retrieve me.

"Ash." I said while opening it slowly and carefully, unsure what might happen next.

Nodding his head and smiling, he greeted me. "It's good to see you well, Raihanna." He said while holding his hand out to lead the way. Slowly I walked into the hall and closed the door. "I hope all is well." He asked as he led the way towards my uncles den.

Glaring at him, I made sure he felt my anger. Pulsing my new-found magic towards him in a wave of invisible magical energy. "That is none of your concern." I said in a harsh tone. I was beginning to feel that pretending to be Raihanna would be easier than I had originally thought.

Suddenly I felt my heartbeat pick up pace and my breathing become uneven. Stopping I tried to control the wave of magic that hit me and threatened to bring me to my knees. It was from Hunter's staff, my mind recognized its power instantly. *I had to be Raihanna*, I told myself, *and Raihanna would not let the staff bother her.* Taking a deep breath, I entered the room.

Hunter stood in his normal place, bent over the large desk with various items scattered across it, his brown hair was greasy and slicked back in a mass of disarray. Aurielle, Lily, and Ashoten sat on the floor to my left in the larger portion of the room, talking about their latest victims and endeavors. As the door closed, it stirred up the smell of the place.

For the most part, it reeked of death and decay, the typical smell of Vampires. Yet, my nose twitched as the sweet smell of pine wafted towards me. Looking to my right, Alkin leaned against the wall talking to Thierry. Suddenly everything went silent, as I felt my breath still, and a slow hum began to echo somewhere in the corner of my mind. Like a nagging sensation creeping across my skin, it echoed within. I was almost too frightened to breathe. It seemed to penetrate my soul and drown out everything around me. For a moment, Alkin turned towards me and shook his head no. Like a million voices speaking at once, the sound of the room returned.

"I brought her just as you asked." The hum in my head instantly stopped. I heard Ash's voice, breaking through its melodramatic hum, slowly I felt able to breathe normally. Looking up from his work, Hunter smiled manically.

"I am very glad to see you alive, my niece." He said as he came around the table and pulled me into a deep embrace.

His evil nature and magic struck me like a rockslide. As he released me, I shook slightly from his sinful nature and its power. For a moment, it felt like his behavior was reaching towards my mind in an effort to consume me. Momentarily I felt my magic encompassed my mind and knew my eyes changed blue then violet in color. "I hope all went well?" My uncle asked, breaking the spell enough for me to answer.

"Everything went well." I said while I struggled to remain in control. The magic that overcame me was confusing, while it drove me to want to kill everyone in the room, it also drove me to want to serve and do as I was told. Placing me in a harsh situation.

"I am sure Alkin told you already, but there was just a minor issue, and it required much healing on my end." I said falling into character and indicating that I had performed the task which Hunter had set forth for me. "I am well healed now and ready to continue my work." I said while bowing deeply, hoping to keep up the farce despite my power raging wantonly within.

Smiling Hunter rounded the table once more. "Good. I am glad all is well. Now we must move forward and in order to do so, Briar must be removed from the picture. Doing this will leave the Wolves powerless since they lack their heir." He said smiling gleefully.

For a moment, I was startled to hear this and glanced at Alkin, unaware that they had not heard word of Deestan being returned to the wolves.

"Raihanna. You, Aurielle, Ashoten and Lily will go to the Werewolves' castle and handle the situation with Briar. Ensure he is dead before you leave. We have to open the portal as soon as possible. I however am having issues deciphering this text. I believe we need to align the staff just right before opening the portal." Hunter said as he placed his hand on the staff that sat on his table.

The large red stone glowed manically at me, while the Dragon and Phoenix carvings held it tight. Hunter had used it to cast the spell on Raihanna that put me on the suicide mission.

"Go and get ready meet at the stables in an hour ready to leave. Alkin, Ash, I want you two to go and investigate a possible weapon that might assist us later." Hunter said as he waved my team away.

***

Entering the halls once more I tried to evade my sister but was unable. "I don't think you were only healing." She stated sarcastically, while Lily turned towards her chambers. Ashoten stood and waited for his mate, my sister. "You seem perfectly fine, I see no injury from you and your magic seems stronger than ever. If I was not mistaken, I would say, you wanted some alone time with Alkin." She said as she departed down the hallway.

Anger filled me and my magic spiked. My eyes flashed blue as I felt myself gather an energy ball in my hand. Gazing down I held a fist size ball of blue energy, I felt the urge to toss it at Aurielle. My magic had once more wrapped itself around my mind and taken control. Fear overcame me as its brute strength channeled into the sphere causing it to flare momentarily. The sheer power of it tried to take full control of my mind, causing me to feel powerless. Vision flickering I began to shake, my emotions stumbled from anger and brought me to tears.

"Go get ready." I heard Alkin say, causing me to turn. He stood near the adjacent wall, leaning against its surface. For a moment, I wanted to go to him and run my hands through his hair.

Instead, I turned and quietly walked the remainder of the hall to my chambers. Closing the door, I collapsed in an emotional mess on the floor. I was tired of this erratic behavior of my emotions and the even more erratic behavior of my magic. Even when I was carrying the girls my emotions were never this unstable. I wanted to go home, I wanted to be with my girls but instead I was being sent out to work and have Briar slain. What was I to do? I couldn't kill the other Elite to prevent them from harming him, nor could I reveal myself. I was stuck and expected to perform the daunting task at hand. Daes had given me orders, return to The Keep, and try and open the portal. *How, though?* He never told me and I never asked but couldn't at this time.

Gathering myself once more, I knew I couldn't just sit and cry about the situation I had to think of something, anything to save my friends from the terrors ahead. I knew I couldn't slay any of the Elite or Hunter, but I wasn't told I couldn't influence events and push them in the direction of such tragedies. This is what I would do, I would try and make the battle go my way and not theirs. Smiling, I left my quarters less fearful of the events to come.

Attack ~ Drake

Reaching the throne room told me something was amiss. The guards rushed towards the front courtyard as Briar moved towards me. "Go to the starlight tower and keep out of sight." He said urgently. "The Vampires have sent several Elite, and I can only assume it is to ensure you are dead. I've already told Avice and her troops to stay out of sight till we know more. Raven's in the tower with Droggen. Hurry." He said as he ran on towards the main entrance.

Realizing the stress of the situation, I ran towards the eastern door and through the hall towards the highest tower of our castle. Rushing up the stairs two steps at a time, I met Droggen, sitting and already watching the events unfold. Raven sat near the window looking towards the courtyard. Taking a seat next to her, she gave me a worried look.

Four Elite—three females who wore the long concealing cloaks and one male who wore his darkened helm—stood scattered amongst an array of regular vampire troops. No longer was Hunter hiding the fact that it was the Vampires leading the Elite. They were engaged in battle with my troops. Drameon stood off to the side near a quiet corner, suddenly he burst forward as if taking chase.

~~*~*~*~*Raillyn*~*~*~*~*~*

As Aurielle and the others ran at their targets, I tried to put off from battle as much as possible. The clash of swords and crackling of magic began to eat away at my calm demeanor. Once more I felt myself begin to shake as my magic took over. My once calm emotions began to rage with the feeling of battle.

The first troop attacked and was easily knocked away, I tried not to kill and instead wound or incapacitate. I was thankful I had enough wits left to control that aspect, and thought maybe it was due to Daes and his power. Rushing towards Lily, I stood back to back with her. Jumping we spiraled upwards, unleashing an array of mixed magic, her Vampire and my Mystic. Several of the Werewolves' guard were beaten back and thrown to the ground. While we descended I made my first move to cause Lily to falter.

As she began to cast a spell, that would release an array of magical arrows. I deliberately knocked her arm, sending her spell amiss. It went crashing into Aurielle and Ashoten, causing them to falter their own onslaught momentarily. Turning, Lily herself made a mistake, I was thankful my sister and her mate were distracted and not aware of the situation which now turned us against each other. Lily was furious that I had purposely caused her to fault her spell and drew her sword towards me instead. The Wolf troops nearby seemed to sense something was amiss and took the opportunity to attack while they could. Drawing my God blade, the very one that had been my mother's, I unleashed my building magic.

It erupted in a wave of blue energy, throwing Lily into the oncoming troops who quickly brought their blade across her neck. Aurielle and Ashoten suddenly aware of the situation changed tactics. No longer were they concerned with the troops but instead they concentrated their attacks towards Briar. Lily had been one of the lower Elite and while it was a loss for us, it would not go unpunished. Ashoten quickly made his way towards me.

"What happened?" He asked rushed as he deflected a blow from a nearby soldier. "She got in the way of my spell." I yelled back hoping he would believe my lie. Smiling, I knew he did.

"She often does, serves her right. Cover Aurielle, I'm going after Briar." He said as he charged once more off in my sister's direction.

As I pulled back to try and follow their lead, I felt a new force enter the battle. Suddenly I blocked the oncoming attack and my blue magic met equally strong and powerful green magic. My father Drameon drove me backwards and towards the very edge of the fighting.

"What are you doing?" He yelled at me as he swung his blade once more at me, this time in a low swing.

Suddenly more in control I responded. "I was told not to kill anyone, not that I couldn't influence things to go my way." I yelled back. "I'm tired of not being able to do anything to stop this madness. I feel Hunter might open the portal sooner if he realizes he's running out of time." I said as I was knocked backwards into another soldier.

Quickly I brought my blade around and spun the soldier head over heels, knocking him unconscious. He landed onto the dirt-covered courtyard. As I looked on towards my father, I realized that Aurielle and Ashoten had been separated. Briar was nowhere in sight and as I watched, Ashoten was suddenly swarmed by an onslaught of new troops.

My sister fought desperately to get to her mate but was pushed further away. Her arrow spell sent scattershot after scattershot into the soldiers, but the Wolves were ready and many had barrier spells in place to deflect them. I realized at that moment that this was why the Werewolves were so apt at killing the Vampires. They learned quickly and were able to change their nature-drawn magic accordingly.

The events unfolding happened so quick, it was less than a few seconds from start to end, Ashoten was cut down. The long Mythril blade had been driven through his neck severing his head. Stunned and unsure what to do I looked towards my sister, who immediately jumped backwards high onto a ledge. Looking back at me I could tell fear gripped her, her once fluid motions were choppy and harsh. My father aware of what was going on jumped after Saibal, who pursued her.

This was my biggest mistake, distracted I felt the sudden sharp bite of metal pierce my armor. Realization hit as I knew only a Wolves blade could do such a thing. My hood was tossed back as my attacker threw me onto the ground and attacked again before realization struck him. My eyes met Briar's wide in shock, as his blade came a hair's length from my heart. Withdrawing it, he looked towards my father unsure what to do. The nearby troops stood in shock and looked at Briar for orders. Knowing if I lay there any longer I would die from blood loss I fell into a blackened portal.

Ancients ~ Drake

Shock crossed my mind as I saw Briar pull back Raillyn's hood and drive his blade deep into her chest. Raven gasped out in shock next to me and pushed at my chest.

"Go, we need to check on her." She said meekly.

Turning to leave, I was sure she was dead and ran with breakneck speed down the stairs and towards the courtyard. As I rushed across the throne room, however, it was Drameon who stopped me. I felt the Wolf in me desperately try and break free. It was almost the full moon and already I was feeling the oncoming the effects. I raged against him as he tossed me onto the ground.

"You cannot go out there, they cannot see you alive. Unless you want Raillyn to die." He said outraged. "Do not mess this up now because you cannot trust us."

"Just tell me if she's alive!" I yelled as Briar and Raven came into the throne room.

"I'm so sorry." He said as he made his way towards me our remaining troops lead by Saibal a few feet behind. Drameon held up a hand before coming to stand before me.

"Follow me?" He asked and turned to walk towards the small den near my chambers.

Reluctantly I followed, glancing back at Raven she had a worried look on her face but went to address Briar about the situation.

Drameon and I walked the halls in silence and entered the den. Again I asked him. "Will she live?" My anger had died down a little by his reaction and calm demeanor, but still it was irritating not knowing.

Nodding he took a seat. "I do not believe that Daes will allow her to die. I would have to go and see for myself, but I had to ensure you would not be seen first." He replied agitated.

Agreeing I sat down.

"Then please go and at least find that out for me." I said stressed. "Even if that's the only thing you can tell me please this time let me know if she lives and don't leave me worrying for years to come."

His eyes met mine and they glowed grey briefly a look of sadness crossed his face. "Again I am sorry I could not tell you any of it sooner, but I did not want your decisions to be influenced knowing Raillyn was Raihanna. However, I will tell you as soon as I know more on her current condition." Drameon said as he gathered his magic summoning a swirling portal of greyish green smoke.

"Wait." I said before he had a chance to go through. "Can I ask you something before you leave? Do you know if Alkin and Raillyn had a blood bond when she was a child?" I asked remembering Howl had told me to ask.

Pausing he looked at me curiously. "Why do you ask that?"

"Because when I was in Silvertine, I saw a ten year old girl and her much older adult mate. Lyth and Howl said they shared a strong mental bond because they had exchanged blood. I guess it would be like the Mystic marks. But I was wondering if Alkin and Raillyn had that when she was a child." I asked again.

"Truthfully, while it's not unheard of to have mate's blood bond early, it's not what Calista and I wanted." He stated showing his father protectiveness. "However, Raillyn told me that she established one with Alkin, just prior to her removal." Turing he left through a portal.

Disarray ~ Raillyn

Pain erupted throughout me as I hit the floor of my grandmother's home. I prayed she was there because I was fearful to cross into Delron's realm in such a state seeking Chaimh. I needed healing, and I knew I was no healer.

Even as a child Lillian had tried to teach me more past the light healing spells and salve and I couldn't keep track of the words, components or grasp the nature she used, eventually I gave up. Thankfully hearing my cry Destiny ran to my side, Chaimh was with her again as she inspected my wound through my armor.

"We have to get this off you." She said while drawing a bright green dagger and running it across the clasps.

Chaimh knelt beside me and helped remove the armor, as carefully as they could. I cried out in pain. For a moment, I was surprised Daes himself was not here. Now that my chest-plate was removed, Destiny inspected my wound better.

"Whoever stabbed you came close to killing you. Let's get her moved to my workshop." She said to Chaimh as he lifted me into his arms gently and carried me into a small room off the hall.

Inside was dark and smelled of nature, herbs, dirt and other unknown scents. A large table sat in the middle of the room, surrounded by smaller tables that held a large array of items; bottles, plants, candles, books and much more. It reminded me of Lillian's workshop where she kept all her healing herbs and salves. I felt terrible and was still losing quite a lot of blood.

No longer fearful, instinctively I felt myself reach for Daes and got nothing. He was either unavailable or had blocked me from his mind. As I was laid on the table, I felt a tear run down my cheek. Now that my body was weakened from blood loss I wanted the magical touch of the only one I knew to bring me relief. My memories, as well as my father and Alkin's words, pounded my head. Tears streamed my face from the pain.

Chaimh and Destiny both noticed. "I will work as fast as I can to relieve the pain." Destiny said as Chaimh brushed my hair away from my face lovingly. Shaking my head, I tried to sit up, and only caused myself more pain.

"Stay down, or you will only hurt yourself more, child." Chaimh said while gently laying me back on the table's hard surface.

Blood poured from the two wounds on my chest as I lay back down. Once more I tried to reach for Daes, and still found nothing. Finally, I spoke up, "Where's my grandfather?" I asked trying to control my tears from running down my face.

Destiny held two different vials, added ingredients to the larger one, then paused momentarily. She seemed focused on something, that's when it happened. Feeling my heart stumble momentarily nearly made me jump off the table. Blood poured once more from my wounds and pooled onto the ground below. Desperately I grabbed Chaimh by the shoulders needing to hold onto something solid. I felt myself begin to lose consciousness and knew if I had anything to say I needed to say it now before the darkness consumed me and prevented me. "Please! Call him or Alkin!" I cried out as I felt my heart stumbled again.

Suddenly Destiny was at my side and laid me down swiftly but gently. "Hold still and let us work. Chaimh, go find her grandfather, please." She said as she poured a green liquid substance over my wound.

It burned and I remember screaming out in pain, my breath caught in my lungs as the liquid entered my wounds. "I'm sorry but we must prevent infection." I heard my grandmother say. "Plus, we were told to not use any magic on you. You are fragile, not only from this wound but also from the balance and sway of your power. If we used magic on you, it would influence the natural process of how you are learning to control it." Destiny said as she turned and grabbed another bottle this one was bright blue in color. "This will soothe I promise." She said as she poured the cool liquid over my wounds.

My grandmother was right, it soothed the burning pain echoing through me from the last concoction. Still the darkness threatened to consume me and fighting it was no longer an option. As I gave into unconsciousness, I felt the familiar pulse of my grandfather's magic enter the room.

Reasons ~ Alkin

Everything I did and do is for her, even if at times I refused to admit it even to myself, it's the truth. Remembering Raillyn when she was young and remembering the carefully created atmosphere her mother raised her in made me smile. Her mother was the sister I never had.

Callie, Leon and I were raised together in Silvertine by her mother Opal, a Drakar. Only the women of the Ancient races were able to survive the birth of a Mystic child. Especially, when the father was a God. The other races died shortly after giving birth, from an absence of magic.

Even then the situation of Opal was a weary one, one that was almost taboo. Opal however did great things, and during the time took myself and Leon in as well, raising the three of us as her own. Callie, who was older than me by only six years, treated me like her little brother. When Leon joined us, I was five.

Callie and Leon shared a father, but Leon had been living with merchants for over fifteen years, and was untrained in magic. Opal had seen issues in this. So in turn, she took him under her wing and decided to raise and train him. As time went on the three of us became inseparable, often sparring and studying together.

Callie was better at spells and weaving them to sway the nature of things around her. Leon was better at manipulating his magic and imbuing it in his blade. The two always tried to outdo each other and often lead to duels in both the magical arts and sparing. My own magic took a darker path. I followed solely in my own father's footsteps and knew death from a young age. It was Callie who noticed my true nature early on. Opal often left her or our nursemaid to watch me when we were young. It was known that Mystics learned magic early so we were trained in control from the time we could walk, but it would never get serious until our magic showed itself.

Callie and I walked the nearby forest in late spring when my magic began to take hold. The birds were chirping and fluttering about from tree to tree. Flowers bloomed and the world seemed so alive. I however was in a dark mood, unhappy about childish things. Regretfully a sudden outburst caused more than just an ill-tempered big sister, it caused several forests animals their deaths as well.

The red flare of my power lashed out at the nearby trees and brush, causing anything that was struck by it an instant death. Callie, thankfully remained unharmed, her Mystic blood and necromantic power, protected her from my outburst. Instead, she stood wide-eyed and shocked as a bird fell to the ground between us. Red smoke billowing from its tiny body as it lay burned against the green grass.

Instantly the forest was silent, as if frightened by my mood and magic, I stood unsure what to do. Not once had I showed any sign that my magic was beginning to grow, and I would need more training.

"Alkin, what have you done?" she asked me as I bent down to examine the bird. I remember thinking if I killed it with my magic maybe I could bring it back and fix what I had done wrong. A childish fancy yes, but I was only a child at the time.

The frozen waters of Death's Realm hit me before Callie could stop me. Standing in its green fog and frozen waters I heard the whirlpool yards away and decided to search for the bird's spirit. Walking the waters for the first time, I unintentionally missed my footing and lost my balance. The fall didn't hurt, nor did the icy waters touch, what hurt was my pride.

The rivers quick flow pulled me under fast, taking me effortlessly over the lip of the whirlpool and into its icy grasp. Around and around, desperately I took a breath, till finally I was pulled under and through a submerged tunnel. Its darkened passage threatened to consume me, and when I thought I would run out of air, it spit me out over a large waterfall. I don't remember how but I know he grabbed me and pulled me to shore.

My father Delron stood, hood undrawn, with a furious look. His bright eyes seemed to glow in red hues, against his pale white nearly translucent skin. His long black hair hung loosely over his black cloak. With high-cheek bones and pointed ears he appeared Elf like, and gave him a very young appearance but his eyes told otherwise. They seemed old and possessed immense power. In his hand was a Dragon, Phoenix staff with a large red bloodstone grasped in their mouth.

The Dragon represented their natural world helpers, who assisted their Mystic kin. While the Phoenix represented their own nature, and a time when the world was a much darker place. Phoenix fire was only able to be cast by the Gods, it was rebirth, and purity. A cleansing to all that was dark. It's said the Gods cleansed the darkened rotted world of Auran with Phoenix fire before creating the Dragons and giving the planet life. An old tale of our creation.

The cold river was what I remembered next. I had backed up so fast I fell back in. Delron had pulled me once more from its icy grasp before it took me downstream. "It's not every day I get to see a child of mine stumble into my realm unannounced." He said mockingly. I sat dumbfounded. "If you were anything, but a Mystic, the river would have killed you, thankfully it likes you." He continued as he stood in one fluid motion and pulled his hood over his face, concealing it.

Standing myself I was unsure what to do, I had known Delron was my father, I was told this much. I was also told that the Gods did not raise their children. My mother had only been a half-demon elf, who had perished at my birth, in fact before my birth. I was told I had to be cut from her body to ensure I lived.

It was all because I possessed magic from this man, before I thought of what to ask or say he spoke again. "I am sure Calista has told on you, isn't her unbalanced nature joyful? Things will be changing soon for you three. You have gone unsupervised for too long." He said matter of fact like. "Do not try and raise the dead like that again." He said sternly. "It was a matter of inconvenience that they died, but it is not a matter of right to raise that which is dead. Only in a dire need is that necessary and only with my approval. Do you understand me?" He asked in an authoritative manner. I nodded my head suddenly uneasy about what I was about to do. "Good, now off you go. I am sure Opal has many studies for you to keep you occupied and out of trouble." He said as he spoke a spell, a red fog like blanket over me enveloped me and instantly tossed me out of Death's Realm and onto the cold surface of Opal's marble floor.

Callie, and Salome, Opal's mate surrounded me. After explaining what happened, Delron was right, Callie had told on me and Opal had left to make arrangements for my training to begin. I would be under the watchful eye of many of the red Drakar, who studied necromancy.

Four basic magic's thrived in Auran, all were connected to the Gods. I was thankful to be with the Drakar at this time, not only would they be able to help me control my power, they would also be able to train me in it.

The Drakar were Half-breeds of the Dragons, which the Gods created to keep magic flowing in the world. Their color, typically seen in the color of their eyes, indicated what magic they were able to cast. Green for healing, land and sea magic. Blue, for harmony, chaos and emotion. Red, for life, death, and Necromancy. Lastly White, for the sky, air, and everything pure. While only the Mystics could utilize all of them, they were limited to their Gods' lineage power being the strongest. I knew my eyes would glow in red hues when I utilized a great amount of energy and that I would never become proficient in manipulating the land and air around me.

Instead, I would manipulate the dead, and could manipulate the living if need be. It would one day be my job to follow my father's orders and slay any undead which were released in the world. In turn, slaying the living that created them as well.

Once I mastered the basics, Solomon, a red Drakar, would take me as his apprentice and further my knowledge of Death, his

Realm and my magic. This was the path I was placed on while Callie and Leon were placed on another.

A year later Delron was right again, things changed fast for Callie. During an outing to a neighboring village for trade goods, she lost control for the first time since her magic took hold. Regardless of years training the natural balance of her power at times seemed to tip uncontrollably. The cost of being an heir of Daes and tied to his chaotic yet harmonious lineage.

The chaotic nature of her power grasped her, as her mind went wild. She had told me about it later since I was still not permitted to leave Silvertine due to my training. While she left many details out she said that her own father stepped in, pulling her temporarily out of Auran. He brought her in control and placed her on the correct path. No longer did she study with the typical blue magic Drakar. Instead she went to her father and trained with him. She quickly became his favorite child and often went for weeks or months to study or serve his cause. I had come to learn that it was adolescence which triggered the outburst of power, and as Leon and I grew we too came to serve our God. Leon often joined Callie on ensuring balance was kept, while I served Delron in keeping the dead actually dead.

Through the years we grew apart only to grow close again, it was constantly like this. Always being separated but always being close, often the three of us shared a house. Even if all three of us were hardly together, it was still a place we could call home. Finally a blue magic Drakar named Howl joined us, later it was Callie's mate Drameon, and eventually Raillyn, their daughter. Even then we never grew apart, Callie was still like my sister but Raillyn was different. Never could I place my finger on it but something deep inside told otherwise.

The Ancient races are funny creatures, the Gods say, often following instincts that are tied to their God or, in other cases, each other. Like the Drakar and Shadow Walkers, Mystics were picky not only about their habits but their family choices as well. Still, I did everything for them and continue to do everything for her now.

Realization ~ Raillyn

The now familiar sensation of the blue crystal awoke me, it pulsed to the beat of my heart and even before opening my eyes I knew where I was. The large blue dome lie high above, stars could be seen high above in the sky beyond. The now familiar blue hue of the room made me feel at peace. Turning my head, I noticed my grandfather sat in a nearby chair, either resting his eyes or sleeping. I wondered how long he had sat with me and how long I had been out. Smiling I tried to sit up and pain echoed through me, causing me to cry out. Looking down revealed that I was bandaged up tightly across the chest.

"Careful, child." Daes said in his cool, smooth tone.

Hearing his voice made me smile. It reminded me of Howl's own smooth voice that held magic in it as he spoke. Daes also spoke with magic, and it seemed to wrap its way into my very soul.

"How long have I been asleep?" I asked laying back down in the large blue bed. Standing and stretching Daes carefully sat beside me on the edge of the bed.

"A few days, Destiny did everything she could without using magic to heal you. I knew staying at Destiny's wouldn't heal you as fast as if I brought you here. I hope you don't mind. Both your father and Alkin have been by to check on you as well. I supposed I should send someone to retrieve them and inform them you are well." He said as he got up to leave.

Sitting up and reaching out to Daes through the pain, I grabbed his hand. "Wait, please." I gasped out.

Immediately my grandfather laid me back down on the bed. A feather sensation tickled my mind as I realized Daes was reading my thoughts.

"Rest, we will have plenty of time to talk after your family knows are safe." He said as he left me in the room to think.

No longer was I fearful of him, but instead I felt a connection begin to take hold deep in my soul. Relaxing, I looked around more carefully. A fireplace sat towards my left where the room seemed to expand well beyond the bed. Another door lay along the wall a few feet away from a nearby dresser. Various bookshelves lined the room full of books, bottles and objects, while an array of weapons hung from the wall near the unlit fireplace.

As I thought what the room might be used for the door opened. Drameon and Alkin rushed in while Daes brought up the rear and closed the door, behind him.

"I told you she was well." He said as my father sat on the bed and took my hand.

Smiling at them, I tried not to move too much and cause unnecessary pain on my part. "I am glad to see you well." Drameon said as he brushed my hair back before kissing my forehead. For a moment I met Alkin's gaze, he stood arms crossed leaning against the wall, near the door.

"After Aurielle returned and said the Wolves guard had killed Lily and Ashoten and wounded you I wasn't sure myself what to do. After her questioning by Hunter, Aurielle imparted the fact that you were not Raihanna and instead Raillyn. She also believed your wounds would lead to your death." He said while shifting uncomfortably.

My nose twitched as I smelled Alkin's scent, the memory of our closeness beckoned me, the crystal in the room to pick up pace. Closing my eyes and not allowing the blue in them to show I steadied my breathing and was able to return to calmness. A skill I now felt I needed to continue working on until I mastered it without my grandfather's presence. Noticing my unease Alkin tipped his head.

"Isn't there anything else you can do to heal her faster? I know you said no magic but if she is to return to The Keep it needs to be soon, Hunter will not wait. He will be tempted on using the staff as an alternative means to open the portal." My father asked while looking at Daes and Alkin.

For a moment, Daes smirked as he played with something behind his back. "Yes, I said no magic. However, Alkin?" He said before turning towards Alkin and placing a bright blue blade in his hand.

"No." Alkin said sternly as he pushed the blade away. The memory of how we healed each other when I was a child brushed my thoughts. Daes wanted me healed with blood, and, of course, my mate's would be the most potent.

"If you won't do it properly then at least spill it into a bowl for her." Daes said as he turned and grabbed a bowl off the table handing it towards Alkin.

For a moment I felt like jumping off the bed, all too aware what may happen if he spilled his blood around me. My breath picked up and I scooted back against the headboard. My father and grandfather look at me curiously. Alkin set the bowl down on the table and swiftly brought the blade across his palm. His blood ran from the open cut and into the bowl. The scent hit me like a tree falling in a forest.

My eyes dilated, and my breathing picked up, I was fully focused on his cut and the blood that came from it. Part of me wanted to go and heal it while another part just wanted to taste it and feel the rush of power that it would bring. Sweat began to run down my face as Alkin placed the dagger on the table and brought his palm to his mouth, to use his saliva and magic to stop the blood.

My head felt like it was going to explode. Static filled my ears and my nostrils flared. Suddenly a cracking sound resonated from the crystal on the table. Its startling sound broke my trance.

Staring at it with clear eyes and an equally clear mind I saw a large jagged crevice through its center. The three men looked at it curiously. Daes smirked as he grabbed Alkin's hand and pulled it from his mouth. The still bleeding wound splattered blood onto the floor and the comforter on the bed.

"You need to just get over this and give her your blood, embrace the bond you two-share and rival in it." He said while releasing Alkin's hand.

"No!" Alkin and I shouted simultaneously. For a moment, I felt like I was slapped on the face. My feelings felt hurt, like I was rejected. A look of unease and sadness spread across my face. Alkin noticed I saw it in his face, he felt disgusted with himself. *Why was my grandfather acting like this? He knew Alkin was my mate but he said to resist the bond...*

"There you have my blood, you can heal her with it." He said while leaving out the door, slamming it behind him.

"I will go after him." My father said following Alkin, knowing I was safe with Daes.

Closing my eyes, I felt a tear running down my cheek. Then the sweet smell of Alkin's blood was directly in front of me. Opening my eyes, I looked at it moving almost rhythmically in the bowl that Daes held. It was entrancing and I felt myself reaching out and taking it.

Holding it in my hands I remembered that **blood was everything to us, that blood was power**. I felt my eyes dilate again and static fill my ears. Before I knew it, I brought the bowl to my lips and drank its contents.

The sweet honey taste danced over my tongue and down my throat. A fire burned deep in my belly, craving more. My nose flared and before I knew it, I was on my feet and across the floor. My wound but a memory... Reaching for the handle, Daes grabbed my wrist, and an electric shock channeled through me and brought me to my knees. It didn't hurt, but it forced my mind and emotions to realign.

"Faen." I cursed as I shook my hand that felt like it had fallen asleep.

"That should hold you over for a few days, help keep those pesky hormones under control." Daes said as he helped me to my feet. Without skipping a beat, he went on. "Alkin needs to come to terms with you. He needs to just accept the fact that you are his mate, and embrace it. I was hoping baiting him on would help." He sighed explaining his behavior. "I will say this though. As long as everything goes according to plan and you follow my order precisely I might be able to grant you a reprieve. In which, you will not have to do anything other than live a balanced life in Auran. However, if things go amiss and issues occur I cannot grant you a reprieve. My magic is lacking from the world due to the slaughter of my line. It has greatly upset the balance of not only the world but every living creature as well."

I nodded my head agreeing. He was right, things were very out of balance.

"After we had removed you from the world, my magic began to die, creating many unsettling events. Events that I have worked effortlessly to aid. However, I will require you to be bonded to me as soon as the portal opens. In turn, this will allow my magic to flow stronger in the world through you." He said with respect and honor in his voice, he began to pace the room.

From my understanding magic of the Gods in our world were like pillars supporting everything. One of those pillars had fallen upon the death of Daes' Mystic line and with it nearly collapsed the balanced structure of the system. That pillar needed to be restored. His magic had been dead in the world for over two hundred years; it created so many unsettling events that plagued my childhood.

The undead had run rampant in Alecien, requiring my father Chaimh, as well as Delron's helpers, his mystic lineage to slay the undead. But this was just one of many issues. Even the people themselves, the races who did not possess ancient blood, were affected. Crops withered and died much faster, rivers ran dry and sickness ran rampant in some parts. Balance desperately needed to be restored and the darkness that had plagued the world lifted.

Nodding my head, I asked something on a lighter note, or I hoped it was easy to explain. "So whose room is this, may I ask?" Catching him by surprise, and pausing for a moment, he smiled. His eyes meeting mine.

"This was your mother's room, long ago when she visited. Upon her death and our recovery of you, it became yours." He said gently as I sat up surprised. "From the moment you entered my home, I made this room as comfortable as I could for you.

Leaving many of your mother's items on the wall and adding a few of my own to assist your chaotic mind. The blue crystal holds a strong force of my magic to ensure as long as you are in my house you will have more control over the balance battle which rages inside you. The skylight I added as well, just because I remembered you loving the stars as a child." My grandfather smiled as he looked up at the stars above. "And since I had nobody else to worry about I spent much time sitting here with you. Talking to you about the world we created, why it was created and why it was essential that balance remained on its surface. In addition, I try and keep the tone of this room and the outside hall dim, twilight in color if you must call it something. The tone is calming and helps put the mind at peace." Smiling up at him, I realized at that moment how much he had come to love me as his granddaughter.

"It was not an easy task I presume." I said quietly, wanting to hear more. Shaking his head, he went on.

"No, you were quite a handful. Even with your magic bound by all of us and your mind put in a coma state your power still lashed on its own accord at the beginning. I allowed no one access to you other than myself and the other Gods. Your father was kept well out of any discussions involving your whereabouts. We did not want him trying to take you back to the world too early and disrupt the plans we had already placed. Chaimh's grandfather was asked to stay in Alecien and try to control the war between the two races. His line was fashioned to be the perfect family and place for you to one day join. Only the war and letting you heal prevented us from returning you sooner, you needed the war to be over and needed a semi-peace to survive. We didn't dare take our chances and release you too soon. If you had perished so would the world. We had created it too perfect in some aspects to reverse many ill effects, but it was realized too late. Even now we can only enter the world to have a child. We cannot stay for any length of time, nor are we able to interfere in any matter other than here. Many ancient spells and barriers prevent us from that. Ancient spells that we do not wish to break unless placed in a desperate situation such as the fall of Auran. I will admit it has been considered, but thankfully was not needed."

I was shocked and yet not surprised that such spells had been placed upon the Gods themselves to prevent incidents. In doing this, the Gods ensured that freewill existed in their world, children and creations. By placing the Mystics, Dragon's and Drakar in charge of following their orders and assisting, it kept the world functioning correctly.

I made the decision then that I would follow my grandfather's orders as best as I could, if not only for myself but for the good of every living creature on Auran. "So you see why it is so crucial things go according to plan." He said as he sat back down.

Nodding my head, I did understand. I was tied up in something that ran deep, deeper than anything I had ever been tied up in before and I knew I had to swim in this violent storm and not let it conquer me.

My magic, mind and power seemed to align perfectly in that moment. "Yes, grandfather, I understand now and want to apologize for how I behaved the first time. It was not my intention at the time to return to The Keep. It's an unsettling place of horror for me and distress. I promise though that from this day forth I will be sure to follow your orders the best I can." I said while meeting his eyes, the blue color I felt was leaving and I began to feel myself return once more to my normal demeanor.

Smiling he stood, reached down and took my hand, pulling me gently upwards, I smiled back at him.

"I would like it if you returned to The Keep. Hunter will not kill you or allow harm to bestow you, even though you are no longer Raihanna. He knows if you die his portal will fall and his staff will in turn fail as well. I will not place a mark upon you at this time. You are still learning to balance your wild nature and it would only disrupt things. However, after the portal is opened will be another matter regardless of how much control you have. I will explain more at a later time. For now please just return to The Keep and continue assisting Hunter in getting the portal open." He said while smiling and releasing my hand.

"Also do not fear Alkin or what you feel towards him. That is perfectly natural and normal for an unbound Ancient. The blood you drank should hold off the worst of its ill effects till later. Right now the longer you stay away from The Keep the antsier Hunter will become."

Nodding in agreement I left through a portal to The Keep, knowing what had to be done and for the first time feeling right about doing it.

Ceremony and Binding ~ Drake

As I stood on the raised dais overstretching the town below my castle, I couldn't help but think how fast things had gone to get here. Pacing the corridors and small den for what seemed like hours, Raven had watched silently knowing there were no words that could quell my fear for Raillyn. Deep in my heart I still loved her, I always would, and I found myself worrying about whether she lived or died. Still, things had to go on.

Raven, dressed in a golden white long gown, stood next to me. My golden pants and matching shirt symbolized life and eternity, that this was forever. Her blackish blue hair was twisted up and held tight by a single intricate hair stick. Red, and matching golden gems were inlaid in it, it had been my mothers.

Smiling up at her I couldn't help but feel a wave of awe when I looked at her. Towards our left the priest from the temple stood, he spoke words of unity, peace, love, and fertility. On our right, the townspeople stood and listened, laying witness to our union. Glancing towards the crowd an array of faces, some happy and others placid.

Lastly out of the corner of my eyes along the farthest back wall, near the alley. I saw Drameon, his ever-changing eyes met mine. Arms casually crossed, he smiled slightly and nodded his head. I took that as his sign that Raillyn was OK. Carefully I took a deep sigh of relief as I looked back at Raven, relief in her eyes as well. She must of seen him also, beaming a smile, I felt she was genuinely happy for me, and for us.

As the words ended, a white leather strap was tied around our hands, binding us together. Quietly as tradition we walked back towards the castle, escorted by those of the village who wished to follow us to the cave entrance. After walking into the tunnel, everything became a blur. Raven and I were out of the tunnels before I could even register what was going on. The white leather band still strapped around our hands would not be removed until we reached the bedroom, to consummate our marriage.

Walking into my bedroom, I saw Briar. He must have been the consort sent to assist us in untying our binds. Smirking, his brown hair spilled over his golden eyes slightly. Carefully he pulled the strands away and came towards us.

This was it, I thought as Briar began to untie the leather strap. Fidgeting nervously I glanced down at Raven. She smiled up at me, she too seemed nervous and stood tense. Both of us knew this was the point of no return. Our people would be hopeful for a child from our union, and we were expected to provide one.

As the last ties fell away, Briar took the band and placed it on the table next to us. Smirking he silently patted my shoulder and left the room, closing the door quietly behind him. Raven's hand touched my shoulder gently, turning towards her I saw a hint of a smile.

"Are you as nervous as I am?" She asked quietly. "I don't know why but I am. I'm a ball of nerves, happy, anxious, curious, but also solemn..." She said trailing off.

"Why?" I asked curious to know why she felt upset.

"Because you're leaving your old life behind. I can't help but feel sad for that, like I share your loss. However, I am eager to begin our life together." She said.

It was time to move on. Raillyn was not mine and never would be. She belonged to Alkin, she was his mate. I had found my own peace in that. Seeing how he treated her and kept her safe while she was in The Keep. Also knowing she had a blood bond with him as a child. In addition, I never felt the deeper connection that I felt towards Raven. This was different, more connected and deeper. Probably because she was a wolf.

Wrapping my hands around her slim waist, I beamed a smile. This was more right than anything else I had done, I thought regretfully. *Raillyn was like an unreachable star, while*

Raven was my sun... Leaning down and brushing my lips across hers, I felt her relax.

As my lips kissed hers and trailed down her neck Raven began to feel warm. She tasted like warm milk with a dab of honey. Her kisses felt so right, her mouth trailed down my own neck. Not being able to resist I reached behind her silky golden white gown and untied it. In turn, she pulled at my shirt, nearly ripping it off my head. Just as her dress fell, I saw her milky white near leucistic skin. The subtle curves of her body gleamed with sweat. Raven's tiny white undershirt and bottoms seemed to stand out against her black hair that now hung loosely around her head and down her chest. Pulling me closer her hands were on my pants as she untied them. My own hands pulled at the last threads of her clothing.

Lightly I brushed my hand across her now bare back. Her eyes lit up like fireflies in the night sky and she giggled a little. Her skin felt smooth and as I traced her shoulder bone she let out a little groan, just as her hands began to explore my body. As the last of our clothes fell away I gently picked her up, breathing raggedly I found myself kissing her with a feverish fire. Her hand seemed to pull me towards her and dig at me, I felt myself pulling her closer. Finding the bed, we continued...

The Keep ~ Raillyn

Walking the halls towards Hunter's chambers I made sure that at this time my hood remained in place. Tired of running, I didn't care about what the others would think when I removed it. And entering Hunter's chambers told me things were once more hushed. Aurielle, Thierry, and Ash lounged on large ornate pillows near the fireplace. Hunter leaned over his table, his staff mere inches away. Alkin leaned, against the wall.

Slamming the door, I pulled off my hood and approached Hunter. All too aware that Thierry and Ash were making a V-line to me, I knew they would not like me in their company. Alkin looked ready to stop them and my sister just stood unsure what to do. It was Hunter who stopped everyone, grabbing his staff and blocking their path.

"No, let her speak." He said while looking at me awaiting an answer.

Reaching for my power, I wanted to prove to Hunter that I meant business. Slowly I felt my eyes begin to glow blue in color, looking around the room I met everyone's eyes.

"I think we both share similar goals, so why don't we continue working together and get this portal open?" I asked openly allowing my magic and eyes to return to normal. Everyone seemed to look towards Hunter and myself awaiting orders from my Uncle.

"Similar goals, you say? And what might those be?" He asked, back to his old ways of toying around.

Coming to stand closer, he held the staff in both hands as if ready to attack. He was taking no chances and neither was Alkin, who had inched closer. If the need arose, I knew, he would pull me through a portal out of harm's way. The tension in the air was thick, no one knew what the other would do, and it caused a strenuous situation.

The staff beat out evil power and made the situation worse. It was a horrid object full of terror and abhorrence. It seemed to affect everyone's mind, making their hatred grow, even myself. I hated my Uncle, wanting nothing more than to see his death, but I knew I could not do it myself. The staff however beckoned me to disobey and to take his life. Shaking my head to clear my thoughts and the burning hate that was building up inside me I spoke.

"We both want the portal open and Daes in the land once more. We might have different reasons why that is, but I don't see why we can't work together to fulfill allowing Daes' magic in the world." I said hoping he would listen and not let his crazy thoughts distract him from the purpose.

Hunter seemed deep in thought and then a twisted smile filled his face. "Well, this might be for the better." He said coming to stand directly in front of me. "You see, I had a little issue after you were sent to kill Lord Drake. The other Elite and I knew you were not dead because the portal and the totems remained so we decided to try to open the portal without you. But for some reason it failed." He said as he began to pace the room.

Ash seemed to calm down and backed up, standing arms crossed listening to Hunter's rant. Looking at Alkin, I wonder why he never told me that they tried to open the portal.

"Oh, don't worry." Hunter said. "Alkin wasn't here when we tried to open it up so he never knew any of it. But now that you are here and are in agreement of opening the portal and summoning Daes, I think we should have another go at opening it." Hunter said as he grabbed his long black cloak and walked to the door opening it gleefully. "Let's go." He said as we, his Elite followed.

***

Perplexed and surprised I followed Hunter and the others towards the stables. Alkin walked right beside me the whole time.

Since I had drank his blood, I felt the pull between us, his magic calling to mine, but I was able to keep the feeling balanced.

The stables sat quietly against the few trees inside the tall walls of the courtyard. Glancing at Alkin, he seemed annoyed. I wanted to reach out and take his hand. Being so close to the others, however, made me afraid to even walk too close. Eager to get this over with, I walked quietly towards the stall and across the dirt path. Near the end was where Raihanna's horse had been kept. As I opened the door, it began to kick and protest, no longer was it the docile horse that I remembered.

Its large hooves pounded the floor leaving small droplets of blood with each deafening slam of its hoof. Its sleek black fur seemed to glow red in color and a sickening smell emanated from its nostrils. No longer able to handle its behavior, I slammed the door, locking it just as hooves smacked the wooden walls, echoing a thunderous clap throughout the stables. Alkin hearing this immediately brought his horse over to investigate.

One of the few living horses in the stables, his large painted Fell Horse stood 22 hands tall and was picture perfect. "What's the issue?" he asked hushed, careful not to touch me.

The horse protested behind the closed door and whinnied loudly as it slammed its hooves into the ground below. The energy that rolled off the beast was filled with hate, the horse hated me. I was different to it and it did not like me. Closing my eyes to steady myself I tried to stop the violent tremors from sweeping across my body. I felt my power rise in protest against the rage sweeping across the stalls.

Other Death Steeds began to violently kick and whinny loudly in their stalls, I seemed to be agitating them and Alkin noticed as well. His loud growl rumbled in his chest, as he walked out of the stables. Quickly I followed him, as I felt my eyes begin to glow blue in color.

"Drink this." Alkin said while shoving a wineskin at me. Carefully I took it, not daring to touch his skin for fear what might happen. "I will get you a living horse, wait here." He said as he walked off quietly.

Suddenly I was aware of Ash, and Aurielle's eyes, avoiding their gaze I drank a large swig of the skin. It was Darah wine, its potent, herb mixed aroma made me smile, and already I was feeling calmer. Taking another sip I allowed myself to savor it for a moment, this was more potent than Howl's and held a hint of tang. *Berries* I thought to myself, *very bitter berries.* As well as a hint of what seemed like hot coals, a warming sensation began to creep through me, and I felt my eyes return to normal.

As I leaned against a nearby tree, I couldn't help but smile. If I drank more it would overpower me and I would be useless. Knowing that could not happen I placed the stopper back in the skin while Alkin came out of the stables leading a small chestnut mare.

"I think this would be more to your liking." He said handing me the reigns.

In turn, I handed him the wine skin and smiled. "Thank you." I said as I mounted up and rode to meet the others.

***

The ride to the Fellshores was peaceful and short. Its marshy landscape and the smell of decaying plants filled my nose. Various different types of vines twined up nearly every tree. Their roots dug deep into the soft soil and wet pools hiding from the sun. Small paths dotted the way, each one a solid land mass of rock and soil, created by magical means eons ago.

Riding on, I noticed the spider-like webs of moss, hanging from some of the nearby trees and the hazy gasses the farther waters gave off. Frogs, crickets and various birds could be heard all around us. Like exiting a haze we cleared the worst of the area and entered the small meadow. The murky waters and muck, gave it a surreal appearance.

Created from wood and vines, from the surrounding forest, the structure for the portal stood tall and magnificent. Its intricately carved sides had taken months if not years to get right. Each rune had to be meticulously crafted, one slight variation or mistake could cause destruction for not only the creator but the casters and surrounding area as well. Years before having Callina, I had gone over this portal's marks ensuring everything was right, luckily no mistakes were found.

***

Dismounting and continuing to follow Hunter quietly, we approached a tall black statue. It stood over ten feet tall and appeared to be pure black onyx, the human-like appearance gave it a rock-man look. It was the ghastly black shadow Alkin and I had released when we charged the staff with Chaimh's spell. It seemed to not be concerned, so we passed it and approached the wooden structure and the main totem.

Ash, Thierry, and Aurielle followed behind quietly as Hunter and Alkin led the way. Hunter's messy brown hair seemed nearly black in color, I noticed now that it appeared to be caked with dried blood. His clothes were no better; they too seemed to be in disarray. The overall smell of him was putrid, and noxious. Almost as if he came in contact with a skunk or another foul animal.

Once he took pride in his appearance and wore only the best, now he seemed to not care and his clothes appeared to be simple and plain. No longer did he wear the finer jewelry and garb that he used to, the once plush leather was now simple cotton and the fine velvet cloak and shirt were nothing more than linen.

"Go ahead and open it, my child." He called to me, breaking my train of thought. I still hated my Uncle, nothing changed that.

Long ago, as a child, he had broken my trust in him while he chased me through the woods in a blood rage. I barely remembered what happened. If it wasn't for Alkin and luck I would have been killed. I fully believe that the Gods made sure I had a safeguard on my magic to prevent unfortunate accidents such as my death from occurring. How else could I have unlocked so much of its power to shock myself out of his grasp at such a young and untrained age? Shaking my head to clear my thoughts, I walked to meet Hunter and Alkin at the main totem.

Its white surface glowed slightly in the sun's light. The bloodstone seemed to be alive giving off red hues to anyone nearby. "So what do I have to do?" I asked suddenly eager to begin.

Hunter drew out a dagger and handed it to me. "Cut your hand open and place it on the stone, then use your magic to reach out to Daes and his power. Here are the words you have to say as you do so. It will create a link between the two and pull his power here to you." Hunter said while handing me a piece of parchment. "At least that is what I suspect..." He said suddenly unsure.

Glancing at him, I became annoyed. He wasn't even sure how to call Daes into the world and that was why he needed me. I was his one tie to Daes. The only one who could actually perform the spell and perform it right. Alkin backed away as I brought the dagger to my hand.

Immediately the blood pooled, a few drops to spilled over the edge to the ground. Steadily I placed it on the large red bloodstone, like touching a cold flame, it began to pulse slightly. Its magic danced under my hand like solid water, or wet sand. Reaching for my power, I felt the gentle tug deep within my soul. Still it felt like it was behind a crystal wall and only slight amounts trickled through a tiny crack at its base.

Speaking the words Hunter had shown me, I felt that wall stress and snap back in place. Suddenly my head exploded in pain, stars burst across my vision and brought me to my knees. I felt darkness begin to envelop me as a deep spell spread across my body. Determined not to allow it to take its hold on me I quickly stood and grabbed the blood stone once more reaching for my power.

Oblivious to everyone around me they let me try again, swiftly this time I reached for my power and allowed my anger to contribute its energy to my rising power. Again I got nothing but a blinding piercing pain erupting across my head and vision.

Stumbling I felt myself fall backwards and into the arms of someone unexpected.

On contact I knew who grabbed me, nearly immediately the pain in my head began to ebb away. Howl's bright blue amulet swung in front of my vision for a moment, illuminated. He turned glared at the Vampire's and Alkin who now stood near the statue shadow figure. The tension seemed intense and I was sure someone would begin a deadly fight if I didn't do something to stop it.

Removing myself from Howl's grasp I stood and glared myself as both Alkin and Howl. "So what happened?" I asked out loud hoping to draw attention to myself.

It was Howl who spoke first, "Well, gorgeous, you seemed to be reaching for a spell you are unable to perform. Instead of utilizing your magic for the spell, your magic decided to utilize you. It took over your mind, forcing you to stop." Howl said before adding. "In other words it's a safeguard to ensure you don't do anything too powerful for your body or mind to handle, and since your magic is slowly returning to you, you are unable to perform such spells." He said matter of fact like before placing a kiss on my cheek.

I felt Alkin's anger as he approached us. "What in the Gods' name are you doing here, Howl?" He yelled as Howl placed himself between us.

The rage from both men brought chaos in my soul. "Doing something that you should have done. Delron smite you for being so ignorant! Did you really think Raillyn could perform such a spell at this time?!" Howl asked, meeting Alkin face to face.

As they argued the tremors increased and my vision obscured as a memory grasped my mind. Howl and Alkin had always been at ends with each other over strenuous situations. Reason for this was because Howl was more cautious than Alkin. Howl felt the delicate balance between chaos and harmony while Alkin only saw it and never truly felt it first-hand. My mother had even mentioned this once, knowing the difference in her two good friends.

Coming out of the slight vision, I heard Alkin yell. "We were given no choice." He said while looking back towards Hunter and the remaining Elite.

Hunter seemed furious by this, his calm misguided demeanor that he portrayed had turned to full bodied anger. In what seemed like a whirlwind of hate he approached us, staff raised ready to strike. Intensely I felt my anger rise, along with it my wild power seemed to peak. Slipping under Howl's protective arm and between my friends, I met Hunter head on, face to face.

As he brought the staff down in a wild un-targeted attack, I quickly reached up and grabbed it, blocking his downward assault. My already wild and chaotic power seemed to flare upon contact with the staff. I felt my eyes burn bright blue as I pulled the staff from Hunter's grasp.

Holding it in two hands, I pushed Hunter back and onto the ground. His Elite charged, ready to attack, but he held up his hand. telling them to stop and hold their ground. The power of the staff radiated through me, I felt nothing but its chaotic nature and it drove a wild stake through my mind and soul. No longer able to feel my own magic. Instead I was drawing only on the staff's power and my mind shifted with the feeling.

Tilting my head to one side, I smiled and drew my dagger out of its sheath. Poised, ready to attack, I knew what I wanted; the power in the staff indicated that. Its electric charge coursed through me, I could sense and feel what it wanted in my mind. No longer was it happy with Hunter and his power. It seemed to have a mind of its own and wanted a more powerful source to wield it. I wanted his blood and death on my hands, and that was all I felt. All my hatred for him seemed to rise and boil over uncontrollably as I dart forwards preparing to take his life.

One step, two' as I got within arm's reach the staff was knocked out of my hand and spiraled out of control towards the Elite, who stood ready a few feet away. Howl desperately pulled me backwards and turned me around to face him. Gently he kissed my forehead and began murmuring a spell in Drakar.

His blue amulet glowed brightly as I felt a subtle shift and the chaos leave my mind and return me to normal. Shaking I felt myself meet his eyes; I had almost killed Hunter, the one thing that Daes told me not to do. No one should die at my hands, the demeanor of my emotions and magic would not handle that on my conscience. It would drive me mad and bring only trouble. I had to learn to control this new nature booming within.

My chaotic mind and magic had to harmonize with the more ordered mind and magic which made me Raillyn. Or I would fall victim to the mindset, ways and old emotions of Raihanna. Finally, I realized the narrow line I was walking. Daes was right. I had a choice on how to live – if I would live a life of harmony and balance and be Raillyn or chaos and destruction and be Raihanna. It frightened me to death and I feared the outcome.

Another memory gripped my mind, this one not so old. Chaimh had often drilled the concept of good and evil into my mind. Telling me I always had a choice on what path I wanted to live, that I only had to fight for it and survive the fight to get it. If I wanted to live as Raillyn, I had to conquer the chaos within and learn to live with it instead of against it. I couldn't just block it out and pray it went away, because each time I did that only caused more issues.

Hunter sat on the mossy grass, laughing maniacally. "I don't know what just happened but if you can display that kind of power while being restricted, I can't wait to see what you can do when your bonds are released." He said in a wild. uncanny tone as he got up and took his staff from Ash.

Turning from Howl, I looked at Alkin and Hunter, and re-gretfully agreed. Nodding my head, Hunter was sadly right. "If we're going to open the portal and allow Daes into the world my magic needs to be aligned, the chaos within me has to be dealt with along with my magic." I said, meeting Howl's eyes.

He pressed his lips thin but nodded in understanding.

"We will leave and find more information on how to reme-dy this issue. You go and do the same. I am sure we can open the portal within the month as long as we play our cards right." I said, hoping we could buy enough time to get this figured out. Everyone seemed in agreement as Alkin, Howl and I opened a portal and silently left to my father's home.

Untold Horrors ~ Raillyn

Finally reaching my father's home, I felt I was able to let my emotions go and not hold back. It was becoming difficult to hold everything in and I felt I was beginning to pay for not trying to remedy this and adjust it accordingly sooner.

Balance that was what I needed... "So what do we do?" I asked leaning against the nearby wall and putting my hand to my head. I felt broken and distraught.

All I wanted was a normal life but I knew that would never happen again; that was over as soon as I ran into Drameon. No, that was over well before when I was taken from Drameon. The ache in my chest brought me to tears. For a moment they moved unnoticed down my cheeks until one fell to the floor. The chaotic roller coaster of my emotions was making me a wreck. It was tiring going from one extreme such as the anger I felt attacking Hunter, to a moment of calm reprieve, to crying like a baby over events that happened long ago. *When would this right itself* I thought as the tears fell faster.

Howl and Alkin seemed to be in conversation between each other over the recent events, so they failed to see my inner battle. Slowly I felt a shift inside, they seemed to twist and turn until slipping into place. The unspeakable chaos that reigned in me from The Keep and life as Raihanna disappeared. It was a good start in controlling the chaos. But, I still had a long road ahead of me, one that would not be easy.

Gazing back towards Alkin and Howl, I felt my eyes shift in response to my mood. No longer in tears, an anxious calm took over my emotions. "So what do we need to do about this? Who should we ask? Do you think Daes would tell me anything?" I asked trying to go over things in my head.

Alkin and Howl both looked at me, concerned, but agreed something had to be done. "I am doubtful Daes would tell you anything. He has a knack of wanting his lineage to discover things on their own. It makes for better learning, he says. Plus it's an emotional high getting there…" Howl said trailing off smiling. "For you I am sure Daes would encourage you to seek out the information by yourself. Not only will it be frustrating but also it will be a very joyous thing to find it out on your own. Without being told."

Alkin looked toward Howl and seemed to agree. "Yeah, I am sure Daes won't say anything concerning this. Even my own father, Delron, always wanted me to discover things on my own or by asking and acquiring information." Alkin brought his fingers to his chin in thought.

Not that I didn't believe them but I felt this might be a different case, but I had to try and ask Daes for help on this. At least, being pointed in the right direction. "I think I need to at least try. It doesn't hurt to ask and if anything, maybe he will tell me where to look, or give me a clue." I said, looking at the two men.

"Go, then. Alkin and I will check on the Wolves, as well as do a little research here and there. We can meet up later, in a few days and share what we have found." Howl said as he pulled me into a deep embrace. For a moment, his left hand seemed absent till he grabbed my butt, and squeezed.

My eyes flew open as I shoved him away, to no avail. *What the hell?* I asked along our mental link. All I got in response was something resembling a smirk. For a moment, his hand ran up my back, under my shirt and across bare skin.

Looking over his shoulder, Alkin stormed forwards and grabbed the back of his hair, pulling him off me. Howl stammered "Ow…Ow…Ow…" as he was pulled back and was almost tossed to the floor.

"Go." Alkin said as I called a portal. Their eyes met in a deadlocked glare; Alkin's eyes ruby red and Howl's vibrant blue. I felt a hint of gratification flash across Howl's mind as I turned to leave. He had provoked Alkin on purpose, to get a rise out of him.

Men ~ Alkin

As I watched Raillyn disappear into her portal, I released Howl. "What in Delron's River do you think you're doing? Do you have a death wish. Drakar?" I asked feeling my anger spike.

Howl turned to face me, laughing slightly before rubbing his head as if I hurt him. "Challenging you." He said to my face before stepping back. "Raillyn is unbalanced because she needs you. She needs your touch, your smell, your blood, but most of all she needs your connection. But you still refuse to acknowledge it and just do what is natural. Bind her to you already!" He yelled at me as he flung his hands in the air.

It felt like a blood vessel popped in my head, my anger radiated, my body was hot and I was shaking. Grabbing Howl by the collar of his shirt I slammed him against the nearby wall.

"Keep your hands off her if you know what's good for you!" I growled back at him. "She is mine!"

"Prove it." He said standing tall. Howl was pushing his luck and challenging me further.

I knew it was meant to be harmless. That he was probably trying to get me to think straight, to get me to do what was right. However, his behavior was having the opposite effect. Raillyn was my mate, she was my charge, and seeing his hands on her infuriated me.

Something snapped in me. I drew my blackened blade and pressed it so hard against his neck I drew blood. "You know you can't kill me. Raillyn will be upset if you do. Plus I don't think your father would be pleased with you." He said calmly, his blue eyes glistening.

It just made me more furious. Red crossed my vision, as I battled to control the anger. Pulling my blade away I quickly sheathed it, trying to reason with my emotions and instincts.

Howl was not a threat to me he was intentionally pushing my buttons to make me move forward and stop fighting our bond.

"No, you're right I should just bind her to me. However, I don't want her to hate me, already she's acting like she's avoiding me. I couldn't handle it if she rejected me altogether. It would be the ultimate slap in the face. Think about it, Howl, look what I have done. I've had to kill her, twice." I shared my most inner worries, the ones I didn't like to bring up. "Plus she's in love with that damn Wolf."

Howl smirked and patted my shoulder. "She doesn't know what she wants anymore. She feels so lost and torn that she can't even begin to understand what's going on. She's confused and refuses to acknowledge her feelings, of both her mind and body. Instead, she just completely blocks them out. You know that only makes it worse and brings out that more primitive side of us. Talk to her, explain what's going on, or even just show her, for Death's sake." He said. "If you don't, I will and you know how hurt she will be."

Meeting his eyes, I knew he spoke the truth. Howl smirked at me. He would tell her and that frightened me more than ever.

Howl had a natural knack, due to his magic, to turn any unbound women on. Even though, they couldn't conceive he often was able to talk them into his bed. Howl was a good man but with the knowledge of his womanizing ways and the situation of my unbound mate. It angered me to the core.

"I will tell her – just keep your hands off of her from now on. If I find you trying to weasel her into your bed with that magic of yours, I will personally remove something you value as dear. Raillyn is my mate and I love her with all my heart and soul." I threatened as he put his hands in the air innocently.

"All right, all right. Truthfully, that would be too weird even for me, I was just playing around. You needed to admit that to yourself, you know? That she is your mate and that you love her. I haven't heard you say anything like that about anyone before. Well, anyone that wasn't family to you." He said.

He was right. Never had I actually admitted my feelings about her out loud. However, now that Howl knew I felt myself relax. I loved Raillyn, I really did. It was more genuine than anything else I had felt before. Sighing, I sat down.

"I think we just need to wait and let Raillyn figure some stuff out on her own before we interfere." I admitted, knowing it's what she needed. "She needs to become familiar with Daes and explore a little on her own. We can't always hold her hand and guide her."

Howl seemed in agreement and sat beside me. "Yeah, she does need to do things on her own. We need to stop treating her like a child."

Meeting his gaze, I knew he was right. I was hoping that ignoring her behavior was best, but it wasn't. I needed to talk to her and confess everything, instead of dodging it. Sitting I pondered his words.

Aeralain ~ Raillyn

Exiting the portal, I found myself in my mother's old room, my room, inside Daes' home. A strange aroma filled the air around me, strange but very delightful. It smelled like someone was cooking soup, but the smell indicated a strong use of magic and herbs. Following the smell lead me into the hall, deep blue magic lights illuminated it and gave off an eerie glow, small statues sat on pedestals and bookshelves lined the walls, while plush ornate carpets lay pristinely along the floors of the wooden house.

As I walked the hall, I noticed a soft yellow glow come from an open door at the end. Slowly I peeked around the corner and saw it was from the glow of a nearby fire. Magic lights illuminated this room as well, and shone like dim suns along the ceiling, giving off enough light to warm the room in a subtle glow. Various tables, benches and pillowed chairs sat around the room near the fire towards my left, while a kitchen, bookshelves, large table, matching chairs, and a weapon rack lay towards my right. This is where I found Daes.

My grandfather stood in the kitchen near a small hearth along what seemed to be an outer wall, stirring a pot simmering over the open fire. Carefully so not to startle him I came into the room, as smiling, he looked up at me. His deep blue eyes met my own ever-changing eyes, and I couldn't help but smile. A sense of harmony entered my mind; my soul seemed to sing in his presence, I was in full control here. I needed to learn to bring this feeling with me and be able to be in this state of mind at home as well.

Brushing his black wavy hair behind his ear, he closed the pot he was stirring. "I thought I sensed your return." He said while coming closer towards me, and around the table. "Please sit, join me for a bite to eat." Pulling out a chair, he waited patiently.

Walking to join him at the table, I found myself happy for this little reprieve from the emotional struggle I constantly felt. Sitting in the chair he had pulled out, he went over towards a cabinet and pulled out two exquisitely crafted Elvin bowls. Leaves, vines and trees lined its terracotta base and rim. Various runes and marks seemed to be drawn across the middle and painted in bright colors.

Daes placed one bowl on the table as he filled the other with the contents of the pot. Handing it to me, he filled the other. Almost, instinctively I stood and retrieved two spoons from a nearby basket. Handing one to my grandfather and placing mine where I had sat earlier, then meeting his eyes, realization struck at what I had done.

Daes seemed to find this comical. "You have spent quite a bit of time here with your mother and me when you were young. I am not surprised you remember little things such as this." He said while raising the spoon slightly.

Smiling slightly, I took my seat and smelled the soup. It seemed like a very pleasant vegetable herb soup. Grabbing a basket of rolls, Daes offered me one. Taking a roll I dipped it in the tomato soup base, scattered with herbs. Tasting it was amazing. The vegetable-like soup was flavored with rosemary, basil, chives, garlic and onion. It was strong but not overpowering, just enough to give it a delectable taste. It was simply the most amazing thing I could ever remember eating. The Den had food similar to this but not as flavorful.

For the time being, I savored every bite and ate in silence. Upon finishing the first bowl, I grabbed another roll and stood. "Can I have another bowl?" I asked him while I noticed his eyes flash violet. "Of course," he said.

Using the large iron ladle, I scooped another bowl full of soup and took my seat once more. My mouth watered at the smell and thought of the soup I would have to learn how to make this at home, because it was absolutely divine.

"So you like the soup?" my grandfather asked, breaking me out of my inner thoughts.

Smiling, I replied. "This is amazing! I have no idea what it is, but it tastes very good! Did you cook this yourself? Can you teach me how to cook things like this?" I asked hopeful.

Laughing slightly, he seemed happy I was happy. "Yes, child, I cooked it. I have become very accustomed and prefer to cook like the Drakar and other Ancients. In fact, I am sure if you asked Alkin he would teach you to cook similar meals." He said between wholehearted belly laughs.

His laughter seemed toxic and I found myself laughing as well. "Alkin cooks like this?" I asked surprised and wondering what other divine meals I could learn to cook and eat. I was never a picky eater, but this food was exotic and my palate seemed to prefer it over the normal Elvin cooking which I was brought up on. "So what's in it?" I asked wondering how Drakar cooked.

Violet flashed across his vision, I was realizing how similar Mystics really were to the Gods themselves. While the Gods' eye color stayed one shade they often flashed various colors indicating their mood, just as their Mystic offspring. My grandfather was thinking.

"That I am not sure how to answer. You see, Ancients and Shadow Walkers share one thing in common: their taste in food. Even the Demons in the Waste cook the same. I have noticed that Mystics prefer this food choice, as well." He said cautiously, he had my attention, I was curious to know what I had been savoring over. "These races cook with items found in nature: herbs, vegetables, fruit and nuts. So, yes, very similar to Elves, however they add meat, and blood to their diet as well. Lastly, they imbue it with magic, empowering it. Often they use blood as a broth in soup and undercook the meat, for taste." His eyes met mine as he mentally gauged how I was going to handle the information.

The soup was a vegetable-based soup as I thought, but it was not cooked with the normal broth. Instead, blood was used in its place. As well as imbuing it with magic and energy, similar to Drakar wine. My mind was blank. Not once had I asked Howl what he ate, or asked about the Shadow Walkers, and now I was enjoying a meal that was typical for their races.

Panic crossed my mind briefly as I felt my balance become disrupted, its sway through me off, but as I came to terms with the idea I figured it wasn't so bad. The food was divine, it really did taste good, and my body seemed to revel in its nourishment. It actually made me wonder if my mother cooked this way when I was young.

Suddenly, reaching towards untold memories I tried to grasp some indication that this had been normal. Flickers of images crossed my mind, my mother had often cooked with the blood of animals. Nothing would ever go to waste from a kill. Bones were used for sewing needles, tools and various other items.

Meat, marrow, blood and good organs were used for cooking. Anything not edible was placed back into the earth and used as nutrients for the soil. This had been how my mother and father began raising me, to respect the planet and all creatures in it. It was the very way Chaimh and Lillian had raised me, excluding the unique cooking.

My emotions seemed to realign as I found myself continue to enjoy the soup. My grandfather seemed to tip his head in curiosity. "My mother used to cook like this, didn't she?" I asked, eager to hear about my mother.

Daes' eyes lit up at this revelation I seemed to have. "Yes, she did; her mother Opal taught her to make various Drakar dishes. Your mother had big plans for you. She had expected to bring you to Silvertine daily for lessons in magic when you got older. Your father's house is just close enough, but at the same time, far enough away to feel jus, the subtle effects of Silvertine's natural magic." He said matter of fact like.

He looked at me more curious, I could tell he contemplated why I was here and what business it involved. As if reading his internal thoughts I asked.

"Is there some kind of direction you can point me in?" I asked hopeful. "Today I tried to open the portal but couldn't I was restricted, so how do I do it?"

Pausing and placing his spoon back into his bowl, his eyes flashed purple. He thought for a moment before answering. "That I cannot tell you directly, you must find out how to break those bonds on your own. I've already told you enough. I will say this though. I believe you can find many answers to your questions in Silvertine. I would ask your grandmother." Daes said with a slight smile to his face.

Connection ~ Raillyn

Exiting the portal, I found Alkin sitting in one of the large overstuffed chairs near a fireplace, speaking to Opal and Solomn. Standing where I was I couldn't hear what they were saying, it was fine though. I was trying to think how to word my questions, to learn how to open the portal.

As I watched I noticed they wore different clothes, fancier ones. Opal had a bright fire-red shirt on with long elegant sleeves, deep brown pants and tall black boots. Solomn and Alkin were similar; both were dressed in a blue shirt with equally long sleeves. Alkin's the color of a deep blue ocean, while Solomn's was bright as a morning sky. Both had black suede pants and black boots. Alkin's scent of pine, moss and rich soil hit me as an instant reminder of his presence. Deep inside I felt an ache I had known was always there, but I disregarded.

My subconscious primitive mind slowly began creeping into my conscious one. My body began to turn hot, like lighting a fire in a stove. Sweat beaded on my skin, beckoning to my mate. For a moment, I shook my head to fight it, but it was no use. I had avoided Alkin and this bond for so long. I was losing myself to its overwhelming magic. I saw Alkin turn his head in my direction. He smelled me, and I knew it. My subconscious threatened to take over, but I refused to lose myself fully. Smiling mischievously, I felt like running to him, jumping into his arms, and tearing off his clothes.

Opal and Solomn seemed to notice our behavior and looked towards Alkin curiously. Closing my eyes, I found myself laughing a little, almost as if I had lost my mind. In a way I was rivaling in this new power, I loved it and wanted to see what would happen in a controlled chaotic situation. Swiftly Alkin stood seemingly unsure about what was going on.

"Raillyn?" I hear Opal question statically. The hairs on my body stood as an electrifying sensation crept over its surface.

Alkin's nostrils flared and I saw his pupils dilate slightly before shifting back to their normal size. "What are you doing here?" he questioned as I felt an irrational behavior over sweep me.

Since I was still unbound, any behavior concerning our bond was not in control. It was like driving a cart around and around with one circular wheel and a square one. It left me unstable, still I needed the bond to move forward and go straight. My head spun as realization hit me, *I won't be able to move forward till we bond.... That's why Daes told me to come here.... He knew I was at the breaking point...*

Tipping my head, I was anxious and excited. It resonated through every fiber in my body. Opal gave Alkin a questioningly look, picking up on my difference in behavior.

"Playing." I said while jumping towards him a few steps.

Standing directly in front of him, he stiffened. I was making him nervous. Wanting to play more I leaned forward, not touching him and not intending to. Instead I gently took a breath and blew air towards him. My core shivered, and my stomach tightened. Reaching for the sensation, I realized what it was. I was on the verge of my cycle, not able to enter it because the bond between Alkin and I was broke, it left me in an even more irrational state.

Closing his eyes, his chest rose as he took in a deep breath. Sweat beaded upon his brow and a shiver ran over his body. Alkin knew I was on the brink of something older than either of us. Something we were powerless to...

Exhaling, my own body tensed as his scent became overpowering. I began to twitch in anticipation, my mind shifted, this time to a more primal state. I would not be responsible for my actions and I wasn't fearful of any of it. Instead, I embraced it and it was exciting.

"We do not have time for this behavior, go jump into the snow and calm yourself down." He said tightening his fists into balls.

Squeezing hard, I knew he drew blood, I could smell it. His eyes shot open, but they betrayed him. They were not red, he wasn't angry at me. Instead, they glowed an eerie hue of violet mixed lightly with pink. Meeting his gaze only made my primal feelings rise, he walked stiffly towards the door. Static increased in my ears as I began moving serpent-like. My motions were fluid, my eyes never left him as he went.

"Don't walk away from me!" I yelled suddenly angered by his words and reaction. Sliding my feet across the floor, as if they were light as a feather, I found myself following.

He was quick though and already out the door by the time I was moving forward. Swiftly I almost jetted across the floor, growling I reached the hall, following his scent.

For a moment, I stopped. He had paused just outside the door, his scent was heavy here. Pheromones hung in the air, the smell of a sweet pine forest, they betrayed his behavior. My body shivered as my mind blanked out momentarily. I was losing myself to my more primal side.

Rounding a corner I saw Alkin summoning a portal, its blackish-red hazy surface swirled largely in front of him. Without turning he began walking through it.

I felt myself rush forward and grab at his sleeve before it slipped into its shadowy embrace.

The smooth material almost slipped from my grip, but I would not let my mate leave me in such a state. He would not have that option, no longer did I want to run from our bond instead I was ready to embrace it. My body burned in memory of my cycle, my vision hazed and my breathing picked up.

Yanking hard, Alkin stumbled backwards through the portal. Tugging at the sleeve, he tried to pull it out of my grip, but I wasn't letting go. Instead, the fury in me took over. Static filled my ears as I went to reprimand my mate for being such an idiot. Again the bordering sensation of my cycle took over. My body shook, I felt on the verge of catching on fire.

Raising my hand I fully intended to smack him as hard as I could across the cheek. Meeting my eyes Alkin's blazed red.

Good! I had angered him! My own anger was boiling over making me seething mad. How could he think I'd be ok with him leaving? It was selfish of him and I wasn't going to stand by and let him leave.

Swinging my hand around it flew quickly towards its target. Brushing his silky chestnut hair and coming inches away from his face, he swiftly grabbed my shoulder with one-hand and my hand with the other. Turning, he slammed me against the nearby wall. His knee went between my legs, preventing my escape. He held both hands in his above my head.

My head hit the wall just as my eyes met his. In a heart wrenching feeling, breathe instantly left my lungs. It seemed to freeze in my chest. Our eyes met vivid violet pink, leaning forward he took in my scent.

That was his mistake. My body tensed with the thrill of what was happening. Blinking slowly a smile crept across my face as I felt his body tense and saw sweat bead on his face. His sweet scent filled my nose and was intoxicating.

My heart stuttered a few times before picking up pace. The air around me shimmered in deep blue hues. Mentally I began to feel Alkin's thoughts. His breath stilled as well. The air around him mimicked his magic color, crimson red. Where our magic mingled together shades of purple swirled euphorically, in what appeared to be deep a mist.

Pushing his knee away with my body, his fingers danced on my cheek. His other hand still held my hands in place, but his grip was less intense. Lightning sparked and danced from his touch. It made my skin tingle and I felt my body almost arching towards his. Placing his forehead against mine, he took in my scent again. Relaxing, I felt him give in. Not wanting to fight our bond any longer he kissed me deeply.

Time was gone, nothing mattered other than this. His other hand released my wrists. Circling his neck, I returned his kisses. I felt my soul link to him in small tendrils, almost like roots of a tree linking to the ground. *This is what I was missing, what should have been...*

It felt like a rush of energy, as my magic searched deep within him, needing, wanting, reaching, to link me to him. Each moment we spent in this trance drew us to the inevitable, an irreversible bond. One that brought tears to my eyes, because I knew I could never escape, that I didn't want to escape.

A kaleidoscope of memories, in unrelenting flashes, began pouring into me. My life, the life I was used to, was a lie. I lost my balance when I went to the Wolves. By doing so, I shifted from harmony to chaos, and later back again in The Keep. Now I was finding myself, finding what was lost, forgotten. I never knew who, or what I was, it always escaped me. The significance behind it all was startling and frightening.

All my memories, even the ones that were locked away, were open to me. He kept nothing from me, going as far as showing me his own memories, from times long ago. Tears filled my eyes as I realized he had always been there, before Chaimh and Lillian, and even during. Always he had protected me, from unseen dangers, risking his own life for my own. It was daunting, and mind numbing.

Only now was I able to see that I was blind. That until I lost it, all of it, I would never be whole. Tears ran down my face and onto the floor below, forgotten. It had been Daes' plan the whole time, for me to find my center.

Dizziness spread, and overwhelmed me, causing me to fall into him. Eyes open wide in shock they just kept coming back. The moment he touched my face sparked what I had lost, reawakened in our long lost bond. I couldn't stop it. I didn't get a choice and never would. It was His ultimate plan all along...

Mentally and physically I gripped the overwhelming surge of our bond. Not able to keep up with my body, my mind was lost to what it was doing. As if being struck by lightning, my mind refused to work and I blanked out.

Bonded ~ Alkin

Intense buzzing filled my ears as I woke up. My head hurt and the dim light behind closed eyelids caused my eyes to ache. I felt like I had drank too much the night before and my body was paying the price now. Physically I felt numb, but slowly sensation was returning. Like tiny needles dancing across my body it slowly awoke.

Squeezing my eyes together and breathing deeply. My breath stilled in my lungs at the scent. The sweet smell of vanilla in an open forest filled me with surprise. Opening my eyes wide in shock, I already knew what happened.

Raillyn lay against me, the warm feeling of her naked body against mine was the first physical sensation I felt. A blanket covered us as we lay on various pillows, creating a makeshift bed. Warmth from the fireplace warmed my left side. It burned brightly, illuminating the room. Chairs, benches and seats, missing their pillows, stood around us. We were in Opal and Solomn's personal den.

Thinking, *I would have to explain myself to my adoptive parents later,* I looked down at Raillyn. Her silky, silvery red hair lay on my bare chest. She was still asleep from the overwhelming surge of our bond.

Relaxing and kissing her head I paused, her scent had changed. It was no longer just her own sweet smell. Now it was mixed perfectly with mine, creating a new invigorating scent. Sweet vanilla, in a rainy evergreen forest, laced with honey filled my nose. Yet there was still something lingering that reverberated a memory of The Keep.

My nose twitched the sweet smell of almond, her cycle had set in. Looking down I vaguely saw bright blue lines across my chest where Raillyn slept. There was no doubt in my mind what happened. We had exchanged blood, marking each other, and in turn we claimed and bound each other. There would be no going back now.

She would only respond to my touch and be offended by other male's advances on her. It also meant her cycle would be upon us. We literally would be racing against the ticking clock of our nature. I was sure she wouldn't be completely balanced until it passed.

Afterwards, though it would more than likely result in a child, we only had a day or two before its overpowering nature gripped us in its thralls. Instead of one night like last night it would be several, leaving us exhausted. Both mentally and physically drained.

This is what we didn't need, and what I knew would happen. All because by dying, her body reset and then she fought what she knew was the truth. Resisting the bond or feeling distraught by it. It didn't matter anymore, I didn't care. I loved her and was happy she chased wildly after me. I just hoped we could get the portal open after she fully aligned her emotions and body. The next couple days would prove shaky.

Suddenly a smile spread across my face, this gave us a few days to live as normal Mystics. I could show her our house and the city while we awaited the inevitable. It was calming and as I thought this, I felt her stir. Unintentionally I found myself rubbing her arm lovingly.

Shifting she put her hand on her head, she was feeling the same effects I had upon waking. Her head spun and her body prickled. Sitting up she placed her hand on my chest for support and stilled as the blanket fell away. Unintentionally she laid her hand on the mark she had put on me, binding us together with blood and magic.

She traced its tribal-like pattern of vines and leaves. Closing my eyes, she was driving me crazy. My body tensed as the burning urge to pull her towards me and kiss her filled my thoughts. She giggled as she sensed my thoughts and I caught the sensation she was going to tease me.

Every muscle froze as she leaned forward and gently ran her tongue across the mark. Letting my breath out slowly I tried to steady myself, she set every fiber in my being aflame from that touch. My body cried out to hers and she found it enchanting and empowering. I allowed her to rival in her new found power over me.

Instinctively I felt myself reaching towards her to show her how it felt. Gently I ran my thumb across the mark I placed on her. She tensed slightly beneath its touch. Smiling, I flipped her over and ran my tongue over it. She whined and wriggled under me by the sensation it created. Her own hands moved up my chest and across my mark. Knowing if this kept up it would throw her into another wave of her cycle I rolled off her.

She whimpered as her overwhelming emotions of love and admiration poured through me. My own emotions love, protectiveness, care, fear and wonder, all the feelings I had kept locked away flooded my mind. I was happy to have her and her me.

She finally fully belonged to me and no one else. The jealousy and hate I felt towards the other males around her diminished. Yes, I would be more primal around the time of her cycle, but life outside that time would be blissful. We lived for one another, we were meant for one another.

"No, please." She said pulling my arm.

Leaning forward, I kissed her. Pulling back I laid my forehead against hers, she rubbed her nose back and forth lovingly across mine.

"You know were playing with fire?" I asked smiling as she reached for my mind.

She felt I was nervous about getting the portal open in time if something came of this. Smiling she put her leg over me and straddled me. Looking at her questioningly I waited, she ran her fingers through my hair as she leaned me down onto the pillow. She knew I was putty in her hands and if she begged enough I would give in.

Hell, she didn't even have to beg. I wanted her to be happy and having an infant to fret over like any normal mother was what she wanted. She never had that luxury, and the desire to have it now was overwhelming. She caught my thoughts and sat up smiling.

Then, like the sudden change in weather, the overwhelming emotions of what had led to this moment filled her head. Grief, guilt and sadness filled her soul from fighting our bond, and going to another man. Tears began to fill her eyes and my heart skipped a beat at her sadness.

"I'm sorry." She whispered. Snuggling her head against my neck, rubbing her back I gently kissed her head.

She needed to grieve for the past. It was part of the process to move forward, to heal. She had lost so much, only to be given a new life and have that ripped from her as well. I hoped this would be the last after the portal closed I prayed things would go our way.

Tears began running down her face, onto my chest. Instinctively she knew I had been the one and only person she could be fully open with emotionally and physically.

"You were always there for me as I grew up, and I never realized that till now." She said showing me her memories. When we first met when she was five. When I saved her from Hunter, and when I assisted her with the dead family in the woods.

In turn I shared my own, the simple act of comforting her while she slept, and trying to keep the nightmares at bay as she grew. The darkness that threatened to fill her soul, even though the memories of it were locked away. Gently I brushed the tears away with light fingertips.

"Don't be sorry, you never knew. Chaimh never raised you to know, it made things easier but at the same time complicated." I said while lovingly lifting her head to mine and kissing her gently.

"I will admit I was furious at first, the fact that Drake had intervened, the fact that he had laid his hands on you after I claimed you. Truthfully I had come close to killing him." I said while looking at her.

She hadn't heard this from either of us. Tilting her head she looked at me curiously. I continued. "I was angry when the Werewolves attacked the troops we had placed around the Shifter's castle. So angry in fact, that I took advantage of an opportunity and took Drake with me to Death's Realm. I admit I lost control and wanted nothing else than to see him die, but thankfully my father snapped me out of it. He cast your friend out of his Realm and in turn I was punished for what I had attempted." She felt my sadness, for not only Drake but for myself as well.

She couldn't bear the thought of either of us suffering or in pain. Understandingly she nuzzled my cheek and kissed it. No words were needed however we liked to hear the other talk.

"What was your punishment for that act?" She asked as she reached for my thoughts.

That I was not proud of, my punishment became her death. Being her mate, I was the one who could anchor her soul to the living world best. Even through dire situations, that Daes intervened in, her chances of survival were greater because of me. I became a pawn to the Gods just as she. She saw it in my mind my sadness and despair at learning I had to kill her not only once, but twice.

The feeling of her deaths, how depressed it left me, lonely and hate filled. I despised myself when she was taken from me, I became dark and uncaring. She brought the best out in me. Leaning forward, she kissed my lips gently.

"I love you regardless of what you've done. It wasn't your choice and you acted out of jealousy over Drake. It's understandable. I forgive you and am thankful to have you with me now. I want to walk by your side till my dying days." She said with affection and tears in her eyes. Embracing her, I pulled her down on top of me.

"Gods, I love you." I said as I felt her smile and relax into me. She was my everything and I was hers. We felt it in every fiber in our being. "If you want another child that bad, we can try all you want for one. However, I think we should wait till your next cycle. The portal needs open and that staff needs to be taken care of."

Physically she sighed; mentally she was disappointed but understanding. "You're right, we need to open the portal, Daes' magic needs to be in the world and soon. Now that my magic is more balanced I can almost feel the land crying. It feels like the hairs on my body are rising out of fear of what it can bring. Something nags at the edge of my mind, still forgotten. I have a feeling if Hunter uses that staff it's going to backfire on him. Yes, undead might run rampant, but they won't be controlled by necromancy."

Nodding my head, I understood what she meant, I too felt the unrest in the land and the draw of the undead.

"That staff seems like it's a God's staff, but I think it's a bind to something much darker. There are stories here in Silvertine of a cave, and inside this cave the Gods cast the shadows and horrors that roamed the world at its birth. The very beings that ruled an entropy world. Clearing the land of its devastation the Gods began creating us, the Ancients, their first creations." I told her, recalling its simple story. "It's said that if those creatures were to ever break free that death and decay would spread rapidly across the land bringing it back into pure chaos."

"A land of pure entropy... A place with no life or death, only chaos, and devastation..." She said almost mimicking my words.

"Yeah. The Gods and their magic keep them in their prison. That being said, Daes' magic has been fading since Alecien's fall, I'm sure those are the creatures Hunter talks about summoning."

"So what do we do?" She asked anxious to finish our task so we could move on. Sitting up I gently placed her on one of the various colored pillows.

"Right now **we** can't do anything." I said putting emphasis on the we. "You can't open the portal when you're brooding, your cycle will kick in here in a day or two and we will be useless until it passes. However, we can place things in motion to get everything setup for afterwards." I said, hinting towards preparing the Wolves for battle with the Vampires, again putting them at war.

This time though they would have the help of Aeralain. Already the Lunar Plane Wolves were allied with Drake and his people. Raven had already made herself known to Lord Drake and from her behavior was interested in him.

Raillyn catching my thoughts tipped her head curiously at me. "Who's Raven?" She asked while reaching for my memories.

An image of the small-framed Werewolf from the Lunar Plane entered my mind. Her long loosely curled hair, black as night hair proved true to her name, while her bright hazel eyes and petite pixie-like face gave her an innocent appearance. However, she was far from innocent. I had seen her fight and her small frame gave her an advantage, allowing her to move more swiftly. Accompanied with her duel short swords, she was a deadly force.

"Lord Cyrin had arranged marriage for Drake and her before his death. However, that was never shared and was too dangerous to reinstate, until now." I said hinting and showing that Drake and her had been mated. "Her personality is very bubbly when she's in a good mood, but dark when she's angry. Sort of like you." I teased her while I showed her of my earlier encounter of Raven.

For a moment Rai paused, saddened, but quickly that changed to relief and happiness. Stretching and going to her knees she lifted her arms above her head, moving like she was made of water, so fluid and graceful. Her hair lay in disarray around her head, but she was beautiful. Going to my knees I ran my hands up her sides, I couldn't resist. Sighing I felt she wanted to get the encounter with Lord Drake over with. Before saying anything, she leaned forward and kissed me.

"I think we should get dressed and go explain ourselves to your mother and father." She said pulling the information of my adoptive parents from my head. "Is that strange? You were raised by my grandmother alongside my mother?" Playfully pushing her over onto the pillows, she jokingly looked at me sternly.

"It gave me a chance to be around you, didn't it?" I retorted as she teasingly threw a pillow at me. Laughing we retrieved our clothes and dressed before going to the hall to find my parents.

Lunar Wolves ~ Raillyn

Since the halls were quiet and dim, we anticipated it was either late night or early morning. Either way I was starving and begged Alkin for food. Smiling he lead me through the halls towards the kitchen, awakening the magic lights the room sprang to life.

Its golden walls and grey stone floors gave the room a homey appearance. Two large tables sat in the middle of the room, baskets hung nearby, holding knives and utensils. Ingredients hung from the walls, herbs, meat, flowers, and other foliage were set to dry, ready for use.

"This is Solomn and Opal's kitchen. I'm sure they will be here first thing in the morning, whenever that is." Alkin said mischievously as he led me into the room and closed the door.

Releasing my hand, he went to a wood stove that stood along the wall. Its large metal surface seemed to radiate heat, indicating embers still charred within. Grabbing some logs, I watched Alkin open the latch and toss them in.

The embers protested, but Alkin was insistent. Kneeling down I felt him call his magic into his breath. Slowly he blew on the embers and they sprang to life, I felt myself smiling as I watched the flames dance around.

"Let me see what there is here." He said as he looked under the table and along a large shelf filled with baskets.

Smiling, he pulled out four rolls and a handful of greens. Searching another basket he pulled out apples. A door lay a few feet away, going to it, Alkin opened the door and walked in.

The room was a walk in frozen room. Almost carved from what appeared to be stone. Meat hung from several hooks on the ceiling, grabbing a square slab of meat came back into the kitchen and closed the door. My eyes were wide as I looked at him.

"It's an ice room carved from the surrounding peaks. Since the ground is always cold here, we can keep meat longer." He said, almost laughing. Smiling, I followed him to the table and sat on its edge. "Since you're so hungry, I plan on making you boar meat pie, it's really easy and doesn't take long to make." He said sensing my stomach rumbling.

He was right I was hungry; I had been fighting the bond so much that I had used a lot of energy when I finally gave in. kicking my feet, I placed my hands behind me and leaned back watching.

Alkin carefully cut up the meat into smaller squares and then chopped up the greens. Grabbing a bowl from below the table he placed all the ingredients together, and chopped the apples. I found myself smiling. His eyes glowed a subtle red hue as he worked. Naturally he used his magic in the way he moved and cooked, placing a little dash in every piece.

Placing the apples into the bowl, he reached for a nearby bottle. Uncorking it released its inner smell, it was blood, what kind I didn't know but I smelled the metallic twinge it carried in the air. Wrinkling my nose, I found myself unsure.

"Oh, don't react like that. I already know you have eaten with Daes at his home and in addition you ate this stuff in The Keep." He said taking note to my inner behavior.

"I just don't like the smell of that blood. Can we cook with any blood?" I asked wondering if even our own could be used in meals.

Alkin paused catching the thought. "Yes, we can cook with any blood, even our own. But I am not cooking with ours right now. It would only cause issues and would give us less time to prepare. When you're not brooding, it's more of a comfort to use our own blood." He said recalling my younger days when I was determined to heal him.

"Yeah, my father knows about that by the way." I said as Alkin laughed and mixed the food together with the blood mixture before adding flour.

"I know, I'm sure he's not thrilled but oh well. Hand me that pan." He said as he showed me mentally which one he needed.

Turning I found it easily hanging on the nearby wall. Hopping off the table, I grabbed its cool metal surface and handed it to him. Making an action as if to grab me I teasingly stood my ground, holding the pan above my head.

"The faster this goes into the oven, the faster you can eat." He teased back.

Feeling defeated I handed him the pan. *All I wanted was a kiss,* I thought to myself, knowing he would catch it. Pretending to not hear my mental complaint he ignored me and poured the mixed ingredients into the pan and placed them in the oven.

Watching intently the fires seemed to lick the bottom of the pan, as Alkin pushed it further back with a long wooden spatula. Looking at me and closed the door, reaching for his mind, it was quiet. He was planning something.

Turning, he grabbed my wrist and pulled me into his arms. I squealed playfully as he kissed me and I felt myself melt into him. His hands slipped down my body and across my thighs. His muscles flexed before he lifted me into his arms. Naturally I encircled him with my legs and he set me on the table. *This was how it all began,* crossed my mind as I inwardly smiled. I felt him smile as well while he ran his hands up my leg.

Suddenly the kitchen door opened, I felt myself jump as Darcia entered the room. Her Elvin face framed with short white blond hair, and ocean blue eyes, met mine. Alkin growled lightly due to the disturbance and leaned his forehead against my head. Darcia didn't seem to care. Instead, she folded her arms and stood waiting. Kissing my cheek he stood upright.

"Darcia." He said nodding his head towards her "I assume good morning is in order?" He half stated, half asked. A laugh from the hall made him pause, it was Opal and Alkin realized it also.

"You don't even know what time it is, do you?" She questioned as she came to stand in the doorway.

Staring at the ceiling, I felt myself smile. Then my cheeks burned red as I blushed from our recent behavior. Leaning into Alkin, I buried my face into his chest.

"I wondered if Raillyn was Callina's mother. You were so secretive about it, but I remember how you two acted when she was young. Even then you could see the bond you two shared." Opal said as she came to stand beside us.

Sitting upright, I looked her in the face and smiled. Alkin stepped back momentarily before turning to check the food. Grabbing the long wooden spatula he pulled the food out. My mouth watered, it appeared undercooked, but the scent of apples, and rosemary meat, mixed with the blood and greens smelled delightful. I hoped it was done.

Placing a fist to my lips I tried to hide my anxiousness. I bit my lip, pulling at the skin hopeful. Opal noticed my behavior regardless, and so did Darcia.

"She's brooding?!" Darcia almost shouted, causing me to look at her alarmed.

"Oh, stop scaring the poor child." A voice said at the door. "So, are we to expect any more grandchildren?" He asked, half teasing.

Looking around Opal, I saw Solomn leaning against the doorway. His relaxed posture reminded me of a serpent as it watched events around him unfold. Darcia didn't seem to relax instead she looked between Opal and me, open-mouthed and distressed.

"Lighten up, Darcia. Regardless of what they want, a week is plenty of time to get the portal open and Daes' power back in the world, the sooner, the better." Opal said as Alkin divvied up the food into five bowls. I was thankful he made enough with more to spare. Handing out the dishes I sat and played with my food.

"We don't plan on another for that very reason. She doesn't peak till tomorrow or so, were hoping to get the Wolves to prepare for an attack against the Vampires before then. Either way we're racing the clock, and will only have a week, minus a few days on our end." Alkin said while rubbing my arm.

I was saddened by the thought of missing this chance for a baby, though I fully understood and agreed with it. *Now is not the time, later would be much better.* I thought, giving myself comfort.

"We will have all the time in the world after the portal is opened, to have babies. Speaking of babies would you mind if I asked Opal and Solomn to take care of Callina for us?" He mentally asked. Giving him a mental smile, I indicated it was fine by me.

Not wanting him to worry I took a bite of food. It tasted good. The meat was undercooked just right to still give it a juicy flavor. The rosemary it had been soaked brought out the apples perfectly. Smiling, Alkin handed me a roll, I couldn't help but smile back.

"Mother, I was wondering if you and father would mind caring for Callina while Raillyn and I dealt with everything going on this week." Alkin asked, already knowing the answer.

Opal's eyes lit up as she grinned from ear to ear. Turning towards her mate, I knew they were talking mentally about the possibility. Solomn sighing made me laugh a little, my grandmother would get her way, whether he was on board or not.

"Yes, we would love to. This will give you some time to get what you need done and not worry about her. Plus in a day or so it will give you the alone time you will need." She said excitedly. Darcia shrugged and eyed me. Finishing the food, I placed the bowl on the table and leaned back.

"So when did you two have Callina? If I may ask?" Darcia questioned curious to know more about how things lead up to now.

"It was when I resided in The Keep, as Raihanna. Truthfully I gave him no choice." I said while smirking and meeting Alkin's eyes.

Returning my smile he smirked. "Oh, you gave me a choice, I just didn't agree with the other option you left me with."

He said leaning forward kissing me, our lips lingered momentarily before he pulled back.

Looking up into his ever changing eyes, I felt myself give him a stern look, half smiling. I felt it, the ticking hands of my cycle wanting to take control of my mind and body again. We needed to hurry. I wasn't sure how long I could stay sane with this growing feeling. Thankfully right now it was only a dull ache, like the first flutters of a heating heart. I knew though it would get worse.

"Before you leave I think you two should go bath, either alone or together; I don't care. You two reek of so many things. If you walked in Silvertine like that, no one would care. But, I have a feeling it might upset the Wolves. They don't seem as open about such things." Opal said, reminding me of their more proper ways.

Smiling, I looked at Alkin mischievously as I hoped off the table and let him lead me through the door and into the hall.

Drake ~ Raillyn

Alkin was taking no chances as we teleported together into the small den south of my old chambers. It felt strange returning after what happened. Returning bound to another man. He held me close to him, regardless of our bath an hour ago, we still reeked.

It was my fault. My brooding was getting closer and closer to its peak and I would smell until it passed. Since Alkin and I had bonded, he would carry a heightened scent also. This was neither a safe nor a good time to be away from home. Already I was feeling the light burn begin to build in my core.

Holding my waist, he led me into the hall as we searched for Drake. The familiar red carpet, with yellow walls, made me smile fondly. It was like seeing an old friend after being apart for a long time. Almost seven years had passed since I walked these halls, *seven years this spring to be exact.*

"Has it really been that long?" I questioned out loud as we walked the empty halls of the northern portion.

"Yes, it has, our youngest's name day is next month, I can't believe she will be four and your oldest will be turning seven this spring." He said mimicking my thoughts.

As we approached a corner the familiar presence of Howl filled my mind. I heard his smooth voice talking, before I heard Droggen reply and Saibal agree. Then a new voice entered the mix the soft melodic tone of a female, her words seemed to hang in the air as she spoke in a high but very feminine tone.

"You know my men will be more than willing to work with yours, Saibal. I will speak to Avice as soon as she arrives with the rest of my troops so you two can work together assembling them. Howl, will you still move your house to my father's land so we can get them here quicker? If we..." She said as we rounded the corner.

Howl leaned casually against the wall, the only one relaxed amongst them, the others stood tense. Bright hazel eyes met mine as blackish blue hair bounced around the slender girls face. Her big eyes appeared wide in shock as she stopped mid-sentence. Glancing at Droggen and Saibal she seemed unsure. Turning they looked for her distress.

"Raillyn?" Droggen said, shocked, as Alkin released me from his grasp and allowed me to go to my friends. Mentally I still felt him keeping tabs but he was not possessive with these people. Nothing was setting his nerves off, at least not yet.

"Lady Raillyn." Saibal said while looking towards Droggen unsure how to react. Thankfully Howl knew what to do and withdrew from his relaxed posture on the wall.

"My little honey bun has returned." He said opening his arms wide and taking me into a deep embrace. I couldn't help but laugh out loud at his comment.

Alkin found it humorous as well and snickered behind me. He knew Howl was not a threat to me, Ayana was his mate and while he hadn't gone to her, he knew where she was. Unintentionally I reached for that information since I knew Alkin was uneasy here. Howl smiled, knowingly before scrunching his eyebrows together.

"I'm surprised you choose to come right now, you reek." He said, noticing my cycle. The Wolves looked at me unsure, as they too noticed something off about me.

"We're not going into that, right now, it's already been a long day." I said reprimanding him gently. This was neither the time nor place to talk about my personal problems. "Where's Drake?" I asked him, cutting to the chase.

"Umm..." Droggen began while biting his lip.

"He's in Silvertine speaking to Geirolf, leader of the Lunar Plane wolves." Turning Howl indicated towards Raven. "This is his daughter, Raven Koray." He said as Raven bowed tentatively.

"It's a pleasure to meet Daes' Mystic. I have heard many things about you and if I might be so bold say we share a few similarities." She said cordially. Reaching for Alkin, I asked if he knew what she meant.

"I've heard rumors but that's it. Ask her and we shall see I guess." He replied.

Looking into her hazel green eyes I asked. "What do you mean by similarities?" Looking to Droggen and Saibal I could tell they already knew.

Raven bowed her head slightly, her blackened hair fell into her face. "My mother was a Mystic of Delron. It was her first cycle and didn't expect it to feel so overpowering. She ran from her mate after he claimed her and met my father. One-thing lead to another and… Well, you know." She said shrugging.

"So what happened?" I asked curiously.

"She returned to her mate only to discover she carried me, they kept it a secret, unsure if I belonged to my father or her mate. She didn't know what she carried. After I was born I clearly was wolf and my mother was forced to return me. My mother and her mate stayed for fifteen year. My father went onto having a son with another Wolf and my mother has a son with her mate. He's of Delron's lineage, Dryten, I don't know if you know him." Turning I looked at Alkin, the name seemed familiar but he hadn't actually met him before just knew who he was.

For some reason, I wasn't surprised at the amount of information she gave me. She was from Aeralain. She probably respected the Ancient races. Especially Mystics, and like our God kin her race answered to them willingly.

"I'm sorry we couldn't meet earlier and hope you don't mind. My father and Lord Cyrin had an agreement before his death. However after speaking to Chancellor Droggen, we found he never told anyone." She looked at him annoyed. "I brought the documents and notes they had written back and forth over the years as proof." Raven sighed sounding exasperated.

From just the few minutes, I had spoken to her I was beginning to see her personality. She was raised as an heir, ready to lead, give orders, organized and stubborn when people didn't listen. Raising my eyebrows she must have taken it the wrong way, she crossed her arms in front of her angrily.

"I looked over everything; it's all Lord Cyrin's handwriting. I even showed it to Drake and Briar and they both agree. Apparently Lord Cyrin was seeking allegiance with the Lunar Plane wolves for help in eradicating the Vampires and securing the shaky peace that presided after the war. Most of the documents are from just after the war up until Drake's twenty-sixth name day, when his father died. Talk of an arranged marriage was even brought up between Drake and Raven since Drake refused to take a mate after his mother's death. The last letter Lord Cyrin wrote said that he would speak to his son after the attack on the Renegade. However, nothing was said because Lord Cyrin died during the attack. No word was sent and in turn no word was replied." Droggen stated nervously as if I might become upset.

For some reason, I found this funny. Raven and her strong-willed personality and Drake's was an excellent combination. His father probably thought so also. Giggling. Alkin caught my thoughts. He seemed pleased I wasn't upset about the situation and instead found humor in it. Beginning to laugh, I leaned against the wall for support.

"You're not mad?" Saibal asked curiously.

Placing my hands to my face, I took a sighing laugh, trying to calm my behavior before it turned erratic. Sighing again, I noticed a change in the air but didn't think much about it. Turning towards the wolves, I smiled wholeheartedly.

"No, I'm not mad, in fact, I'm a little relieved. Drake is a good man, he's a strong leader. He's caring, loving, and funny, you name it, and he's really just overall a nice person. But while I admit I love him it's not in a mate way. It's different, I can't explain it. With Alkin I feel a deep connection that runs to my very soul, it's comforting and I'm never left wondering what he's thinking or going to do. Instead, I just know. Truthfully it was a little unnerving with Drake, not knowing what he was thinking or what he was planning. I'm happy to hear he has a headstrong mate to keep him in order." I said as a fit of giggles took over.

"You will have to excuse her behavior, she's not herself today. The reason she keeps laughing is because she think your personalities are perfect for each other." Alkin said as he left his spot along the wall and took me into his arms.

Turning I rested my cheek on his chest and took in his scent. Smiling, my senses seemed tickled and I couldn't help but bury my face further. My hearing heightened and my senses narrowed, attuned to Alkin. My body quivered slightly as I realized the first waves of my cycle were hours away.

Sweat beaded on my forehead as I felt it try and capture my mind. Already I was feeling its effects. Looking up and meeting Alkin's gaze, I knew he sensed it also. Raven giggled slightly behind me, turning slightly I met her eyes and tipped my head curiously.

"You're a brave one, leaving Aeralain, let alone Silvertine, like that." She said teasingly and giggly. "My mother was terrible when she brooded. I can't tell you how thankful I am, not having to worry about that like my mother." She said on a calmer note, almost matter of fact.

It was strange being around an outspoken female who was used to Ancients in Alecien. Looking at her face, I knew mine was beet red as I blushed in embarrassment. Raven stood redfaced fighting a smile and I found myself laughing suddenly at her behavior.

"Well, I'm glad to see you two getting along so soon." Said a familiar voice behind Alkin.

Turning simultaneously Alkin and I looked at Drake. His black hair was free and hung lightly over his shoulders. His vivid green eyes seemed to sparkle. It was odd seeing Drake, I felt unsure how to react or even what to do. Drake approached and for a moment I thought him and Alkin would argue. Alkin's familiar touch reassured me. *I have spoken to him about the situation, while he doesn't know yet you are bound to me, he knows you are my mate.* Alkin released me and stepped back to allow Drake and I to talk.

"So you've heard my father wanted me to consent to an arranged marriage?" He asked seemingly curious to hear my thoughts on the subject. "And that I agreed?"

I didn't know what to say and stood stuttering for a moment. "Ahh... You heard all that didn't you?" I asked knowingly. The look in his eyes gave it away. He had been there the whole time listening.

"Will you walk with me?" He asked extending his arm. Unsure I felt myself reach mentally for Alkin as well as turning to look physically at him. He nodded his head. *"Go, you two have much to talk about."* Smiling I nodded back and gently reached out, taking Drake's arm.

"Wait till we're on the balcony to speak." He whispered into my ear.

Silently I let him lead me through the halls, through the small den and out onto the balcony. It was early night here, the darkened skies were dotted with the last rays of sun. Oranges mixed with deep purple as it went black and stars appeared one by one.

Drake seemed different, older. He wasn't pretending to be funny or play around instead he walked with authority and maturity. It was strange, and his nature made me feel uncomfortable.

For a moment I felt off balance, my magic shifted and so did my mood. It was confusing, one moment I felt like I was dripping wet and the next I felt bone dry. Feeling myself panic sweat began to run down my face. Shakily I went to my knees to prevent any further change, hoping this wasn't the first ill effects of what was to come.

Instantly I felt Drake's arms around me. They were strong, muscular, but they were not Alkin's I didn't feel the love from them as I did with his. Instead I felt nothing. Meeting his eyes, I felt tears run down my face.

"I'm sorry." I said crying into his shoulder. "I'm so sorry, I do love you but I can't feel like myself around you. I feel only half of who I am..." I admitted while the tears continued to streak my face. Being around Drake, I hadn't embraced the Mystic way of life, one that I was sheltered from as a child. Now that I had seen it and was exposed to its freedom while I lived in The Keep and recently in Silvertine, there was no doubting how I felt.

"It's not your fault, don't think it is. Neither of us were prepared for how Mystics really lived, and no one knew my father had already set up an arranged marriage for me. I was hesitant to agree though. I didn't want you hurt if I said yes. Plus we haven't had much time to talk since you returned from The Keep. Truthfully I didn't know what to expect or what to tell our daughter. However, I had to do what was right for our people, Deestan told me that. So I agreed..." He said while he brushed my hair affectionately. "I will always love you, but you are bound to Alkin, he is your mate and I feel terrible already for what happened. You were ripped away from so much as a child, I don't want to stand between you and what you are entitled to." He said stating my Mystic heritage.

"Figures she would say that, she's a very smart girl... Just so you know I will always love you too, and we can always be friends. I want you happy, and I think Raven can make you happy. As far as Deestan, we can make it work. If you don't object, I would like her to study in Silvertine as well as here. If you still intend on her taking the throne, it will be good for her to know the old ways as well as Alecien's." I said nervous on Drake's thoughts about our child. He seemed startled for a moment.

"Of course I would still let her take the throne, that is as long as she wants it. She is first born, it's her birthright, and nothing will take that from her. Also, if you want her to visit Silvertine I'm sure we can make it work. Howl doesn't plan on removing his portal from here so she can use that." He said as grief and understanding filled my mind.

Tears rolled down my face. I was happy, sad, grief-stricken, and I didn't know what else all at once. Emotionally I was a mess. Taking a deep breath I tried to stop myself from crying, overall I was so thankful for Drake and so heartbroken I couldn't love him.

He was my last connection to my prior life, to my life living with Chaimh. In a way, I felt that letting go of him was saying goodbye to that life forever. Like a part of you died and would never return.

Gasping for air between sobs, I felt terrible and to make matters worse my stomach ached. Gently Drake pulled my arm over his head and swept me off my feet. Cradling me, he walked us to a nearby table and chairs. Silently I sniffled in his arms. Gently he helped me in the chair moments before I felt Alkin's presence. He stood by one of the columns near the door.

Instantly my tears stopped and my vision focused on him. Already I smelled his scent and felt my pupils dilate. My stomach growled. I was hungry again even though I had eaten just a few hours ago. Releasing me, Drake stepped back as if unsure what to do.

"Don't worry, you're ok." Alkin said leaving his spot and coming towards me. "I just felt she was having some issues and we still have business here before we can return home." He said reaching his hand towards my face.

His hand hummed and radiated heat, it was invigorating and hair rising. Placing it upon my cheek, it radiated down my neck and through my core. It felt as if I touched fire, but it didn't burn. Instead it warmed. Relaxing I felt my mind shift back into balance. Taking a big sigh, I blinked my eyes several times.

Alkin leaned down and laid his forehead against mine. "Just a little longer and we will return to Silvertine and I'll get you some food before we relax. I know you're hungry." Gently he kissed me before standing again.

"If you two are hungry I can have the maids bring some food." Drake said politely. Alkin shook his head.

"While we appreciate the offer, she won't be able to stomach Alecien food right now. She's brooding and we don't have much time." Alkin said matter of fact like.

I knew he was right. I had spent too long in The Keep with the rich Drakar cooking of Nora and Alkin. My body had become accustomed to its sweet flavors and exotic nature, and right now it craved it. Even thinking about the bland Alecien food I had grown up on soured my stomach.

Drake looked at me curiously as I saw his nose twitch. He was taking in my scent. Understanding crossed his face as he looked at Alkin.

"What are your plans with the Vampire's now that Raven is here? Or better yet what are your overall plans altogether?" Alkin asked getting straight to the point.

"Our plan is to attack Hunter in the next few days and try and dismantle the portal, so he can't summon any more creatures into this world." Drake replied. "As far as altogether I don't know beyond that right now. Why?"

Alkin paced for a moment. I caught his thoughts and shared his concern. *If the Wolves attacked Hunter now, it might cause more problems.*

"Can you hold off on the attack? Say an extra day or so?" Alkin questioned tossing numbers around in his head.

We had five days, six tops to get the portal open and the staff away from Hunter. That was if everything went well and no issues occurred. Drake seemed to weigh his choices.

"I'm sure we could hold off a few more days. It will give Raven more time. She's already stressed about fully integrating Avice and her troops into ours. While we're the same race, we have very different views." Drake stated as Alkin caught something he wasn't saying.

"And?" he asked. *Sounds like Aeralain...* I thought for a moment. "What are the terms of this agreement, if I may ask?" Alkin went on, I was curious to know more, suddenly wanting to create a controlled chaos. Mentally Alkin chuckled, catching my thought, and shook his head.

"Just that I will allow the Aeralain tribes to establish trade and packs with our people, in addition there were several who showed interest in returning if the Vampire problem was taken care of. I hate saying it, but this is the perfect opportunity to kill a few birds with one stone." Drake said while smiling.

"What's Deestan think of Raven?" I asked curiously. I wanted to see my girls so bad, but I knew until the portal was open it wasn't safe.

Drake smiled. "She likes her, finds her interesting that they both have something in common. I often find Raven staying up late and talking to her in bed. They share stories and Raven treats her like a daughter." Compassion filled his voice and a smile spread across my face.

Tears filled my eyes as I realized something. *Raven with Drake was good, it felt right. Already Deestan had been happy to be back with her father, now she had a stepmother who loved and cherished her.* She had stability in the unstable world of my Ancient blood. *The path we're on is the right one.* My soul sung as my emotions and magic resonated in harmony.

"Good. I'm glad to hear that. Hold off your attack for us, we will return and help as soon as possible but we will be indisposed for a few days." I said indicating what he probably already smelled and suspected.

"That sounds fine. The day after we will begin to move our troops towards the portal, I'm sure by the time we get there you two will be able to join us. I will be happy when this is over and those Vampires are gone." He stated. Alkin and I mentally couldn't help but agree.

Our Time ~ Drake

Going to find Raven, I left the balcony, and walked through my room. Carefully I avoided the table that Raven and I had pulled into the middle of the room to work, and sidestepped around the paper, inkwell, and pens we had scattered about. Opening the hall door, I heard Raven's melodic voice talking to Deestan. Hearing the two of them made me smile. They had become good friends lately, and Deestan began to confide in her.

"I heard my mother was here... Are the whispers true? Is she?" I heard Deestan question.

My hand grasped the cold metal door handle and gently pushed it open. The girls turned and looked at me as I entered the room. Raven's black hair fell into her face as a worried gaze met my eyes. She looked unsure how to answer Deestan's question.

Sighing, I went to sit next to them. Raven sat on the edge of Deestan's bed like they did every night. It became routine for Raven to put her to bed. Usually they read, but tonight I could tell they decided to talk instead.

"It's not Raihanna, if that's what you mean." I said cautiously. Still unsure if she meant Raillyn, or the imitation who cared for her in The Keep.

My daughter nodded her head, chin set strong, and face solid. She seemed to be contemplating my words and their meaning. "Raillyn..." She whispered. "That's what everyone said, and that it's been six years since she was last here. I want to see my real mother." She almost begged.

Thinning my lips, I sighed and looked at Raven. "I'm sorry baby, your mother thinks it's best if she stays away till everything is safe. There are nasty things in the world and she doesn't want them to hurt you." I said truthfully. I was sure Raillyn wanted Deestan safe and these creatures Hunter wanted to summon were pure evil. She wouldn't want these creatures to find their way to her family.

Deestan turned her face upwards in that stubborn chin expression, and sternly said. "I know of unspeakable horrors. I grew up in The Keep with those Vampires. I know how horrible it can be." She said reminding me that even though she appeared to be a little girl mentally she was mature for her age. *Alkin and Rai had raised her like her sister, as a Mystic.* I thought to myself as I sighed.

"I know." I said gently reaching my hand out to brush her strawberry blonde hair behind her elf-like ears. "However there are worse things than Vampires. Creatures that the Vampires think they can control. However, the truth is I don't think anyone can control them. Your mother is trying to stop these creatures from breaking free and coming into the world." I said trying to tell her half the truth. "When everything is better she'll visit, when she's sure everything is safe, and no harm will come to you for being here."

Raven reached out and clasped her hand in mine, smiling fondly between me and my daughter.

"Ohh, alright." Deestan finally said before snuggling down into her bed and pulling the green sapling designed quilt to her chin.

Slowly I leaned down and kissed the top of her head before standing and eyeing Raven. Carefully she did the same, whispering "I love you" into Deestan's ear. My face beamed as I smiled down at them. Glancing at me Raven stood, taking my hand and smiling back. Saying my own, "I love you" to Deestan we quietly made our way to the door.

Quietly we made our way to my room, our room now, before saying anything out loud. As the door closed, Raven spoke. "I wish she could see her mother, it breaks my heart that she asks every night for her and every night I have to tell her no." She said while embracing me and burying her face into my chest.

"I know and I don't know how to approach it either. I know Raillyn doesn't want to endanger her..." I said trailing off and pulling Raven's chin up so her eyes met mine. "All we can do is wait and try and end this as soon as we can." I said before leaning down and kissing her on the lips.

Moments Reprieve ~ Alkin

Our home was along the southern steep which overlooked the lower region of the Turbid Still. We had bid Drake farewell moments ago and I had pulled her through a portal towards home. She was thankful how the situation turned out for Drake and Deestan. Drake had even said after the portal was taken care of we would talk further on the details.

"I've been to our home before, haven't I?" Raillyn questioned me, recalling when she teleported to it while seeking me out. I couldn't help but smile.

"Yes you have been there before, but I don't think you remember it very well, you were a little preoccupied at the time." I whispered into her ear causing her to blush and smile as I recalled the events myself.

"It's not my fault you're distracting." She teased back.

Many Drakar came and went, some seemed surprised to see us, and shock crossed their faces. Most were busy going about their own business to notice. It still made me nervous, and I kept Raillyn close to my side. It was a rare sight to see a Mystic, let alone Daes' last, and everyone in the city would know her at first sight. Evening was the busier time of day; if my other plan worked we would explore the city tonight, before retiring in our home.

The simple wooden buildings that stood around us lined every street, this was the market district, food was sold here. The textile district was fancier than this, most of the local artists had decorated it with their wares, or students donated their time and studies to do repairs. Some even designed new more exquisite sculptures, buildings or art. This was how our city was run.

Students often took apprenticeship under the merchants, temples, or archives owners. Very few were allowed to take apprenticeship under city leaders or elders, those who did were considered to possess a special skill which only could expand in such a situation. Later these students would take up the trade they studied under. They were our future, our leaders, hunters, crafters and suppliers.

Rounding a corner, I saw our home. Most of the houses in this area seemed to appear almost hive-like, dome buildings built from trees, wood and other items from nature. Raillyn's eyes met mine as I felt her excitement boom. In that instant, she knew which house was ours. Her eyes lit up as she smiled at me. Slowly, arm in arm, we approached the elegantly carved door, her curiosity grew.

Long ago after I had left Opal and Solomn's home for one of my own, I decided I wanted an Elvin-styled house. I hired the best woodcarvers for the job, and the door spoke how meticulously carved it was. Leaf, vine and flower patterns weaved around the door in circular patterns. The handle was a single vine with slight leaves.

Placing my hand on the familiar surface, I felt the magic within react. Recognizing my presence it granted me entrance, but before going in gently I placed Raillyn's hand on the door. She looked at me surprised as the magic danced across her skin and searched deep within her.

Waiting, I spoke the words to allow her permanent access, even when I was not home. The door and her hand flared momentarily red in color as it accepted her. The magic within would recognize her blood and power from now on. Grasping the intricate leaf handle, I opened the door and lead them in. Even within, the house was dome like. The main room was a vast chamber with tree-like rafters, vines and a banister.

The banister twined upwards tree-like forming a staircase, that spiraled into the smaller region of the top dome. Here the bedrooms lay, doors on the outer walls gave way to additional unseen space. Each room was decorated with a vine tree-like bed, tendrils held up canopies, lights decorated the room in the elegance of nature. The kitchen, workshop, baths and study were connected much the same, but on ground level. My room, our room, lay on the top-most floor. That I would save for last.

Raillyn looked around, I felt her excitement and saw it on her face. Going towards the fireplace, she paused at the table, running her fingers over its hard surface. She recognized the room, the table, chairs, and the location of all the doors from her last visit.

"Glad to see someone didn't let the blood stain its surface." She said before returning to my embrace and kissing me deeply, fully catching me off guard.

Full-heartedly I returned her kiss, her sheer joy to the fact that this home filled her mind. To Raillyn everything was perfect. Releasing me, she smiled before peeking into the kitchen and the smaller rooms dotting the lower chamber.

Climbing the stairs, I stayed close, not wanting her to go past the second floor to our room. That I wanted to be saved till later, when the moon was up and the stars were out. It had been meticulously created, unconsciously with her in mind, and it had become my gift to her. It was our sanctuary of calm and peace in the chaos that we now shared together.

The doors were all open and each room resembled the other. I had planned this out as well, not wanting any future children to squabble over something being different or better in their mind than a sibling. A large tree-like bed sat in the middle with vines running up its four large posts, holding a white canopy overhead. A bookshelf, table and chair sat along the adjacent wall while a chest sat at the foot of the bed. Two tall windows lined the eastern wall to bring in the light from a newly risen morning sun.

Smiling I felt Raillyn's curiosity peek as she turned towards the stairs. Slowly I pulled at her, bringing her gently away and kissing her again. Already it was so hard to keep my hands off her, I craved just being in constant contact with her and she mine. However, I didn't want her cycle to control us. I wanted to treasure our moments together, and court her properly. Even if it was just a little.

"Not yet. That I want to show you tonight, after we have had something to eat." Smiling I pulled her against me, it was difficult to resist her presence so close to mine. She was still unbalanced, but I had endured this feeling since I had first brought her into The Keep, I could continue to do so until she was ready.

Naturally she leaned into me further. Memories of her mother and father flashed across her vision. She knew how she felt was natural, and it was reassuring to her. Placing her hands on my chest, she looked up into my eyes.

"So what is there to eat?" She said touching my thoughts.

Brushing her cheek with my thumb, I was half tempted to steal a kiss on her puckered lips again, but decided against it. We already walked a precarious line.

"Truthfully, I was going to suggest we go out into the city tonight. I'm sure a few of my old friends wouldn't mind making a meal for us." I said while smiling down at her.

Instantly I felt the gentle pull between us, she was searching my intentions, not wanting to hide anything from her I left my whole mind open. Satisfied she kissed me gently.

"Ok let's go see the city. It will be nice. Daes wants me to relax and allow my magic to finish realigning." She said while taking in my scent.

She knew this was the only time I could give her total relaxation, no worries for tomorrow or any duties we might face. This would be our time and I was going to make sure she was happy. Laying my cheek upon her head, we relaxed for a moment.

Our Time ~ Raillyn

Alkin lead me out into the city. Looking at the perfect night sky, darkness had fallen while we were exploring the house. Magic lights illuminated the streets, different areas of the city had different color lights, red, white, green, and blue, the colors of what I knew now as the primary magic colors, the God's magic.

Brushing Alkin's mind revealed that the Drakar were very focused on the Gods and serving them appropriately, they would never deny a request from their God or a Mystic of their lineage. I was beginning to understand life outside Alecien was very different, more relaxed and bound to the old ways.

It made me sad how much I loved it, and thankful for this reprieve. All too soon we would have to continue our work, open the portal and pray for a good outcome. I ignored those feelings, tonight was our night and I wanted to see how life was in Silvertine. How life was supposed to be for us.

We entered the market district and small shops lined the bright cobbled stone streets, this region seemed to have all four different colored lights. It seemed magical and I felt the city's magic dance in everything around. One small stall caught my eye, it had jewelry of all kinds. But the thing that stopped me was the gentle pull of magic.

Even from where we stood a few feet away I felt its gentle tug. Something there was calling me. I didn't have to speak a word, Alkin slowly lead me through the light crowd, to the stall. Immediately I saw it, a small blue charm, with a tear drop stone and silver chain. For a single moment I felt my eyes shift to mimic its color, Alkin took note of the slight shift and picked up the amulet bringing it closer.

He spoke to the shopkeeper about it, but I barely made out what they were saying, my full attention was to the necklace. Without a word, Alkin handed the man four gold coins, an outrageous amount for any item in my mind. His reaction was just as shocking, he smiled and slightly laughed.

"I gave him extra." He said mentally, as he clasped it around me. It hung perfectly and almost mimicked the necklace, which I knew Alkin kept hidden beneath his shirt, next to the mark I had placed on him long ago in The Keep. His amulet held a stone red, mine blue, each another reminder of our lineage.

Pulling me back into the small crowd, I felt a calming sensation coming from the necklace, just like the turquoise ring I wore on my finger. Each item was imbued with magic from Daes, probably from one of his dragons. As we walked, I noticed Alkin was leading us towards another large beehive-like building. It's brown sphere roof billowed with smoke as we entered it smelled wonderful.

A woman with silver hair stood behind a counter while several patrons sat at tables around what appeared to be a tavern. The bar was circular and lined the outer wall nearly all around. Rafters hung from the ceiling dark and unknowingly hiding anything that might be up there. Soft glows illuminated each table, like the gentle glow from a softly lit candle. The silver haired lady turned to see who had come in.

Immediately her face lit up, her eyes, deep red in color glowed as she slide over the bar top after shouting "Alkin's back!" through the door behind her in Drakar.

Looking at Alkin, I wasn't sure what to expect; she was excitable and quickly closed the few feet between us before coming to a stop and bowing deeply before Alkin and me. Pulling me closer Alkin smiled.

"Hello, Lena, glad to see you're doing well." He said as a man entered the room to see what all the commotion was about.

His eyes reflected pools of deep emeralds, while his hair was bright yellow, both had Elvish like features. He dried his hands on a rag as he came around the bar before stopping and nodding towards Alkin. The two men shook hands.

"It has been quite some time my friend, what can we do for you tonight?" The man said while giving me a curious look.

Lena seemed to be very curious in me and immediately reached out and took my hand, shaking it in the process. Alkin gave me a reassuring thought and nudge as he released me.

"My names Lena, I'm friends with Alkin, but it's been ages since he has been here. I'm one of Delron's Drakar, my mate and I assist Alkin when he needs the help. And…" She paused as she looked at me closer, pausing a moment on the blue amulet Alkin had just purchased for me.

One word escaped her lips as she met my eyes. "Daes." She said silently and shocked. Her mate who had been talking to Alkin paused and looked at me with surprise. I felt myself withdraw for a moment unsure what to do, physically I leaned towards Alkin and took his hand reassuringly.

The man pulled Lena towards the back room while Alkin and I followed behind them. The large room was a kitchen; fires, pots, tables and food were everywhere. It was messy but very clean at the same time. Closing the door, Lena continued.

"Why didn't you say something sooner?!" She shouted at Alkin. "Your mate is Calista and Drameon's daughter?!" she raved on as she paced the room.

Her mate laughed slightly as I mentally asked Alkin if she was ok. "Don't worry," Her mate said reassuringly. "The room is spelled so no one can hear us talk."

As she paced, she continued to rave on about the situation. "The great Alkin who swore he would never take a mate or have any girl for that matter is tied down to Daes' last Mystic." Lena said as she paused and crossed her arms waiting.

"Yes, you're right, however, stop scaring my mate, you are very eradicate today. What stirred up your scales?" He asked giving her a questioning look.

She seemed to go silent and went to stand by her mate, "We're expecting our first." He said lovingly while looking down at Lena. I felt Alkin's response before he said it.

He was surprised and happy for them. "And here you go on badgering me about my behavior, when I recall you telling me you couldn't stand children." He said teasingly.

Lena seemed to blush and fold into her mate just as I found myself doing to Alkin recently. "Things change," she said in a quieter manner. "It was the Den, the nursery, I was sent to help out for a few weeks and it triggered my brooding cycle. It was very hard to resist that temptation, and I found myself wanting a child of my own. A little life to hold in our arms and who depended on us, I wanted the love of an infant. And I wasn't going to have Ezar tell me no." She said smiling up at him. "Plus we had been talking about it before I went to the nursery to help. We knew going would disrupt things, so it just assisted in what would have happened anyway." She said hinting at the idea of mates avoiding the nurseries unless they are prepared to want a child.

Alkin confirmed this *"It can trigger magic deep within, it's part of the bond mates share. Young Ancients, such as you, are more susceptible to the magic. Think of fledglings and their hormones. Often being around infants for a long period, and not having one recently, can trigger the feeling and want to have another."* He said mentally to me. *"And you my dear are young in the terms of Ancients. I can hold my own against that magic, but I am sure you cannot, and you would place me in a difficult situation."* He said while gently nibbling my ear with his teeth.

Determination crossed my face and he felt it flow off me. "I would still like to see it, regardless. I'm not as young as you think, remember I was born before the war." I said tartly, even though consciously I only really lived for forty odd years, still... "But for now I would like something to eat, all this food in the room makes me hungry." I said smiling to him.

Lena and her mate Ezar both smiled simultaneously, "Of course my dear, there is plenty of Leeche Soup tonight. I have called our apprentices to come mind the tavern so we can eat without interruptions tonight." Lena said with a sparkle in her eye as she grabbed my hand and began leading me towards another door, Callina let go of her father's leg and followed quietly behind me.

The men stayed behind and Alkin waved reassuringly as Lena lead me into a large den room. A fireplace sat near the door and various chairs, benches and pillows dotted the room. While a large table and chairs lay close to the fire. Casually I sat on a nearby pillow and made myself at home. Lena smiled at me as she sat nearby.

"I'm so glad Alkin has you, he seems so happy." She said as I heard Alkin and Ezar coming into the room.

Ezar held a large tray with five bowls of the Leeche Soup. It was white in color but had red dots that appeared bead-like mixed in. There was also a large plate of freshly cooked bread rolls. Alkin brought us each a bowl of soup and roll before sitting down and joining us.

Tasting the soup, I discovered it was very much like the stew we ate in The Keep except it had more flavor. The sweet taste of vegetables mixed with a red herbal meat, reminded me of Daes' soup. Alkin felt my thoughts and commented. *"I will just have to teach you to cook like this."* He said mentally, while reaching down to squeeze my hand.

After finishing Alkin took my empty bowl and thanked his friends for the meal. When he returned, I sighed and thought how different the Den here might be.

Laughing slightly, he met my eyes, as a sigh escaped him. "I guess for you we should go see the Den here." My face lit up from his comment. I nearly toppled him over as I hugged him.

I had only been in the Den in The Keep or the Den near the castle with the Wolves but never one that belonged to the Ancient races. I was eager to see the differences. As I had already heard, this one had a nursery. He kissed my head as I let go and allowed him to stand.

Pulling me to my feet, we bid our friends farewell and went out into the gentle glowing streets. All was dark except for the subtle glow of the magic lights which guided our way. The streets were quiet, few people wandered their stone paths, and those who did were mostly dancers. Dressed in their icy earth-tone colored pants, skirts and tops Medallions, small coins, and beautifully colored beads, decorated the edges of the fabric.

A couple dressed similar in starlight silver pants and top, with sparkly beads reflecting nearby light approached us. In their hands were small fire sticks that seemed to pop and crackle in pretty colors. Alkin was not surprised or startled at their behavior as they handed each of us one, bowed slightly and went on their way.

Tipping my head as they left, I looked at the fire stick crackling away in deep shades of red, while Alkin's was blue. They made me smile. I could feel power deep within as if the stick and substance that caused the colors to change and flare were created with magic. "The dancers share these on clear winter nights. It is said that the Gods have a clearer view of the world on nights like these. The dancers pay homage to the Gods by sharing their light by these fire sticks." He said as they began to die down and fizzle out.

As my fire stick died out I looked at Alkin, "Do you think the Gods are watching more clearly tonight?" I asked still aware that all too soon life would return to normal and we would once more be serving the Gods in their plan.

He felt the shift of my emotions and sighed. "I'm sure they are. This gives you a break from the stress that you have been put through. More importantly it gives you a sense of the old ways and should help you better understand the Gods. So I don't think they care what we do as long as eventually we do as we're told." He said smirking as he continued to lead me along the cobblestone streets.

The dancers Den was huge here. Not only was it one large circular white hive, but three, the middle being the largest. One single door was seen along its lustrous surface. Alkin gently knocked on the door and waited. Within moments, a male dancer opened the door.

Bright blue, vibrant eyes met ours and waist-length deep red hair, lightly braided almost wrapped around his waist. Instantly I felt myself almost laugh as I remembered who he was. It was Lyth, Celeste's mate.

He leaned lazily against the door frame. "And to what do we owe a visit from Daes' little mystic?" he questioned, before going on. "Before I can let either of you in I need to make sure you are both Den mates." He said while Alkin seemed to sigh and release his hand from my waist.

"Oh, come on, Lyth, you know better." I said sarcastically. Eyeing me, he grabbed my hand.

"Yes I know however there are ears listening..." He said mentally to me. I nodded and glanced at Alkin.

Reaching into his pouch he withdrew a small silver token, it was the same dancers token which Stasha had given me in the Werewolves Den. Rummaging in my pouch, I found mine as well and showed him.

"Tell your Den master that Ratu Raillyn and Raja Alkin are here to pay homage to our Den." Alkin said carefully and tactfully.

Pulling me close as we entered the large room, I looked around. Just like the Werewolves' Den this Den was decorated in bright colors, the four colors of the Gods magic, pillows and a large fireplace lay in the middle of the room burning bright and fiercely. Various dancers, lay around the hearth, danced or were settling down for the night.

Vibrant eyes looked our way, Drakar eyes. All in various shades of red, silver, and green, very few had blue. Daes' Drakar line had even suffered when his magic left the world, remembering what Howl told me. Smiling and glancing towards Alkin I let him lead me through the room.

Two large arches lay on either side of the huge circular shaped dome. "Follow me, Den-master Droe will expect to see you." Lyth said as we walked through the large arch on the left of the room.

No one seemed bothered as we walked and entered an equally decorated room. Towards the back, kids could be heard laughing, crying and playing. We walked towards the noise, and around a corner. Lyth opened the half door and lead us in. A tall man with black-silver hair and bright silver eyes, that appeared gem like, stood holding an infant and smiling at a lady holding another baby the same size.

"Our Den master's mate bore twins earlier this week. Two of the four infants Silvertine has currently." Lyth said as he led us towards Droe.

The room appeared to be one of many; several half doors lined the room. This room, which after reaching towards Alkin's mind, indicated that this was the main room. Each age was separated. Older children, older than seven or eight, were appointed to be apprentices and went out into the city to study their arts. Children between the ages three and seven studied here in the Den, while their parents worked. Currently there were around twenty children spread out in age.

Droe's mate met my eyes as she rocked her infant, bright forest green eyes met mine as her brown hair flowed in wavy curls around her. Smiling up at us, I couldn't help but stare at the baby in her arms and smile back. Alkin grabbed my hand and pulled me close as Lyth stopped and bowed. "I bring you Ratu Raillyn and Raja Alkin." He said stating that Alkin was Solomn and Opal's child and I was his mate.

Droe extended a hand and shook Alkin's while he nodded towards me.

"So you are Alkin's mate?" Droe's mate asked curiously. "And Daes' Mystic?"

"Loren." Droe interrupted her. "I am sure all of Silvertine doesn't need to know that she is here. And I am sure Alkin would not agree with that information leaving the Den." He said.

Alkin's arms crept around me as he pulled me close.

"I'm sure half of Silvertine knows already, Droe. Information like this doesn't stay quiet for long." She said tartly as she smiled at me.

Alkin, however, raised an eyebrow at the matter. "I am sure you are right, Loren, but I would still like to try and keep that information as quiet as possible." He said while smirking and kissing the top of my head.

The infant in Droe's arms began to wail and Loren laughed as he seemed unsure what to do. He rocked the infant, but still its wails carried on. "I think she needs a new nappy." He said nervously.

"Trade me babes and I will change her." His mate said while the baby in her arms slept silently.

Reaching my hand out I gently placed it on Droe's arm, stopping him. "I'll change her if you want. That way the other one stays asleep for you."

Loren was surprised and Droe looked relieved. "The infants room is through that door. If you really want to that's fine with us." He said. "I appreciate it, I am not used to such small babies yet. I find it funny that older children don't scare me as much, but my own tiny ones frighten me deeply."

Loren and Alkin both laughed at Droe as I took the baby into my arms. "You get used to it." Alkin said as I went to change the babe.

The infant room was dimly lit; tiny carved oak cradles almost nut shaped lined the room. There were two infants in the room each rocked by an adult, who smiled and nodded to me quietly. A table sat in the room with extra nappies on it, so I went and placed a fresh one on the now happy baby.

She was content with being changed and cooed as I held her against my neck. Suddenly I felt myself missing the baby days. I was in The Keep for both my girls' infant years, never having complete freedom to snuggle and care for them the way I wanted. Thankfully Alkin hadn't been as tied up in the Elite as I was during the time and gave the girls plenty of love and attention when I was not able to. Something I regretted, but that I couldn't change.

Coming out of the room, Alkin caught my thoughts. *"Don't think about it, my dear. We will have our own time for babies later. I promise you, but for now there are other things that need taken care of."* He said reminding me of the tough situation we faced.

For a brief moment, I felt shunned and the baby seemed to react suddenly to my change in mood, crying out again for her parents. Loren reached out to take her as the cries escalated. *A reason I would not be happy not to have an infant at this time.* I thought to myself, as Alkin caught my words. *I don't feel that mentally I could handle the cries of one so demanding.* My mood was darker and I felt the balance in my soul tip towards how I felt and acted in The Keep.

Coming over and taking my hand, Alkin pulled it to his lips; I felt myself relaxing and the balance in my mind returning to its normal state. *"I think it's time we head home."* He said mentally.

Bowing my head, I thanked the Den Master. "Thank you for allowing us into your den, Droe and Loren. We hope to see you again, but it is getting late and we have an early morning."

Droe and his mate smiled. "Understandable." He said. "Mystics are often very busy; good luck in the tasks you perform for the Gods. May your light guide you." He said, bowing back at me. Loren tipped her head and smiled in return.

Alkin pulled me into his arms. "Thank you again, my friends, and we hope next time we can stay longer." He said while tipping his head and smiling.

Turning we walked back through the Den, and past sleeping dancers curled up in furs and blankets on the floor. It was like a giant snake pit, everyone seemed to be sleeping so close to each other. Approaching the main door we saw Lyth.

His red hair flowed around him as he walked towards us. "I hope all is well. Maybe next time, if you don't mind that is, we can have a little chat." He said while his blue eyes flashed brightly.

I couldn't help but laugh, he was a Drakar of Daes and being close to him helped realign my mood. I nodded my head in agreement as he went to open the door. Walking out into the dark streets, we turned to wave goodbye. "Just remember if you need anything, just ask and I will try my hardest to be of assistance to you." Lyth said before closing the door.

Our night was coming to an end and I was a little saddened about having to return to serving Daes. I just wanted a break. I just wanted a normal life for a while. Like what my parents had, but then again what I remembered was when my mother was granted her reprieve. In addition to the few months where she had returned to work, that ended in chaos.

Knowing I was following my mother's footsteps slightly frightened me. The Vampires were ruthless and as long as the portal remained closed I knew they wouldn't kill me. But after it was open was another story, I wasn't sure what would happen. This made me wonder what my mother was up to before her death. What Daes' overall plan was. *Something I will have to ask...* I thought to myself.

Alkin took note to my internal struggle and thoughts. "Yes, if you want to know more about what your mother was up to before her death, you will have to ask Daes. She never told me nor from what I know, your father. Something was amiss and needed correcting that was all I know. But, that's normal for your line. Nothing seemed strange or different from any other time your mother had a task." Alkin said as we approached the house.

The subtle glow of magic lights lit the window panes as we stopped at the door. Alkin gave me a reassuring nod and mental indication that he wanted me to open it. Smiling I laid my hand upon it and pushed my magic outwards into the door, just as Alkin had before. Already I was learning and adjusting to the Mystic way of life. Recognizing my power it clicked open and I reached down and turned the handle.

Pulling me into the room, Alkin hugged me in the crook of his arm and whispered into my ear. "Before we sleep I would like to dance with you, if that's all right." He said while I paused and looked up at him questioningly.

My thoughts went from giddy excitement to unease. "Isn't this playing with fire?" I asked him teasingly.

Laughing, I allowed him to pull me towards the stairs. "A little yes but it is something I have always wanted to do. As I said I can hold my own against my magic, it is you who has trouble."

He replied teasing me back before pulling me closer towards him. "I want you to close your eyes." He said while smirking and raising an eyebrow.

Skimming his thoughts told me he didn't want me to see the room until I was fully into it. So humoring him I closed my eyes and waited. Touching his mind again briefly, I sensed Alkin's anticipation, gently he scooped me up into his arms and we went up the stairs.

His strong arms held me tight, but also were gentle. As if gently holding onto a glass doll and frightened of dropping it. I was giddy and excited I couldn't wait to see why this place was so carefully guarded from his mind. I had seen his room as a child and remembered it vividly. So what preparations had he made in this room with me in mind?

Alkin shifted my weight and slowed his pace. Lifting his leg up, he propped me on it momentarily and used one hand to open the door. Lifting me again we moved forward a light click sound indicated the door closed. Gradually I was set my feet, Alkin's mental mind gently brushed mine, like butterfly wings. A slight smiled lit up my face as he indicated to open my eyes.

Slowly I did so and the site that struck me was amazing. The room itself was dome-like, just like I remembered and similar to the room at Daes'. The pale ivory four-poster bed with the white netted canopy sat in the middle of the room. At its end sat a large deep mahogany chest, while towards my left a matching dresser and wardrobe lay along the wall. Lastly a large bookshelf full of various sized books sat next to an intricately carved Dragon and Phoenix mantled hearth.

Two large glass paned doors sat open and led out to a balcony. From what I could hear outside there was a pond or some sort of spring. I didn't remember that as a child, but the sound trickling of water falling into a pool was calming. Looking at Alkin, I took a step further into the room. He sensed every thought that ran through my mind. It was still perfect, and I loved it!

Going out the open doors, I looked towards the sound of the water. A small natural spring sat against the balconies surface. The balcony itself appeared to have been carved out of the mountain. Deep groves ran down the side like channels guiding the water.

"If you don't remember. It's fed by a natural hot spring." He said as I began to notice a slight sulfur smell about the water. The smell I remembered and stirred memories of playing in the pool as a rebellious child.

Turning back to Alkin I immediately hugged him deeply. "I remember and I love it!" I said while opening my mind to him. "I want to make a deal with you. Since you want to dance with me, I'll agree as long as you wear your Den attire." I said deviously suddenly wanting to just have more time and not worry about what was to come.

The emotions he portrayed back were surprise and intentness. I knew he would agree, even if it was just to please me. Looking at him with determination in my eyes, I felt him give in. Taking a big breath in and sighing he smiled.

"All right, stay out here and I will go dress, but in turn you will be required to wear a Den outfit as well." He said while smirking and going into the room.

Part of me wanted to follow while another part of me ached, I watched him go to the mahogany dresser and pullout deep crimson red pants, which appeared nearly black in color. He untied the top of his shirt just below the neck and pulled it over his head. His long chestnut hair fell loosely over his face, as the muscles across his chest rippled with motion. Briefly his hair fell into his eyes, and I couldn't help but smirk. Again I thought something I had in The Keep, *what did I do to deserve him?* He was my everything and I was happy to have him. As he began to untie his pants, he looked towards me questioningly. Almost as if he caught my thoughts. Sighing I pried myself away, as well as withdrew from his mind.

Walking around gave me a sense of relief and watching the natural pool, trickle and bubble made me wonder how hot it was.

Reaching out I ran my fingers in the warm water. It felt soothing. So many things had been put into making his home, our home, perfect. Sensing Alkin's presence, I stood up and turned to face him.

He leaned against the door frame lazily, his nearly black crimson pants seemed to glisten in the light of the moon. Around his waist was a blue dancer's belt, small gold coins dotted its surface, while his chest remained bare. His hair, which looked dark in the dim light, was pulled back and secured with a leather strap. He was dressed exactly how he was when he came to the Wolves Den. Kissing the top of my head I looked up and he smiled at me.

"Go get your outfit on. I laid one out on the bed for you." He said while indicating it wasn't the outfit he hadn't wanted, but one that would do.

Looking at him curiously, he caught my thoughts. What did he mean by not the one he wanted? Closing his eyes and smirking he laughed slightly. "I had planned on acquiring you a deep blue outfit but the dancers making it are still adding the beading." He said matter of fact like.

Nodding my head I backed up and went into the room. On the bed lay a chocolate brown skirt, long belt and tiny top. The belt and top were dotted with small gold coins. Picking up the material it felt like satin, as it slipped in my grasp slightly.

Pulling off my shirt, I paused for a moment, Alkin's eyes were skyward but I felt the gentle brush of his mind ensuring my safety. *I will never escape him.* I thought to myself smiling, as I pulled off my undershirt, tossing it to the ground. Grabbing the top, I pulled the chest piece over my head, and tried to secure the small brown top around my neck and back. My stomach remained nearly bare. A fine layer of see-through material lay over it with the small coins. Pulling off my pants and pulling on my skirt made me stop for a moment.

There had been very few times in my life that I had worn anything other than pants. Not once did I think that till now, and it didn't bother me. Alkin was the first person, since Chaimh and Lillian, to get me into a skirt.

Lost in thought and trying to tie my belt Alkin's hands reached out and took it from me, securing it. As he did so I leaned down and stole my own kiss, gently on his hair. His hair smelled lightly of wood burning on an open flame. Grinning he stood upright and pulled me towards him.

We started dancing slow at first, something I was familiar with, the song of morning that welcomes and blesses the day. Smiling we moved side by side mimicking each other's steps as we moved into more upbeat dances. It had been years since I had danced, since I was with the Wolves and carried Deestan. Dancing now felt amazing. Our magic twisted and spun around us with each step, becoming a mass of swirling energy.

My head spun from the sheer amount of power we generated in the room and every sense was focused on us. Nothing else mattered. Sweat began to trickle down my face as Alkin switched pace. Brushing his mind indicated he too was caught up in the energy and power we produced. Red and blue magic twisted around us at every step, barely mixing when we danced close.

All logic was tossed aside as we danced on. He took my hands and twirled me around into his grasp. Stepping into a more dangerous more sensual beat, one that Stasha had spoken of and I had seen performed between mates. His hands ran down across my hips and down my thighs, moving the material of the dress. It slide over my body and only added to the sensation of the dance.

Naturally and instinctively I spun around Alkin as he twisted around me. This was a primal dance that invoked magic and made the bond we shared resonate in pure bliss. Again his hands tried to run down my sides and across my waist but I turned into him. Twisting this game against him I ran my hands up his chest, barely letting my nails touch the surface. Then I spun away.

Breathing heavy I felt myself began to fall into the pattern of balance. My magic attuned to my emotions. One step in front of the other I came to meet him, I could feel the magic between us. It almost seemed like it was calling to him. He twisted me around once more, until I found myself leaning into him, taking in his scent.

It was sweet the smell of nature itself on a warm spring day, yet it was mixed with mine. My heartbeat picked up pace. Before being able to stop myself I leaned forward and kissed his bare chest, lightly running my tongue over the surface. The taste of his sweat on my lips stole my breath away. My heart raced faster as I spun away from him, needing a moment away.

Pausing for a moment, I leaned my back against the wall, trying to control myself. However I was losing. Palms down, head tipped, and a foot resting near my thigh. I sat watching as my eyes followed his every move. I was lost in the energy of the power we generated, and the lingering taste of him on my lips. My mind focused purely on him and his mind said the same about me. I couldn't think about anything else, nothing else mattered.

Noticing I had stopped, he quickly spun over towards me. His chestnut hair spun along with him as his arms circled around my waist, pulling me into a deep embrace. Like butter, I melted into him. He laid kisses along my neck and shoulder, and traced the path with his tongue. Magic danced across our skin, it tingled as I felt the deep pull of my magic reaching for his.

The mark he had laid on me burned, setting fire to my chest. Each line, spiral and leaf pattern ignited in an icy flame. For a moment he pulled back, curious as to why I reached out along our mental path. I felt the fire infest his mind and try to consume him, just as it was me. Shaking his head, I could tell he tossed logic aside. Our lips met in a pure inferno, everything burned my mind went blank and equally so was Alkin's. My hands frantically began to untie his belt, as mine fell to the ground.

Wrapping my right leg around his waist I felt his left hand trace my thigh and slip under my skirt. His belt clattered loudly onto the floor, as my hands worked at his ties. The tie around my neck slipped away, just as his right hand moved towards the one on my back.

For a few short seconds, nothing else mattered to me but Alkin. His kisses traced my neck and stopped briefly, hovering above the Mystic mark he laid on me. I felt his need to taste my blood there and open his mark up with a dagger for me. Every fiber in my body reached for him, reached for that need.

A loud resonating knock sounded from the door. Briefly I felt him pull his mind out of the energy that engulfed it. He seemed to struggle for a sense of control.

"Not now." I heard Alkin say feverishly as his lips met mine once more.

Again the knock sounded, this time louder, as well as the sound of the handle jiggling.

"Solomn and Opal are in the main room and wish to speak to you." Howl's voice sounded through the closed door.

Alkin brushed the stray strands of hair away from my face and kissed me once more. Regrettably pulling back, we rested forehead to forehead trying to catch our breath and clear our minds. The energy continued, beckoning us to keep going, but I knew we couldn't.

Like a fog leaving an open harbor in the morning light. Alkin was able to bring his mind and magic back into control within a few short moments. Me on the other hand. I felt the rage of power rake its way through my soul and mind. Shaking with shock and the overall feeling of what the power brought on. I was supposed to be resting and this wild magic didn't help matters.

Releasing my leg, he sensed my thoughts. "How do we avoid this?" I asked truthfully wishing we didn't need to.

Alkin picked my sash up off the floor and secured it to my waist as I began to retie the strap around my neck. Struggling with it, I allowed Alkin to help. As I tried to tame my hair, he reached down and retrieved his sash, placing it around his waist once more, before turning towards me.

Running his hand and thumb across my cheek, he kissed my forehead. "We avoid it for as long as we can. The portal has to be opened. It's a situation that's going to need a delicate hand and an understanding mind, for everyone involved." He said before turning towards the door.

I knew what Alkin meant. We had to fight this nagging sensation, our natural instincts and pray for a good outcome. At least until I was able to safely open the portal and we were able to take care of Hunter and the Elite.

Sighing, Alkin walked over towards the door and spoke a spell to unlock it. Curiously I reached for his mind. Unbeknownst to me until now, I caught that he had locked the door while he dressed.

"I don't dance for anyone, other than you my poppet." He said while he pulled me into his arms once more.

"And I don't wear dresses or skirts, other than for you, and now I have to go out there like this..." I said tartly in return.

Snickering momentarily, he pulled me towards the door. "You look amazing and if anyone has issues with what you wear, they can deal with me." He said as he opened it, only to reveal an irritated Howl leaning against the nearby wall.

Raising his eyebrow, he looked at curiously. "Took you two long enough, I hope I interrupted something." He said as he descended the stairs. "Come on, they want to make this quick since it's late."

Following Howl, we wound down the spiral enclosed stairs. Exiting near Callina's room along the balcony, we looked below, Opal, and Solomn stood looking up at us curiously.

"We have news that should be exciting to you two." Solomn said while smiling. "Darcia has found several books that refer to the Gods and items of power. She will be here in the morning with them. She said they might help with opening the portal sooner rather than later."

Opal eyed me questioningly as her mate spoke. Alkin and Howl descended the stairs to join them, I stood still, unsure what to do and suddenly exhausted. Slowly, taking one step at a time I went to join them. I had expended quite a bit of magic dancing and was feeling the ill effects of not being at full power. I needed rest, and food to recharge. It made me feel almost childish as Alkin pulled me into him.

The feeling of utter drainage was almost overwhelming, my head ached, and stars lightly danced across my vision. The last time this feeling encompassed me was when I was carrying Callina, in The Keep. My power had begun to wane and I over-exerted myself, causing me to lose consciousness. Almost giving Alkin a heart attack.

As I stood and lingered in Alkin's arms, I began to notice a slight change taking place deep within. My head spun momentarily and I closed everyone out of my mind. "Raillyn, are you all right?" Opal said with concern, noting my behavior.

Taking a deep breath and holding onto Alkin tighter, I felt myself slip towards unconsciousness. Worried but not surprised, Alkin anticipated this might happen and held me closer. Pushing the darkness aside, pain echoed in my head giving me a splitting headache.

"Yeah, just tired." I admitted as I laid my head against Alkin's chest. *"You are going to carry me to bed after this and let me sleep in tomorrow."* I said mentally, bringing a smile to his face.

"Of course, just let me chase these three away and I will do anything you say." He said deviously but knowing he meant well.

Gently and non-intrusive I felt Howl brush my mind only to discover I was mentally and magically drained. *"You've exhausted your energy, what have you two been doing? Have you eaten recently?"* Howl asked mentally as I felt Alkin eavesdrop in and give him a threatening look.

Opal and Solomn seemed to sense the tension in the room rise. However, I felt the need to intervene, it wasn't Howl's concern if I ate or how I expended my magic. Alkin stepped in front of me momentarily, putting himself between Howl and I.

"We might have guarded and ensured Calista's protection as if we were all siblings, but Raillyn is different. You let me worry about her for now, Howl. She might be Daes' lineage heir and I know you are obligated to protect her, but she is well protected with me. You need to back down when I'm with her and let me do my job." Alkin said staring Howl down.

Looking across towards Solomn and Opal they stood quiet, unsurprised. Alkin's natural instincts were raging inside him. Telling him I needed to be protected, and it put his senses on edge knowing I was close to my cycle.

"Is she protected from you? Can you ensure there will be no issues that might arise to stop us from opening the portal? That's what we need to do, but in order to do that Raillyn needs to be rested and taken care of." Howl said as Alkin's eyes burned red.

Overwhelmed with the energy in the room and the emotions raging between Alkin and Howl, I felt overly exhausted. The room spun and my vision hazed, spiraling towards the floor. I felt Alkin catch me, cradling me in his arms, I knew I was safe and allowed the darkness to consume me.

Calm ~ Alkin

Opal let out a cry as she collapsed, into my arms. Gently I held her close, picking her up and cradling her in my arms, where she knew she was safe. Howl, for a moment was furious, while Solomn held onto Opal, stopping her from running to Raillyn.

Everyone in the room loved her and cared for her, they were all her family, and I had to understand that as well.

"Is she all right?" Opal asked, knowing how I often thought.

Cradling Raillyn closer, I rested my cheek against her forehead before laying a kiss upon it. Her scent of honeysuckle, thyme and vanilla wafted and mingled with my own.

"She's fine, just a little overwhelmed. I had planned on letting her get some sleep tonight." I said indicating we had been interrupted from that.

The thought killed me; if Raillyn and I weren't able to avoid this bond then we might bring another child into the chaos of this world and that was unacceptable. The portal had to be taken care of at all costs, even if in the end the Wolves hated us for using them as pawns in our game.

Solomn caught my thought. I felt it in his mind through our Mystic mark. He eyed me knowingly.

"Let us hope it does not come down to that, but yes I have to agree. Do what is best for Raillyn, she is an Ancient and Daes' last mystic. The Wolves will either just have to accept what they forgot. That being the old ways or they will not have help from anyone in Aeralain." He said while Opal caught his thoughts and agreed.

Relaxing, Howl took a deep breath. "Perhaps you should leave Raillyn here tomorrow and go elsewhere. Darcia and I can protect her while you go and do something else. Maybe spend the day with Opal and Solomn. You two are walking a dangerous path right now. Truthfully I thought you two would be fine to-gether but after retrieving you earlier, I'm beginning to think otherwise." Howl said curiously.

Closing my eyes I sighed. "You're right, this is the only time we both will be in the most control of our magic." I admitted, knowing deep down that something was going to give.

"Perhaps we should take our leave, my dear." Solomn said, breaking my train of thought. "I agree with Howl. I would like to see you visit us tomorrow. Let Howl and Darcia tend to Raillyn, they can teach her with no distractions. She can listen to some stories, cook and most importantly, relax." He said while smiling at Opal.

Nodding my head, I agreed. It would be best. Everyone seemed to relax with my decision.

"If that's the case I'm just going to stay here, if you don't mind." Howl said curiously.

"That would be fine. I will plan to be home tomorrow at sunrise. I am sure Raillyn will sleep late. If you'll excuse me, I will see you all in the morning." I said, suddenly tired myself.

Cradling Raillyn in my arms, I walked up the tree-like staircase and onto the balcony. Below Opal and Solomn said goodnight and left. Howl made himself comfortable on the padded bench near the fireplace. Everything was quieting down when I pushed open the door to the enclosed stairs.

It was dimly lit by small orange magic lights that hung like little candle flames. Spiraling upwards I gently brushed Raillyn's hair and kissed it lovingly. *What was I going to do with her?* I knew Howl was right. We could only fight it for so long.

Approaching our bedroom, the door stood open and the moon gently shone in from the large panes across the room. Carefully kicking it closed I took Rai over to the bed and balanced her on my knee. Gently I tossed back the covers. Sitting her down on the bed, I gently removed her sash and lay in atop the chest at the foot of the bed. She would sleep easier without its weight on her waist.

Placing her head down on the pillow, she took a deep breath and rolled onto her left side. Removing my own belt, I hung it over the chair. Going to the other side of the bed, the paned doors stood slightly open. The scent of the night filled the room.

The northern forests, small animals, and the strong smell of Drakar. A coppery rustic smell, *almost like smelling magic, if magic had a scent*. I thought. Not bothering to change clothes, I carefully climbed into bed and placed my hands behind my head.

Laying on my back and looking up towards the white canopy, I noticed it danced in the light breeze of the night. Then the bed shifted, bringing my attention back to Raillyn. Slowly she closed the space between us in sleep and laid her head and hand against my chest. She settled into a deeper sleep against me, listening to my heartbeat and taking in my scent she instinctively knew it was where she belonged.

Gently holding her, I kissed her hair before closing my eyes and escaping into sleep's welcoming embrace. A smile lay on my lips as I realized the smell of the room was taking on a mixture of our combined scents. The magic of our house was reacting with her magic and was ensuring anyone who entered would know her scent and that she ruled this house. *Tomorrow would be a good day,* I thought as I fell asleep.

Answers ~ Raillyn

The sweet smell of bread and something tart awoke me the next morning. As I opened my eyes, I knew I wouldn't find Alkin home. However, I still reached for his mind; he was visiting Opal.

"Do you need me?" He asked noticing my presence. Mentally I indicated I was all right and felt a mental smile in return. *"Howl and Darcia are in the main room, I will be home when I can. Solomn and I are doing some work here today."* He said while he withdrew and focused his attention elsewhere.

Turning back towards the room, I shifted out of the white satin bed and laid my feet on the hardwood floor. Still in my Den attire, other than my missing sash, I stood up and looked for it. It lay on the back of a nearby chair, Alkin must have removed it last night.

Smirking, I turned back towards the room and searched for clothes. Going to the dresser along the wall, I opened it. The smooth hard surface slide out gently, the wood within gave off a pine scent. It made me smile.

In the dresser, I found various items. Removing a pair of simple blue pants and a nice long-sleeved white shirt, I ran the material between my fingers. It was smooth but not shiny like silk. After untying my top I placed it on top of the dresser, then slipped off my skirt and did the same. Grabbing the blue pants I put them on before reaching for the smooth shirt. Carefully I pulled the it over my head.

Alkin's shirt hung slightly off my shoulders, on both sides. It was also slightly too big around my waist. Frowning, I spied something that would help fix this. Pulling Alkin's crimson red sash off the back of a nearby chair, I smiled. It brought my outfit together just right; after tying it around me I went to the door.

The tiny coins clanked together gently as I descended the stairs and entered the large room. Standing on the balcony, I saw Darcia sitting in one of the large red plush chairs. Books were strewn out around in piles on the floor and a strange aroma smelled delightful. Sounds coming from the kitchen and the subtle brush across my mind indicated Howl was cooking.

They both took note to my presence. "You look like a mess," Darcia said without even looking up from her reading. "Alkin said he had business around Silvertine this morning and for us keep you occupied and resting. But I'm sure you know that already. Anyway, there are tons of books here that refer to the Gods. If you want to do a little reading before breakfast, you can join me."

Emerging from the kitchen, Howl dried his hands with a rag. His piercing blue eyes met mine as he smirked. "Food will be done soon, I figured after whatever it was you two did last night you needed something other than sleep to replenish your exhausted power." He said while looking at me curiously.

Breathing a big sigh, I descended the stairs. He was right, never before had I felt as magically exhausted as I had now. Between dancing, fretting over Daes' task, the portal, and the dark creatures Hunter wanted to summon was exhausting. And of course never before did I have to battle with my inner feelings and magic against natural instincts.

Howl and Darcia both eyed me as I stood in the middle of the room, deep in thought.

"Oh, stop it, you two!" I said tartly, knowing Howl was brushing my mind to ensure I was ok and Darcia felt the subtle shift of my emotions. All because we followed Daes.

"All Alkin and I did was dance a little. I just forgot how much energy it uses and was unprepared with the magic I have coursing through me now. This is an adjustment for me. While I'm used to my magic. I'm not used to it being controlled by my emotions, and sometimes I can't control it. It's much better now, but I still feel like a child because of it." I admitted.

They both seemed to understand my words. Children were often bound with bonds that prevented their magic from lashing out or from being controlled by their emotions. My magic had done this before the information shock broke the barrier around my magic. Now I was left to pick up the pieces and form my own sense of secureness, that I slowly seemed to be doing naturally.

Smiling Howl patted my back. "I fully understand, and that's why we're looking through these books. Hopefully, with plenty of rest and good food you will be back to normal soon." He paused and smiled, sarcastically. "If you want you can join me in the kitchen and I can show you how to make some amazing dishes."

As Howl went back into the kitchen, he tossed the rag on his shoulder. Turning he looked at me deviously before disappearing behind the door. Darcia seemed rather annoyed and went back to her reading. I felt anxious, hungry, and unable to focus.

"I'm going to talk to Howl while food is being made. I'm going to be completely useless till I eat something anyway." I said while going to the kitchen door and walking in, and closing it behind me.

Howl stood, in the middle of the room, next to a large fireplace and a large pot hanging over the fire. Looking high above was a roofed opening, which allowed the smoke to exit and fresh air to enter. There was magic in this room, which seemed to channel the smoke and fire accordingly.

Three large tables sat around the walls of the room while windows filled the eastern and western walls. A door towards my left lead down to an underground area. Cabinets, an icebox and shelves, lined the Southern wall near the door. They appeared to be fully stocked with food, drink and ingredients.

"I knew you couldn't resist." Howl said as he stirred the large pot. "Come and look, learn." He said with his back turned towards me.

Going to stand near him I felt the gentle pull of magic, he was infusing the pot and food with its very essence. His eyes glowed bright blue, it seemed almost natural. As if he didn't intend to infuse the food but his magic took over and did it for him.

There was a gentle tug and I couldn't help smile at the sudden want I had to cook and assist him. It was Daes' magic. I knew at that moment we would feed off each other's power and work well together. Turning towards the table, I saw potatoes sitting, waiting to be cut.

"Want me to cut the potatoes?" I asked while turning and finding a knife in the basket on the bottom shelf of the table.

Howl smirked as he went to retrieve some diced onions, adding it to the pot, "I've added onions to the oil base, there is meat on the table that needs cut, and the potatoes need to be sliced into circles. If you can do that I will take care of the meat, I have bread already cooking and a berry jam simmering."

Nodding my head, I turned towards the table and began to cut the potatoes into circles while Howl went and diced up the meat into fine pieces. Coming to check on me, he held up one of the circles in his fingers.

"I'm surprised you know how to cook so well. Then again, it's cutting and I don't think you're foreign to that." He said indicating back to my days in The Keep, as Raihanna.

Eyeing him sternly but jokingly, I tossed a smaller piece at him. "Just because I lived in The Keep doesn't mean I don't know my way around a kitchen."

Instantly I knew those were the wrong words. I saw it in the link we shared and across his face. He smiled obnoxiously and tried to keep his laughter at bay.

"What I mean is my mother Lillian and her daughters were all earth mages. My mother was a magnificent healer while my sisters were both superb at cooking. While I didn't care for either, I spent plenty of time assisting them and I was better at the cooking than healing." Admitting I was a terrible healer.

"That just makes it funnier." Howl said while laughing out loud.

I heard Darcia from the other room yell at Howl. "Stop picking on her, Howl, be nice!"

"It's just that your father's a healer, and I expected you had acquired some of his skill at the very least." He said before returning to the task at hand.

Sighing, Howl scooped the potatoes into his hands and put them into the pot with the oil. Slowly he began to sauté them, turning their white appearance yellow in color. Next he took the minced meat he had placed into a bowl and gently added them. Stirring for just a moment, he reached for a large blue bottle. Popping the cork, he added red liquid to the contents of the pot, leaving about half the bottle left.

"Here, stir this gently." He said while handing me the ladle and going over towards what I could only assume was the berry jam, he had simmering.

Gently I stirred the pot and tried not to think about the food; it still was an adjustment, regardless of taste or smell. Slowly I began to fall into a rhythm and without even realizing it I felt my magic begin to work its way into the cooking. Turning I knew Howl realized it also.

"Good! See, you're learning. Keep it up and as soon as this jam is finished it will be added to the rest." He said before turning his attention back towards the jam.

It was almost trance-like, relaxing, and energizing at the same time. Howl and I worked in unison, our magic fed off each other, imbuing the ingredients we worked with. It truly was an amazing process and I couldn't wait to learn more.

Carefully, Howl brought over the smaller pot and poured the jam into the potato, onion and blood mixture. Almost instantly the food began to thicken, Howl gently held the ladle with me and assisted in stirring in the jam just right. I couldn't help but smile eagerly at him, never had I done anything like this before and I loved it.

He felt my excitement and eagerness. Noticing a change in the mixture he extinguished the fire with a flick of his hand. Instantly it blew out and a slight breeze wafted across the room. Looking at him, I recognized the spell. He was manipulating the elements around him.

Twisting them with his magic to do his bidding, just now he twisted the very air around us with his magic. Removing it from the fire, he contained its location and the brute force of it caused the fire to die instantly. I hadn't done any of this magic since living with the Wolves. Maybe I could do some training exercises today as well while I waited for Alkin to return.

Howl went over towards the oven and brought out three loaves of warm bread. Placing each on a plate, along with a knife and spoon he placed them onto the table. Catching his thoughts, I grabbed three bowls from the nearby shelf, and began ladling the potato jam mixture into the bowls.

I handed each full bowl to him and he laid them next to the loaf of bread. When I was done, I was suddenly tired. Looking at Howl, he held two of the plates, with the bowls on top, and waited for me. I grabbed the last and followed him out of the room.

"It's normal to be tired after cooking, you used up energy by assisting me, but you will get it back and then some after you eat and rest." He said as we walked into the large hive-like room and towards the table.

Darcia placed her book down when Howl laid the plate in front of her. Carrying my plate to a nearby chair, I sat at the table and joined her. Howl took his own seat.

The sweet tartness of the food smelled amazing. Darcia and Howl both sliced their bread into smaller pieces before using the spoon to scoop the mixture onto the bread before eating it. Having never eaten this before, I copied their actions, slicing my own bread before spooning the mixture onto it.

The first bite was incredible, my tongue danced with the energy we produced. It was a sigh of relief to realize I was finding my place in this new world, with Ancients like me. The thought was surprising and caught me off guard. I had to return to Alecien, there was still so much left undone.

We finished eating in silence, it was nice and relaxing. Howl offered to take my plate, and I let him. He returned quickly and sat back in his spot.

"Feel better?" he asked, while he eyed me curiously.

"I do, I'm still tired but its better. The food was tasty." I said while leaning back in my chair before eyeing the books.

"Should we get started and look for information pertaining to the Gods?" I asked while standing and picking up the closest book before sitting down in the deep red chair next to the fireplace.

Howl nodded while Darcia and him stood and retrieved their own books and sat down. Silently we worked and read; most of the information I already knew. The gods created Dragons to assist in keeping balance in the world. Each Mystic and Drakar followed a personality similar to their God. Nothing was new information.

As I read I began to grow tired. As my eyelids became heavy I heard Darcia ask a question. Nearly asleep I didn't hear her. "Huh?" I asked startled from sleep.

"I said I have to agree with you and Howl. This is annoying. We know that the Gods created all living things, that each of them have a staff they wield..." Darcia's words trailed off as I began to close my eyes.

"I've never seen Daes' staff..." I mumbled before falling asleep in the deep red chair. My book fell to the ground before I allowed sleep to overcome me.

Time Away ~ Alkin

Entering my parent's home, I smelled the distinct smell of a Wolf. *Oh today was going to be a long day.* I thought as I opened the Dragon doors into the main den. Solomn and Opal sat near the fireplace. Lord Drake and Saibal sat in the adjacent chairs speaking to them about how different the weather and time is.

That's right, it's late evening in Alecien, while it's just morning here. All eyes turned towards me when I closed the door, crossed my arms and stood waiting.

Solomn sensing my unease was the first to speak. "We seemed to acquire some unexpected visitors. Claude brought them just a few minutes ago. I guess Drameon told him to do so." He said matter of fact.

Lord Drake looked at me and raised an eyebrow. We couldn't call each other friends but thankfully we both held a somewhat shaky respect for one another concerning Raillyn. Sighing he took a seat back near Saibal. Slowly I unfolded my arms and went to sit near my parents.

"So why are you late, Alkin?" my mother asked me curiously. My father however knew.

Smirking, I leaned back and recalled why I was late. It took me longer than anticipated to leave Raillyn. A growing need to stay and be there when she awoke resided inside me. Thankfully I was able to pull myself away.

Afterwards, I needed to get out and clear my head. After an hour walking the textile district, the fresh air helped me think again. Everything was realigning in Raillyn, even her cycle. I sensed it, I didn't know how long we had, until I would have to disappear or send her away to keep us sane.

Knowing what was to eventually come, I decided to swing by Lena and Ezar's and grab a pint of Dragon fire ale. The burning sensation of its potent herbs and alcohol would help numb the burning I had to return to Raillyn. Thankfully they didn't ask anything and let me be on my way. Yet even after I drank its contents down swiftly, it only numbed the sensation. *God's I saw why Howl drank more often lately.*

"I needed to clear my head, mother, so I visited Lena and Ezar and had an early morning drink with them." I said hinting at my inner fears about Raillyn brooding soon.

Frowning slightly, Opal turned her attention back towards the Wolves. "So, Lord Drake, our granddaughter has been well?"

"She is well." Drake said, confident before a worried look crossed his face. "She misses her sister and mother, which brings me to why I am here. We have been making connections here in Aeralain with the half-breeds and some of the Lunar Wolf clans. I was wondering if it would be possible for Deestan to visit and maybe study a little here? I think it would benefit her as well as our people if she knew the old ways and the new."

Solomn, Opal and I were all surprised by this. Drake was adjusting well to the new information and the old ways. My mother and father spoke mentally to one another. I sensed it through the mental link we shared from my Mystic mark on them.

"Of course she can." Opal said elated to finally get a chance to meet her great-granddaughter.

Drake seemed to relax, Saibal nodded his head in understanding, just as the door opened. Lyth strolled into the room before pausing and smiling. Tipping his head at Drake and his friend he bowed at my parents before coming to stand next to me.

"I just wanted to swing by and let you know we might be later or earlier than anticipated tonight. Celeste is attending one of the boys from the market. He fell from the Temple's roof and has injured himself internally. Hopefully, he will make a full recovery." He said before turning to leave.

Nodding my head, I hoped the boy would be all right. "Thank you for letting me know. Please give his family my prayers, I pray the boy lives. Hopefully, we will see you tonight after

I return home." I said while he walked out the door. Two maids who stood to next to the door closed them carefully as they disappeared into the hall with Lyth, returning to their work.

Thankfully another maid entered the room from the hall near the dining hall. "Lunch will be served shortly. If you could accompany me to the dining hall, I would be happy to serve you." She stated in the Drakar language.

Drake and Saibal looked towards us unknowingly.

"Come, you can join us for lunch." Solomn said as he stood with Opal and led the way. Waiting for Drake and his friend to follow, I trailed behind, hoping all was well with Raillyn.

Friends and Family ~ Raillyn

Groggily, I opened my eyes and looked around the room. The sun shone through the paned windows and indicated it was midday. *I must have slept all morning.* I thought as I saw Howl emerge from the kitchen with Darcia. They carried three bowls and bread.

"Here." Darcia said, handing one to me along with a small loaf of bread. "We figured we'd let you sleep. After we read a little more about the Gods staves and finding several books pertaining to the creation, we decided to make some lunch."

Taking the bowl and bread I was thankful they went ahead and did this. I was hungry again. Blinking my eyes several times I quietly ate.

Darcia took my bowl into the kitchen when I was done. As she returned, I noticed Howl eyeing me curiously and felt the gentle tug of our link indicating he had a question.

"So what did you mean when you said you never saw Daes' staff?" He asked while Darcia returned and took a seat nearby.

Looking at both of them, I shrugged. "I've never seen a staff in his home. What little bit I have seen anyway. I've seen Destiny and Delron's but never Daes'. Why?"

They both eyed each other nervously. A sudden uneasy feeling took over. "He's supposed to have a Dragon-Phoenix staff isn't he?" I asked suddenly aware all the Gods I had seen had one with a large stone pertaining to their magic color on top. After meeting Destiny and knowing Delron, they kept their staves close, but Daes had none.

Simultaneously, they both nodded their heads. "Yeah, from all the books and everything your mother said he has a large Dragon-Phoenix staff with a blue sapphire on top. He's never had it with him?" Howl asked, showing me the image he had in his memories from my mother showing him.

The staffs were identical. Destiny's and Delron's however the stones cut was different. I had seen a staff that looked eerily similar to it, except its gem was blood red. Hunter had it, a wave of memories filled my mind. I felt Howl follow along hoping to help. The staff loved my power, craved it, and fed off it. It loved my blood even more. It was pure chaos...

As the memory of how it nearly killed me faded, I met Howl's eyes. Hunter had Daes' staff. I felt it in my soul, my very being knew it belonged to him. Even if the stone wasn't his, the staff was. Unknowingly I felt myself reach for a portal spell so I could speak to Daes himself about this. I found nothing but a wall. They had blocked off their realm, preventing my entry.

Darcia stood stunned, having seen the memory though Howl. "We have to get it away from him before he does something stupid." She said as she began flipping through books.

Startled, I looked at her. "And how are we supposed to do that? That staff is evil, pure chaos, it almost killed me." I said, hoping there was another way.

"It almost killed you because you weren't in control of your magic. However, that has changed and you are the only one on this world who has a chance to wield it." Darcia began to say as she found the page she was looking for. "See it says here that the Gods' staves possess the magic of the Gods themselves, that it contains unspeakable power of their magic. They imbued and created these items at the beginning when they made the world. When they rid the world of total entropy. It's another safeguard, it says here that if a God's linage is endangered, the staff can be sent to Auran as a temporary substitute to keep their magic in the world and prevent it from dying. But it can only be done while their lineage still resides in the world." She said while eyeing us. "So Daes must have done this before you were removed from the world. Knowing he would be left with no choice other than to pray his staff would hold the balance of Harmony and Chaos. However, if you say the staff is evil I wonder what happened.

Something or someone changed the alignment on the staff from neutral to chaotic. In turn, someone removed the sapphire from on top and replaced it with another. If it's not controlled, the power of Daes' staff will destroy the world. It will seep into the hearts of everyone around it and feed off their evil nature. It will be like a chaotic plague, slowly darkening souls and turning them evil. There will be nothing left, no life or death, just emptiness." Darcia said while reading the text.

I looked at Howl, unsure what to do. I had imbued the bloodstone that resided on top of it. And because of that, he knew how much I hated that staff but it made sense. If it was evil and would consume good within people around it, then it would slowly corrupt the world and turn it to pure entropy. Feeling obligated and knowing it was what I was here for, I knew I had to control the staff and its evil nature. But how would I get it away from Hunter unless he died?

Howl caught my thoughts. "Don't worry about that. When the time comes, we will get you the staff." He said while looking at Darcia. "Also, don't fear it; you are Daes heir, his prodigy in a sense, born with his magic." He said as I met his eyes fearful. He smirked. "I caught it in your thoughts. Whether you realize it or not, Daes crafted you so perfectly, and carefully."

Instantly I understood why the realm of the gods was blocked from me. They could not intervene. It was left up to us.

"It would be horrid if the creatures of chaos he spoke of broke free while we tried to control Hunter and his Vampires." I said suddenly aware of what else we needed to do before peace could ensue. "We need to find out more about these creatures he kept talking about."

Darcia handed a book to me and Howl and we got to work. For the next few hours, we poured over the texts in search of a location of the creatures. Finally after nearly four hours Howl found something.

"Here," He said in excitement, "it says the Gods locked the creatures away in the largest mountain of the Aneross Peaks."

"That's in Alecien, and when I was in The Keep Hunter was "given" the staff by who he claimed was Daes. He said it was acquired up north." The gears in my head were turning. "Do you think Daes placed his staff near the cave? Possibly where these creatures are kept to ensure they remained there and somehow Hunter discovered its location and in turn the staff?" I asked knowing I would have to get Hunter to talk and tell me the truth about this eventually.

I could tell Howl thought the same thing. "Sounds like that might be the case." He said while looking towards Darcia. "Looks like after you are recovered we will have to pay Hunter a little visit, maybe we can get him to tell us where he acquired it? I'm sure he will if he believes it will assist in opening the portal. Bluff our way for the information. I don't think it's a good idea to take the staff from him until we check on these creatures first." Howl concluded while sitting back in the chair.

"I agree. The staff might be linked to the cave now and with its chaotic nature it might need to be wielded in chaos to be controlled properly. If you tried to wield it and force harmony on it, it might cause the bonds on the cave to shatter, releasing those creatures into the world." Darcia said while stretching.

Her words made me wonder, I needed to wield the staff in a controlled chaos. But I couldn't fall into chaos unless I thought and acted like Raihanna. Evil, heartless and deadly. I couldn't do that. I wanted to use the staff instead for good. If I used it in chaos it would control me, I just felt it.

Sighing, I reached my arms up and stretched. "Can I ask you something, Howl?" I said relaxing and feeling better.

Raising an eyebrow, he looked at me questioningly. "Sure, I guess." He said curiously.

Folding my arms, I knew he was right, I was curious. "Where is my sister and the Shifters? I haven't seen them since I returned to normal. I know they visit the Wolves, but what's going on?" I asked curious to know where Alihandra was and needing a slight distraction to clear my thoughts.

Howl ran his hand through his hair and held his neck. By the look on his face, he was debating on how to answer. "Well, they were, how shall I say this, relocated by Lucine." Howl said before crossing his arms.

"Lucine?!" I asked eager to know why the Lunar Goddess chose to intervene in the Shifters' business.

"Yes, Lucine. They prayed to her and asked to be removed from their realm. However, she had a better solution. She told them to relocate to the Winter Shores." Darcia stated while still reading.

Looking towards Howl, he shrugged his shoulder. "Yeah, basically she's right. They left on a ship to the northernmost continent, and that's where they have been living since. I guess they like it there and they have tons of space."

Chewing on my lip momentarily, I had to agree. While I was sad to hear they left the larger areas of Auran I was happy they found a place where they felt they belonged. "Can I see her?" I asked Howl hopeful.

He glanced towards Darcia, eyebrows raised. She didn't stop reading but crinkled her nose a little. "I guess." He replied.

"Yay!" I said smiling big and reaching out to hug Howl. "You said to relax, and I haven't seen my sister in ages. I can relax and catch up a little with her then!"

Darcia put the book down, her bright blue eyes met mine and stopped me momentarily. "Just don't be gone too long. Lyth and Celeste will be here soon, and I'm sure Alkin won't be far behind them. We still have to prepare dinner and I am not doing it alone." She said tartly before sticking her tongue out and going back to reading.

Looking back at Howl, he held out his hand, waiting. I felt a tingle of excitement course through me at the thought of going and seeing my sister after so long. Reaching out and taking Howl's hand only made that sensation stronger. His magic danced across my skin, and made my head spin. As he called his magic and created a portal, I watched as the misty blue spirals grew and grew. Finally, it was large enough for us to enter and he lead me through.

Exiting the portal I was met with stone walls. It appeared similar to The Keep. It felt cold, and at first glance barren. However as Howl lead me through the grey halls and around a corner I saw vibrant tapestries across the frozen stone. For a second, I stood amazed then the sound of footsteps and voices echoed from further down the hall. Quietly he placed his hand over my mouth and pulled me into a room. Mentally he indicated I needed to be silent.

"No one can know you are here. Do you understand me?" He said hushed as the voices grew louder. One unmistakably was Alihandra's.

Quietly nodding my head he released me, and gently putting me behind him, he stood between me and the door. *Only Alihandra can know you're here.* I heard him say in my head.

Outside I heard the voice of a lady getting fainter. Then shortly after I heard Alihandra. "I'll speak to you later about it." She called out a split second before I heard the door open and close.

I tried to peek around Howl, but he was like an immovable wall. Quietly I heard him say "Shhh," and felt his arm move. I could only assume he placed his finger across his lips. Slowly I felt him shift his weight and begin to move aside. Folding my hands in front of me, I waited patiently, unsure how I would be perceived.

As Howl moved aside, I was able to see my sister and the room. Her auburn hair hung down around her face, framing it, and her yellowish hazel eyes seemed to lightly glow. The room appeared to be a bedroom. A large deep-purple bed sat in the left corner next to a closed window while a fireplace, table, chair and bookshelves lined the right wall. A simple cherry wood chest sat at the foot of the bed, intricately carved with various forest animals.

The moment Alihandra's eyes saw me he mouth hung open, as tears caught in her eyes. "Raillyn." I heard her whisper, while placing a hand over her mouth, as if uttering my name was something wrong.

She glanced at Howl, and in turn so did I. Sharply he nodded, and Ali left her spot on the floor and ran to me, arms outstretched. As soon as she got close enough, she hugged me tight, and I threw my arms around her.

"I missed you so much!" She said excited but hushed. "We don't have much time; my handmaid will be back. Are you well? How have you been? I have a son now!" She said everything at once trying to say everything before running out of time.

Pulling back, my face felt wet, tears ran down from my eyes, and blurred my vision. Running the back of my hand across them, I was able to get most of them off. "I'm fine, I've been well, and I have another daughter...." I began to say before I realized she probably would misinterpret it. "What I mean is I have a child with Alkin." I said more hushed.

Drying her own tears, she nodded her head. "I know—he told me. He came here and told me you were expecting, after you passed out on him in The Keep. Alkin's a good guy, he really is, he loves you more than you will ever believe." She said hugging me again. "I just had to tell you that. I felt you needed to hear it from me."

Meeting her eyes, I looked at her curiously. "He told you? How did you know, and Drake never knew anything?" I asked confused.

Alihandra laughed a little, as she wiped more tears away. "Alkin was the one to help us leave Alecien. At the time, we didn't know he was the same Demon the Wolves were hunting. At least not until later. When he came to help us get all our people on the ship to sail here, he told us he was working for the Gods. I knew you disappeared and he said he'd find you and Leeda and that he would keep you both safe. After that, we hardly talked to the Wolves one on one so it was difficult to share information. Howl kept us mostly up to date with what was going on and he also brought messages back and forth for us.... Well, I should say most messages because a few he burned instead. Telling us they were too risky to deliver. He also brought me Leeda when you released her into the den." She said sighing.

Looking at Howl, he shrugged his shoulders. "What can I say, you didn't need to tell the Wolves you were talking to Alkin and they didn't need to know he was working for the Gods, or that Raihanna was really Raillyn. And especially that she gave the Den your daughter." Howl began before placing his hand up just as I was about to speak. "And yes, she knew, I told her everything. She knows you were betrothed to Alkin as a child, and that he's your mate. She also knows that Drake and Raven were betrothed and are now mated. Why do you think they're here and not in communication with the Wolves anymore?" Howl said jokingly.

Alihandra gave him a stern annoyed look, one that she always gave me when I tried to be funny. "I get it now but still you don't have to act like that about it." She said smacking his arm. "Just remember I can go get Aya if I need to put you in line." She said teasing him.

"Aya?" I asked curiously.

Wide-eyed Howl looked at her with the most serious face I'd ever seen. His tone became low and authoritative. "That's not funny. She's here because she needs to be around people who understand her better. Not for you to threaten me with, and cause a confusing situation."

"Who's Aya?" I asked again trying to reach for Howl's mental mind for answers.

He rubbed his face and seemed as if he was debating how to answer me. Glancing at Alihandra, she laughed slightly. "His fiery-haired princess."

Tipping my head I looked at Howl. "Aya's the girl from your memory? Isn't she?" I asked as I heard the door creak and begin to open. Panic rose inside as I felt Howl grab my arm and pull me behind him. His magic quickly boomed out as I felt him call a sudden portal. Then before I could say anything further, he pulled me through it with him.

Glancing back, my sister waved understandably. Looking at the door, a fiery red-haired fledgling peeked her head in, the same girl from Howl's memory. Her eyes fell on the portal, wide-eyed and open-mouthed, she looked shocked and surprised. She was young maybe twenty or so, her small pixie-like face was framed with high-cheek bones and pointed ears. However, her magic felt different, a collided power of something familiar yet strange. As the portal closed around me, I saw Alihandra run towards her.

Then everything changed and we stood in Alkin's kitchen. Pulling my hand out of his grip, I was determined to try and finish my visit. Regardless if he didn't want to be seen or not.

Calling my magic I quickly created a portal and went through. Darkness surrounded me, after I went through, to the point that I had to call a magic orb. Holding the illuminated orb above my head brightened up the surrounding forest. The bright blue light gave it an eerie appearance. Tall pines stood all around, it wasn't as cold here as it was in Silvertine either. It seemed warmer. I suddenly heard a snap of a twig behind me. I was not alone.

Turning towards the sound, a ferocious growl rumbled from a nearby bush. Peering closer a large black wolf jumped out and nearly bit its teeth into my arm. I felt it's hot breath inches away. Screaming I instinctively brought out my blade and slashed at the creature. Knocking it off in another direction and nearly slicing it in half it now lay dying on the soft mossy floor. Ruby red blood spilling from a gash along its stomach.

Taking a few deep breaths to calm my nerves. I sighed, I felt sorry for the creature. I knew I could not heal it and I didn't mean to hurt it. Kneeling beside the timber wolf I placed my hand along its neck, it whimpered in pain, as it breathed ruggedly. Bringing my dagger around I delivered a final blow. My sword went deep in its heart, stopping it. Like feeling a feather lift off from my hand. I felt its spirit escape and leave its body, just as its last breath escaped its jaws.

Sighing and wiping the blood from my hands and blade on the moss-covered ground. I felt the prick of a sword at my back. "Stand up slowly and turn around." Commanded a gruff yet young voice.

Dispelling my light orb and sheathing my blade, I slowly turned around hands to my side. Several bright green orbs suddenly brightened the forest. Two men dressed in all black with sleek long black hair and deep brown and honey eyes. Both of them looked at me cautiously, swords pointed at me. Suddenly nervous the two men spoke a strange yet familiar language, Shadow Walkers.

Leaning forward to reply to them and tell them what I was, the honey-eyed man raised his blade to my throat. "You will not say a word unless you want to die. Now walk!" he said while pointing towards a path just beyond the orbs light.

Quietly I walked and hopped I was being brought to Zian and that I would have a chance to speak to Finn. A bit of useful information I had acquired from Howl's memories. Searching for more, I tried to reach out and make contact with him. Our link seemed to vibrate, as if he registered my attempt, but he felt far away.

Sighing, I continued walking in silence; neither man said anything as we walked on. Their swords never left my back as we neared a large wooden wall. Small trees and spikes made up the parameter, and was twice the height of a man.

Rounding the wall and walking its tall oaken length brought us to its equally large gates. Torches burned brightly beside each door, and guards stood ready to attack at a moment's notice. The strong smell of Shadow Walker filled my nose as I was lead through the gates and into the quiet streets beyond.

Darkened houses filled them, no torches burned here, only the moonlight lit our path. Simple wooden and stone houses lined the path, all dim. Finally we reached a large house on the edge of another gate and the forest. The two men lead me up the steps and opened the door.

The house beyond was a simple wood structure, but held exquisite furniture, rugs, tables, and chairs. It's bright yellow walls seemed to stand out against the red of the wood. Two other men sat near a fireplace, one I recognized as Claude. His long wavy black hair, and deep honey eyes met mine in surprise. Thankful to see a familiar face, I decided I was tired of not speaking up.

"Finally!" I said as I disregarded the blades and walked towards Claude and who I could only seem to assume was Finn. The deep brown-eyed man brought his sword around just as the honey-eyed man came towards me. His arm was extended and ready to grab me. Having enough of this endeavor, I used my magic to create a barrier between me and them.

Summoning the magic towards my hand I expanded it outwards. Creating a blue shield like structure that deflected the blade, causing blue sparks to fly off its surface. While it detoured the other man, like bug spray does a mosquito. Both men looked up at me shocked and stunned, I knew my eyes glowed blue with my power. The man Claude was speaking to stood and immediately took action.

"Ethan! Owen! You two will stop this nonsense this moment and leave! I suggest you two take a little trip and visit Master Cole. And do a little more research on Mystics before you return to patrol." He said sternly as the men bowed and left. Watching them go I lowered the barrier before turning towards Claude. He stood next to the taller man with deep brown hair and brown eyes.

Raising my eyebrows, I smiled.

"I am sorry for that incident and hope you can forgive my people." He spoke sincerely but authoritatively. "My name is Finn and I am the leader of the Shadow Walkers." He said while holding out his hand.

Reaching out we shook hands. Before I had a chance to turn towards Claude, he spoke. "What are you doing here?" he asked stunned. "Better yet, does Howl know you're here?"

Finn looked back at me. "I can only assume Mystic you are tied to Howl?" He asked raising an eyebrow.

"Yes I'm a Mystic of Daes and Howl is one of my guards." They both looked surprised. I was curious to know why. "Why does that matter?"

Shaking his head Finn didn't appear to be happy. "That doesn't matter right now. If you wish to go to back to your own kind then I have to ask you to use Howl's house. It would be in your best interest to leave Zian since you are unaccompanied by your guard." He began saying. As I started to protest he held up his hand. "It is not that I do not wish for you to remain in my village, but you will make my people uneasy. They do not take well to Mystics, especially Daes'. Don't get me wrong, we are very respectful and understanding to your kind, but you tend to bring trouble and we do not wish it." He said very blunt.

Mentally I felt like I had been blindsided, but physically I remained composed.

"I will personally escort you to his current portal here and you can take leave tonight." Finn said while going towards the door and opening it, waiting for me to follow him.

Slightly shocked at his behavior, I followed, Claude stayed close as I walked down the wooden steps and onto the dirt covered streets. As Finn descended the stairs, a group of males walked by and bowed before going on. Everyone on the street was male, no females were seen. Looking towards the wood and stone buildings all the shutters on them remained closed. Claude came up beside me as Finn began walking swiftly away.

Following Finn, I felt Claude step even closer. "Try and blend in." He whispered, as several males eyed us suspiciously. Claude carefully pulled me towards him and into the crook of his arm, as we walked on. Suddenly uneasy I let him hold me close to him and guide me through the village.

Rounding a darkened corner, I saw the familiar two-storied house that belonged to Howl. As we approached it I heard the creek of a shutter window. Turning towards the sound I saw a lady peeking through curiously, honey-colored hair hung in her face as her eyes met mine. Claude pulled me onwards as he lead me towards the door, watching as she hastily closed the shutters.

"Howl has a reputation here for being a ladies' man." Claude said while he reached for the door handle and led me into the familiar den.

Finn stayed on the stoop outside, out of the way. "Here you go." He said, "I expect you to be on your way and not return unless Howl is with you. In fact I recommend it for your own sake." Finn said as he turned to walk away sharply. "Claude, let us finish our talk back at my house. We lead Howl's newest fancy to his home, so let us take our leave of the affairs."

Claude took a deep sigh as he tipped his head towards me in a short bow. "Sorry about all this, Finn is not used to dealing with women who are not from his village." He said as he closed the door and left me standing in Howl's den, flabbergasted.

The creek of wood boards behind me made me jump. I had been so focused on what was happening, and worried about it all that I had closed off my mind. Turning towards the sound, I saw Howl leaning against the wall casually, arms crossed.

"So you ended up in Zian? Or close to it?" He said raising his eyebrows. "I would of told you but you ran off too fast. The Winter Shores are inaccessible to those that are not trained to get there. Or those too lazy to get a boat."

Marching towards him I wasn't happy. "How was I supposed to know, and why in the world did I end up near Zian anyway? What is wrong with those people?" I almost shouted still nervous over what just happened and being escorted through a very male village.

Smirking Howl answered. "That's how things are done there. Females are guarded and protected after night falls. No female is allowed outdoors by themselves, let alone outside the village. For a little history lesson, they are cared for by their father or brother till they are of age. Then they are married off to their mate for a dowry. After that her mate tends to her safety." He said, while brushing something off his hand.

"So basically they are sold into marriage?" I asked mouth wide open in shock.

"It's more complicated than that, but to outsiders, yes it seems so. Now you see why I disliked the village and Finn." Howl concluded tartly. "Come on, let's go back to Alkin's." He said while reaching out and taking my hand, dragging me through a portal.

Just as before we teleported into Alkin's kitchen and stood next to the large center hearth. Sighing Howl picked up a spoon, before placing it onto the table again, almost worriedly.

Courtyard ~ Alkin

Exiting the palace my feet touched the dirt-covered ground. All around us were tall stone walls and a small stable. The evening air was cool and crickets could be heard off in the distance. The wind blew slightly from the north and brought a crisp breeze with it.

Lord Drake stood, holding the reins of a chestnut mare. Deestan carefully held onto Callina who sat in front of her. "Ready?" He asked the girls as Deestan held tighter.

During lunch, Opal and Solomn had allowed the girls an evening together before Lord Drake was supposed to return home. Looking at my daughter she appeared nervous.

Callina's face and emotions were of excitement and fear, she had never been on a horse before in her life and somehow because of her sister and Lord Drake they got her on one. Leaning against the nearby wall I watched. I wanted to see my daughter ride her first horse, and wished Raillyn was here to see, *I will show her later*, I thought to myself.

Swiftly Deestan kicked the horse into motion, Callina let out an ear-piercing scream and Drake lead the horse around in circles. Deestan was a natural on horseback. She rode with such poise and confidence. Our daughter on the other hand, was like me on horseback, uncomfortable and antsy.

While I rode horses when I was required to, I disliked it and preferred walking or wagons instead. Callina continued to scream, and as Deestan tried to pick up speed, she also tried to reassure her.

"There is nothing to cry about, Callie, I won't let you fall." She said as her cries escalated.

My ears perked when Deestan said 'Callie'; *when did this happen?* I wondered to myself.

Not worried about the situation and hoping Callina would calm down on her own I continued to watch. The subtle pull of Mystic magic, Delron's magic, made me realize I couldn't just sit and watch any longer. Like a storm building to a peak, I felt Callina begin to gather energy. I had known her magic would start showing itself soon, only time would tell and now it seemed to be slowly making itself known. We would have to up her studies with Solomn, meaning she would be spending more time in the palace as she learned to control the basics.

Not wanting her magic to lash out as mine did at her age, I approached Drake as he began slowing the horse to a halt. "Come now, Callina, riding a horse isn't that frightening." I said making my presence known.

Callina should have known I was there, but she was so worked up she was failing at realizing anything but the need to be upset. She squalled at the top of her lungs, just as she did as an infant. Carefully Drake pulled her from the horse and placed her on the ground.

Immediately she collapsed into a sitting position, as she continued her screaming. Her cries were so dramatic that she had to pause between sobs and gasp for breath. Her face was bright red, almost purple as she covered her eyes with her hands, as tears fell. Looking around we had seemed to gather many looks, as people came to see what was happening. Many of the assistants in grey were watching. It had been decades since a Mystic child was in Silvertine, so many were curious.

"Callina, stop the tears and come here." I said leaning down to her level, hoping she would listen.

It had always been Raillyn who was good at soothing these fits, not me, so I felt cautious on what I could do to remedy this. Getting up, she ran full force into my arms. Her mind seemed to calm briefly before I felt her continue with her tantrum. She pushed the emotion of safety and calm away and continued her wails.

"She was so excited to get on the horse before we came out here. It was Deestan that was able to get her up there." Drake said while helping Deestan down.

She ran over and gave me a slight hug, before reaching out and brushing Callina's hair back. "Callina, it's ok; you're off the horse. It really wasn't that bad, if you would have just relaxed you would have had fun." Deestan said while rubbing her sister's hair.

I failed to sense Callina's reaction. Siblings being siblings, she shoved at her sister, knocking Deestan from her feet. Her crying escalated once more and my parenting instincts took over. Pulling her face around so her eyes met mine I sternly spoke to her. My eyes glowed red.

"That was not nice; you need to go tell your sister you're sorry." I said as she knocked my left hand away from her face.

Grabbing her hand she crumbled to the ground in a full blown fit. She kicked and screamed as I pulled her towards the wall, where I placed her to continue her screaming. Determination crossed her face as she began to call her magic to assist her in this fit.

"My goodness." I heard Drake say before I turned to deal with my child.

Immediately I grabbed her wrists and summoned my own magic, directing it into a solid shape. It twined around her wrists forming small lines. The bangle like lines glowed red in color, the more she tried to reach and summon her magic the brighter they got. I had bound her magic to her so she was unable to lash out at anyone. Realization crossed her face as her eyes met mine.

"I-WANT-MOMMY!!" She cried between sobs, as she threw herself once more onto the ground and continued her tantrum. Ignoring her and knowing she would eventually stop I turned my attention back to Drake and Deestan.

"Sorry about that, she's never tried to use her magic like this before. I have a feeling it because of recent events." I said while looking back at Callina as she laid on the ground crying into her arm.

Sighing Drake seemed to understand. "How's Raillyn doing?" He asked apprehensively.

Smiling I replied. "She is well, but overwhelmed. Like you, she is trying to understand everything around her and why it happened the way it did. She feels like she was given the short end of the staff when she was taken away and wants the chance to make up for lost time. However, until everything with Hunter and the Elite are settled, she can't live how she wants." I said trying to summarize things so I didn't say too much but enough so Drake understood.

Nodding his head in understanding, he looked down at Deestan as I turned to check on Callina. Her cries had subsided and she lay quite on the ground, listening. Going over and bending down I brushed her hair.

"Come now, no more tears." I said as she looked up at me, her face dusty with dirt and tear residue.

Getting up, she crawled into my arms. "I want mommy." She said in a calmer tone. "Take me to mommy." Her eyes met mine as she tried to avoid the situation at hand.

Placing her back on the ground I shook my head. "First I think you need to apologize to your sister. We do not let our magic lash out at others." I said sternly as my own father had said to me long ago. "Those marks on your wrists will remain there until you learn to control your magic and not allow such things to happen."

Her eyes met mine in shock, but she nodded her head and went to her sister. Hugging her gently she murmured into her shoulder. "I'm sorry." She said as she withdrew and looked on the verge of tears again.

Standing I laid my hand on her head. "At this moment I can't take you to your mother, she isn't feeling well. However, I can take you to the Den to play with the other children." I said hoping she understood.

Looking at her own father I could tell Deestan was formulating notions of her own. "I want to go, too!" She asked almost bouncing up and down. "I want to see the Drakar Den!" She begged as Callina looked up at me hopefully.

"I can only speak for Callina but I think it's best if you stayed here." I said trying not to say it too harshly. "I don't feel comfortable yet, taking the Alecien Werewolf heir into the Drakar city."

Drake nodded in agreement, and thankfully stood his ground. "I believe since your mother is having a hard time with her magic, it would be best for you to stay home. Callina needs to study and Silvertine is the safest place she can do that. I have told you that was the reason she had to study here while you studied at home." He said lovingly but sternly. Deestan nodded her head in understanding.

"Be sure to let Raillyn know we miss her." He said while clasping my arm in a handshake. Nodding my head I picked up Callina who had been pulling at my arm. Smiling, I slightly bowed my head as we walked into the palace, knowing Drake and Deestan would return home and I would take Callina to the Den.

Night Life ~ Raillyn

"Let's get dinner going and we can talk." Howl said while patting my shoulder and going about the room.

Sighing myself, I followed.

Immediately he grabbed a large bottle of what appeared to be spirits and drank it down heavily. Removing the bottle and wiping his mouth, he seemed to relax. "Sorry," he said. "As you know I started trailing Ayana; this seems to be the only thing stopping me from going to her. She's young and I want her to have time to finish her studies before I bring her to Silvertine. We still haven't met, I'm afraid if I do I will frighten her and cause unnecessary issues. Plus I fear Finn will drag her to the village." He said while taking another drink. "That's why we left so suddenly from your sister's. I convinced Alihandra to house her so I knew she would be around safe people. Unreachable from the Shadow Walkers as well. Aya..." He said quietly.

I didn't know what to say. He fled because of similar issues that Alkin and I were having. Howl felt the same way that we did. It was an adjustment that needed a gently hand.

"She's part Shadow Walker, you know?" he said, breaking my train of thought. "Because of that I can't claim her unless I tell Finn. However, if Finn finds out, he will command she be returned to Zian and given a chance to find a Shadow Walker mate. He wouldn't believe me if I told him she was mine anyway. I earned a sour reputation for women there. Not that I broke any laws, but they saw my carousing habits outside the village as evil and unnatural. If I walked into the village with Ayana, no one would believe me because of it. They would see her as another fancy of mine and she would be taken from me and I know that would be devastating for anyone involved." He said sorting out his problems. "I'm patient and since I haven't met her and struck the bond between us, I can wait and sort this all out before I go after her. Maybe in a few years it will be easier."

I was doubtful of his words. We both knew that even though the cord was not struck between them I felt his desire and need to go to her. Like Alkin and I, he was fighting the inevitable.

"Let's do an exercise while we cook. No words, instead we will use the mental link we share through that little Mystic mark you placed on me." He said smiling with a sense of slyness.

It sounded fun and I agreed mentally. Silently we worked and I handed him ingredients and prepared meat. Mincing it just as he had earlier, but adding my own twist. A touch of thyme and lemon grass. When I was done I let him work on the main dish, while I took charge of making flat bread.

Carefully adding vanilla and honey, a wonderful mixture of fragrances, to the dough. I couldn't help but smile, it smelled delightful. After kneading it and rolling it out I let the dough settle. And turned back to the minced meat. Carefully I added some bottled blood to the mixture and added the contents into a pan.

Placing the pan over the fire, I sautéed the ingredients together, adding more thyme and lemon grass. After they began turning golden in color I removed them from the heat. Allowing them to cool, I noticed Howl was cutting up lettuce and other greens, adding them to a large bowl. Uncut fruit lay next to him and an empty bowl.

Turning back to my work, I separated the dough into six different balls and rolled them flat. Carefully I added the meat mixture to each flat circle, then folding the dough I sealed each into a ball. All that was left was cooking them, so I placed them into the oven to brown.

Howl still added ingredients to the salad, as he tossed it and added herbs. *"Can you dice and soak these strawberries for me?"* He asked mentally while he began cutting apples. Nodding mentally, I grabbed a new knife and began slicing the strawberries up, greens and all. As I did so, the kitchen door opened swiftly. Startled, I jumped as the blade went across my hand.

"My Gods!" I yelled as Lyth walked into the room casually, Celeste a few steps behind him. "Ow, my hand!" I yelled as I looked down and realized I had sliced it good.

"Well, so much for our exercise. Let me see." Howl said as he took my hand into his and looked at the cut.

My hand was covered in blood, I had cut it deep. Placing a bowl under my hand Celeste came over and took it into hers. Gently she turned it over and examined the cut. Reaching into her pouch she pulled out several herbs and crushed them in her hands. I caught Lyth read her mind and hand her a glass of water and a rag.

"Here let me see." She said as she put the herbs into the water before dipping the rag into it and wringing it out.

As soon as she placed the rag on my hand it burned, but the blood began to subside immediately. Lyth took over cutting the rest of the strawberries as Howl took the bowl and added some bottled blood to my own. Celeste looked at them curiously.

"No use letting good blood go to waste." Howl said while Lyth looked at him mischievously.

"Plus I think it will be funny to see Alkin unnerved a little. He needs frazzled now and again. It's been too long since we caused issues on purpose." Lyth said sarcastically.

Looking at Celeste, she was shaking her head. "Boys." She said. "They always try to outdo one another and when that doesn't work they torture each other. Are you ok with them doing this? It's not going to hurt anything, just will ruffle Alkin's nerves a little."

"What smells amazing?" Lyth said as Howl added the strawberries to the blood mixture.

Sighing I knew I wouldn't win, plus it might be fun to see Alkin a little frazzled. Lyth let Howl finish up and went over to the oven. Opening it carefully, he grabbed a wooden pallets and removed the meat bread before placing each on a plate and topping them with the strawberry mix. Smiling, he turned back towards us.

"Tell me you made this, Raillyn." He asked curiously eyeing Celeste and me.

Looking at Howl, I stood stunned. "Yeah, we decided to do an exercise and I sort of let my magic tell me what to add and do." I said looking towards Celeste, who thinned her lips.

"Howl, you knew she would do this, you planned to frazzle Alkin way before we came." She said sternly as we heard the front door open.

"Too late." Howl said as Celeste gently smacked at Lyth teasingly.

Sighing Lyth's presence was felt in my mind briefly. *"Don't worry it's not that bad, but you did add ingredients that mimic your scent to the food. For mates, it makes for a tempting dish and since dinner is primarily made with your magic and now blood. It will make him feel how much you love him."* He said as the kitchen door opened and Alkin walked in.

Hearing the hint behind his voice, what he lacked to say was that it would cause Alkin to want me closer to him, and feel more at ease with me naturally. That was ok except if he started to relax too much and not control the situation. Then we were both going to be in trouble.

Turning and looking at Alkin my mind went blank, I saw it on his face, he smelled the difference in the room, and the cooking. Smiling Howl patted me on the back.

"You have to admit Raillyn does a great job cooking, smells wonderful. Let's go eat." He said while Lyth and him began to carry the plates of food to the larger room.

Turning slowly, I felt the gentle tendrils of Alkin's mental touch. Unsure what to say or react from what I had caused, I grabbed the salad bowl and followed the others into the room, leaving Celeste and Alkin to be the last out of the kitchen.

That's when I noticed it, even the larger room held a distinct scent, a different scent. It was an amazing array of the combined scents from Alkin and I. The room smelled like a fresh spring day, with flowers and herbs.

A part of me deep within stilled and began to tick. I felt it, an odd sensation of warmth began to warm from my belly out. It was calming but at the same time feverish. Suddenly I took a deep breath before sitting down at the table next to Alkin. Aware I had blocked everyone in the room from my mind. I smiled and went back to my normal thought pattern.

"You made this?" Alkin asked mentally as he took a bite of the meat bread with strawberry topping.

Mentally I nodded yes in reply and smiled at him. Then momentarily I saw him tense. He too blocked me from his mind. Startled, I stared at him wide-eyed. Howl and Lyth took note as well as Celeste.

Reaching out I brushed Alkin's face, his ever-changing eyes met mine as he opened his mind backup to me. Reaching up he took my hand lovingly into his and relaxed. Leaning forward, he stole a quick kiss before pulling back and resting his hand on my cheek.

"You make amazing food, my dear." He said in total control.

My face lit up and I smiled so big I couldn't help but laugh a little. The warm feeling spread out once more and made me feel like I was standing near a lit fireplace. Alkin returned to his meal and continued eating. Smiling, I began to enjoy mine.

The bread was sweet, and with the strawberry blood and meat mixture it tasted infused with power. Like a second heart beat, the ticking seemed to pick up pace, and reminded me of waves lapping gently against the shore.

After we all finished Lyth and Howl removed the plates as I stood to stretch. "I think while it's still quiet I'm going to go upstairs and soak in that hot spring." I said while unintentionally reaching down and playing with a strand of Alkin's hair.

Pulling my hand back, Alkin smirked at me as I went to the stairs and up to our room. Entering it , I noticed that it too held the stronger scent of Alkin and I, the smell of pure spring, herbs and sweet smelling flowers.

Smiling I closed the door and removed my clothes. The cool air, of the soon to be winter gently bite my skin as I stepped onto the balcony. The steamy waters looked warm and welcoming, and as I stepped in, small snowflakes began to fall from the cloudy skies.

Sitting down in the warm waters, I noticed the snow melted before touching the water's surface. A mist lightly enveloped the pool causing me to feel relaxed. Slowly I closed my eyes and rested against the mossy edge. I let my thoughts linger and smiled as I thought of Alkin.

The sudden sound of a door awoke me, *I must have fallen asleep,* I thought to myself as I sat up in the pools warm waters. The snow was lightly falling still and as I went to the other side of the pool, for a towel that lay on the edge of a chair, I heard Alkin.

"Rai?" He called into the room silently as I heard him near the balcony.

Before I crossed the pool however, Alkin stepped out of the room. Our eyes met and I saw him tense slightly before turning and going back into the room. Wanting to stop him, I swiftly crossed the remainder pool and climbed out of the water, pulling the towel around me as I did so.

My feet crossed the snow-covered surface of the balcony and left watery prints that melted as I walked. Chilled by the sudden shift in temperature, my body tingled. Crossing the threshold of our room I closed the doors, blocking out the chill. Shivering slightly I turned to look for Alkin, reaching for his mind I realized he blocked me.

He stood leaning against the wall, head in his hands. I didn't care, it wasn't the first time he had seen me with no clothes. Going to him I gently lay my hand on his shoulder, turning his eyes mirrored a foggy purple color. Shivering again from the cold, he noticed and instantly took me into his arms.

Holding me close, he turned me towards the wall concealing me. My back lay against its hard surface as I felt Alkin open his mind to me. *"Don't move and I will warm you with my mag-*

ic. " He said as I felt him drawing on his power from deep within. A red fog began to swirl up from our feet, circling around us. Similar to the fog that had captured me in Death's Realm so long ago. It tingled and warmed at the touch.

Meeting Alkin's eyes, I realized how precarious the line he walked was. He struggled with control and so did I. Refusing to do nothing and stand still, I gently reached up and laid my hand on his cheek. I felt his composure crumble, between the food I cooked and the accidental addition of my blood to the mix, it made a dangerous combination.

Pressing me against the wall, his lips met mine. My towel fell away as I reached up and circled my hands around his head. A burning began to radiate from my stomach, the ticking sped up and burned. Spreading through every vein in my body. Feeling his desire I jumped into his arms, he held me close and pressed me further against the wall, before pulling me away.

His kisses began to trail down my neck as he turned and laid me onto the beds soft surface. His familiar weight rested atop my body as the burning sensation began to radiate and sear its way through my body. I recognized its sensation.

The radiating heat indicated the beginning of my cycle, the burning desire which would prepare us for two days of its unrelenting fire, the peak. Placing my hand on Alkin's chest, I felt myself begin to lose myself to the power of its magic. He was right; I was young and still powerless against its ground-splitting force.

His mind snapped back to sanity as he too recognized the shift inside me. Instantly I felt him withdraw and close his mind to me. Releasing me from his grasp and standing, he took deep steadying breaths. The magic continued to dance across my skin. Closing my eyes I tried to gain control, to calm the fire that resided in my magic and my very soul.

"Get dressed." Alkin said as he went out the balcony doors, closing them behind him.

Sitting up, my head spun slightly but it seemed that my magic was ebbing, giving me more control. Sighing about what almost happened and my obligations I went to the dresser and pulled out a simple red nightshift. Lastly, I pulled on a pair of black boots.

When I was more presentable, I went to the balcony doors and followed Alkin out into the snow. He stood along the right side opposite of the warm pools water. The snow was still lightly falling as I followed his tracks around towards what appeared to be a wraparound portion of the balcony. Alkin stood leaning on the rail, looking out over the city. I didn't even know this part of the balcony was here, but the view was amazing.

We were so high up that we saw many of the rooftops from the nearby temples. You could see the Den from here, people hustled in and out. Children played in the snow near the large fountain, their laughs echoed joyfully through the streets.

In awe, I walked over towards him and leaned against the rail. He looked at me and smiled, knowing I was enchanted by the beauty of the city itself. As I watched the snowflakes began to get bigger, looking skyward was mesmerizing.

The snowflakes danced and twinkled as they fell. Living in Alecien I had never seen snowflakes this large. We had snow, but it never stuck around in the region where we lived, it was too warm. This was amazing and I marveled in their glory, just as I did as a child.

Noticing a slight change in the air around me, I felt the subtle shift indicating Alkin was using magic. His mind still closed to me, I saw him reach up and catch a snowflake in this hands. Bringing them down in front of me, he smiled as he opened them. Inside, the snowflake solidified into a red crystal-like shape. It was amazing and taking it from his hand, so solid. Touching it triggered a memory. He used to do this for me when I was young, I used to have a dozen or so.

"It will keep like that, and when we get inside I will put it on a chain for you to wear." He said lovingly as he placed his hand on the small of my back, and led me back inside.

Just as he promised after he closed the outside door, he went over to the dresser and opened a small box that lay on top.

Carefully he pulled out a small silver chain before replacing the lid. Bringing it over to me I handed him the snowflake and he secured it to the tiny chain, before holding it up for me to see.

Smiling I turned around so he could place it around my neck. It lay perfectly against my chest. Turning back, I noticed something bothered him.

"My apologies for tonight," He said calmly. "I think we're both tired and need some sleep."

Holding out his hand, I allowed him to take me over to the bed. Letting go, I felt just how tired I was. My eyes felt leaden and burned with the need for sleep. Pulling back the covers I slipped into the white satin sheets, just as Alkin did on his side. Not daring to close the space between us, I rolled onto my stomach before ensuring the snowflake was safe. Gently rubbing it between my fingers I fell asleep.

***

Opening my eyes, it was still the middle of the night. Yet, I knew why I had awoke even before opening my eyes to meet the darkness of the room. My body burned.

It was the same sensation I had when I was in the Wolves castle and The Keep, so long ago. Fingers of what felt like fire pulsated throughout my whole body, and a dull ache radiated from the pit of my stomach. My vision was hazy and upon looking down at Alkin it only made the combined sensations worse.

"*That was it...*" I thought suddenly. *"I needed chaos, the only time I ever fell into a controlled chaos was when I cycled... And both my mind and body fell head first into my magic... I need to leave, while I can still utilize this power."*

Gripping my fists into tight balls, I went to my feet, before blanking out. When I realized what was going on again I realized my body was still consciously doing stuff, but my mind couldn't or wouldn't keep up and instead it temporarily shut down. This reminded me of my time in The Keep.

For two days, in Issia, I had moments like this. Where Alkin and I did not remember a thing and yet something had occurred. It was the natural flow of our bodies and the bond we shared. *I'm surprised he was able to not bind me then.* Recalling the situation only caused my mind to stutter momentarily.

My head lay in my hands, as I sat in the stairwell going towards the balcony. Thankfully my body was working unconsciously with my mind for the time being, letting me leave. Yet, I knew it would only be a matter of time before it would flip, willing me to stay instead. I needed to find something that would keep me on my driven path to get the staff.

Again my mind stutters in the beginning thralls of my brooding cycle. Pressing my hands to my forehead, hoping to regain control of my mind I found myself in the main room. Howl held my shoulders, steadying me. Briefly I saw a bottle in his hand. The image seemed staticky, and jumped about, causing it to become two at times. Looking towards Howl was no better, he spoke to me but I heard no words. Everything was silent other than the unrelenting static of my magic.

Suddenly as my mind began to stutter once more, something was pressed to my lips. It was the bottle, and its contents felt like drinking fire. Yet, I allowed him to pour it into me. The static sound popped as my hearing returned.

"This will help calm your body and dull your mind to the point where you won't go in and out as badly." Howl said quietly into my ear.

Just as when we formed our Mystic bond, he held me in front of him, keeping me upright. Taking the bottle from his hand, he released me. Quickly I drank down the rest of its contents. It hurt, my throat felt like it was on fire, but then again so did my body. Thankfully though that sensation was calming, dissipating for the time being, I was feeling sane again.

Having drained the bottle, I handed it to Howl and took a seat in the nearby chair. Its soft pillowy surface was a welcome relief. Sighing I leaned back,the closing my eyes briefly.

"Feel better?" He asked. Opening my eyes, I smiled at him. Everything was still there, the burning need to return to Alkin, my mind wanting to escape and hide, me knowing I had to get the staff now, or it would be too late. But it was all dulled, muffled by the wine.

"Much better, thanks. I have to get out of here. We can't afford this right now. This is the only time I can wield Daes' staff in chaos. Or I should say in a controlled chaos. That's why my grandfather told me to just get over it and bond with Alkin. He knew it's what I needed to wield his staff in its current state and not have it kill me." I said as Howl looked at me only half-surprised.

"I wondered if that was the case. However, you can't get the staff half drunk, I don't think it would help any of us. Once you hold it, I'm sure it will try and control you. Plus we don't really know what will happen when you gain control of it." He said while pulling out another bottle and taking a swig.

"Yes but that's the thing, if I don't do this now we will lose the chance and Auran might not survive." I pleaded, knowing this was the only way.

Howl sighed and rubbed his neck. "Fine, but let's get Celeste to give you a drought instead of the wine. Plus Lyth can go with us." He said while calling a portal, I looked at him curiously wondering why he was summoning a portal to Lyth and Celeste's home. "Easier this way." He said while pulling me through. "So how do you plan to get Hunter to give you the staff. Do you really think he will just hand it over to you?" Howl asked as we entered a small room.

"Actually, yes." I began while looking around the room.

Its deep mahogany walls seemed to glow in a subtle firelight. The room seemed small or perhaps it just appeared that way. To my left was a lighted hall that took a sharp corner as soon as you entered it. Along the right wall was an enclosed fireplace. A large metal grate stood enclosing the flames and hiding most of the light.

"I expect if I tell Hunter that I need the staff to summon Daes, and if he feels my chaotic nature, he will hand it over. I plan on telling him that he needs to give me the staff so I can stabilize its power while they move towards the portal. Afterwards, I plan on having you tell Drake to do the same..." I said knowing I was deliberately throwing Alecien into another war by doing this.

Then the final stage of degeneration would occur. If we were lucky, it would reverse the tide and bring reparation. If not, Auran would be lost and dissolve back into the ravaging chaos that it was born from. Back to a land with no end and no beginning. The fire in my belly began to burn once more. I knew my eyes glowed vividly, matching Daes' bright blue eyes.

A door burst open and Lyth came rushing into the room. My hearing turned to static, and my vision hazed. Another wave was threatening to consume me. "Keep me here..." I begged out loud, as Celeste appeared through the same door.

My mind stuttered and blanked. When I came too, Lyth had me pinned to the wall, and was giving me his blood. Consciously my mind cleared as I saw Howl run a dagger over my wrist. The rush of our newly forming bond, him becoming another one of my guardians, sent my mind reeling. It hurt to breathe, and I felt like my blood was boiling, devouring me from the inside out. The stuttering was relentless. For a moment, my mind blanked and everything went eerily still, my eyes flew open as I felt an overwhelming sensation takeover. I was falling... Or my mind felt like I was. Even though my body was anchored to Lyth and our blood exchange, I felt disconnected and distant.

Then the stillness faded, almost as suddenly as it began. The overwhelming fire threatened to consume my body and soul. The fiery stabbing pain that echoed through my body was driving me mad. I was being thrown further into pure chaos, yet because of my current link to Lyth I was consciously aware of what was going on and it was mind numbing.

Another wave of terror tried to still my breathe and abandon my mind, a fiery liquid was poured down my throat. Howl and Lyth held tight, restraining me from Celeste's fiery brew. Like a burning cold, it's magic seeped into every fiber of my body. Again my mind tipped and chaos erupted within my soul. The eerie silence returned and a calming cold crept into my very being. For a moment, my mind struggled with it, but then images of darkness, terror and a burned world entered my mind.

Once the world was filled with nothing, no life, no death, no time, and no end. It was pure chaos and terror, nothing was still, instead everything fought in an endless cycle of hate and pain. Black shadows hunted the living, or nearly living beings. They preyed on the weak and consumed their flesh, leaving them alive as their victims were devoured whole. It was purgatory.

My bones felt like an icy skeleton, yet my skin burned with the fires of the land. The pain was like being shattered glass, broken over and over with no end. My mind lurched as my body shook unremittingly. Memories... These were more memories... Daes' memories of the begin time...

In that instant, I realized what was needed. *The staff couldn't be wielded unless the user was in pure chaos....* I had to be Raihanna to wield the staff, I had to be evil-minded and hate-filled... Sorrow filled my heart at the thought. *Would I survive this?* However, if I survived or not, I knew the world would fall if I didn't succeed. This stillness was the land and its magic waiting, and dying. Again my mind stumbled as I fell into a portal. Whether or not Lyth and Howl followed I didn't know, but I had to get the staff from Hunter and I had to get it now, before those creatures were released.

Power ~ Raillyn

The stillness crept into my body like a subtle knife. Thankfully it made things easier, Hunter saw it as evil and gleefully surrendered the staff to me. As I left The Keep he assembled his remaining Elite and troops to march on the portal.

As soon as my hands touched the staff I was sure it would kill me. It shattered and fragmented my very being. I became a witness to its controlling power, as it shoved my conscious mind aside for its own purposes. In a way, I was thankful, because it drove the mind numbing pain aside with it, but enveloped me in the eerie stillness and silence. Making me wonder if I would even survive long enough to do what was needed.

The power utilized my body so well it was frightening. Manipulating it through Daes' magic and blood running in my veins, I became its puppet. Its power encompassed me and drove me forward through watery mirages. Through the flashes, I found myself outside a large vast cave. Nothingness was felt within. The vast icy opening resembled a hungry, vicious mouth. Ice and rock crags jutted outward along the floor and top rim. The darkness within seemed abhorrent, and abnormal. Giving off an eerie feeling of unease. It was enough to deter anyone from going in and yet that's what I did.

Into the icy mirror walls of darkness, I walked. My hand reached out and touched its surface, but I felt nothing. Then a sound was heard. Gnawing, grinding and slurping. As if a dog chewed on a bone and ate at a dead carcass, it echoed in the cave. Proceeding towards it, I found what it was.

A being made of pure shadows with no real distinct features and burning flame eye sockets stood over a deer. Ahead, shadowy lacy arms, and legs were visible, and teeth. Bloody twisted teeth dripping with flesh and gore. The deer bleated, still alive as it was being devoured. Its belly was torn open and its insides were strewn everywhere. It was a sight of pure horror. A sight that mimicked Daes' memories of the beginning. The shadow twisted it's head and smiled a horrific grin before opening its mouth and letting out a blood-curdling screech.

Almost too fast for my mind to recognize, it turned on the deer and in one swift motion, ripped its head off. The terror-filled bleat of the deer's last cry echoed in the nothingness of the cave. Blood splattered the mirrored walls and sprayed me with its warmth. Then the crawling jitter sounds began. Like arachnids creeping over stone, the shadows crawled and everything went dark.

Something enveloped my body in an icy embrace. Like a heavy fog crawling over moors it took me. Down, we went, into the icy caverns and through solid walls. The feeling of being nothing but air, yet being enclosed by solid walls was repulsive. *I could be trapped here...* crossed my mind as I began to panic. It didn't matter though. I had no control, my mind screamed and thrashed for domination and yet the staff's power didn't care.

Finally, we stopped, the heaviness that enveloped me receded and left my body kneeling on a hard surface. The air felt open, thankfully we were not within the walls any longer. A haunting *eeee, raahaaa, ruuhh*, sound filled the open space. Louder and louder the sound became, deafening my hearing. Skittering across the ice and shuffling was heard. Then it all stopped.

A bright magic light filled the cave, illuminating its icy surface in a reddish-blue appearance. Ledges of all sizes filled the walls, the darkened shadows sat upon them. Various shapes and sizes but all shared the fiery eyes, and vicious teeth. Like clouds of blackened tar, they sat. Some stuck out long, red-pointed tongues, licking their lips and cried or screamed an ear piercing sound. It was loud enough to shatter glass and yet, they weren't the worst.

Standing several paces away was an ashen-skinned man. As if he had been burned from the inside out and charred. His flesh was a sickening shade of burnt grey. Dirty blonde, wiry hair hung around his face like a wired rope of twisted slime. His body looked like a bloated corpse that washed upon a seaside shore. And eyes blackened red, within rings of amazingly clear, pure cerulean blue.

His arms were crossed as he smiled a haunting smile. Something about this man called to me, my magic seemed to rejoice and resonate in happiness at the sight of him. However, part of me shuddered in fear. His very being was evil, and hate filled. His soul twisted and tormented. Dark and corrupt, his magic seemed to twine around the room as if he owned the place.

"You wonder why you're here, don't you?" He said putting his hands to his side and walking towards me. "Well, I'll tell you. You're here because of me. You're drawn to my power, even if it's depraved. I was one of the handful of beings Daes created in the begin days that survived the onslaught of overwhelming power."

Like a marionette doll waiting for its handler, my body stood still yet my mind reeled. *He was one of the first beings created by the gods?* Yet he was so grotesque and decayed. *What happened and why was he in the cave with the darkened horrors?* He sauntered towards me like a leopard preparing to pounce.

I felt myself shift. "That is not why I'm here. It involves you, but not in the sense that you believe."

A mocking laughter echoed through the cavern. The man threw his head back and joined in the laughter of the creatures. His belly laugh was bone chilling and haunting. It left a creeping cold stillness to my soul.

"You really think it's that simple?" He asked slinking closer like a python ready to attack.

His muscles tensed a split second before he uncoiled and sprang towards me. My mind screamed in horror as his eyes blazed red with madness. This was why he was here, he was filled with chaos. Whatever possessed my body refused to stand down.

Holding my ground, but purposely letting my guard down, icy fingers enclosed around my neck. The cold bit into my skin like icicles piercing my body. It crept into my soul, into the darkened space of emptiness where my conscious mind lay. A prisoner, a witness to all events. However as the tendrils of cold began to encircle me, a blue orb of warmth burst forth, keeping them at bay.

"Each step you take to opening the portal is one step closer towards your death." He stated as something snapped within. Like walls breaking from a sudden blow, I felt the shift.

The power controlling my body swiftly took over. Manipulating Daes' magic, a crystal barrier was erected between us and the shadows. It's icy surface sprang up like a bubble being blown into the wind. Screams filled the cavern as the darkened creatures leaped towards the barrier. Claws and teeth screeched across the solid shield. That's when it happened, the force keeping me in the shadows thrust me forth into a duel consciousness of my physical self. I was still a puppet, but the sensation of touch returned.

Sluggish and hazy like, I began to feel the chill of the cave. The air felt thick and so cold that my chest burned with each breathe I took. The bit of a knife across my wrist and the brute force of my hand twisting his arm back in an inhuman way, while pushing him back, brought me fully to. Like a cork being pulled from a bottle, I felt a pop. I was finally physically aware of everything, even though I remained a puppet. Looking down for a second, his face went rigid in pain, then his magic peaked and reached out towards mine. For a moment his cold nature met mine, but my fire didn't give way to his ice. Instead his faded.

His arm went limp in my hands as he fell to his knees, head going down as he fell forward like a rag doll. Meeting my eyes, he seemed placid, and uncaring. The cool, roped-lined metal hilt of my sword met my hand. Quickly I pulled it from its sheath and thrust it down into his leg. Metal scrapping into ice screamed around us as my blade pinned him to the icy floor below. Black blood began pooling out of the wound. Both thigh and shin were pierced through by my blade. There was no hope to move unless it was removed. Again his eyes met mine and flashed orange, then purple in surprise.

"Kill me then, if that is what you want. Then you will reign as leader of these creatures. For they cannot survive without chaos."

Circling him, dagger raised. He closed his eyes as if preparing himself for the final blow. Smiling, I reached out and grasped his hair, it felt like thin, wet ropes of dried hemp, brittle yet slimy. Yanking his head back with such force as to break his neck, I felt my demeanor tip. I wanted to kill him. In that split second the thought of ruling these creatures of darkness and shadow made me excited.

Preparing for a killing blow, I smiled as I pressed the blade against his skin. My whole body felt giddy and static-charged with power. Yet there was some underlying reason for it, something my unconscious knew that my conscious mind did not. Leaning forward, I whispered into his ear. The smell of bloated flesh, a smell far worse than that of a rancid skunk filled my nose.

"I know...." I heard my voice whisper. "But just remember... Chaos cannot survive without order, and when the two collide harmony is created."

His eyes shot open in horror as the blade ran across his neck, deep, but not deep enough for a killing blow. My still bleeding wrist slide across his lips, as I bent down and lapped at his open wound. Instantly pain shot through my body, like a tempered sword shooting through ice.

A new heat began radiating through my core, this one was more terrifying than before. Flashes of a young boy, with golden hair and bright blue ever-changing eyes, crossed my vision. Images of Silvertine, smaller looking, and more village like skittered around me. A dark-haired Drakar, much older than the boy reached out happily and took his hand in hers. Smiling, her silver eyes seems to glow like bright stars.

Then the image skipped, the boy was older, he held a bloodied infant in his arms. It was small, much smaller than a newborn. The black haired woman wept, and large, bloodied lines marked her body. As if someone had cut her up and down, in some places ugly yellow black bruises seemed to be trying to heal. I felt the man mentally withdraw in pain and agony. Tears of hate radiated through his mind, this was his life prior to this cave. And Demons had ended that prior life. I felt it, and saw it. The man went mad with rage.

Turning to attack and fight the Demons who brought such hate to his family, he stormed the Deleon Waste. Only to find a large Ancient Demon with a fiery whip and broad hellish blade. A creature that inhabits the abyss and deepest region beyond the gate of Death's Realm. Some Necromancer had brought him back into the world and in turn he wreaked havoc on the living. In the end this being twisted the man's nature, corrupting it and turning his hate against himself. Understanding sank in.

My core became an inferno of fire and ice. Something clicked into place, like a key fitting just right in a lock. My magic and mind became one. Its power ran up the staff in such a fierce inferno that its brutality surged outwards causing the ground in the caves to quake.

The red bloodstone that was charged with my family's blood and power shattered with the force, spattering outwards in an array of colors that swirled and mingled in the air around us. Still my body went on, exchanging blood with the chaotic creature of darkness. One I knew nothing about.

That's when I noticed everything was silent, other than the ground rumbling, the other creatures were deafened out or gone. It was as if he and I were the only two that remained. Chaos and order. The ground lurched once more, causing me to hold the staff tighter. Raising my head and glancing at the glittering shards of broken crystal, I saw they began to dance in the air.

As if coming together and becoming whole, four groups began to take shape, each the color of the Gods' magic. Twisting and turning their colors blazed bright. Green, red, silver and blue they formed their own separate orbs. Large marble-like spheres floated in the air before us. Like balls of frozen ice, they glowed and glimmered, dimming and brightening with their own magic. Then they shot up through the barrier and out of sight, all but the blue sphere.

Briefly it floated down and touched my forehead, what felt like a blessing my body felt at peace, true peace. As if being removed from the world I knew, I felt engulfed with magic. I had become a tool, and was being utilized like one to bring peace into the world. To help create a balanced world for all living things. That's when I realized, I was no longer in the cave, no longer surrounded by the chaotic souls that inhabited the barren horrors of the darkness.

Instead, I was surrounded in a haze, there was no substance, no ground, no nothing. Other than a scattered array of blue stars streaking across the vast grey white air. Wiping the dripping blood from my lips, I looked around.

The blue orb was gone, and the bright blue stars began racing through the sky, swirling and twisting around me. Like a whirlwind of raw power, it began taking shape. The stars became small tendrils of thread, weaving up and under around and around, into a tightly wound ball.

Instinctively I held out my hand as the ball solidified into a solid mass. On contact, it flared such a bright blue I thought it would burn or blind. Closing my eyes and shielding them with the staff, another key like sensation slipped into place. My hand now empty just held the staff, the bright light faded and an old being I hadn't seen since Raihanna stood before me.

The blue dragon from the caverns below the Wolves territory glowed fiercely with the power of Daes before taking human shape. Pale blue-white hair, almond-shaped vivid blue eyes made him standout against any other race. However, his skin was the biggest stand out, it appeared like tiny glittering tan scales of glimmering blue hues. I had never seen a creature or human like this. Like plucking a high noted string, his name echoed in my mind. *Razul...* I knew I was safe. Like a dagger piercing my mind and heart, darkness enveloped me, as I fell into his outstretched arms. *Razul..... Daes' Dragon....*

Power Restored ~ Howl

Lyth and I had been searching for Raillyn for hours, but we found no trace. She had visited Hunter, took the staff and literally disappeared. Neither of us were able to trace her and we feared waking Alkin, just yet. Walking the halls of the palace, I knew there was only one other I could go to. One who would help still Alkin's wrath once he found his mate missing yet again.

Pushing open the four spiraling dragon doors, Lyth was just paces behind me. Opal nestled in one of the overstuffed chairs staring at the fire, her dark hair fell into her sorrowful face. She glanced at us, as the doors shut behind us.

"You feel it too? That Raillyn is missing?" Lyth said quietly.

Slowly she nodded her head. "I felt something, as if glass shattered into a million pieces. It was a pulse of his magic, of Daes' – I would know it anywhere..." She trailed off before standing and coming towards us. "Does Alkin know?"

I diverted my eyes, "No, not yet. Does Solomn?" Opal did the same, no, she hadn't told him. Only Daes' lineage was being affected by whatever was happening.

"We went looking for Raillyn after she left, but couldn't find her." Lyth said. "I don't know what happened but one minute everything was fine then the next everything went deathly still. Almost like something shattered inside me."

I nodded my head. "Yes, and we can't find her, nor are we able to trace her. It's as if she's vanished. I went to Hunter but he's gone, his Elite and troops are marching on the portal and werewolves as we speak. It's as if Alecien has been thrown into total anarchy once more."

Opal's eyes became soft, as pools of tears began to creep into the corners. "I haven't felt this way since Callie died. This heart wrenching feeling of nothingness is utter torment. It's just as before, just like when all his Mystics died." She cried. "We've lost haven't we? Raillyn is gone from us and Daes' magic will never be restored..." Opal cried as she slid to the floor, placing her head in her hands and sobbing uncontrollably.

A loud bang indicated the door had been roughly thrown open, heavy footsteps echoed in the darkened room. I didn't need to turn to know who entered. "Where is she?!" Alkin yelled while coming to stand by us. "And why do you three look like someone has died?!"

Opal raised her head to her adopted son and met his eyes. I could tell he regretted his words and flinched at his own anger. "I'm sorry, mother." He said as she stood and let him take her into his arms. "What's going on? I woke up and Raillyn was missing. So I went to the Wolves, hoping she was there. Only to discover they are preparing to engage the Vampires in battle at the portal."

"We don't know. None of us have answers. Something happened with Daes' magic... It felt as if a ball of glass was thrown against a stone wall, shattering it. It was painful and numbing." We all looked at each other unsure what to do.

~~*~*~*~ *Razul*~*~*~*~*~

After taking Raillyn to Daes, I began to wonder what price she was going to have to pay to restore his magic into the world. Her mind was in shambles, her body tormented, and her soul on the verge of breaking. *Just like before...* Daes said it was a necessity that balance had to be restored from what created the chaos in the first place. In other words, Alecien had to be at war and Daes' bloodline had to be in shambles... It was tricky and if everything didn't go as planned would be devastating.

Quietly I watched as Daes and Delron tried to keep her in the living world. The overwhelming force of magic threatened to break her soul in pieces and end her life. The only thing to ensure that she wouldn't go willingly into death was to bind her to a task. In essence binding her to the Gods to perform their will. Daes created the first-blood tie with her, his intricate blacked blue symbol ran up her back marking her as his chattel. Its ancient pattered of twists and turns was familiar to me, I myself had the same pattern dotting my back. Never would she be the same after today. However, that wasn't enough.

Keeping hushed, I only heard the murmurs of what might come, death, destruction, devastation, and entropy if she failed. None that the world could afford. She had to be kept alive, but the cost would be great. I just watched, knowing better than to intervene.

Daes ordered Delron to give her his potent blood, securing her soul from death if she survived its toxic mix. Eyes wide I watched. The Death God's blood was like drinking a deadly cocktail of the most potent herbs and mixtures the world had to offer. Even if she did survive this, what would that leave her with? In the end, it would eat away at her body and in the end she would die. Just as in The Keep with the construct spell, they were sealing her fate to death.

I had to close my eyes as Delron drew his blade across his wrist, a haunting hiss escaped the wound as if steam meet cold air. My own soul shuddered and a tear escaped my eye. *This wasn't fair...* However, I knew it was the only way. Alecien had to be in devastation and Daes' line had to be near extinction for this to work properly. It was because this time Raillyn wasn't a child, now she was the adult...

Opening my eyes, I watched as Delron fed her his blood. She grimaced and tried to pull back, but Daes' magic soothed her and made her accept the toxic mix.

"Go, and tell Alkin and Lyth to annihilate the Vampires in Alecien. They have become too overpopulated. Tell them that it's time to intervene." Daes ordered. Nodding my head, I turned and left through an open portal. Before it closed around me, I heard Daes' voice once more. "Do not mention what you have seen here..." Sighing I mentally nodded my head and agreed.

~*~*~*~*~*~*Howl*~*~*~*~*~*

As we stood around in silence, a portal was felt opening behind us. A tall man, with shoulder-length, white-blue hair, almond blue eyes, and a haunting shade of tan, blue scaly skin stepped out. He smiled slightly as he cocked his head and nodded at us. Opal gasped at the sight and left Alkin's arms.

"Razul..." She said going to him before he held up his hand, stopping her.

"I come on strict orders. Alkin, Lyth, go assist the Werewolves. Help annihilate the Vampires in battle. They have become over-populated in Alecien. The Gods have deemed it fit for us to assist in their termination." He said as if repeating orders.

Lyth tensed for a moment as if he was about to obey till Alkin marched towards him. "First off. Tell me where she is, Razul? Where is Raillyn!" He yelled with such force that the items on nearby shelves shook with his power.

Razul stood unintimidated. He was Daes' most trusted Dragon, the oldest that still lived. He was ultimately a pet to the Gods. Whatever Daes told him to do he would obey, without question. Even if that was to kill his own mother, or father. However I doubted this being still had parents. He was as old as time itself.

"She's with Daes, and he will bring her back when he sees fit. Other than that I cannot tell you what is going on, it is not my place." He said before turning and motioning towards the door. "I can say this, you two need to hurry. Help tip the balance of this war in our favor or else chaos will erupt once more. The past has a way of repeating what was never fully healed. This is one of those cases."

I saw Alkin tense. After being around him for so long I knew he wanted to argue, but he wouldn't. He'd been told what to do by Razul before, when Calista was alive. He knew in the end either way, he would obey. That it was quicker and easier if he obeyed sooner rather than later. We learned that too late the first time. After taking too much time and losing the first war. We were too preoccupied, then worrying too much about Drameon and where Raillyn went to help tip the tides of war in our favor. This time, however, things would be different. Seeing Razul before me verified we had not lost… yet.

Alkin nodded his head and left with Lyth. After the door closed, Razul turned towards us. Coming close to Opal he smiled sinisterly. "For you, my dear." He said taking Opal's hand into his, just as another portal of blackened blue mist opened up.

Through the swirling mist walked Daes, and in his arms was Raillyn, pale and unconscious. In her hands lay Daes' staff of power, whole and glowing brightly. Daes' vivid blue eyes met mine. The last time he had walked this land was almost two-hundred and fifty years ago. Opal looked at him and Raillyn in shock, tears filled her eyes as she went to them. Shakily she reached out and stroked Raillyn's hair before I followed.

I had never seen Opal so distraught, and never had I seen Raillyn looking so haggard. She was beyond limp, it was as if she was dead. "She's not…." Opal began thinking the same thing.

Daes shook his head, his black hair fell into his face as he looked down at her. "No, she lives, for now, anyway. I cannot guarantee though what will happen. Which is why I am here." He said gently passing Raillyn to me.

Carefully I took her from him shifting my weight to accompany hers. Daes' cool skin brushed mine as a surge of power passed between us. He smiled knowingly, before drawing on his magic.

A small blue orb faintly glowed like a fiery ball. It wisped around as if it was made of pure flames. Dancing in Daes hands, he looked at Opal as she grabbed his free arm, and cried into his chest. His strong arm encircled her as he placed his head on hers.

"I propose a deal of great value to you my dear, shall you agree." He said as she looked up to meet his eyes.

I had always known their history but never seen the two interact together. They had history together, and for some reason or another, Daes truly loved her, more than just as a creation of his. This was why Calista was favored, in a sense they both loved each other. Maybe that was why Opal had only successfully carried Ivy with Solomn. Deep down she had feelings for another man, one she could never really truly physically touch. I shifted uncomfortably for a moment before Daes went on. This was taboo, and went against everything I knew. Making even me feel troubled.

"This tiny blue flame is our daughter's soul. Everything she was and everything she could be. It is her very living essence and I have been keeping it safe since her death."

Opal's eyes went wide, as her crying ceased. For a moment, I stood shocked as well.

"Call it a debt I promised her."

Her eyes met his and then looked back at the soul orb.

"If you agree to help bring Calista back I can guarantee Raillyn's safety as well. If not, everything might be lost. Delron has already done all he dared with keeping Raillyn in the living. Only time will tell now..." He said trailing off.

Looking down at Raillyn, I heard Opal choke back tears as she placed her hand over her mouth. Stepping forward I had my own questions. "But if Raillyn dies, won't your magic?" I asked looking back at her ashen face.

Flicking his hand, the blue flames disappeared. He strolled towards me and brushed Raillyn's hair from her face. "I have put countless hours into her well-being. I am not giving up on her easily, plus I cannot afford to lose her now. But if the worst should happen we need to be prepared." He said as the door opened again and in came Celeste.

Her bright hair swirled around her as her emerald green eyes met mine in shock. Slowing her pace she looked at Daes then Raillyn. Hurrying, she made her way to me. "I don't know what's going on but what happened to Raillyn?" She asked taking on her healer's demeanor.

Before anyone could stop her, she began using her magic to examine Raillyn's body. Daes said nothing and instead just sighed. A split second later her eyes flew open as she turned to look at Daes. He held up his hand stopping her from what she began saying.

"Don't say a word. I know... All of us have done everything we can already. If Raillyn lives, she will be in control of my staff until more Mystics are born or grow into power. Essentially I molded her too perfect and she is more like our first creations than a Mystic now..." He said with regret to his voice.

We had heard stories of the Gods' first creations. When the Gods created time, and gave meaning to life and existence. Born from their magic, and blood to keep peace on earth, these Mystics were essentially true demigods. Keepers of the peace and rulers of their own magic.

Their job was to ensure their Gods' magic flowed and functioned correctly in the world, as well as follow the Gods' tasks. The purebred Dragons accompanied them, no questions asked. Just as they had the Gods when they walked the land making it whole and good. they walked beside these demigods as their guardians and assistants.

Daes had broken not only one taboo with Calista's conception, but also with Raillyn. That's when it hit me. Raillyn never was a true Mystic, and neither was Calista. Calista was born directly from Daes' power, she was like one of the God's creations, in her own sense.

Mingling an Ancient's power with the Gods resulted in such a being. Then Raillyn... If Daes did not intervene and ensure a safe pregnancy with Calista, she would have never been able to carry her. In turn, if Daes didn't intervene when Raillyn was three she would have died due to the lack of power. That was the issue with their first creations. Most died from lack of power or diluted power. They were incompatible for life on this earth. Daes had doomed them both to an existence of redeeming more power for their own lives. When Calista failed, it fell onto Raillyn's shoulders. Now she had Daes' staff and he even said she couldn't survive without it until more of his power possessed the world.

"I can't believe you... You've known this whole time what you were doing and you knew Raillyn and Calista's fate since before either of their births! Why! How could you be so evil and cruel to your own offspring!?!" I yelled as I saw his eyes begin to glow an off shade of red.

"Do you think I enjoyed knowing their fate? Or why they had to be created? I hated the knowledge surrounding their births and wished it could be different. But there was no stopping it. This world is still at a tipping point and has been for the past few eras. Order cannot exist without chaos. If either order or chaos ceased then the world would fall back into the nothingness. Calista and Raillyn were not the first! Drameon actually was and then Alkin, Varg, and Nora..." Daes said in his anger, before calming down.

"So how many are there?" I asked suddenly stumbling onto what we had fought so fiercely for when the first war broke out.

Daes sighed momentarily as Opal looked at the floor.

"There were at least two from each lineage at the time. There was hope for more to be born, seeing that they had mates between their own. That and mingling Ancients' blood with the Gods' that would leave a viable race to support the greater good of the land and the Gods themselves." She began hesitantly. Looking at Daes he nodded his head, and she continued. "Just like when the first beings were created in the land, so it was meant for these children to be similar. They would become the voice of the Gods and hidden workers for their lineage. They would become the single tie between the land and the Gods, working their magic more intently for the greater good. By working side by side with their creators. It was a way to restore order, to restore the Mystic race to what it should be. Instead of having such diluted power and blood." Opal uttered quietly.

"Ahh..." I began, before Celeste chimed in.

"That's why we're so drawn to them, that we agree so willingly to follow their orders. We've created ties and alliances with them and we never even knew. But since you said something, I can see the difference. We're family with them, we're not just friends or protectors like normal Drakar are to Ancients. We actually created our own family unit and fight fiercely for each other." She said, drifting off.

She was right, it was different with Drameon, and his family. Even Alkin and Nora were different, but now we understood why. It was making sense.

"Leon then..." I uttered.

Opal nodded her head. "Yes, Leon was Daes' second child born back into this world. I had the privilege of raising three and assisting in Nora. They were all born around the same time. It made things easier when there were others around. Drameon grew up around Varg and Rhaine. Alkin doesn't know, but Drameon does; he spends so much time with his mother I don't see how he doesn't know."

"If Raillyn doesn't survive and Opal agrees to my bargain then I will personally hold her soul until she can be reborn. I hope it doesn't come down to that because we will lose much more than what you see." Daes said as Celeste nodded her head.

"What can we do to help then?" Celeste said while nodding at me.

"Give Opal and I a moment to discuss this in private. Please, if you could take Raillyn to her mother's room here in the palace, I will be there as soon as I can. My time is limited here and already runs short." He said while taking both of Opal's hands in his and kissing them gently.

Meeting Celeste's eyes, we both nodded and walked out of the room. Razul followed quietly behind us, closing the doors as we left. The monotone halls were quiet and everything was still. My mind was numb, so much had happened in such a short amount of time and we still weren't in the clear. Almost mindlessly I entered Calista's old room.

It was still adorned in the blues and greens of her youth. It was funny how Ancients were. Preferring one color over another, which usually indicated their mate's magic color. This was how

Calista had always been. She loved green. The idea of walking in a vast forest was pure bliss for her, and she loved the smell of lilies.

Looking down at Raillyn, I wondered if she would live. She was so still as I placed her upon a vast bed covered with a large green sapling quilt. Her hands gripped the staff so tight I doubted anyone other than Daes or Razul could remove it. In a sense, it comforted me, knowing she instinctively held onto the one thing keeping her alive. Keeping her in this world.

For a moment I felt my demeanor break, I wanted to drown myself in Darah wine or worse Fires breath. Anything to take the edge away. "What do we do?" I asked no one in particular.

Razul sighed and glanced at Celeste. "We do as we're told, and continue to fight for the ones we love, and the future we hope for." She said with determination in her voice.

I shook my head. How could she be so sure about everything? I had witnessed first-hand the last war, and it ended badly. Why would things be different this time around? Already I felt like I had failed again, but this time with Raillyn.

"I don't think she will die. And I know it sounds bad but, too much time has been spent into shaping Raillyn. Daes won't let her go so easily. That's why he insists to restore Calista. He feels he owes her a debt. Owes her the life that should have been, hopefully in a world of peace..." Razul said quietly.

"But at what price must that peace be paid with?" I yelled frustrated. I had lost Calista, who became like a sister, to the same "peace task." Now her daughter lay in the same position.

"Nothing is free in life, everything comes with a price that must be paid. However, magic and power come with the highest prices of all. Whether Raillyn lives or dies she will pay a price, one way or another." Razul stated matter of fact like.

"How can you be so calm? You've always been this way and it drives me insane!" I said grabbing his shoulders and shoving him into the nearby wall. Celeste let out a squeal as a nearby portrait fell to the ground.

Razul's eyes lit up bright blue as he shoved me away. "You of all people should know I appear calm but my emotions are far from still. I obey and do as I'm told." He said putting his face in mine. His scales shimmered in deep blue hues, as his eyes glowed with fire. I of all people knew not to anger a Dragon, even in human form.

Before I had time to retort a shift in the air occurred. Like tranquility striking a windblown lake, everything went still. The air seemed to crackle and stir with a familiar power. As the rustle of sheets caused me to turn.

Raillyn sat upright, staff in hand beside her she placed her head in her other hand. "You two need to stop, you're making my head hurt." She said meekly, as I noticed her eyes barely shift color. Like Daes' the blue never seemed to fade, and instead hues illuminated them briefly before returning.

Celeste ran over towards her and placed a hand on her head. "You feel fine, no fever." She said as Raillyn looked her in the eyes.

"What happened?" She asked as she slid back down on the bed. "I feel so tired, and there is a disturbance in the magic near here. Something that shouldn't be..." Her eyes closed as the door swiftly opened.

Daes strolled into the room in one fell swoop. Strutting across the floor as if he owned the place. His black hair hung around his Elf-like face and piercing blue eyes. While his blackened leather armor seemed slightly shambled, and his shirt remained united. Giving sight to a muscular chest no normal race on Auran could obtain. As he entered the room, a wave of calmness echoed in his wake. Raillyn sat back up like a bolt of energy entered her body, and jolting her into animation.

"The disturbance is because I'm still here, child." He said, smiling before going on. "And I'm glad to see you are awake. Thankful to say the least. I truly wondered if you would survive that ordeal." He said while sitting on the edge of the bed.

Her eyes were wide, mind closed to me, but I could still read the subtle changes in her posture. She was frightened, and whatever horrors accompanied her ordeal had scared her mentally. Placing the staff in her lap, her hands covered her face as a gut wrenching cry erupted from her.

Daes reached out and held her close as she cried into his chest. "Why?" She cried as he lovingly kissed her hair. "Why, and what in the world was that man?" She asked pulling back and looking to Daes for answers.

Daes diverted his eyes momentarily before looking back at her and answering. "That was Phury, my oldest creation still alive today. He merged with the very Demon he set out to kill. Actually it was after he killed it, he summoned its soul into his own. We had no choice but to lock him up within those walls." He said as if recounting a story of sorts.

"Am I connected to that creature now?" She said as her demeanor finally began breaking through, allowing me to see what she had seen. Brief flashes of a hazy figure with wiry hair and blackened red blue eyes exchanged blood with her. She had pinned him to a cavern floor, like a trapped mouse in a cage.

Daes shook his head and smiled slightly. "Order cannot exist without chaos. You of all people know this. Phury had a very chaotic life. While you were raised by Chaimh and Lillian in a more balanced one. In a way you two are very much alike. Aside from that, no you do not have a substantial link with him. If he were to ever escape you could track him, but nothing else." He said, seemingly calming her fears.

Momentarily she glanced at the staff. "This is yours, I guess, then..." She began before Daes raised his hand, stopping her.

"No until my power is fully restored in this land, it is yours. You are my one true blooded child that still walks this land." He said as she met his eyes.

I saw it in the way her face twitched and her eyebrows went up. She was so much like Calista it wasn't even funny. She wanted to cry as she realized what Daes meant.

"I cannot guarantee how long that will be." She said hushed, hoping only he would hear.

Leaning forward, he kissed her forehead. "Much sooner than you think my dear. You only have to be patient and hold on. The staff will become like a familiar friend over time." He said smiling at her.

Briefly a smile crossed her face before she looked at him, concerned. "What happened to you?" She asked Daes, her ears twitched a little as I felt her reach towards his mind.

Her face blanked and so did her mind as she pulled back from the flashes of intimacy she saw between her grandparents. "My mother?"

Daes nodded and smirked at her while pulling a strand of hair behind his ear. "Yes, as a precaution, if you die I will be sure you're reborn."

Raillyn looked down at the staff in her hands, a loose tear ran down her nose and onto it. "But Alkin, Callina?"

Reaching out, Daes turned her face to his. "If the time comes for me to take your soul, I will tell them. He will wait for you, I know he will. He'd never leave your daughter to grow up alone in this world." He said with all seriousness before his face softened. "Plus I don't think Alkin will be able to resist picking on Calista since the tables would be turned."

"Are you going to tell my father?" She asked.

Daes shook his head. "I think for now it will stay between my lineage. Opal isn't even telling Solomn yet."

There were so many questions to ask concerning this choice, but one stood out. "Will she remember anything from before?" I asked curiously.

His weighty face met mine, a certain reserve seemed to glow in his eyes. Swirls of blue hues danced around them, as he frowned. "No."

So in other words everything would go back the way it was, or supposed to be. Essentially the Gods were resetting what went wrong and were going to let their children and creations pay the price. But with a debt owed concerning some.

"So I wouldn't remember anything either would I?" She asked looking back down at the staff.

Daes reached out a brushed her hair aside. "No." he replied saddened.

"So what do we do?" Raillyn asked, breaking my train of thought. If neither of them remembered what would happen with those that did?

Daes took Raillyn's hand and gently pulled her to her feet. Like a dancer ready to perform on stage, she stood graceful, and strong. Staff in hand she grasped it tightly and smiled at her grandfather. All appearance of tears and sadness gone. Whatever was shared was only between them, it made me wonder what we would do.

"I'm going after Ash and Hunter. I won't kill my uncle, but Ash is mine, he condemned my mother to death and I will have my revenge." She said leaving Daes' side who stood smirking as she walked with authority and power. She must have read Daes' mind and gotten the information from him. It made me wonder if she intended to kill him or to continue following Daes' orders not to.

In that instant, I saw how meticulously she was shaped. Neither Mystic or God but somewhere in between. It made me wonder what would come of this old recreated race.

Walking up to me, she looked me in the eyes. "Did you know it was Ash who tortured my mother in the cellar?" She asked.

Trying to remember back, I wasn't even in the same room as Calista for most of the time. In addition, I was poisoned and barely lucid myself till I received a partial treatment before being converted. I remembered a black-haired man, but his face escaped me. However, I knew he wasn't Vampire, he was a rogue Shadow Walker. I could smell it. It was part of the reason I wanted treatment in Silvertine. I couldn't bear that part of me any longer, not after being tortured and nearly killed by one.

Raillyn read my memories as I recalled them. Shaking my head, no, she knew what I meant. "I want to accompany you in killing Ash then. I don't think it's safe to do it alone, he's cunning and vicious when cornered."

"I wouldn't have it any other way." She said smiling up at me. "Grandfather, thank you again, and I will try my best to finish this task." She smiled back at him before calling a portal and leaving through it staff in hand. Nodding to Daes I followed behind her, determined to correct this wrong.

The Marsh Lands ~ Alkin

Lyth and I followed the now familiar trail towards the portal. Long threads of green moss hung from the leafless trees as we passed a bubbling bog of swampy water. It's hissing stench smelled of marsh gas, rotten eggs mixed with wet animal. Finally we saw the clearing, the place that would mark the final battle.

Drake and a few of his troops circled the tall black shadow that Raihanna had released from my father's realm. They appeared to be uneasy about it. But the stone-like structure stood unmoving, seemingly unanimated. Lyth picked up pace and went beside the troops.

"Well, lookie here." He said while reaching out to touch the creature. For a moment it rumbled and took a step back, tipping its head towards Lyth like a puppet looking at its master. The nearby troops jumped back, and drew swords. Pointing them directly at Lyth and the shadow. "It's not every day you get to see one of the greater shadows." He said as the blacked cloud creature resumed its standing form, unmoving once more.

As Lyth smiled at the troops they seemed to relax a little. "What is that?" Drake asked as he came over towards us, holding up a hand indicating for the troops to stand down.

"Like Lyth said it's a greater shadow. Once an Ancient of some sort who turned evil and died. Rai awoke it when she was in The Keep and released it. It won't hurt anyone unless commanded too, and only Raillyn or her guardians can do that." I said while looking at Lyth who smiled gleefully.

"Don't worry I'll keep this baby in line." He said excited. "There's only three of us other than Raillyn that can control this thing, and I'm the only one not busy at the moment. So you have nothing to fear.

Drake looked at him apprehensively and sighed. "Raven and Avice said they saw Vampires just on the other side of the swamp. We don't have much time. But if this thing can fight, will you control it to help us?" He asked trying to get everything ready for the battle.

Nodding my head I looked at Lyth, who agreed as well. "Good, where's Raillyn and Howl?" He asked while looking around.

The portal stood behind him, the white wood structure arched more than twenty feet high. White steps lead up to the platform where the staff Raillyn and I created lay. Drake still thought this portal was evil, yet it wasn't. It would bring Daes' magic back into the world and soon. Even the very air seemed to feel it and tingled with electrifying energy.

"She's not here. She and Howl had some business to finish. I'm sure they will be here as soon as they are able." I said hoping Daes was right and that Raillyn was ok and would soon accompany us.

"They're coming!" Raven said as she ran towards us. Her black hair shone in blue streaks where the sun hit it.

Sweat beaded her brow as she drew her sword. Drake nodded his head as he did the same. Off in the distance the sound of footfalls echoed in the surrounding woods. Gently rhythmic sloshing could be heard, as what I assumed was the Vampires wading through the murky marsh. Turning my head I heard Drake holler at his troops. There was no use being quiet, they could smell we were there, and hear our beating heart.

Troops rushed all around surrounding Raven and Drake. Avice and Saibal worked side by side, rallying the remaining troops into the surrounding woods and around the clearing. Like a well-oiled machine the Wolves went into motion, just as the first Vampire appeared.

They circled him, and quickly attacked, as more appeared. Swords clashed as blows were exchanged between both sides. Vampires, tore into flesh as they attacked and ripped their teeth into arms and necks. Blood splattered around us, and Lyth patted the greater shadow into motion.

Groaning like a rusty gear the creature turned towards Lyth and spoke. "What do you command, master?" It asked in a rugged, dry voice. It reminded me of a husked corpse talked well after it's been mummified.

"You see those Vampires?" He asked the shadow. "I want you to kill them, but only the Vampires. Leave the living alone." He said carefully wording what he said.

The creature's giant black clouded head nodded as its elephant legs began moving forward. "Yes, master..." It trailed off as its giant elongated tree trunk of an arm swiped at the first Vampire in its path. Like swatting a gnat the Vampire flew through the air, smacking into a tree.

It spittled blood and grabbed at its chest, where a branch impaled him. Black red blood oozed out of the wound and steamed the air around the hole. The blackened shadow leapt at him as soon as its giant feet rumbled into place. The cloudy arms reached out and ripped off the Vampires head. Blood sprayed everything around, as the Vampire let out a dying scream.

Lifting the dripping head high over his head. The greater shadow let the blood spill into its mouth, taking the Vampires last life energy. A twisted mouth of razor sharp teeth smiled as red fires burned in the creatures eyes, giving it a maddened appearance. Like a cat attacking a mouse, it jumped off the tree and picked up another Vampire. Picking it up with its two shadowy hands the shadow bit it in half, sucking in its blood as it did so.

"Well..." Lyth said as we watched the shadow disappear into the mass of battle. "That thing is pure chaos."

I had no words for what happened. I hated these creatures, they were horrifying and blood thirsty. And like Lyth said they were pure chaos. "Can you control it?" I asked hesitant about what we released into the battlefield.

"Let's hope so." He replied.

Drawing my blade, Lyth did the same. It was time to follow orders. To help annihilate the Vampires and ultimately tip the odds in our favor. Bringing my blade up I blocked an attack, just as Lyth swung under my blade and sliced my attacker. I was on the lookout for Hunter and Ash, and so was Lyth. They were the leaders in this whole fiasco, once they died the remaining Vampires may scatter.

History repeats ~ Raillyn

My head hurt, and swam with the vile drug that was used to knock me out. I felt sluggish, cold, violently ill and weak. Hunter had taken the staff, its power was no longer felt near me. A door clicked open, squeezing my eyes, light poured into the room, making my head pound.

"Keh, I see you're awake." I heard Ash say as his cold hand grabbed my face and forced me towards him. "How does it feel to be in the same place where your mother died? We could have a little fun if you want." He said as he forced his mouth onto mine.

His lips felt cold, dead, and overall just sickening. He had done this in The Keep when I was Raihanna as well, but this time I didn't have the strength to fight him. My body wretched as I tried to break free. For a moment, he let go, and I heard him take a swig of a bottle, trying to open my eyes, they felt swollen. Leaving me only able to squint. Everything hurt and the light from his magic was only making me feel worse.

Once more his mouth met mine as he tried to slip his tongue in, cool liquid followed. It felt like fire, and pure agony. I tried to struggle, but he held on tight. Raking his fingers in my hair he held me in place. Still trying to fight him I did the only thing I felt I could and bit down.

Foul-tasting warm blood filled my mouth, it tasted rotten or stale. Almost reminding me of spoiled juice mixed with milk. It was horrid, and made me wretch.

Pulling away, I felt the back of his hand slam me onto the cold stone floor. It was a welcome relief from before, but my stomach rolled and, trying to regain my balance, I felt it protest. Bile rose in my throat and burned as I vomited onto the floor.

He was poisoning me, I just knew it. He slipped me something deadly and it was making me weak and sick. Ash stood behind me snickering, before I felt his hand in my hair once more. Yanking me back, he whispered into my ear.

"It's Dragonbane and Willow Tears, a deadly combination if you have Drakar blood in your veins. Too much and it will still your beating heart." He laughed as the door opened.

Carefully opening my eyes I saw Hunter walk in, Daes' staff in hand, its blue glow no longer illuminated the stone. Instead it was dull. For a moment, I took the time to glance around. I was in one of the cellar's various torture chambers.

Mossy green stone walls splattered with black and red blood, and a wooden door with bars. A table was near the door, I knew what was on there without even looking. My time in The Keep taught me a thing or two about the cellar. Hooks, knives, pliers, picks, and other tools used to torture victims lay dirty and blood-stained on its surface.

Closing my eyes I wanted to cry. They were going to torture me. A sharp sting along my shoulder brought my attention back to Ash. A knife ran along my skin, as he cut Howl's blue mark, tracing each line with the poisoned blade.

Searing pain and angry red welts boiled on my skin. Smiling, he drove the blade into muscle. I tried to reach up, but I was so out of it, I almost fell over. I heard myself cry out, either physically or mentally I don't know. The poison coursed stronger in my veins and darkness tried to consume me. A darkness I would welcome at this moment.

"Don't kill this one, Ash. We need her still to open the portal and bring us those creatures." Hunter said.

"Yeah, yeah I know, but she has to be beaten into submission for that. We have to bring out Raihanna in her before she will do something like that. Raillyn's too good and sweet to ever create chaos. Isn't that right, Raillyn?" Ash said yanking me off the floor by my hair.

For a moment I felt a smidgen of power from the staff, it reacted to my anger towards Ash and Hunter. A small static charge sent a shockwave through me, and the staff flared momentarily, illuminating the room in a foggy blue haze. The pain of my hair being pulled lessened and wood clattering onto the floor echoed in the room.

"Get out of here!" I heard Ash yell. "And take that thing with you! I didn't have any problems with her until you showed up. Don't worry I won't kill this Mystic, but I do plan to have my fill of fun with her." He said as he brought my mouth to his and slipped me more poison.

At this rate, he would kill me, and it made me wonder. *Was this how my mother died?* His mouth ran down my chin then his teeth sank deep into my neck. Grimacing at the pain, I felt him drink at my blood. My mind became foggy, and moments of being lucid caused me to slip in and out. Overall I felt like I was adrift in an abysmal sea of darkness. I wanted to feel hate, I wanted to lash out and hurt. But I couldn't. The poison coursed too strongly through my body and prevented it.

"I never got to toy around with your mother, but I will say her blood was just as tasty as yours. You, however, I have always wanted to do bad things to. If only you gave me a chance as Raihanna maybe I wouldn't be so cruel to you now." Ash said as I felt him cut away at my clothes. "You have such soft skin..." I heard him say as he bit me again, piercing the soft flesh near my breast.

A tear escaped my eyes as I laid there like a doll. Blood loss and poison coursing through me left me feeling paralyzed. Ash would have his way with me whether I liked it or not and he knew it. His hand traveled down my body and across my tender skin. Thankfully my mind slipped away only becoming lucid briefly now and again.

Stinging pain and agony filled my body and bones, as Ash sliced at my flesh and drank my blood. The cold stone floor on my bare skin only added to the pain. Parts of my body that shouldn't hurt, burned. Vomiting onto the floor, I knew I looked like a mess. I tried to concentrate on something, anything to elude the pain, but I couldn't. I wanted to cry, and sadly I wanted to die...

The River of Death nipped at my back as the torture went on. However, I couldn't escape to it. Not yet anyway, I needed to take the portal apart and fully release Daes' magic into the world, and sadly only I was the one strong enough to do it. Then I would accept my fate. Either way I didn't see myself escaping this alive. My weakened state and the force it took to dismantle the portal releasing his power would kill me, or Hunter and Ash would. Again my mind slipped from me and the welcome relief of unconsciousness encased me.

If it was hours or days later, I awoke to the gentle sway and clopping of horse hooves. My body felt leadened, but I was able to make slow movements. I lifted my hand towards my face and looked at it. It was distorted and hazy. Looking up I noticed I was enclosed under a cloak or blanket, and leaned against who I could only assume was Ash.

My body hurt, and as I looked at my hand, I saw how much damage he had done. Cuts lined my arm, appearing almost pattern like. Reaching to touch my neck, I felt an array of bite marks. This was why rogue Shadow Walkers were killed, they were too deadly and often kidnapped women and tried to keep them as theirs. They were no better than the Vampires.

For a moment, my head pounded in pain as I began hearing the clash of steel against steel. I must have groaned because Ash shifted his weight and lifted the material slightly to look at me. He smiled viciously as he reached out and brushed my hair away from my face.

"Don't worry, dear, we're almost to the portal. After you open it and release those creatures into the world, we can go home and I will be sure to heal you properly." He said while gently kissing the top of my head.

Part of me wanted to withdraw, but the more sensible part told me not to. I was sure if I rejected him outright, instead of pretending to be OK with everything, I would end up right back in the cellar. That thought made me shiver in fear.

Closing my eyes, I didn't want to remember that place, or what Ash had wrought on me down in the dark halls. I felt dirty, abused, and infected. Part of me still wanted to die just to forget, but another part of me didn't. I had missed out on so much in my life, and what was supposed to be, that I didn't want to miss anymore. *I wish I could have the unreachable... I wish I could have back my missed time...* A tear escaped my eye as we rode on.

Why was I the one being punished? Why was I the one paying such high prices for my father's intervention? None of it made sense in my fog-induced state. And that's when I realized. I hated everything.

I hated my father for intervening and me having to pay such high prices for his punishment. I hated the fact that only I could realign the upset of balance and magic in the world. I hated the Vampires. I hated that I now had a weakness, the staff and that when taken from me, I was worthless. I hated that I grew up with Chaimh and Lillian. And I hated that I missed growing up in Silvertine, beside Alkin, my family and my friends. Most of all I hated my life and myself. I hated what I had become.

Ash did it, he tipped me over the already teetering edge. In the end, I really became the very thing they wanted. A vessel filled with hate. I really was Raihanna. The scary thing... I was OK with it, because I knew I was going to die. I had found my own peace in what I had become, and what I was shaped into. I had found my own balance in my chaotic upside down twisted world. I only wished Alkin would forgive me. Forgive me for giving up...

I didn't have it in me anymore, I couldn't fight, I didn't want to fight. I just wanted it to end. After everything I had been through, I just didn't care anymore.

The steady sway of riding stopped, that's what brought me out of my inner thoughts. Everything felt in slow motion as the cloak was pulled back. My vision was distorted, as if looking through bent glass I could barely see. Looking around, I noticed we were at the portal.

All around us Wolves and Vampires fought, both Aeralain and Alecien. I recognized no one as they clashed swords and claws, and teeth tore flesh. Remotely I felt Alkin and Drake's presence off in the distance of the moors, but I knew I couldn't reach out to call them.

Looking at the tall wooden portal, my inner thoughts still told me it was a farce. That this trick would never work. They would never get what they wanted, regardless of how corrupt they turned me. I would never release total anarchy onto the world.

Someone grabbed my hand and helped me down. Turning to look, it was Hunter. His slimy slicked-back hair was almost clean, and his clothes were nice. As if his own corruption had never taken place. But his aura was black and twisted. It reminded me of the creatures in the cave. Evil and heartless souls of nothing.

"Welcome, niece. I'm glad you choose to come to your senses. I hope you're ready for opening the portal." He said as Ash climbed down off the horse and came to stand next to me.

Faking a smile, I didn't say a word. Instead I nodded my head. Ash grabbed the staff from Hunter and placed it in my hands. The steady blue glow began to pulse and match my heartbeat. For a moment I swayed, I wasn't used to this power yet. It radiated up my arm and neck penetrating my mind like a bolt piercing my skull.

Closing my eyes, I placed my hand on the totem's sunstone. It boomed with power, just as Daes' staff lit up like a beacon in a grey foggy harbor. It beamed skyward, as if trying to reach the stars. The power spiraling outward surprised me, I was never thinking it would be this simple to spread his power in the world. No something was wrong....

My head ached and images of the cave reverberated in my mind. One moment I felt hot the next cold. Daes never said what would happen when the portal expelled his power back into the world. Realigning the world on its path of balance, and the gentle sway of chaos and harmony.

That's when it struck me. A gut-wrenching feeling tore through my heart, it stuttered from the brute force of the power. Opening my eyes, the world around me was a blue whirlwind of pure magic. I alone stood in the whirlwind, Hunter, Ash, the battle and portal were gone. It spiraled around me in streaking shades. Some opaque and some intense, pure bliss.

It was the magic from the staff, Daes' magic trying to break free and become strong enough to realign what should be. *What should be...* For a moment I swayed uneasily on my feet, pain echoed in my soul, causing me to cry out in agony. Looking down, I noticed something was wrong; my skin no longer the subtle color of the living resembled Phury's grey and death like.

None of this should have been, and we came full cycle to correct it. Instead of my mother it was me paying the price. The land was once more in ruins and the Vampires and Wolves were at war again.

Darkness threatened to encompass me once more. It's gentle embrace promised relief from this boggling and draining situation. It wasn't enough though, I wanted the pain to stop, to disappear, and I wanted it all to end...

The cold embrace of an icy hand brought me out of the darkness. Opening my eyes, Phury stood before me. His wiry blonde hair, darkened blue, red eyes full with blackened hate gazed at me as he smirked.

"What are you doing here? How are you here?" I asked frightened. He never could leave the cave unless chaos reigned.

Being of Daes' lineage, he must of caught my thoughts. "Alecien is in anarchy, my dear. It has come full circle and the power of the staff called me."

I looked at the staff and noticed it was no longer pure blue. Instead it mirrored a reddish blue ball of swirling power. *Chaos and harmony meshed together, but not one...* I thought to myself.

My mind blanked momentarily, then Phury's hand encompassed mine and helped hold me and the staff tight. "I think we both want the same thing. I think harmony and chaos can balance each other out..." He said while looking towards the cyclone of power. My mind connected to his so purely it made me jump. Flashes of images of when he was little flickered across my vision.

A little boy, happy, bright-eyed and full of life ran up to a black-haired woman, with silver eyes. She reached out to him and held him close. Then images of an older fledgling, or young adult, lashing out his magic in hate and anger, broke through. Something was wrong, I felt it along the link.

A huge red, black-skinned figure stood over him, his hands encompassed a small bloody bundle. Phury snapped, his hate was so strong that his magic became whip like, attacking the tall figure. Static and fuzzy images that I couldn't make out filled my mind before a new one became clear.

The black-haired woman, sat on the floor, crying. Bright blue lines marred her skin where his magic had touched her. She begged him to stop, but he didn't. His mind was in shambles, he felt disconnected from reality, living in a made up world. He felt confused and lost, and it thrust him over the edge into madness. He became twisted and corrupt. As suddenly as the images appeared they disappeared and once again I was looking Phury in the eyes.

Blinking I looked around me, the whirlwind was warped, twisted and hazed with our combined magic. A tear escaped my eye. This was not the fate I wanted. I couldn't bear my homeland becoming filled with such a hatred that it fell into darkness. I couldn't allow the release of those creatures on the world. Left to torment the living, and end life as we knew it.

However, no matter what I tried to tell myself I always circled back to one thing. Phury was right, harmony and chaos could balance each other out. I was at peace with dying and knowing my fate. Phury was not at peace, and from what I knew, he wanted total anarchy. What would it cost to create balance?

"What do you want, Phury?" I questioned mentally to him.

"I want what you want, peace, death, I don't care what you call it. I am tired of living in a world centered on one thing. I am tired of being held prisoner in an endless nothingness. If I am to live that way then, the rest of the world can join me." His reply boomed in my head. He was angry still for being locked up, and who could blame him? Living so long in chaos and entropy

would do that to you. The girl from his memory, though, what happened to her...

Pushing the image of her into his mind I had to find out. *"What happened?!"* I yelled back. *"Don't you care about her?!"*

His demeanor shattered briefly as I saw a black-cloaked figure with star-like silver hair and one I recognized all too well. The same cloaked figure who dropped me off to Chaimh and Lillian so long ago. *Lucine...* She came for the woman and took her away. Her lucid skin reached out and took her child from the living world, and anger flared in her starry eyes.

"For this act you shall forever be alone," She said as she threw an icicle at his heart. Piercing it and sealing his fate. She faded from his view, taking the woman with her just as Phury lost consciousness. *Marceline...* he had cried out as he fell into the darkness of his hate filled world.

That was it, his weakness. Marceline was his mate who he too was removed from in his anger filled life. Phury and I had lived very similar, and for a moment I felt sorry for him. He and I were both ripped violently away from our family, friends and even our mates. What lead to his removal and hate filled destiny escaped me but we were the same...

Taking Phury's hand I no longer cared. If I did, I would of never been able to make the choice for the world as a whole. I admit I would be selfish, but in this choice I couldn't be. I saw what happened when one was selfish, and someone had to step up and correct the wrong of it.

Phury met my eyes and nodded. He too felt what needed to be done. Our hands grasped the staff as we poured our whole selves into its power. This is what was needed for releasing Daes' magic. My resolve and pure harmony of my fate and his anger filled hate of chaos. It would be an act of pure selfishness on both our parts.

I felt it, Phury's chaotic magic ate away at me. It poured through every cell in my body and utilized it. *This would kill me...* I thought as I felt my heart burn and stutter. Raising my head, I felt my magic release. In turn, it ate away at Phury as well. My back tingled and pain erupted along my shoulder bone. The blackened wings I hadn't called upon for years spread from my back and encompassed me.

Looking towards Phury he too had wings, pure white. *Harmony and chaos...* They enclosed us in their feathery embrace like a gentle blanket. A reverting crack resonated outside our shield, and within my soul. The strength of it brought me to my knees, Phury too must have experienced it. We both knealt, panting, as feathers began to swirl around us in a cyclone of black, white and blue hues. My body hurt, my mind felt foggy and the river of death bite at my skin.

Like lightning striking sand, something broke inside me, shattered like glass being thrown against stone. I felt my last breath leave my lungs as darkness encompassed me. Falling forward, I felt Phury fall as well. This was it, our time was up and we had carried out what Daes wanted. Paying with our lives.....

Power unleashed ~ Alkin

The cyclone of magic barred Howl and me from Raillyn. I only prayed Phury wouldn't kill her. After tossing Ash's lifeless body off the platform, the ground began to quake. The once magnificent portal turned brown and began to float away like grains of sand on the wind. Even the swirl of pure magic that spun around began to fade.

That's when I saw it; twisting in the dark and light blue magic of harmony and chaos were feathers, black and white. Swirling around individually amongst the magic. A lightweight feeling encompassed me, looking at Howl his eyes were wide, he felt it too.

"Daes' magic is spreading, I feel it, it's building." He said as I gazed back at the whirlwind.

That's when it happened, the cyclone stopped in mid-spin. The magic hung in the air, sparkles of power, mixed with grains of sand. It was beautiful. White and black feathers hung in a shimmering array, of blue mist. Like Darah wine being thrown into a hearth, the beauty exploded outwards.

Placing my arm up, I protected my face from the sand, and anything else flying at us. It felt like being tossed into water, a clear cooling water that hushed everything. When the wind stopped I looked where Raillyn and Phury had stood.

Now Daes stood, head tipped and smiling. His black hair bordered his strong face as his vibrant blue eyes met mine. For a moment, he looked at the floor of the platform. A blanket of black and white feathers lay over two objects. I could only assume it was Raillyn and Phury. Reaching down, Daes smirked at me. His hand touched the blanket and lifted the edge.

For a moment he paused, his eyebrows furrowed worriedly, as he glanced at the blanket. Quickly I tried to run towards him.

My feet felt heavy, and my legs weak, something was wrong. My chest ached, but didn't burn, something in my soul said there was a problem. Daes looked at me once more, his face was stone, no indication as to what he felt. Before I reached him, he disappeared, taking the blanket and its contents with him.

Digging my feet into the ground, I came to a stop. Footsteps behind me indicated Howl had followed. Running my hands through my hair, I took a deep breath.

"What happened?" I asked Howl, hoping he was able to decipher more since he was one of Daes' Drakar.

"I don't know, Daes hasn't walked this land for over two hundred and fifty years."

Howl's face was placid, his eyes were so vivid and glazed over, he seemed drunk. Thinking that, he probably was, he was drunk on the immense power being unleashed. Footsteps behind me indicated the arrival of another. Looking behind me, I saw Razul; his eyes too were glazed over, but I knew better, he handled Daes' power better than a Drakar.

"Where is she, Razul?" I asked him, knowing he knew what I meant.

"He has her, there is a debt he owes to your mate." He said meeting my eyes.

For a moment, I reached towards my father's land only to find it blocked from my reach. Furious I grabbed Razul's shirt and pulled him at me, almost shaking him in anger.

"What the hell is going on where is she? What debt?!" I yelled as Howl looked at me.

Razul laughed at my behavior. "He said if she died he would hold her soul so she can be reborn. Her mother already lives and things are returning from whence they came. Look at your mark Alkin." He said as I released him, stunned by his words.

Looking down I saw the mark Raillyn and I shared was gone, but it didn't feel as if she was. *I never felt her die, not like when I had to kill her in The Keep.* No, something else was going on and I was determined to find out what it was.

"What do you mean, Calista's alive?" I asked baffled.

It was Howl that answered. "We weren't supposed to tell you. Opal's is pregnant with Calista. I'm sure by now Solomn knows anyway. But Daes held Calista's soul till he felt it was time for her to be reborn, as a precaution. This way if Raillyn died she in turn could be reborn as well." Howl said monotoned. "We should go see Opal, and tell her Daes took Raillyn."

Nodding my head, I felt in a fog. *Was Raillyn really dead? Would she really be able to be reborn? Why and how long will it be before I see her again? And she won't even remember me, everything would start from the beginning again. Drameon will make changes....* I groaned as I followed Howl through Razul's portal.

Entering my mother's den, I closed my eyes and took a deep steady breath. Hearing my mother gasp, made me look at her. "Dear Gods, Alkin, you're a mess!" She said as I looked down at my clothes. They were torn and blood-stained from the battle and slaying of the Vampires. Thankfully the blood wasn't all mine, only the small cut on my arm bled slightly. And my boots had tracked mud onto the floor.

"Sorry, mother." I said slipping them off and letting the maid remove them. "Why didn't you tell us?" I questioned about recent events.

"I told him, Daes took Phury and Raillyn." Razul said casually.

Opal looked at him, shocked, but nodded her head in understanding. "I see so we should expect a visit I suppose." She said quietly.

Silently the door opened, turning to look I saw Drameon and Celeste enter the room. As the door began to shut I saw Solomn grab it and follow them in.

"What's going on?" Drameon asked. "Where's my daughter?"

"And where's Lyth?" Celeste asked sounding worried.

Closing, my eyes I shook my head. I didn't know what to tell them. I hadn't seen Lyth since we split up in the mass of the attack. Looking at my mother she too seemed concerned. A single tear ran down her cheek. If Raillyn was gone then we all knew what would happen, eventually she would be reborn.

Opal hugged herself and rubbed her hands up and down her arms as if she was cold. "Drameon, there's something I need to tell you. I'm..."

"I have them." A cool voice interrupted from the edge of the room, out of the shadows.

Entering the light, I knew who it was even before I saw him. Daes' cool blue eyes reflected the dancing fire light and the blue glow from his staff in hand. His blackened hair hung slightly in his face, covering his elven ears. His face was blank, lips pressed thin.

"Phury and Raillyn are with Lyth and Destiny, in my home. Sorry, Celeste but I needed a familiar Drakar for Raillyn, she was a little uneasy around Chaimh and Lillian." His words caught the attention of everyone in the room. Staring at him questioningly I was sure others shared my confusion.

For a moment my head spun, as I reached for the blood bond I always shared with Raillyn. Briefly it registered something, yet blocked me from her, and static filled my head. She was with Lyth that was all I caught. Daes spoke the truth.

"What do you mean she was uneasy around Chaimh and Lillian?" Drameon questioned.

My eyebrows furrowed as I tried to read between the lines. Looking towards my mother she turned her head down, blue eyes meeting the floor, she knew what happened. I saw it on her face, in how she pulled nervously at her lip. Her hand went to her mouth as I heard her cry. Face turned downward, Solomn went to his mate while Daes stood unwavering.

Solomn seemed shocked but not surprised. He raised his eyebrows before taking Opal into his arms. Closing his eyes, I knew that look. He was talking mentally to my mother, figuring everything out.

Drameon, Howl, Celeste, and I looked between Opal and Daes, expecting answers. "Nothing will be said until you two men go clean yourselves up." He said raising his eyebrow towards Howl and I. For a moment I wanted to protest. I was getting angry having to jump through hoops for answers, but that's how the Gods worked especially Daes, unless you were his favorite.

Clenching my fists together, I had been around Daes enough with Calista to know when not to argue. Meeting Daes' eyes, he stood tall and unwavering, arms crossed he stared sternly at me. Glancing at Howl, he looked defeated and didn't seem to want to argue either. Nodding my head I sighed as Howl turned towards the door. Silently we walked into the hall and down the quiet halls towards the washroom.

One of the maids wearing the grey clothes of an assistant, passed us in the opaque halls. Bowing I asked her to bring garments to the bath, for Howl and I. Quietly she nodded and walked on. As we approached the darkened wooden door. I held it open and sighed as Howl entered and I followed.

The palace, like the city, had a communal bath, even the Den bathed in the gender-separated bath house of the city. Its white and black marble floor was a little chilly, at first. The closer I got to the large pool, the warmer the stone became. Kicking off my boots, and removing my clothes I stepped down into the cool water, just on the edge. The warm steps leading down into the pool felt hot but didn't burn.

Tall pillars stood holding up what almost looked like an underground cavern like ceiling, made of shimmering gems, and stone. The water here always remained warm, by being fed by the hot springs below. This bath had little to no issues, since it was enclosed. The larger outdoor one of the city, occasionally had a problem or two. However they were typically minor.

On occasion, the rare fledgling would try and sneak into the opposite sex' bath to take a peek at their mate. Guards were posted to try and deter this, but fledglings often were rebellious. Other than that, it was our way of life.

Sitting on the utmost step I grabbed the copper basin nearby. It was chilly in the open air but quickly adjusted temperatures, as I dipped it in the water. I wanted to be fast and get this done. Pouring the water over my head. It ran across my nose, causing me to shake my head, and almost sneeze. Tipping a few more over me, I grabbed the soap and washed up. Its lavender scent smelled relaxing, and calmed my nerves. I still didn't know what was going to happen, or how Raillyn would react to everything.

After putting the soap down, I refilled the basin a few times, rinsing off. Unlike Howl, I decided against getting into the actual water. Not that I wasn't comfortable or anything, but I felt it was a time-wasting effort.

Leaving the pool, I grabbed a towel, and dried off. Garments lay on a wooden chair near the door where the maid must have left them. Grabbing the black pants, I tossed the towel into a nearby wooden basket. As I dressed Howl got out and dried off. All in all, it had been only ten minutes or so before we were back in the room awaiting an answer.

Daes looked at me smirking before he spoke. "Good, I don't want you to frighten the poor child when I bring her back." He finally said. "Stating that, Drameon, how would you like to take on another child to raise?" He questioned turning to look at Drameon, who looked blindsided.

Raise another child? What does he mean? For a moment, my mind raced. I was tired of riddles I wanted answers. Ready to speak up, Drameon stopped me.

"I guess, but what's going on and what child?" He asked cautiously.

"Phury, and of course Raillyn, unless you can't handle it. If not then Alkin can take Raillyn, and Lyth will take Phury."

"What?!" Celeste shirked. "Phury? You've got to be kidding me? What in Delron's River is going on, Daes? This isn't a game anymore! Tell us what happened!" She shouted losing her calm demeanor.

Smirking, Daes slowly met all our eyes. Gazing around the room his smile faded. A solemn look crossed his face, "I can't really explain it. Other than Phury and Raillyn's magic canceled each other out and brought balance upon the world and themselves." He paused for a moment before going on. Crossing his arms he paced a few steps. "Both of them were reverted back to a time before chaos touched their hearts and mind, back when they were innocent and balanced. Neither of them remember any recent events. Raillyn remembers everything up to the moment her mother left to accomplish the very task she carried out. And Phury remembers living here in Silvertine and visiting his friend Marceline. The very one who Lucine removed from the world after Phury tried to kill her. Since he has no memory of losing his mind and heart to the darkness, Lucine said she would release her. But all of you will follow our directions and not let either child know what you know of their prior, more recent lives." Daes said looking at us.

My mind went blank. Raillyn remembered nothing again from her past. *No, not nothing, she remembered what she should have always remembered. What she should have never forgotten. She was exactly where she began. Three years old and fully ignorant to the realm of Alecien. That meant Vampires still scared her, the old stories of Shadow Walkers hunting rouges filled her mind.* In a sense it was a sigh of relief, much better than the alternative.

Laughing hysterically for a moment, I couldn't help myself. My fit left me breathless and gasping for air. "I think keeping those thoughts from her will be the easiest." I said between laughs. "Plus I'm sure if we aren't careful and lock them away in our mind, than you Gods will make us forget. Won't you?" I asked seriously. Everyone was looking at me shocked. Smiling I met Daes' eyes. "I'm right, aren't I?" I asked again.

Smirking he nodded his head. "Yes, you're right. So. Drameon, will you take your daughter and Phury or not?" He asked crossing his arms in front of him.

Again Drameon seemed hesitant. "Well, if Drameon won't take Raillyn and Phury I will." I stated sternly. I would not stand by and ideally watch her fall back into chaos this time around. No, I wanted her to live how she was meant to live.

Drameon looked at me annoyed. He knew I meant well but since Raillyn was a child again, things were bound to be stressed between us. *Back to the typical parent vs. mate mentality.* I sighed to myself before running a hand through my hair, and glancing at Celeste who snickered slightly. By the way, her green eyes gleamed she too thought the same thing. *Back to the old way of life.*

"If I take them, will you intervene again? Or let us have a reprieve after recent events?" He asked tentatively.

Daes placed his hand on his chin in thought. "I already promised Raillyn a reprieve, so I will hold to that. I can promise at the very least fifty years. At that time, we can see where every-thing stands and I may grant you more." He said, stating his terms, and placing his hands on his hips. "This way it allows all the children to grow up, and if we're lucky, have their own."

It was a fair deal, and yes he was right. Fifty years was plenty of time to put everything back in order. To the way it was meant to be.

In a sense, my heart leapt for joy, I'd get to see Raillyn grow up, and we would have the chance to do things right this time around. On the other hand my heart ached, Callina still did-n't know I was her father and at this point probably never would. In a sense, I felt myself wanting to grieve for what should have been with her, but celebrate what will be from here on out.

Looking at Drameon, we awaited his answer. I could tell by how he placed his hand to his lips that he was considering his op-tions. "And what about Marceline?" He asked.

Smiling softly, Daes answered. "Just like Alkin, she will reside in her own dwelling of choice. I'm sure she will build a bond with him just like your daughter and her mate." He said. Drameon frowned a little.

Yep, right back to where we left off.... I thought. He hated the idea of his only daughter forming a bond with her mate early. Even though it was all part of the typical lifestyle, he thought he could avoid it.

Nodding his head, I saw his defeat. Drameon took a big sigh, laughing a little he smiled. "I see I don't have much choice in this matter. This is a sigh of relief, to how things have been recently. Of course, I will raise them."

Daes returned the smile. "Told you the pain and torment would be well worth the wait." Tipping my head, this was the first I had heard of Drameon's punishment. It made me wonder how much he actually went through before reaching this point. "Since there are no adult mystics of my lineage alive currently my time grows short. I shall have Lyth and Marceline bring the children shortly." Reaching out his hand, Daes grabbed Drameon's, shaking it respectfully. "Glad you choose to stay with us, my friend." He said before releasing his hand and opening a portal, leaving.

For a moment, we all stood around baffled. I felt full of so many emotions I didn't know how to react. Smiling and chuckling to myself, I took a seat near my mother.

Looking at Drameon, smiling, I said. "Well, at least I still have all her lovies. After you went off the deep end, I went to your house and saved them. Figuring Raillyn wouldn't be in your care anymore."

Sighing, he returned the smile as he came and sat next to me.

Return ~ Raillyn

Sitting up I rubbed my eyes and yawned. It had been a busy day. Grandfather brought me to his house and told me something went wrong, that my mother was to be reborn and that grandmother already was pregnant with her. It was confusing, but he said it was ok and that we would be friends after she was born.

Yawning again, I looked at Phury. His golden hair fell into his face as he slept. Pale skin that matched my own seemed illuminated against the deep blue bed. Reaching out I poked him.

"Phury, wake up." I said as I poked him again, my own golden hair falling into my face. "Wake up, wake up!" I almost shouted.

His hand smacked mine away. "No, don't want to." He said as he rolled over.

Pushing his shoulder, I helped him keep rolling. Right over the edge of the bed. Giggling to myself, he thumped to the floor. For a moment I sat quiet and listened, before I looked over the edge. A blue pillow met my face, knocking me off balance, I too fell. Phury laughed as I landed on top of him, and rolled off. Reaching out my hand grasped another pillow, grabbing it I swung it at him as he hit me again with his.

For a few minutes, we sat hitting each other playfully. As we did so the door creaked opened. Instantly we both stopped, we didn't need to look to know grandfather was there. His power swept through the room like a wave over dry dirt. Phury's ever changing eyes met my own as we smiled at each other mischievously. More softly he swung and hit me in the head once more with the pillow. Smiling I followed suit and did the same.

"All right you two, it's time to go home." He said, coming over to us and kneeling down.

Frowning that our fun was spoiled I put the pillow on the floor and stood, eager to return to Silvertine. Grandfather's house was boring and there were no toys here. Phury seemed eager to return as well, our magic link told me he too was bored.

"I want you two to be good, things haven't been ideal lately so it may be a few weeks before things return to normal. But at least they aren't chaotic any longer and everything has calmed down." He said, running his fingers through my hair, trying to fix its disarray.

Smiling, I nodded my head and threw my arms around his neck. His strong arm hugged me back as I felt Phury join us. For a moment, the three of us just embraced. It was peaceful, calming, and a solid rock amongst the uncertainty of what we were walking into.

"We'll be good." I said pulling back and looking at Phury.

He nodded his head, "Promise?" He said as Lyth and Marceline entered the room.

"We ready to go?" She asked as she pulled her pale brown hair behind her elf-like ear.

"Since you two have been so well-behaved I think we can talk Celeste into making cookies when we get back, for snack." Lyth said smiling at us. His long red hair hung in a loose but high ponytail, making him look much younger.

Raising my eyebrows and smiling wide, I looked towards Phury. His ever-changing eyes mirroring my own. He too looked excited, as we thought the same thing. "And ice cream?" We both asked simultaneously.

Ice cream and cookies was our favorite, especially the soft ice cream in the market. It was yummy, taking the still-warm cookies and scooping the soft ice cream on it and eating it like a sandwich. It was gooey and melty, but tasted so good.

Crossing his arms Lyth took a deep breath, before hanging his head down. "Oh, all right, special snack for a special day then." He said raising his head and smiling at us, his blue eyes glinting in delight.

Excited, I ran to Lyth as Phury ran to Marceline. "And stay up late?" I heard Phury ask as Lyth picked me up and hugged me. Eyes wide open, I nodded my head, hoping he would say yes.

"Now you two are pushing it." He said while shifting me to his right side, his left hand ruffled my newly fixed hair from grandfather. "Let's see how things go first, I don't even know where everyone is or will be tonight." He said as I looked toward Phury and Marceline, who was giving Phury a nose kiss.

Seeing that, I felt myself miss Alkin; we always gave each other nose kisses. Her silvery star eyes softened as she looked at me and smiled gently. Almost as if she knew what I was thinking, and in a sense probably did through Phury.

"Let's go home." I said ready for things to return to normal.

Grandfather reached his hand out and shook Lyth and Marceline's hand, and ruffled Phury's and my hair. Holding his hand out he called his magic. Like a swirling whirlpool, his magic shot out in a single location before spreading and spiraling about, expanding until it was large enough for someone to walk through.

Lyth looked towards grandfather once more before nodding his head and walking through it. The portal tingled my skin slightly as its magic danced over me. As it disappeared, I saw we were in my grandmother's den. The bright red, blue, silver, and green pillows lined the furniture. Alkin, Celeste, Solomn, father, and my grandmother sat on the large pillowed benches. Howl leaned against the wall nearby.

As the portal closed I wriggled around, till Lyth put me down. The moment my feet hit the ground I ran to Alkin and my father. Smiling I was eager to share my news.

"Papa, papa, Alkin, Alkin!" I shouted stopping in front of them. "Lyth said we were good so we could have cookies and ice cream. Can we go now?" I asked as Phury came running to stand beside me.

For a moment, Alkin turned and glanced at my father before looking back at me. Reaching out he grabbed me by the waist and pulled him onto his lap, his arms encircled me as he shifted my weight in a tight embrace. For a moment I stilled, unsure why he was acting like this.

"I am so glad you are safe." He said holding me tighter and taking in my scent. Relaxing I circled my arms around him and took his scent in as well. Alkin was my rock when my parents were away, my protector, and my savior. "Of course we can go get ice cream." He said kissing the top of my head. "Also." Alkin said reaching behind his back. "This little guy has missed you." Pulling out my ratty red Drakar plushy. A half-human, half-dragon, red scaled stuffed toy. Alkin had bought it for me as a baby when I refused to let it go, ever since I carried it everywhere.

"Corin!" I almost shouted, grabbing my plushy from his hands and hugging it to my chest. "Thank you." I said hugging Alkin again.

Returning to my feet and beaming a smile at him, I turned and ran to my father. "Papa, can Phury and I stay up late also?" I asked as he picked me up and hugged me tight.

Releasing me and ruffling my hair, he smiled. "We'll see. We have to go to Alkin's and get the rest of your toys and decide what's going on first." My father said as I looked around the room.

I saw Howl move slowly towards Alkin, his black hair framed his solemn face. Taking a deep breath it was good to be home. All my friends and family were there. Watching Howl, his blue eyes looked down before meeting Alkin's again. Pausing, I saw a little hand go from gripping Howl's leg to Alkin's. Tipping my head, I wondered who this was.

Trying to wriggle free of my father's grasp, while he talked to my grandmother. He wearily placed me on my feet. "Behave." He said as I went over to Alkin and Howl.

Glancing at Alkin his mind was blocked from me, but his face seemed worried. Carefully I reached out and touched the hand, a little girl with dark curly hair, and ever changing eyes peeked out from behind his leg. *Another mystic child...* I thought to myself.

"Hi," I said smiling at her. "I'm Raillyn. What's your name?" I asked as she looked up at Alkin and then back at me. Slowly he stepped aside and gently released her fingers from his leg. For a moment, the girl seemed panicked and scared. "It's ok." I reassured her. "Where's your mommy and daddy?" I asked her worried.

She frowned and looked towards the ground. "My name's Callina, my mommy died in the Vampire's keep in Alecien, and I don't know who my daddy is. Alkin and my mommy kept me safe in The Keep. Before my mommy died she released me to the Den's care, but Alkin said he was going to take care of me now." She said quietly.

Tipping my head I thought for a moment, my magic reached out towards her naturally. She was sad, confused and overall overwhelmed. "Alecien?" I asked knowing that was were a lot of Vampires lived. "Is it scary over there? There's no Shadow Walkers there to kill Vampires, are there?"

She shook her head. "I hated The Keep, hated the Vampires. It's quieter here." She said, meeting my eyes.

"Do you want to be friends? You want to get some ice cream and cookies with us?" I asked smiling.

Still staring at me she bit her lip nervously, before glancing towards Alkin. Looking at him myself, he raised his eyebrows and smiled at both of us. Callina happily met my eyes and nodded her head. For a moment, Alkin sighed as he reached down and took each of our hands.

Together we walked out of the den and down the opaque halls towards the main door. Looking behind me, Lyth, Celeste, Marceline, Phury, and my father followed. Howl stood, leaning against the door frame, smiling. "I'll go on ahead and inform Drake and Raven of recent events." He called out to us before turning to talk to grandmother and Solomn.

"Who's Drake and Raven?" I asked looking up at Alkin as we walked into the open streets.

Scrunching the corner of his mouth he seemed to ponder my question before answering. "He's a friend of mine and we need to go speak to them tonight. They have a little girl. Deestan, Callina's half-sister." He said almost carefully.

Furrowing my brows I tried to reach for my link to Alkin, but something was wrong. I didn't like how Alkin was acting, he seemed tense or stressed out. He kept his mind blocked from mine. Pulling on his hand, I dug my feet into the multi-colored stone bricks that lined the street.

"Tell me!" I demanded causing everyone to stop and look at me surprised. Alkin knew what I meant, I didn't like him keeping things from me and he was very quiet mentally lately.

Eyes closed Alkin took a deep breath and pressed his lips thin. "There's nothing to tell, they're friends of mine and we will see them later." Sighing he rubbed the bridge of his nose. "I'm sorry, babe, it's been a very long day and I'm just stressed out." He said, reaching his hand out to me, almost apologetically.

Biting my lip, I nodded and took it. It had been a long day and everyone was tired. The walk was short, and we reached the market plaza. Stalls were set up along the brick roads, some small and some large. The large circle one with the bright multi-scarf canopy was the ice cream and sweets stall. Eagerly, Phury took my hand and ran towards it. Before getting out of reach I grabbed Callina's hand and dragged her along.

Nearing the stall we looked at the different kinds of ice cream. Various flavors and colors filled the small ice table that they sat in. Nigel, a blue Drakar, ran the booth and kept it cold with his magic, smiled at us. Gazing at the table and different flavors I quickly found my favorite – red raspberry fire berry blend. "I want that kind." I said before running to the other side to find a cookie.

Before going too far, I spotted something better than a cookie, a cookie cone. "I want it in the cookie cone!" I shouted loudly as the adults neared us.

Alkin chuckled as he patted me on the head. "Ok, we'll take a double scoop of the fire berry blend, in the cookie cone. Phury, Callina what do you want?" He asked as he pulled out his coin bag.

"I want vanilla, please and I don't want cookie I want the dark brown cone." Callina said quietly.

"Marceline, I want the silver star kind in the cookie cone!" Phury shouted eagerly.

"Don't worry about Phury." Marceline said, paying for his sweets.

Smiling, Alkin nodded his head in understanding, and ordered a berry blue in a cookie cone for himself. Paying for the three cones, Callina and I went to sit nearby at the fountain. It's four dragons stood magnificently in the suns dimming light.

"So who's Deestan?" I asked Callina as Phury climbed onto Marceline's lap and took his cone carefully from her. Alkin smiled at me as he waited for Lyth and Celeste.

"She's my sister, I think the adults don't like to talk about her mom. She had the same name that you do." Callina whispered in my ear.

Tipping my head sideways, I thought about that for a moment. It kind of made me feel strange, but after a moment it passed. There were lots of people that shared names. Like Elsa, Mauve, Breckon, and Locke. Why should I care if someone had my name on the other side of the world.

"Oh, well, is your sister fun?" I asked eager to know more about her.

Callina nodded her head as Alkin and the others joined us. Handing her the vanilla ice cream, Alkin sat next to me. Like Phury, I climbed onto his lap before taking my cone. Leaning back I happily licked the cold but hot-tasting ice cream. That's why I loved the fire berry, it was so cold, and yet so hot at the same time.

Kicking my feet I looked up at Alkin as he ate his cone, he looked down at me and smiled. Above us the sky was dimming and the air was growing cold. The warm days of summer and fall had resided, leaving us with chilly soon to be winter nights.

Bright reds, purples, pink, and blues lite up the evening sky as the sun descended further into the horizon. Eating my cookie cone and sitting on the edge of the fountain made me happy. The smooth chocolate danced in my mouth and melted like fudge. When it was all gone, I yawned and rubbed my eyes.

The bright opaque colors in the sky began to grow dark, indicating it was getting very late. Late to set and early to rise is how the sun worked in the colder months. Some nights in the dead of winter the sun never seemed to be awake long. The evening was the sunniest time we had right now.

Strong, fit arms circled me and hugged me tight while slightly rocking me from side to side. "Rahhhh." Alkin said playfully as he kissed my cheek. Fidgeting I laughed as he did so. "You ready to go see our friends? Callina, you want to come? Phury, do you want to come?" He asked as Phury snuggled against Marceline.

"I want to stay with Marcy." He said as he closed his eyes. Reaching for our link indicated he was still tired. Whatever he had been through before being brought to Grandfather's had been more exhausting than my endeavor.

Marceline, patted his back gently, as she spoke. "I'll take him home to Drameon. He's still tired from his adventure." She said while standing and cradling him against her.

"We'll stay as well." Celeste said as she smiled towards Lyth. "I'm sure Drameon could use our help making sure everything is where it should be."

Gently Alkin patted my leg, indicating he wanted me up. "Sounds like a plan. If you could tell Drameon we don't plan to stay long and that I'll bring Raillyn home shortly, I'd appreciate it." He said as Callina and I took his hand. Marceline nodded quietly before turning down the path leading towards home. Celeste and Lyth agreed as they followed. As they left Alkin he called a portal, and lead us through.

Exiting it, we walked into a giant white and gold pillared room. A table and several chairs, made out of dark wood, were directly in front of me, standing around the table were several people, Howl included.

"Sissy." Callina, joyfully cried out and ran towards an older girl, who stood next to a black-haired man and woman. A brown-haired man covered his mouth and chuckled a little at the way the two behaved. Callina and her sister jumped up and down happily, while hugging and laughing.

The man and woman next to them looked down and smiled, before turning towards us. For a moment their scent hit me, they smelled like Wolves, but more musky. "It's good to see you again. Howl informed us on what occurred." He said while holding out his hand. Howl came towards us, standing by Alkin and I.

Stepping forward, Alkin shook his hand, before they turned and looked at me. For a moment I felt scared. *Why were they looking at me like that? Curiously?* Scratching my arm nervously, I ducked behind Howl, stopping and grabbing his pants while I did so. Whining a little into the leg of his pants, he reached down and poked my side.

"Come on, sunshine! There's nothing to be afraid of." He said, smiling as he poked me again.

Squeaking, I let go and ran to Alkin's leg. Squeezing it tightly with one hand I batted Howl's hand away with the other. Both chuckled momentarily. As I looked up at Alkin, he smiled down at me. Reaching out and taking my hand, he pulled me around in front. Still frightened around these new people, I tried to climb up his body and into his arms.

Sighing he gave in and just picked me up. As soon as he did so I quickly buried my face into his shoulder and neck.. "Sorry, she's a little shy." He said as I heard footsteps behind me. Panicked, I pressed myself against Alkin as hard as I could, it just made him chuckle more.

He shifted my weight and turned me so I was on his left hip, facing outwards. Covering my eyes with my hands, a hand touched my shoulder. It wasn't his, I sensed its difference. It seemed colder, not hot like Alkin usually did, and the skin was rougher, more calloused. Immediately I froze, unsure what to do. The hand rubbed my shoulder gently, I felt Alkin's mental touch, trying to reassure me.

"I am so happy she's ok. Raillyn, would you like to go play with Deestan and Callina?" The male voice asked me.

Opening my hands slightly, I saw the man Alkin called Drake smiling and touching my shoulder. The black-haired lady called Raven stood beside him, smiling at me.

Quietly I glanced at Alkin then Howl. "I want to stay here." I said softly, burying my face back into Alkin's neck, as he adjusted my weight again. His shoulders rose and fell as he sighed.

"So how are things here?" I heard him ask, his voice rumbled in his chest and sounded underwater like.

Peeking, I was curious. Drake stood running his hand through his hair, his other hand was encircled around Raven's waist. A black wolf print insignia ring was on his finger. "Quiet, actually. That blast of light took out many of the nearby Vampires. Any remaining ones my troops disposed of. Then we set fire to The Keep. Well-burned, what we could at least. If there are still Vampires here, they are far and few." He said casually. "I still can't believe that was just two days ago. It seems like ages have passed." His voice wavered and seemed distant.

"So now what?" Raven asked with a chipper voice.

Alkin's shoulder raised and fell quickly as he shrugged. "Daes gave us fifty years' reprieve, I guess that's what was promised if all worked out. So for now we just live and not worry. I know it won't last forever, the scales will tip again and we will be needed before too long. Plus fifty years really isn't all that long if you think about it." Alkin said solemnly.

Drake and Raven smiled and nodded their heads before turning to look towards Callina and Deestan. "I'd like Deestan to study in Silvertine if that option is still open. I want her to continue to unite the two continents in peace, and if possible I'd like her younger brother or sister to study there as well." Drake said while placing a hand across Raven's lower belly. His dark eyes glinted in eagerness.

Alkin looked at them curiously. "We just found out, if I had known earlier, she would have never fought at the portal." He replied as Raven smiled, eyes aglow, and cheeks red.

"I'm glad to hear you have a little one on the way. And of course he or she may study in Silvertine. I think the world needs to reunite, things need to return to the old ways." He said as I rubbed my eye sleepily.

Yawning, Drake smiled and reached his hand out, laying it on my cheek. "Tired?" He asked hushed.

Nodding my head at him, I heard Alkin laugh. "I think we should get going. I have to talk to Drameon and see where this little miss will sleep tonight."

"I wanna stay with you Alkin..." I started to say before Alkin interrupted me, placing a finger across my lips.

"I understand that but you really should stay with your father..." He said, as I looked down to avoid his gaze. I only got away with it for a moment, gently he pulled my chin up to look him in the eyes.

Averting them downward again, I chewed on my lip. "But mama's not there anymore. Can Celeste and Lyth come over?" I asked curiously.

Alkin rubbed the bridge of his nose before running his hand through his hair sighing. "Let's go find Marceline and Phury then go see your father." He said pulling me into an embrace. Quietly I agreed and gave him a mental response.

"Alkin, can I stay tonight with Deestan?" Callina shouted from the other side of the room.

Drake sighed himself, and as I looked at him, I saw his head shaking back and forth and a smile across his face. "It's fine with us." He said, looking towards Raven.

"I'll bring her home in the morning if you want." Howl said from the pillar he leaned against. "Well, since it's so late there and early here I'll bring her back tomorrow night." He said, snickering a little.

Tipping my head, I looked at Howl questioningly. "Well, little bird, Alecien is on the other side of Auran. It's still daytime here, but at home it's very late at night."

I think I had an ah-ha look on my face 'cause Howl and Alkin laughed a little. It made sense, but I couldn't think more in depth about it. I was exhausted and ready for bed.

"Ok, we'll do that." Alkin said while reaching out and shaking Howl's hand. Afterwards, he shook Drake and Raven's before looking back at me. "Ready to go home?" Sleepily I rubbed my eyes and laid my head against his shoulder. Mentally indicating I was ready for sleep.

Alkin summoned a portal and carried me through. My eyes felt heavy as I yawned. I was losing and my eyes closed one last time as I fell asleep.

Choice ~ Alkin

After laying Raillyn down in her bed and tossing the green sapling comforter over her, I turned and went to the living room. Drameon, Celeste, and Lyth waited around the table talking quietly about the recent events. We had been given a second chance, but I was finding it hard keeping memories locked away without hurting her.

Running my fingers through my hair, I paced the room and ran over my options. None of them I liked, but I couldn't keep this up so I choose the lesser of two evils. Pausing I crossed my arms in front of me and looked at my friends.

"I'm going to my father to have him muffle my memories of what's happened over the last fifty years. I can't just block her out and it's not safe for her to be in my mind." I said regretfully. "I don't want to forget but I can't have her know the truth. So I'm going to see what can be done to gently fix this."

No one said a word. Instead they just stared at me. For a moment Celeste quickly looked at Lyth before looking back at me. He sighed for a moment before coming and patting my shoulder.

"That's probably best. Just after you left to Alecien, Daes and Destiny hazed our memories. I guess Howl's was hazed as well, for the same reason. If you do, this none of the Ancients will have a clear memory of her anymore." Lyth said as I bit my lip for a moment.

He was right this would erase the prior persona of Raillyn, leaving the Wolves and few Aleciens with the only remaining clear memory of her. In a way, it felt haunting and finite. Pushing those thoughts aside, I couldn't think of that now. I had to do this or something, it wasn't fair to her and would become worse as she grew. If I wanted her to have the life she should of had, I needed to do this.

"I know." I said shrugging his hand off and opening a portal to my father's home.

***

The dim cavern was filled with crystals lining both the walls and ceiling above. Their darkened red shapes stood out of the natural stone walls. In the center of the room was a monstrous black caldron. Green bubbling liquid swirled around the rim, nearly overflowing. Various tables lined the room surrounding it. Sulfites, herbs, weapons, liquids, and trinkets lay upon them. On a shelf in the corner lay soul orbs, each glowed in accordance with their God's tie. Blue, green, red, and silver.

Delron entered the room through a door near the shelf. In his hand were more soul orbs. This was his nearly constant work, constructing and reconstructing souls that were to be born into Auran. Gently he placed each soul orb upon the shelf. His black hair that almost matched my own wisped into his face. After the orbs were out if his hand he brushed it behind his ear with his fingers.

"I can only guess you are here for the same treatment your friends have had." He said without even looking at me. Instead, he stared at two blue soul orbs that lay together, side by side. Sighing heavily he turned to face me. His ruby red eyes met my ever-changing ones.

In turn, I sighed. "I can't keep her locked out of my head forever and with everything that's happened I can't just not think about it all." I admitted. "Trust me if there was another way I'd take it but if hazing my memories and blurring them is the only option then so be it. It's not fair to Raillyn."

My father rubbed his chin with his leucistic hand and nodded his head. Grabbing a nearby bowl he walked towards the caldron. The bowl was a rough, lumpy metal, it's opaque orange rim shimmered slightly in the light. Reaching out he took an iron ladle off the nearby table. Gently he dipped it into the ominous green liquid.

- 346 -

For a moment, it bubbled sinisterly. My father taught me this stuff was deadly to the touch that it was used to strip a soul from a mortal body. I fidgeted uncomfortably a little, shifting from my left to right foot. Delron moved around the table nonchalantly adding dashes and pinches of various ingredients and herbs. Some I didn't even recognize that only grew in the Gods world.

"You know, I mixed a draught similar to this for Raillyn. After she was wounded and lay dying on Destiny's table." He said meeting my eyes for a moment before continuing his work. "However hers was different. It anchored her soul to her body."

That caught my attention more than anything. The Gods making these draughts to save their own was nothing new, but using it to anchor a soul to a body was different. "What?" Was all I managed to spit out flabbergasted.

"After she shared blood with Phury, it began killing her. It tore her body up from the inside out. Daes was losing her. So myself and Ryaku, my assistant, mixed a special draught for her. I had to use my blood. It was the only way to save her." He said grabbing a dagger and slicing his hand with it.

That made it worse, my father's blood was toxic to anyone outside his lineage. It was literally a slow-acting poison. It would freeze the body from the inside out. slowly killing whoever consumed it, and eventually still a beating heart.

His ruby red blood fell from his hand and into the draught. Wisps of steam meandered upwards from the slowly bubbling green liquid. The more blood that fell the more the liquid bubbled, almost boiling, releasing its steam into the air.

"Either way it all worked out in the end. You all did your job meticulously and mercilessly. I am proud of you, my son, and such deeds do not go unpaid." He said patting me on the shoulder and giving me the bowl nefore going and taking a goblet off the table, bringing it to his lips. "Drink up, I will not speak anymore on what occurred. What happened, happened and no one even us can change that."

Looking at the bowl, I knew he was right. Nothing could change what happened, not even the Gods. Sighing, I thought of the old Raillyn for the last time. Of our first actual meeting, when she was five. I thought of her when she was older, and when I knocked her out of the tree in the woods before, Drake interfered. It was by chance I met her then, and bad timing on my part. I was glad to have a chance to forget that, it still angered me.

Reminiscing on the short time we had. Her throwing accusations in my face and me threatening her in the council room because she didn't carry my child. The short-lived "normal time" we had in the Den when Deestan was born. Our time in The Keep, how we behaved so naturally around each other it was hard to believe she was in a construct body at times. Then what she had become, the bright-eyed cheerful little girl I had lost when chaos filled her life and broke her heart and soul.

Closing my eyes, I felt a tear run down my cheek. That's when it struck me, she was different, and I loved her so much because of it. *Never again...* I thought tossing back the liquid, drinking it down.

It seared the back of my throat and burned all the way to my stomach. When I breathed out the air was grey in color. My head exploded in pain. Stars danced across my vision as everything began to become staticky. Images of Raillyn and Raihanna raced across my mind.

"I assure you, you will not regret this. The time that was lost has now been restored and in turn your happiness. Prodigies..." I heard my father say before darkness consumed me.

~Epilogue~

15 years later ~ Raillyn

So much had happened over the last fifteen years. Phury, Calista, Callina, and I were raised side by side. Deestan visited weekly and joined in on our lessons, as well as took up an apprenticeship at the Silvertine Den. She told us she wanted to aspire to become the Werewolves Den Master, today she rules the Den side by side with Stasha. This left her little brother, Dracken ruling the Alecien Wolves. Callina has taken up apprenticeship with the Gemcrafters and makes breathtaking necklaces.

Last night was one of the nights where we had spent our time in Alecien in Deestan's Den. Talking, dancing and just having fun being fledglings away from our parents, but under the watchful eye of friends. Like Aeralian, the Dens in Alecien began to allow rulers to join as Denmate. So Deestan's parents were never far away.

After returning home, Calista, Phury and I ended up falling asleep in the library of father's house. This was not unnatural and father often found the three of us doing this often. No one ever said anything. However, today I heard his voice breaking through the fog of sleep.

Yawning wide, I heard him talking quietly to Phury. "Are you awake?" I heard him say as I rubbed the sleep grit out of my eyes and sat up slowly.

My father's familiar silver hair, and ever-changing eyes glanced at me before he went to Calista. Looking at Phury I yawned again. He didn't look thrilled and through our mental link, he wasn't. His shoulder-length golden hair hung in his eyes, as he huddled under a blanket up to his neck. His own ever-changing eyes met mine as he reached for our link. *"I hope there is a good reason we're up before the sun."*

Rolling my eyes I agreed, and looked back at my father. Gently he brushed Calista's near black hair out of her face and kissed her forehead. She stretched and reached up for him, bringing him into a deep hug. "Why are you waking us up so early?" She asked before kissing his cheek.

Pulling away slowly from her, he stood and looked at us. "Because Destiny has called me away and I need to leave now. However before I do I wanted to talk to the three of you."

Tipping my head, all three of our curiosity peeked. The small link the three of us shared by being Daes' Mystics vibrated with energy. None of the Gods had called upon us, not like this anyway. We trained with them, and visited now and again but that was all.

"What's going on?" Phury asked, pulling his bare arms and chest out of his blanket. Drameon glanced at him and furrowed his brows.

"Don't even start." Calista said knowing what he was going to say. "Yes, were getting older. Yes, I know you think it's inappropriate for fledglings to dress in whatever we want around each other. And that it bugs you to no end when we wear only underclothes around the house. However, we don't care. It's not like we don't know what each other look like or anything. Nothing is private between us. So get over it already. Think of it like we created our own unique Den that's just the three of us." She concluded, while I smirked and giggled to myself.

All the adults hated us walking around the house practically naked around each other. Like children, fledglings still didn't feel the need to dress in normal attire, or any attire at all. Aside from the satin tops and shorts girls wore or just the satin or cloth shorts Phury had. But Calista was right, we didn't care. And it wasn't like we did it in front of our mates or outside the house, well at least Phury and I didn't.

Calista always tried to provoke Drameon. In her mind, and her argument about it all, was that she was fifteen and only had about eight years to be courted properly. However, being four years older, father still had refused to allow Alkin to begin courting me. Phury was the same way, he wasn't allowed to begin courting Marceline either.

"Regardless, of that." He said sighing and rubbing his brow. "I haven't been informed about what is going on. But I'll be gone for a few days, and I expect you three to behave." The excitement between Phury and I spiked, while Calista was saddened.

"Can't I go too?" She asked solemnly.

Father shook his head. "No I'm sorry, but since I don't know what's going on, you need to stay here. With that being said. Yes, I know this is the first time you will have freedom, and to be home alone. However, Lyth and Celeste will be by in a few hours to check on you three. Also your grandparents know you are home alone. That means you are expected to behave." He concluded sternly.

Phury and I looked at each other with a spark of mischievousness in our eyes. We haven't had freedom like this. It was exciting and it meant we could do whatever we wanted. As if father read our mind, which he may have been informed by Calista, he spoke.

"No that does not mean you can do whatever you want. Alkin and Marceline also know you are home alone. They have agreed to keep an eye on things here and make sure you stay out of trouble."

Phury wrinkled his nose at Calista as father bent down and kissed her cheek. "I expect you three to behave, please." He said standing once more.

Frowning we looked at each other and sighed. "Ok." we all said simultaneously. Nodding his head, he left into the hall and towards the front door.

Hearing the click of the lock indicated his departure, and smiling widely I jumped out of my blanket. "I'm getting dressed." I yelled as I ran down the hall, practically into the wall and towards my room, to retrieve real clothes.

Almost slamming into the chest at the foot of my bed, I turned and opened the cherry dresser, rummaging for pants and a shirt. In the next bedroom over, I heard something fall to the ground and thud loudly. It sounded like Phury was doing the same. Pulling a red shirt over my head and pink undershirt. I pulled out a pair of pants and hiked them up tying them around my waist.

Light footsteps echoed in the hall, as Calista came and stood in the doorframe. "You know your dad said to behave." She said trying to sound stern.

"Yes, mother." I said tartly, as Phury peeked his head into the room around Calista.

"Wanna go outside the walls? We can tell the guards we need herbs, and just go blow things up or something in the forest." He said as he nearly fell over pulling a pair of brown pants over his undershorts.

I couldn't help but laugh. His shirt was disarrayed in a half-on half, off-fashion. One arm through a sleeve the other not. He grabbed his dark leather boots and slipped them on without socks, and pulled his other arm through his sleeve.

Grabbing my own boots, I quickly did the same. "Yeah lets go." I don't care where but let's blow something up." I said extremely excited to do something fun for a change. Without adults telling us no.

Calista sighed as she pulled a blue shirt and black pants out of my dresser. Her dark hair fell loosely and nearly perfect as she pulled the shirt over her head and reached for socks. "Fine if that's where you're going I'll come too." She said pulling them over her feet and then securing boots over them.

Out of the three of us she looked the best dressed, Phury and I looked more like wild children that had run through a windblown meadow. Our hair was disarrayed and our clothes looked untidy. Sighing she shook her head and walked to the door. Smiling, Phury and I followed.

As we entered the still-darkened streets we kept to the shadows. The red, blue, silver, and green bricked streets were illuminated by pale magic lamps. The moon was high in the sky, probably just after midnight as we walked towards the large iron and wood gates. Two Drakar guards stood, both in armor of iron and Mythril. Glancing towards us, I bit my lip nervously.

"Hello, my good men." Phury said as he rushed forward. If we were going to get out of town it was going to be because of him. Females typically were not allowed to leave so late at night unless accompanied by a male, and we were fledglings. "Such a fine night to be out for a stroll. The girls and I need to go gather night lilies. We don't want to cause any trouble and only expect to be gone for an hour, if that's alright with you." He concluded.

Night lilies were a perfect excuse. The only way to find the correct ones, and not regular lilies was to pick them at night, because of their ultraviolet glow. One of the guards glanced at me and Calista, smiling I nodded my head. "I need the flowers to make a mixture for school." I said hopeful he would let us pass.

For a moment they appeared like they would protest, but then waved us on. "Just be back before the sun's up or else we will have to alert your grandparents." They said as Phury grabbed my arm and lead us through the gate.

Outside and away from the wall, I squealed excitedly. "I can't believe they just let us out like that!" I said as Calista rolled her eyes at me.

"You two need to calm down or else we will get in trouble." She said seriously.

"Nah, it's ok." Phury said. "Plus it was a perfect excuse. Raillyn advanced to studying alchemy with Howl and this is a typical ingredient in fire wine. So with her being his pupil it's a feasible reason to need them." He said calmly as we walked deeper into the woods.

The tall pine trees of the Turbid Still loomed over us. Their needles, moss, and decaying matter lay scattered across the forest floor. It was dark here but with the moon so full we didn't need a light to guide our way. Phury flicked his golden hair back as he walked on. It made me laugh a little as I remembered how many people swore we were twins. Most of the time we just went with it, the real story was to confusing.

Through the maze of trees we approached a meadow. This is where Howl had taken us to practice our magic. It was open enough to see everything around for a mile on both sides, but closed enough that no one else could see us. Plus it was far enough away that Silvertine wouldn't hear or see.

The meadow was surrounded by unlit torches, each standing as tall or taller than us. This was the sparring ring, as Howl so cleverly called it. Phury, Calista, Callina and myself often went one on one here or against Howl, perfecting our skills. Knee high brush lay outside the ring, along with a few carelessly placed night lilies.

Stepping across the threshold of moss-covered forest to grass-covered meadow, I paused. Twenty feet or so away stood a girl, fiery red hair reflected in the moonlit. She knelt in a doeskin jerkin and pants. Carefully she picked the few scattered night lilies, giving off a blue and purple glow. Turning I looked at Phury, he looked worried, and I knew he saw her too. Cautiously he grabbed my waist, and pulled me behind him, beside Calista.

Placing himself between us and her he took up a protective demeanor. Mentally he told us to draw our daggers, as he did the same. Being fledglings we were not allowed to use heavier weapons, or swords. To me it felt stupid, especially in a case like this.

Phury took a few steps forward towards the girl. "Hey." He called out to her. She looked up at him startled, as she dropped the lily that was in her hand. If fell to the ground and bounced in a blue light. "What are you doing here?"

The girl stood frightened and looked around almost as if she wanted to escape. However Phury wasn't going to allow that. He moved forward fast, faster than she could decide where she was going and caught her arm. "What are you doing here?" He asked worried.

The girl looked young, no more than a few hundred years old. Her elf-like face made her appear Drakar, but her energy said otherwise. Through Phury I noticed her eyes were blue. She glanced around frightened, almost on the verge of tears. Calista touched my shoulder, *"Let's go."* She said mentally to me, as she pushed me along.

When we got closer I noticed she breathed heavily, and placed a hand to her head. "What's wrong?" I asked noticing her energy spike and fall like crashing waves.

Shaking her head, I looked at Phury sternly. Sighing, he let go.

"I got lost." She began. "I was visiting Aeralain with a friend of mine but we got separated. I came across this meadow and couldn't help but pick these flowers." She concluded innocently enough.

Looking her in the eyes. I was curious to know something. "What are you?" I asked her genuinely interested.

Calista bumped into me. "It's not polite to ask that stuff." She said sarcastically.

Just then a twig snapped off in the distance, sending us all on alert. Phury turned his attention towards the unlit torches. Calling his magic into his hand, a bright blue light began to take shape. As if it was clay, it wavered in shape as is whirled around.

Raising his arm he threw it at the closest torch. Blue light erupted from the wick. Pointing his arm towards the other torches, the fire spread out, and streamed across the open space. One by one it spread like wildfire until the whole ring was aglow. Then he waited silently until another twig snapped.

A small tremor raked through the earth causing a light earthquake. The ground shifted around us as it rolled, and threw dirt. The girl grabbed my arm fearful of what she knew had found us.

"It's a Vampire." She said. "I'm a Shadow Walker, but I have Drakar blood. It wants me." She said almost screaming, as we held onto each other for support. A crash off towards our left caused me to turn. A black figure leapt out of the shadows, jumping skyward.

Immediately I called fire from a nearby torch to my hand. It streamed into my hand into a ball of blue flame. Phury leapt towards the shadow grabbing it by the tattered remains of a shirt. The creatures tried to resist, and scratched at him, however Phury held him far enough away to not be harmed.

Snarling at the creature, Phury spun him into the light. Pale grey skin stretched loosely off a bony frame. Gnarled rope-like hair hung like wire around the sunken eyed and hollowed faced man. Calista grabbed the girl and held her close as I threw the fireball at the strange man. Immediately Phury tossed the creature aside and called the air. It began to spiral and spin around the figure. The ball of flame quickly got caught up by Phury's wind. Like a whirlwind of fire it engulfed the creature and spun around him.

Phury stood to my left with a grin on his face, shrieks and screams echoed inside the cyclone of fiery blue magic. "I think we should get back to town before he calls friends, or we find out this doesn't kill him."

Nodding my head, I turned back towards the path. Calista and the bright redhead were already a few paces ahead of me, racing along the path. Running to catch up, I turned back to glance at Phury. He smiled as the meadow faded from view. Breathing heavily, I turned back around, and ran on.

The snapping of twigs caused me to run faster. I felt Phury, and Calista's fear as well. *There may be more Vampires...* We quickened our pace, as Calista pulled the girl along. Feet pounding the ground, we raced up the hill and towards the gate.

Phury passed me and eventually Calista, he was always quicker. Grabbing one of the guards, I knew he told them what happened. His partner reached to a horn on his waist. Bringing it to his lips he blew into the spiraled goat horn. Its shrill echoed hauntingly as we raced through the gate, and into the streets. As soon as we passed its threshold, it slammed closed behind us.

Not stopping, we raced on. running across the bricked streets; our footsteps echoed as we ran. Our plan was to head towards the house, however we bumped into Lyth. His eyebrows scrunched together as he frowned at us.

"I don't suppose you have something to do with the horns sounding do you?" He asked as Celeste appeared from around a corner.

Stopping and bending over, I knew we would be safe this far into town and we could stop running. That we were being silly for even running so far anyway. No Vampire had ever been able to enter town, they were slaughtered at the gate by spells and arrows. Breathing deeply, my chest burned. Phury sat on the ground next to me and tried to steady his breath as well.

The girl turned towards Calista and apologized. "I'm sorry, I didn't know they followed me." She said while taking deep breaths between words.

"And who are you?" Celeste questioned, her green eyes almost glowed with anger as she met the girl's blue eyes. "What in the world did you three do? We leave you alone for a few hours and you can't even stay out of trouble." She said, as she grabbed my arm and pulled me upwards.

Lyth snickered a little until Celeste swatted his arm gently. "At least they didn't do anything too bad. So they went outside the gate and ran into some trouble. I bet they won't leave town again before sunrise." He said before laughing at us.

Frowning, I looked at Phury, irritated. Yes, Lyth was right, we wouldn't plan to leave town anytime soon before daylight again after that little mishap. All three of us agreed mentally to that.

"Opal and Solomn are expecting you to be brought to them as soon as you're found, so let's go. I don't know if they informed your grandfather that you were missing yet or not. But, you can explain who this is and what you did there." She said while pointing towards the tall white building that stood in the middle of town. The palace where my grandparents lived.

Kicking a nearby pebble, I scrunched my nose and walked the familiar path towards the main door. I knew everyone followed behind me, our footsteps echoed along the quiet streets.

Even this early there was hardly anyone up. The darkened sky was just becoming bright as the sun began to rise.

Looking skyward I hoped Alkin wouldn't be at the palace, but knowing my luck he probably was. Mentally I felt the three of us hope Daes wasn't informed. Not only would we be in trouble with our grandparents but our one day mates wouldn't be thrilled either. However, if Grandfather knew he would add a punishment.

Lyth bumped my arm and mentally picked on me. *"Oh it's not that bad. I'm sorry you got caught so fast. I tried to deter Celeste from going to your dads, but she insisted you three would do something stupid."* He said as he opened the door that lead into the opaque grey walls of the palace.

Looking at Lyth with a *"Really..."* look, I rolled my eyes, regretting our decision to go outside the wall. Nearing the dragon-spiraled door, I glanced at the girl. We still didn't know who she was. Only that she was a Drakar and Shadow Walker; that meant she was a half-breed. She stared at the floor, keeping quiet.

Lyth opened the door and walked in, we followed and Celeste brought up the rear. "I found them." He said as I saw Opal and Solomn in one of the many pillowed benches.

Before turning towards the fireplace I knew who stood there. Howl and Alkin stood near the Dragon-Phoenix mantled hearth. As soon as the door closed they spoke up, as well as Marceline, who stood on the other side of the room near Darcia.

Closing my eyes, I sighed, knowing that if everyone was here that we were in big trouble. "Where have you three been? We were just about ready to call Daes and who is this?" Marceline asked loudly cutting everyone else out.

Looking at the girl she stood wide-eyed and stared towards Alkin and Howl. In fact she stared right at Howl, and looking at him he looked shocked. "You." She said quietly, as she walked towards him.

For a moment Howl looked like a bird trapped in a cage, trying to escape. His eyes grew wide as he tried to hide behind

Alkin. "Oh no, I'm not getting in the middle of this." He said as he walked away from Howl and over towards me.

The redhead raised her hand and slapped Howl across the face, his cheek lit up as bright as the fire in her hair. My mouth dropped as I felt everyone's shock.

"Hello, Ayana." Howl said while rubbing his cheek. His black hair fell into his face and across his piercing blue eyes. "Didn't get enough of me and had to come back for more. Huh?" He questioned as he jumped back.

The girl, Ayana, muffled a scream as she tried to grab him. "You infuriate me! Four years ago you got me drunk in Liedan! I never got drunk before in my life, but whatever you had sure did the trick and then some." She said as she swung at him again.

Carefully Howl ducked and backed further out of her reach. Holding up his hands he tried to calm her down. "It was Fire wine, a Drakar-based wine, I didn't know you were Drakar enough to have it affect you. I thought you were more Shadow Walker and that you would leave me alone." He said as she began to call a blue fireball to her hand.

Eyes wide, I watched in shock. What was going on and who was this Ayana? Alkin's hand slipped around my waist and pulled me closer, causing me to look away. His black hair hung into his face as he smirked.

"Uh-Oh." I heard Calista say, as I turned my attention back towards Howl and Ayana.

The blue fireball was growing in size, and flaring erratically, like it often did in an untrained hand. I saw and felt Howl notice also, quickly he changed directions and instead of running he grabbed Ayana's hand, extinguishing the fireball on contact. Blue smoke streamed through their fingers as he held her tight, restricting her movement.

"Calm down and I'll let you go." He said calmly but sternly. "I truthfully don't know what happened in Liedan four years ago. Perhaps you can enlighten me, child?" He said as I saw her relax.

"I'm not a child. Even if I was born after the war in Alecien." She said as he released her. "And what do you mean you don't remember? All I know is that one moment we were in the bar drinking and the next I woke up in a room that looked like a Dragon's horde."

That peaked my interest, no one had seen inside Howl's room but he always bragged about it being famous with the ladies.

"There were gems, metal chunks, baubles, feathers and Gods know what else hanging from the ceiling, and scattered across tables. Not to mention various bottles of potions, and fragrances strewn about."

Howl looked like he was ready to jump at her to keep her quiet. By Howls reaction and mental shock, she was right. She had been in Howl's room.

Howl rubbed the bridge of his nose irritated as we stared on quietly. "And you just left?" He asked carefully as he dropped his hand and met her eyes.

"Yes." She said taking a step back. "When I got back to the Inn where my friend waited she said I was gone for several days and asked what happened, but I had no answer for her. All I can think of is that you drugged me, you evil man." She said, angry again.

Something sunk in at that moment, Phury laughed out loud, as Opal and Solomn looked at each other. I glanced up at Alkin in shock, as one phrase echoed along the mental link of Daes' bloodline. *Howl has a mate... and it had been four years since they had seen each other...*

My stomach shook as I belly laughed, this was hilarious. Howl swore he would never have a mate and yet he did, she was a feisty half-breed. The funniest thing of all was that obviously they had sparked the mate bond between them, and shared a bed together.

Taking a few deep breaths, I tried to calm down enough to stop laughing. Looking towards Calista, she snickered as well.

"Don't think this will get you out of trouble." Alkin said sternly while crossing his arms and looking at me.

Being nineteen, and only a few years away from adulthood, I knew what the mate bond meant just as much as he did. Watching Ayana and Howl, made me wonder how life would soon be like for us when we came of age.

Reaching up and wrapping my arms around Alkin's neck I smiled up at him. His broad elf-like face, lined with his silky black hair, already made my stomach flutter with love. My time as a fledgling was limited. Already we shared secrets between the two of us that my father didn't know about. Already I put my whole heart and trust into this man. Even though he wasn't yet my mate, he was the love of my life. We had been through so much together, and would stand by each other through much more.

Alkin was my rock, my safety, and my mate. Standing on my tiptoes I couldn't help but steal a kiss, one of the many things that my father hated and said I was too young for. Typically Alkin withdrew and respected my father's wishes. Today however, he placed a hand on my cheek and returned the sweet kiss. My heart and soul felt whole in his arms, and I was at true peace with the man I loved.

***

When your life comes to an end,
Who will be the one to tell it?
                    ~Nahdia Swedersky~

~*~*~

www.ingramcontent.com/pod-product-compliance
Lightning Source LLC
Chambersburg PA
CBHW071511260626
47170CB00002B/335